S0-CRG-916

DEFIANT ANGEL

"You looked so innocent, I had not the heart to wake you."

Katrina cursed her heart for pounding so furiously and so loudly.

"As I watched you sleep, I wondered if such innocence could be real," Rafe murmured, his gaze falling upon her lips.

"You're still delirious," Katrina said.

"I wondered," he continued, "if you could be the same woman who has haunted my dreams of the past week. The woman who, during my fever, tossed her clothes aside and pressed against me . . ."

Katrina touched her fingers to the warmth of his lips. "Please . . ." she pleaded.

He caught her hand and kissed each pink-tipped finger. "Do not fear me," he said raggedly, moving over her until her head was caged between his elbows. "Never fear me, my little Katrina."

Other Books in
THE AVON ROMANCE Series

Avon Books are available at special quantity discounts for bulk purchases for sales promotions, premiums, fund raising or educational use. Special books, or book excerpts, can also be created to fit specific needs.

For details write or telephone the office of the Director of Special Markets, Avon Books, Dept. FP, 105 Madison Avenue, New York, New York 10016, 212-481-5653.

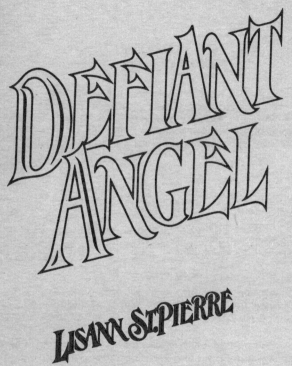

DEFIANT ANGEL

LISANN ST. PIERRE

AVON
PUBLISHERS OF BARD, CAMELOT, DISCUS AND FLARE BOOKS

DEFIANT ANGEL is an original publication of Avon Books. This work has never before appeared in book form. This work is a novel. Any similarity to actual persons or events is purely coincidental.

AVON BOOKS
A division of
The Hearst Corporation
105 Madison Avenue
New York, New York 10016

Copyright © 1988 by Lisa A. Verge
Published by arrangement with the author
Library of Congress Catalog Card Number: 87-91680
ISBN: 0-380-75511-4

All rights reserved, which includes the right to reproduce this book or portions thereof in any form whatsoever except as provided by the U.S. Copyright Law. For information address Yvonne Hubbs Literary Agency, 5321 Roper Avenue, Fair Oaks, California 95628.

First Avon Books Printing: March 1988

AVON TRADEMARK REG. U.S. PAT. OFF. AND IN OTHER COUNTRIES, MARCA REGISTRADA, HECHO EN U.S.A.

Printed in the U.S.A.

K-R 10 9 8 7 6 5 4 3 2 1

*This novel is dedicated to
Thomas Patrick*

Chapter 1

"Do what you like. I care little whether you come or not." Katrina Dubois tossed a shimmering plait of blond hair over one thin, jutting shoulder, ignoring her companions' glances of anger and ill-concealed fear.

" 'Tis foolish to venture into the darkness on such a night," Charlotte whispered. "The fair is nearly over. Who knows what men have wandered into the woods?"

"You're all frightened of your own shadows," Katrina retorted. " 'Tis only half the distance through these woods to the chateau, yet you insist on taking the road though it isn't any brighter or any safer!"

"Charlotte is right," Marie insisted, planting her plump hands on her hips. "Only yesterday there were reports of brigands just outside of Poitiers."

"We hear of new 'brigands' every time a beggar enters the town," Katrina said nonchalantly. "I'm weary of such rumors."

"Not rumors," Marie responded. "The Marquis de Noailles's lands have been attacked, and those lands are not many leagues distant."

"But have the duke's lands been touched?" Katrina returned, her green eyes flashing at the plump girl. "The Duke de Poitiers's grain is probably the best protected in France." She threw up her hands in frustration. "Don't you see? Any brigands that foolishly may be lurking in these woods will be near the road where the merchants bring their grain carts." Katrina scanned the girls' stubborn faces. Looking beyond them into the light of the marketplace, another, more convincing argument came to

1

mind. "Besides, it's far safer in the woods than in the center of that market."

The girls glanced over their shoulders to the fair, not one hundred paces from where they stood. From the light of bonfires they could see the stream of exuberant townsfolk milling among the carts of wandering merchants, stopping to watch a bear-leader and his pet.

"We can get home just as easily by the road as through the woods," Marie insisted. The other girls bobbed their heads in agreement.

Katrina glanced anxiously at the night sky, gauging the time by the stars. "If we don't leave soon by either route, we won't be back before Tante Helene's curfew."

"Are there really brigands in the forest?" Anne, the youngest girl, lifted frightened eyes in her pockmarked face.

"Hundreds of them," Marie said. "And they lurk in the trunks of trees, waiting for young girls to wander into their branches."

"Stop, Marie," Katrina said impatiently. "You'll frighten the girl."

"She should be frightened!" Marie insisted. "You, Katrina, may be some strange child of the forest who has no fear of mortals, but we're not. We were born of woman—not found in some straw basket in the middle of briars—"

"Marie, hush!" cautioned Charlotte.

"No, I will not hush!" Marie continued. "We will not go into the forest because we fear what lurks there at night," she concluded.

"You speak foolishness," Katrina replied. "You fear what you do not know—"

"While you, dear Katrina, wander fearlessly through the forests where wild beasts, brigands, and beggars make their home, as if you were the daughter of fairies and wood sprites, protected by the trees!"

Katrina's eyes flared at the dark-haired woman, but she tightened her lips in determination. She hardly knew why she was going to such great lengths to convince her companions to come with her. Perhaps she desired their company more than she would admit to herself. She glanced toward the sparse trees that heralded the border of the woods. She had never feared the forest, but tonight it did not beckon her kindly, as usual. Tonight dark secrets lurked in the trees, and though she ached to discover those secrets, a cold internal voice warned her not to seek them. Katrina shook her head at her fanciful wanderings. Perhaps the chalky wine she had sipped had affected her more than she realized.

"Very well," she said in resignation, turning her back to the girls. "You shall go your way, and I shall go mine. We'll see who returns earlier and in better health."

She marched with determination toward the dark, ominous edge of the woods. What did it matter if she walked alone? After seventeen years in the kitchens of the Duke de Poitiers, she still couldn't call one of these servants her friend. They were such frightened, suspicious girls. Katrina smiled at their flights of fancy. She knew they thought her some kind of fairy, born of wolves and left in the forest for Tante Helene to find, for how could a normal babe survive the cold of winter in the middle of the woods?

Katrina pulled her black shawl tightly around her shoulders as she entered the cool forest. Engulfed by the darkness, she breathed easier, the foreboding that had darkened her thoughts vanishing into the shadows. Neither in the bright of the day nor in the blackest of nights had she ever come to harm in the protection of these woods. How many times had she run along the crooked paths, hair unbound, chasing rabbits or following a lost doe? How many books, borrowed from Father Hytier's small library or the duke's larger one, had she read in the shade of an elm? Perhaps she did have a touch of magic in her blood to remain unmolested for so long in a place that all villagers feared.

Shaking her head at her foolishness, she strode confidently among the tall, straight trees. The brittle nettles snapped under her bare, callused feet, catching in the rough calico of her faded dress. A restless night wind ruffled the treetops, releasing the pungent scent of pine resin.

" 'Tis a good sign," she mused aloud. "Perhaps this year's harvest will be better than last." It had to be so, for the harvest of 1788 was meager, indeed. Not a day went by this past winter without a beggar appearing at the duke's kitchen, his bony arms raised for food or alms. Although Katrina slipped them scraps whenever she could, there wasn't much to give, food being such a precious commodity. Many beggars were becoming desperate.

Fearing that carts of grain and flour would be attacked, the intendant of the region sent guards to protect the goods traveling along the forest-shrouded road from the farms to the village. Yet the guards were nearly as burdensome as the brigands because they claimed their pay in grain.

Katrina's own fortune was thrown starkly in relief in this year of famine, which was far worse than any other of the seventeen years she had seen. Tante Helene, though often strict in her ways, sheltered her and fed her well without demanding a word of gratitude. Katrina felt a stab of remorse and quickened her step, thinking for a guilty moment of Tante Helene's worry if she should return late from the fair.

"Ah, 'tis a girl!"

Katrina swung around at the sound of the voice and peered into the darkness, her heart thumping erratically.

"Who's there?" she cried. Fear gripped her as firmly as the greasy hand that suddenly clamped over her mouth.

" 'Tis a girl," the man behind her repeated, pulling her stiffening body against his own. "And a fine one." A second form emerged from the shadows and approached her.

Katrina's eyes widened in fright. Her captor's sweaty male scent attacked her senses, spurring her to action. As she bit into his hand, nearly gagging from the filth, he trapped her arms behind her back.

"Little bitch!" he cursed, sucking on his injured hand but still holding her against him with his free one.

"Let me go!" she cried, trying to pull her trapped arms free. "Have you no better sport than to molest a girl?" Her shawl fell off her head in the struggles, and the second man gasped.

"Look at her hair!" he exclaimed, staring at the length of golden braid.

"Fool! Help me with this wench. Would you have such a piece running away from us?" The second man rushed in and, capturing Katrina's waist-length hair in his hand, yanked her head back roughly.

"She's a beauty," the man said, his loose lips gaping as he gazed at her. "But she hardly looks more than twelve."

"No, she's far older than that." Her first captor grasped Katrina's bodice. Shocked by his brutal touch, she kicked out wildly at the man, but he moved away easily. "She's ripe, all right."

The second man released Katrina's hair, and she pulled away from him, regaining her balance. The other man held her wrists tightly with his hand while he gazed intimately at her body. Although she tilted her chin defiantly, her heart pounded in terror.

Brigands? she wondered, noting the men's rough linen shirts and dirty breeches. They had no horses, no guns, and, as far as she could see, no other cohorts. *Wouldn't Marie laugh if she could see me now?* She shook the wry thought from her head and looked furtively for a means of escape.

"Don't think of escaping, wench," the first man warned, leering and moving closer to her. "It'll be far easier for you if you just relax."

"I want her first," the second man said, rubbing the front of his breeches.

Katrina's stomach turned at the sight, and she renewed her struggles. "Don't touch me, swine," she spat, kicking her abductor firmly in the shin. He yelped and jerked her arms. Katrina groaned at the pain shooting to her shoulders. The man stepped in front of her and began to loosen his breeches, his lips curving under the dirt-encrusted mustache.

" 'Tis indeed a fine piece, Roland," he said, lifting her chin up higher by yanking her hair. "She's got skin untouched by the pox and eyes like spring leaves."

" 'Tis not her eyes I want to see," the second man groaned. "Rip that damned dress off her."

The first man stared down at Katrina, interest renewed in his eyes. She boldly returned his stare, though she dreaded the hands that would soon be tearing her dress from her body.

Yet the man continued to stare at her face, a strange spark lighting the depths of his yellowed eyes. Emboldened, Katrina tried to pull away from him, but he brought her easily to her knees.

"What are you waiting for, Bertrand?" Roland asked impatiently, his eyes fixed on her bodice. "Let's get the wench on her back—"

"Not so fast," the other man said, holding a hand to ward his friend off. "I have a better plan."

"What better plan than rolling her?" he asked harshly, his breath ragged. "She's got me all hot—"

"Think, Roland," Bertrand interrupted. "Think what the marquis would say if we gave him such a piece."

"We'll give her to him after," Roland said sharply. "I have need of her now."

"Fool!" her captor cursed. "You know the marquis never touches whores. This girl is a virgin if ever I saw one. Let's bring her to him and see how grateful he is."

"I still say we roll her first," Roland continued, his watery eyes fixed on Katrina. "How will the marquis know?"

"He will know when we bring her to him with dirt on her behind and blood on her thighs," Bertrand answered, his hand tightening around her wrists. "This girl could be worth . . . thirty or forty louis."

The words checked Roland, and he regarded his partner with interest. "Thirty or forty louis, you say?" Roland asked, staring down at Katrina's bent form. "Do you think she's worth so much?"

Bertrand grasped her chin and yanked it to face his companion. "Look at that face," he said. "If the marquis refuses my price, well"—he shrugged—"then we'll have our way with her."

Roland pressed his lips together and moved away from Katrina. "Very well," he agreed. "But if the marquis refuses, she's mine first."

Katrina stumbled on the unfamiliar ground as her abductors yanked her along unmercifully, her wrists bound tightly with biting rope. The dim flicker of lanterns wavered ahead, and as they approached the light, she recognized the dark, looming shape of a fine carriage. Her eyes widened. The men had mentioned a marquis, but she had thought the name a mockery. Her heart leaped with sudden hope. If this man—this marquis—was indeed a nobleman of fine breeding, he might take pity on her.

"Whoa, there!" her captor yelled. The click of muskets echoed loudly above his voice. "It is only myself, Bertrand, and Roland." The silence stretched as the two men slowed to a nervous stop.

"Who is the third?" someone called from the trees.

"A . . . gift for the marquis, if she pleases him." Slowly, the muskets lowered, and the three moved carefully into the circle of light surrounding the carriage. A tall man dressed in garish gold-trimmed livery stepped before them. He glanced briefly at Katrina, his lips curling in distaste at the sight of her bound wrists.

"Did you see any brigands?" the man asked sharply.

Roland and Bertrand shifted uncomfortably. "We looked all through the forest from here to the village," Roland said carefully. "We saw no one but this wench."

The liveried man turned his attention to Katrina and stared again at the rope. "Must you bind her so?" he said. "The marquis will not take kindly to a marred prize."

" 'Tis not his property yet!" Bertrand objected, but he closed his mouth at the servant's icy glare and loosened Katrina's binds. He glanced briefly at her face. "Mind you don't try to escape. You'll be shot down in a moment."

"Stop muttering," the servant said haughtily, eyeing Katrina critically. She lifted insolent eyes to his and turned, frustrating his attempts to view her backside. The man frowned and moved toward the carriage. "Come with me," he said, gesturing to her, but Bertrand's arm shot out to stop her.

"Not so fast," he said harshly. "The girl is ours. We want money, or we won't hand her over."

"You'll get nothing until the marquis approves. Now, step aside." The servant held out a hand to Katrina.

She glanced around quickly, searching in vain for a means of escape. Her gaze rested on the waiting carriage, and doubts clouded her thoughts. Few aristocrats would even acknowledge the presence of a peasant, much less aid one in times of trouble. Yet there were exceptions: the Duke de Poitiers, for one, generously helped the people of his lands in times of trouble. Perhaps this marquis . . . Nodding decisively, Katrina pushed Bertrand's hand away and followed the servant to the edge of the carriage.

"Monsieur, I have brought a gift for you." The servant spoke quietly into the darkness of the carriage. Katrina started, the full impact of her situation finally hitting her with those words. Her stomach knotted.

No sound came from the carriage. Katrina waited in the silence, the golden light casting strange shadows upon the ground. Her heart fluttered madly as a leather-clad hand emerged from beneath the carriage blinds and gripped the sill, tightened, then

went lax. The end of a dark cane emerged from the blinds and
moved the stiff material away, leaving a small opening. She
gasped.

Two lights penetrated her soul from the black depths of the
berline. She could not see the shape of this marquis's head, or
his body. All she could see, all she could sense, were two seering
pinpoints of evil fixed on her soul. She staggered as if physically
attacked. The marquis's probing stare froze her to the spot, and
she stood like a rabbit under a snake's mesmerizing gaze.

One long, gloved finger lifted, and the liveried servant nodded
sharply.

"Very well, Monsieur," the servant said, moving toward Bertrand and Roland. Katrina watched as the leather curtain fell in
its stiff folds. Her heart began to beat again.

"Here," the servant said curtly, tossing a small bag to her
captors. "That's more than enough for the wench."

Bertrand quickly snatched the bag and weighed it heavily in
his hand. A slow smile spread above his encrusted beard. "I
hope the marquis enjoys her," he said, his eyes falling upon
Katrina. "When he tires of her—"

"Begone!" the servant said harshly. "We have no need of
you."

Katrina watched with rising terror as the two men nodded and
bowed their way out of the circle of light. She took one hesitant
step after them, away from the carriage and the evil that seemed
to emanate from its center.

The servant grasped her wrist. "The marquis will not be
cheated of his prize," he stated as his eyes traveled dispassionately over her upturned face. She flinched at their coldness but
did not turn away. His hand rested lightly on her arm, yet when
he turned to lead her to the carriage she found his grip inescap-
able.

"But—but—Monsieur," she pleaded, finding her voice again.
"I am not a woman to be sold for an evening of . . . of . . ."

"If you were, we would toss you to the wolves tonight," the
servant replied. "The marquis does not like whores. His tastes
are much more . . . refined."

Indignant, Katrina tried to wrench her arm away, but her efforts were in vain. "I am a free woman! A servant in the Duke
de Poitiers's kitchens—"

"For your own safety, keep that information to yourself," the servant warned, dragging her inexorably closer to the dull shine of the carriage door. "Else the marquis might see the need to stop your wagging tongue."

The door opened before she could utter another word, and her skin felt scorched from the evil heat that seemed to exude from the gaping door. Her eyes fell upon a length of leg covered in shimmering white hose. *At least he has the legs of a man, not those of a beast.* Unable to meet the marquis's eyes, she stepped back instinctively, but the servant's grip tightened. With one swift motion, he swept her off her dragging, heavy feet and deposited her in the center of the carriage. Katrina leaped for the door as it closed with a decisive click.

She gripped the smooth edges of the door, pressing herself against it. The hairs of her neck prickled as she felt the marquis scrutinizing her.

"So reluctant." His deep, echoing voice sent shivers to her neck. "Most would think it a privilege to grace my carriage."

"I—I know not who you are, Monsieur," Katrina said, cursing her quivering voice. "Those men . . . those men abducted me in the forest and dragged me here against my will."

"No matter," the marquis continued, ignoring her words. "Before this ride is through, you will understand the honor I bestow upon you."

She whirled to face him. "Honor?" she burst out, then caught her breath. The eyes she had only sensed from outside the carriage were now so close; they glared at her with an unsettling intensity. With the rest of his face shrouded in the darkness of the carriage, it seemed as if some strange beast were watching her with wild eyes through a curtain of forest darkness.

"I have chosen you, child, to serve me tonight," the marquis explained. "Tonight I am your seigneur—and I will exercise my seigneurial rights."

"You are not the Duke de Poitiers," Katrina said, pressing against the far end of the carriage. "I am a servant of the Duke de Poitiers."

The marquis's eyes hardened to granite. As he moved closer to her, his hot breath fell upon her face. "Do you not know me?" he asked, incredulous.

"No," she responded, pressing still farther against the leather-bound seats. "I have told you—"

"I am the Marquis de Noailles."

The Marquis de Noailles! The most feared and hated man in the province. Katrina's eyes widened at his words.

"I see you know my name," he said, moving back.

Katrina turned away. Why was he in Poitou and not at Versailles, as was his wont? And why, in God's name, was he out in the middle of the forest in the dark of night?

The marquis pulled the leather shade aside and nodded. The servant's face appeared in the opening.

"Tell the driver to go on. If the other scouts were coming back, they would have returned by now." The servant nodded.

"Oh, but no, Monsieur!" The near hysterical voice came from the driver's box atop the carriage. "You can't go on! Surely the scouts have been killed by brigands. Why else would they not come to get their pay?"

"Do you question the marquis's orders?" the liveried servant interrupted. "Ride on, and not another word."

"Oh, Monsieur, please, have mercy!" The carriage lurched to one side as the driver climbed down from the box. "These men are desperate. They have killed for a mere bag of grain! They travel at night, waiting for such a caravan as ours. You must see that the scouts have been killed, or worse, have warned the brigands. No, Monsieur, you must stay, for to go is madness—"

The liveried servant lifted one brow in question to his master. Without hesitation, the marquis gave a frigid nod. Katrina briefly saw the dull gleam of a pistol in the servant's hand as a single shot stilled the hysterical voice. She started and reached for the door.

"No." The marquis's long fingers closed brutally over her arm and pulled her back into the carriage. "You stay, lest your fate be the same."

Horror washed over Katrina as she heard a last, dying moan.

"You kill so easily," she said breathlessly, her heart pounding painfully in her chest.

The edges of his lips twisted in a distorted smile. "He was naught but a peasant, child," he said calmly. "One less begging mouth to feed."

The carriage jolted forward, and Katrina wrenched her arm from the marquis's tightening grip. Hopes of compassion, barely born, withered and died.

Katrina struggled to understand what had happened to her. Only moments ago she had been walking peacefully through the forest, and now she sat in a plush berline, prisoner to a man who killed on whim. She turned away from him, wishing she could dissolve into the night.

If she had only listened to that inner voice that had warned her to stay out of the forest tonight. Surely this was a fate she could have avoided. A nagging thought hovered in the back of her mind, telling her the night was not yet over. She turned to the marquis, hugging her arms to her chest as she again realized why she was here.

"You have the look of a frightened hare as the hounds close in." The marquis's gaze scanned her slight form. "I shall call you *lapin.*" His hands, hidden by the blackness of the carriage, closed suddenly over her arms, and she jumped. His fingers tightened and dug into her skin.

"Monsieur . . ." she pleaded, her voice trembling. Off balance from the movement of the carriage, Katrina could not fight as he dragged her off the seat to kneel before him. His knees closed in, pressing against her ribs, and she gasped as he increased the pressure. The heavy, floral scent of his perfume washed over her in waves, sending her senses spinning. Instinctively, she struck out.

Her hand was caught midair in an unmerciful grip. She still could barely see him, and she searched the darkness, wondering where his hands would touch next.

"You wish to see me better, *lapin?*" he taunted. Katrina struggled, pinioned between his knees. "I can see you well enough—your hair lights the darkness. I can see the smoothness of your face, the curve of your breasts—"

"I wish . . . to be left alone . . . Monsieur!" She gasped as his knees tightened till she could hardly breathe. His harsh laughter echoed in the swaying carriage.

"I care naught for your wishes," he said. "I warn you—take care, *lapin,* for I will have no qualms about killing you as easily as my servant killed the carriage driver."

Katrina stilled in his grasp, terror freezing her blood. The marquis forced her closer to his loins. Strange, twisted images tumbled in her head. She was naught but a kitchen servant, he, a marquis. No one would dare question his actions. This man would take her tonight, in a way no man had ever taken her, and she would accept—or die.

The marquis held the leather curtains open, and the golden light of the lanterns attached to the outside of the carriage blinded her. She lifted a hand to block the light.

"No." He thrust her hand away. "I will see you."

Katrina gasped. Even in the light of the lantern, his eyes blazed icily at her from wrinkled sockets. His sallow skin sank below short, small cheekbones. He turned briefly toward the window, and she saw a long, jagged scar pulling the skin of his face on the left side.

Abruptly, he struck her, and she was thrown against the opposite seat.

"I will not tolerate such disgust from your eyes," the marquis said bitterly. He reached for her again and drew her up against him.

"M-Monsieur . . ." she stuttered, pressing against the hardness of his barrellike chest. Her head swam from the blow.

"Your coloring is strange for someone from these parts," the marquis said sharply, his eyes sweeping over her face. He grabbed her jaw with one brutal hand and tilted her head toward the light. "Your skin is unflawed." He reached down to pinch her breasts. "Yet you are not a child."

Katrina's insides churned, and she stiffened at the nobleman's intimate touch. He pinched her breasts again, harder, making her cringe in pain. His eyes warned her not to cry out.

With one deliberate movement, the marquis removed her linen fichu, then tightened his knees and brought her full between his thighs. She sucked in her breath at the feel of his arousal beneath his breeches. He laughed as her young body recoiled.

"A virgin, aren't you?" the marquis asked, finding his answer in the green depths of her eyes. "I have a virgin to entertain me this evening." His eyes swept the ragged edge of her bodice, dipping over the arch of her young, swelling breasts.

"Yes, I'm a virgin," Katrina said, finding her voice despite her terror. "Why me . . . why, when others would more willingly fulfill your needs?"

"You are convenient, *lapin*," he said swiftly.

He ignored her hands pressing against his chest. "There is another, waiting at my chateau. But I grow weary of her and"— he pressed himself against her abdomen, a smile twisting his face—"I have an urgent need."

One hand dipped beneath her bodice, and brutally massaged her breast. She could not help the scream of revulsion that ripped from her throat. Throwing her head back, she rained ineffective blows upon his chest. The marquis struck her, then pinioned her fallen body below his upon the carriage floor.

"Fool!" he spat, crushing her with his weight. "Do you think my men will come and save you? They laugh at your screams. If you displease me, I will give you to them after I'm finished."

Katrina heard him through a thick gray fog, her head and jaw throbbing from his blows. She sagged beneath him and closed her eyes as his hands traveled freely over her body.

But her eyes flashed open again as he pulled the bodice of her dress down, pressing her breasts above the edge. They jutted up from the pressure, and the marquis smiled before lowering his thin mouth to suck on their peaks.

This cannot be happening! Katrina squeezed her eyes shut against the sight of the knotty, barrel-chested man poised over her half-naked body. Her hands weakly pressed against his shoulders, but he did not feel her efforts, and Katrina shuddered as one smooth, long-fingered hand pushed her skirts up to her waist.

The marquis sat back, reaching up to open the curtains wide. The golden light fell upon her breasts, well-formed and firm, and he gazed at them in appreciation. He admired the golden mound between her fine, coltish legs, which she had pressed together instinctively.

"No modesty, *lapin*," he said, breathing raggedly. This country twit was having quite an effect on him. Blood pulsated through his loins. Mindlessly he reached down to untie his breeches, his eyes still fixed upon the length of flesh splayed on the carriage floor.

Katrina's eyes hardened on the aristocrat who was gazing upon what no man had ever seen. She would not, could not, let him touch her. Her body shrank from his gaze, her terror of his touch greater than her fear of his threats.

She sat up abruptly, her skirts falling over her loins, and pushed against him. Off balance, the marquis fell sharply against the door as she rose.

"And what do you mean to do, *lapin?*" the marquis demanded angrily as he grabbed her skirts. "Throw yourself out of a moving carriage?"

Katrina clutched the door, swaying with the movement of the carriage, resisting the pull of the marquis as his hands clamped about her waist. He dragged her down to the floor, turned her around, and slapped her.

"You need a stronger lesson than most, foolish one." He struck her again and stared down at her glazed eyes. "Must I kill you and then take your body?" He laughed harshly, pushing his breeches to his knees. "Either way I'll have you."

Katrina gasped at the monstrosity jutting from between the man's thighs. She struggled away, but he struck her again, harder, and she fell back onto the floor.

Her head spun in dizzying circles. She was only vaguely aware that the marquis had pulled her chemise up over her waist and was probing that secret place between her thighs. She struggled with the blackness that threatened to engulf her, fighting to rise above it, only to cringe in terror as he began to lower himself upon her.

The sound of pounding hooves brought the marquis sharply to his knees. He cursed loudly and pulled the leather curtain open.

"What's the matter?" he yelled to the approaching horseman. The carriage stopped abruptly, and Katrina rose to her elbows, shaking her head to clear it.

"Horsemen, Monsieur!" a rider cried out, pulling alongside the carriage. "Several of them. Ahead—"

"No, not ahead, Marquis!" a deep, resonant voice called from the edge of the road. "We are here, now. I suggest you order your men to drop their weapons before we kill them on the spot."

Chapter 2

The marquis released a string of curses and struggled with his breeches. The rider glanced into the carriage, his eyes widening at the sight of Katrina.

Starting, she quickly threw her skirts down and adjusted her bodice. She searched through the carriage for her fichu and hastily threw it about her neck. The marquis pulled his breeches over the softening evidence of his lust and turned flashing, angry eyes to her.

"I must put aside this pleasure for now, *lapin*," he said hoarsely, struggling with the ties at his waist, "for there is another I must attend to." He crushed her jaw in his hand and brought her face inches from his. "You will remain silent," he ordered. "One word from you, and I will ensure your death . . . after every one of my men has had you."

His eyes held no compromise, and Katrina swallowed. "I have little choice, Monsieur," she said. "It is either you or a band of brigands."

The marquis's eyes darkened at the girl's unwitting insult, but he turned away, far more important things on his mind. He stared out the carriage window at the fence of trees alongside the road, observing the bayonets that glinted in the light of the lanterns. The marquis nodded to his rider, and the man gave the order to drop their weapons.

"Wise choice, Marquis." The brigand's voice become louder as the speaker moved out of the circle of trees and into the light. "Had you hesitated a moment more, I would have killed them all."

Over the marquis's shoulder, Katrina saw three riders emerg-

15

ing from the woods, dark linens and the common tricorn covering most of their faces. The front rider sat proudly upon his mount, his wide shoulders nearly blocking the view of the two who flanked him. A musket rested easily upon his thigh. Other riders emerged from the trees, surrounding the carriage and the few mounted men that guarded it.

"Now, Marquis, I will see you out of the carriage," the leader said, his voice rumbling with a hint of amusement, "for I know you have much gold warming beneath your seats."

"Your sources are thorough, brigand," the marquis spat. He rose from his seat and opened the door. The riders moved closer. Slamming the door firmly behind him, the marquis walked a few steps from the carriage and glared insolently up at the leader. "You're a fool if you think you can get away with this," he explained calmly. "You're stealing the king's taxes."

"The king's taxes, are they?" The brigand's laugh rumbled. " 'Tis not the king's taxes I'm taking, Marquis, but the people's earnings."

"You should watch your speech, brigand, for already I know your political views." The marquis casually brushed away a piece of fluff on his waistcoat. "You must be one of the plague of republicans that have—"

"I suggest you drop the gun, Marquis," the leader said tightly, his musket suddenly pointing directly at the aristocrat's heart. "I wouldn't like to kill you so easily."

The marquis gauged the brigand's eyes. He glanced warily at the musket and dropped the gun he had pulled from his waistcoat. Katrina moved closer to the window to watch.

"Come out of the carriage, else you will die also," the leader said suddenly.

Katrina started as she found the musket pointed directly at her, and her eyes lifted fearfully to the shadows beneath the man's tricorn. She pushed the carriage door and fell ungracefully to the hard earth, to the amusement of the brigands.

"Why, Marquis," the brigand said, urging his horse closer. He watched warily as Katrina dusted her skirt off, her cheeks flaming. The light of the lanterns caught in her disheveled plait and danced among the gleaming strands. "It seems you've brought me two treasures tonight."

The leader of the brigands sucked in his breath as the girl

lifted startled green eyes to him. Defiance burned in their depths, though bruises had begun to darken on her chin.

"I had no idea you preferred children to grown women, Marquis," the brigand said harshly, his eyes roving over the slight girl's common dress and signs of obvious ill-treatment. "Certainly you could find a more worthy opponent to battle."

The marquis's eyes glinted maliciously at the brigand's perusal. "Do you find yourself worthy, brigand?" he asked. "For I would enjoy such a battle."

The brigand urged his horse dangerously close to the marquis, his hatred obvious in the glittering depths of his eyes.

"I, too, would enjoy such a battle, Marquis, and the time will come when we shall face one another," the leader said. He gestured to two other brigands, who dismounted and moved past Katrina into the carriage.

Katrina watched the strong back of the leader with growing interest. There was no doubting that his dark eyes had sparked with rage when he had noticed her face. Absently, she touched her sore jaw and gingerly pressed the swelling. Perhaps . . . perhaps he would take pity on her and save her from this satanic marquis.

Foolishness! she told herself, straightening. What better treatment would she get from brigands? Her eyes lifted to the leader again. He spoke well for a common thief. Too well. And what had the marquis said about republicans?

The two brigands dragged out roughly made sacks that hung heavily in their hands. The linens stretched tautly across their faces as they smiled.

"High pay for such easy work," one said, glancing toward his leader, who nodded briefly.

"Your punishment will be far more dear," the marquis snapped, his eyes resting on the gold-filled sacks. "For when the king discovers this, he will surely scour all of France to find you."

"Your threats are useless, Marquis," the leader said. "For I know this money goes only to your coffers, not to those of the king. The king doesn't know of it, for you have not told him of the new taxes you force on your lands."

"You do not know everything, brigand," the marquis said dangerously. "And your ignorance will be your death."

Not deigning to reply, the leader's eyes moved to linger on the slight, golden-haired figure. "The girl." He pointed toward her, gesturing to his men. "Bring her here."

Katrina flashed defiant eyes at the leader and crossed her arms stubbornly before her. "I have been ordered altogether too much tonight," she said evenly, finding courage in her plans. She would find out which was the better of two evils: to be attacked by the marquis, or to put her fate in the hands of this brigand. She glanced warily at the brigand, whose eyes narrowed in what seemed like amusement.

"The girl is of no use to you," the marquis said carefully. "Or have *you* developed a taste for children?"

The brigand's amusement vanished, and he leveled a withering glare at the marquis. "I do not care for men who beat those who are weaker than they are," the brigand said harshly. "I am taking the rabbit away from the wolf."

"Aptly put," Katrina said wryly, "for this man has already compared me to a quivering rabbit. But I must say I do not fancy to be taken from a single wolf to be given to a pack of dogs."

The leader's eyes hardened as the men behind him stifled their laughter. "You prefer this"—he waved a hand toward the marquis—"to your freedom?"

Katrina tilted her head, her plait falling over one shoulder and reaching nearly to her knees. "How do I know you will not treat me as badly as he has?" she retorted. "In one evening, I have been captured against my will, dragged to this aristocrat, threatened, beaten, and nearly raped! Can you promise better treatment?"

The leader watched the girl with mounting amusement. Though her face was bruised and her eyes wary with shock, she still rallied enough strength to banter with villains and thieves. His eyes sparkled as he studied her.

"I promise you your freedom should you come with us."

"And should I accept the promises of thieves?" she said suddenly. She cast a glance at the marquis. "No more than I would accept one of an aristocrat." The brigand to the leader's left burst out in laughter.

"She's a quick one," he said to the leader.

"I am surprised," the leader responded, "for the marquis could hardly handle a tongue as sharp as hers."

The marquis's eyes were filled with murderous hate, and he stared at Katrina, the threat of vengeance lurking in the depths of his gaze. She stepped back from the intensity of his look, unconsciously stepping closer to the brigand.

"No more of this nonsense," the leader ordered, glancing at his men, who began moving into the darkness. "We have tarried too long, though the visit has certainly been entertaining." His eyes rested on Katrina. "You will come with us."

She inched away from the two brigands who approached her, then she struggled as they locked her arms behind her and dragged her to the horse.

"Stop!" she cried sharply. "I have been dragged about all night. Please, let me go!" Surprised, the brigands released her, and Katrina rubbed her bruised and rope-burned wrists. Reluctantly, she moved to the leader's side and gazed above the huge horse into the man's face.

Closer now, Katrina could see the ebony depths of his eyes under the strong black brows. They watched her curiously, and she sucked in her breath at their warm, probing stare. She felt as if he looked past her eyes and into her soul. Clutching her chest in surprise, she stepped back.

"Come," he said gently. He lifted an arm and held out his hand.

She noticed the dark hairs on his knuckles, the strong, firm wrist. She glanced briefly at the marquis, then quickly took the brigand's hand. It closed about her own.

The brigand's head shot up abruptly, and he searched the darkness beyond the carriage. The horses moved restlessly, and Katrina pressed against his mare.

The marquis smiled. "I told you your ignorance would be your folly," he said smugly, folding his arms across his chest. "Do you think I would go on such a dangerous mission without being prepared?" In the next moment, the undeniable sound of horses' hooves rumbled down the road, and the brigands moved quickly into the forest.

"Spread out," the leader barked. "They will not find us all." Roughly, he tightened his grip on Katrina's hand and pulled her upward.

Katrina gasped as she flew through the air to land sidesaddle on the horse's back. She nestled between the brigand's firm thighs, and as the mount moved beneath her, she instinctively twisted to clutch the man's linen shirt.

"Hold tight," he ordered, then glanced toward the marquis. "This encounter is not over, Marquis. We have much to settle between us."

The marquis laughed, a sardonic rumble that sent Katrina stiffening against the stranger. "It will be settled soon enough," the aristocrat responded.

But the brigand had already turned his horse and headed into the forest. All Katrina could hear above the horse's pounding hooves was the sharp report of a gun. . . .

Rafael Etienne Beaulieu cursed as he felt a ball rip through his upper thigh. He squeezed his eyes shut at the fiery pain and pulled the small woman roughly against his body. She clung desperately to his shirt, jolted by the horse's rapid pace. Rafe gritted his teeth against the waves of pain emanating from the wound and leaned low over his horse, urging her on to greater speed. He had to make some headway before the marquis's mercenaries crashed through the forest. He could not see Duarte and Renauldo, only the small puffs of dust rising from their passing.

His mare, Rebel, lagged farther and farther behind Rafe's men, weighed down by the two she carried. Rafe twisted to scan the forest behind them, but there was no sign of the marquis's men. He pulled up briefly on Rebel's reins, and Katrina straightened beside him.

"What . . . what are you doing?" Katrina asked breathlessly, her face flushed with the exhilaration of the ride. Rafe turned to glance into her up-tilted eyes.

"They're still following," he said. "I can hear their horses." Katrina strained her ears but could hear only the horses of the other brigands as they scattered through the forest.

"But . . . but should we linger?" she asked. Abruptly, he slipped off the horse and reached up for her. His hands clasped her waist firmly and placed her on the ground. Trying to regain her equilibrium after the ride, Katrina leaned against the horse as the brigand fumbled with a pack attached to the saddle.

"Rebel will not outrun those men, not with two riders, no matter how small the second." He hit the horse roughly on the rump, and the animal leaped into the depths of the forest.

"What are you doing?" Katrina gasped, a note of hysteria entering her voice. "They'll certainly find us!"

"Not yet," he said, moving swiftly toward her. He clutched her arm and dragged her into a nest of briars. She pushed away the clinging branches as they pulled and tore at her dress. Rafe ruthlessly dragged her deeper into the darkness, and Katrina's heart suddenly began to thump in terror. Could he mean to . . . was he . . .

She yanked her arm away. "I will not go with you!" she cried, realizing his intent with a burst of clarity. "I will not—"

"Hush, wench, before I gag you," he said sharply. "You wouldn't like to return to the marquis."

"The marquis or a brigand, is that my choice?" she demanded angrily. The man stopped his brisk pace and dragged her roughly against his chest.

Katrina gasped. His body pressed rock hard against her, and she suddenly realized the power and enormity of the man to whom she had entrusted her life. His eyes, deep-set and dark as coals, gazed into her own, his face only inches from hers. The linen mask that had earlier concealed much of his face, now hung limply around his neck. His skin, dark and clean-shaven, stretched tautly over smooth cheekbones and caught in the small cleft of his chin. But it was his lips that arrested her attention: they were drawn in an angry white line.

"If you say one more word, I'll find a way to silence you," he said softly. His eyes belied his tone.

"I thought you had no taste for small girls," she said, remembering his words to the marquis.

His lips curved in a half smile. "Ah, but you are no girl, *petite.*" He glanced at her figure. "That became quite obvious when I pulled you upon my horse."

She sucked in her breath and pulled away from him. "You promised me my freedom."

"And you'll have it, if you remain quiet," he said carefully. "If you make even one small noise, we will both be discovered, and I don't intend to die alone."

Katrina's eyes widened at the threat, and she pushed against the wide expanse of the brigand's chest. To her surprise, he released her, moving away and easing himself upon the ground.

She watched with horror as he pulled a gleaming knife from his pack and ripped his breeches at the top of his thigh.

His leg was dark and shining.

"You're hurt!" She gasped as she saw the gleam of blood on his hands. "You're bleeding!"

The man eyed her briefly and removed his tricorn. "The marquis is a deadly shot," he said calmly. "I am fortunate that his aim was not even better."

Katrina moved toward him, forgetting for the moment who and what he was. She knelt beside him and leaned down to stare at his leg. "We must wash this soon and bind it." She glanced at his darkly stained hose. "You have lost much blood."

Rafe watched her golden head as she leaned closer to the wound high up on his thigh, tentatively pushing aside the ragged material. A small smile flittered across his pained face. "For an innocent, your fingers probe with skill," he mused.

Katrina started and straightened beside him. She tore her gaze away from where her hands had just been. "I only wished to look at your wound, Monsieur," she said defensively. "Unless you chose to bleed to death from it—"

"No, no," he objected, "continue your ministrations." His lips, white with pain, stretched over a whiter smile. "I was enjoying them."

Flushing, Katrina returned to her examination. She carefully kept her hands away from the edges of his breeches, but could not help pressing against the rock-hard thigh, which twitched periodically from the pain.

"You're fortunate: the ball didn't lodge in your leg," she said after a minute. "I will not have to dig for lead."

The brigand's eyes flickered. "And are you skilled in such surgery, little one?" he asked, watching her carefully.

"I've never done such a thing, but I have seen it done. My guardian is skilled in the ways of healing and has taught me much." Katrina rummaged through the pack that the brigand had taken with him. She stiffened as she heard the click of a gun.

"I don't trust you, little one," he said hoarsely. "There is no reason for you to nurse me, especially since my death would guarantee you your freedom."

Katrina stared fearfully at the gun. "It seems you must trust me, brigand,'' she said, ''for I seem to be your only hope now. You cannot possibly escape those men while you lie here bleeding to death.''

Rafe examined her in the dim starlight. Her wide, tilted green eyes brimmed with innocence, and her hair, undone now from the rough ride, cascaded in a river of light around her face. Her breasts rose in sweet arcs above her bodice, her fichu having been lost somewhere in the woods. She was right; he had no choice but to trust her. But to trust a stranger who had nothing to gain by his survival—that was a foolish thing to do.

''My men will return to find me,'' he lied. His men had their orders, which included leaving all wounded behind. Their work was too important to risk more men than necessary.

The girl shrugged a thin shoulder, unaware of the enticing movement of her breast. ''Then I must rely on your gratitude,'' she said quietly. ''But I cannot leave a wounded man in the woods to die.''

The brigand smiled softly and lowered his gun. ''You are an innocent, indeed.''

Katrina looked away from his intense scrutiny and continued her search through the bag. She drew out a small flask. ''Is this wine?'' she asked.

He shook his head. ''Brandy, but that will do as well as wine.'' He reached for the flask and lifted it to his lips.

Her hand stayed him. ''Not much,'' she warned, gently retrieving the flask as the first gulp of liquid burned his throat. ''I need it for your leg.''

The brigand's hand engulfed her own, and Katrina nearly melted at the warmth. ''What is your name, little one?'' he asked, leaning toward her.

She breathed deeply of the cold night air and pulled her hand away from his. A breeze ruffled her hair, loosening the light scent of Tante Helene's special soap. ''Katrina Dubois,'' she said shyly.

'' 'Tis a pretty name for a pretty woman.''

Katrina abruptly pushed him back against the trunk of a tree. ''You do not have the fever yet,'' she said sharply, ''thus you have no excuse for such ravings.'' Mercilessly, she poured the brandy over the open wound. Clenching his eyes shut, Rafe flung his head back against the tree, but no sound of pain emerged from his lips.

"Cruel wench," he hissed when his muscles relaxed. His eyes opened slowly, then watched with interest as Katrina lifted her skirts. "You tempt me sorely, Katrina," he said, her name rolling strangely off his tongue. "I am wounded, yet you wantonly lift your skirts—"

"To get cloth to bind your wound," she finished, ripping the edge of her ragged petticoat. This man's soft, rolling voice played havoc with her pulse. "How I'm going to explain my current state of *déshabillé* to my aunt when I return home is beyond me."

"I approve of your dress," the brigand teased, gritting his teeth as she lifted his leg and slid the linen beneath him. His eyes roved over her bodice.

"I've lost both my fichu and the shawl that Tante Helene gave me not a year ago." She knew she was chattering inanely, but she was oddly disturbed by his banter. She flushed as she was forced to reach between his thighs for the other end of the linen. His breath fell warmly on her cheek as she leaned over him.

Suddenly, the brigand clutched her shoulders and pulled her against his hard chest.

"Hush, *petite*," he whispered. "I hear riders."

Swallowing nervously, she twisted her head to listen, too, but all she could hear was his heart pounding hard and even beneath the smooth linen of his shirt. She spread her fingers over his chest and let his warmth ease her ice-cold terror. His scent was clean and spicy, not the thick, earthy scent she expected. For a moment she relaxed against him, her cheek pressed against the finely woven fabric.

His arms tightened around her. He lifted a hand and tentatively ran it through the silken thickness of her hair. Then, gently, he pushed her away.

"The marquis's men have passed by, but I fear they'll double back and find us." His voice rumbled pleasantly through his chest. He reached down and finished the makeshift bandage. "We'll have to find a place to hide and defend ourselves."

"But . . . but you can't walk with your leg like that," she objected. He rose to a standing position and grabbed the saddle pack. "It will bleed even worse."

"If we do not move, then I will be killed, and you, my pretty little Katrina, will be brutally raped by a dozen mercenaries." He watched her face carefully. "Now, come before I am forced to draw a gun on you."

"I have little choice, brigand," she retorted, the anger and frustration of the evening spilling over. "At least you are . . . incapacitated . . . for a while."

A grin split the darkness of his face. "Don't be so sure of that, Katrina," he warned her. He glanced around, lifted his fingers to his lips, and whistled. She started and ran to him, pulling on his arm.

"What are you doing?" she asked incredulously. "Surely the men will hear that!"

"Perhaps," the brigand said. "But Rebel, my horse, will hear it first."

"Your horse?"

"Yes," he explained. "She's well trained for battle. In a minute or two, she'll find her way here."

Katrina turned away from the man, releasing his muscular arm.

"What is it, little one?" he said, his tone taunting her. "Afraid I may take advantage of you?"

She shook her head vehemently, flashing angry eyes at him. "I know well that you'll soon faint from a loss of blood if you don't get off that wounded leg of yours. Then I'll be able to do what I please."

His laugh echoed seductively. "You have spirit," he said, laugh lines lingering around the edges of his pain-filled eyes. He continued to stare at her as his smile dimmed. "For your sake, temper that spirit with wisdom."

Katrina bit her lower lip in indecision. She knew she could easily run from this man and perhaps find her way back to the chateau. But to leave a man wounded in the cold of night, whether the man be noble or thief, was not in her nature. She lifted her eyes to him, and found him still staring at her in an unsettling manner.

"What thoughts cloud your eyes, *petite?*" he asked softly. But before she could respond, the bushes rustled not far from where they stood, and Rafe tensed in anticipation as Katrina rushed to hide behind him. Rafe raised his gun, then lowered it as Rebel burst through the trees, tossing her head. "You're a fine horse," the brigand said gently, moving to caress the mare's side.

Katrina breathed a heavy sigh of relief. "This night will be the death of me," she murmured, clutching her breast.

"Come, Katrina," Rafe said. "It's time for us to put some distance between ourselves and the marquis's men."

She hesitated a moment, then, making a decision, moved quickly to his side. She noticed the beads of sweat on his brow, the pallor of his face. His eyes probed her own sharply.

"I know a place where you can stay, where no one will find you," she said, placing a hand on his clammy skin. "Not far from the duke's chateau is a small church—Father Hytier's church. Behind it, in the depths of the forest, is an old shed that I think even the good *curé* has forgotten about. It will provide some shelter, and no one knows of it but me." She rushed on, encouraged by the light in his eyes. "You can stay there while you heal. I'll bring you food and tend you."

"And why would you risk so much, *petite?*" he asked, his voice hard. "For the reward that will be placed upon my head?"

"You have little faith," she said defiantly. "I am . . . grateful. After all, you saved me from the marquis."

"To hold you for a similar punishment, for all you know," he threatened. "You know nothing of me."

"I know you're wounded," she retorted. "I wouldn't leave a wounded animal untended."

His dark eyes crinkled in a pained smile. "So now you compare me to an animal." Amusement laced his words. "Very well, little one. Take me to this shed." He clutched the saddle, straining as he pulled himself up by his arms.

Katrina watched the muscles bulging beneath the taut shirt. Disturbed by her train of thought, she turned her attention to his wounded leg and found the linen already soaked with blood.

"You've managed to undo any good I've done," she said, pointing to his bleeding limb. "You must rest soon." She reached for his outstretched hand. With a strength that belied his injury, the brigand pulled her up between his thighs. Embarrassed by the intimacy of the situation, she tried to move away, but he smiled and tightened his grasp.

"No use squirming now, *petite,*" he said huskily. "For you're my captive. If you try to deceive me, I'll have no qualms about killing you.''

Katrina twisted to stare into his black eyes. Now no smile marred the smoothness of his face. ''No need to worry, Monsieur,'' she said, her tone half serious, half mocking. ''I will lead you to safety.''

Chapter 3

"Took your time, Katrina," Tante Helene said good-naturedly as Katrina entered the hazy kitchens.

"You're hardly fair," Katrina retorted. "There's little thyme so early in the season. It took me hours to find a good under-shrub."

"I smell the rosemary." Tante Helene moved close to Katrina's straw basket and picked among the contents. "What else have you found?"

"Little. Some dried pods, a few parsley sprigs." With a sigh, Katrina handed Tante Helene the basket and sat down on one of the rough wooden benches. "I expected little more."

Tante Helene flashed dark eyes at the younger girl, noticing the circles beneath her eyes. "You've a tongue like a wasp this morn, Katrina. I thought a walk in the woods would do you good. I see it hasn't."

Katrina shifted uncomfortably, as restless as a bird. The dark bruise that marred her skin throbbed painfully. "I'm sorry, Tante. It's just . . . all the girls talk about are the brigands. After last night's alert, they're worse than ever."

Tante Helene deposited the straw basket of greens upon the wooden table and paced the length of the kitchen. "Rightly so," she said, a tremor of worry coloring her voice. She reached for a loaf of bread and brought it to the table, slicing a thick piece for Katrina. "The brigands that attacked the marquis's carriage did so on the duke's own lands."

"The border of the duke's lands, Tante," Katrina corrected automatically. "Still at least a league away."

"Nonetheless," Tante Helene said firmly, pushing a strand of

28

her peppered hair back into the uncompromising chignon, "it is good the intendant of Poitiers has sent men down to search the lands."

"The intendant?" Katrina gasped.

Tante Helene gave her the bread and glanced strangely at her. "Perhaps you have not heard." The woman settled on the bench, arranging her skirts neatly. "The marquis has requested that both the Duke de Poitiers and the intendant of the city send their men out to search for the brigands."

"But . . . the brigands will be leagues away by now."

"Perhaps. But the Marquis de Noailles arrived here today, in a grand black carriage—"

"The Marquis de Noailles?" Katrina nearly choked on the words, her eyes widening. "Here?"

"Are you ill, child?" Tante Helene asked, her gaze narrowing on Katrina's pale face. "You're repeating everything I say."

Katrina shook her head, more to clear it than to answer Tante Helene's question.

"The marquis is here now," Tante Helene repeated. "And the duchess, by all accounts, is up in arms. She's got all the house servants plus a few from the kitchen scouring every piece of gilt-bronze molding in that huge chateau."

Katrina stood up abruptly and moved to the doorway, staring off at the chateau. It seemed it should look different because such an evil man had entered through its stone portal, but the walls still shone sandy and smooth. Katrina was not afraid that the marquis would find her here: such an aristocrat would never go near the kitchens. No, her fears were centered on the discovery of her wounded charge, now lying in danger a short walk from where she stood.

Katrina's heart jumped as a servant in blue and silver livery burst through the servants' entrance of the chateau and hurried to the kitchens. She stepped aside as he swept by her without a glance and crossed to Tante Helene, who held out to him a plate of ham baked in sugar. More servants followed the first, and Katrina rushed to help the older woman arrange the food. Her stomach growled in hunger as a servant snatched a plate of pigeon legs from her grasp. He eyed her insolently, then swept off to the chateau.

"They're annoyed," Tante Helene explained, whispering until

the last servant left the kitchens, "because several kitchen maids were allowed into the chateau."

"Heaven forbid that lowly, unliveried servants should deign to enter such hallowed halls," Katrina said sarcastically, her mind far from the surly men.

Tante Helene smiled. "Father Hytier taught you well, Kat." She moved to clean the mess from the servants' hasty entrance and exit. "There are times when I don't understand a word you're saying."

"All this preparation is for the Marquis de Noailles?" Katrina blurted out, wandering to a pan where pieces of warm ham still lay at the bottom. She reached in and claimed a sticky piece.

"Oui. The duchess thinks this is the king's court at Versailles, not a country chateau," Tante Helene remarked, gathering the food that remained. Wiping away the beads of sweat that gathered and ran down her face, she moved away from the fire and brought a chunk of nearly red meat to the table for slicing. "She doesn't think that all this food would do more good in the village, where beggars starve, rather than in her enormous belly."

"Tante Helene!" Katrina exclaimed, catching a piece of the meat and bringing it quickly to her lips. "What if she overheard!"

Tante Helene laughed heartily and dropped the knife onto the counter. "Hell will freeze before that aristocrat sets foot behind the chateau," she remarked. "I've been told that there was a time when the duke used to come back here to rally his harvesters, but that was before his first wife died. Since then, he barely leaves the chateau." She shook her head and resumed her work. "I wager he isn't pleased with the marquis's arrival.

"Neither am I. How long will he stay, do you think?"

"Since when can I predict the whims of an aristocrat?" Tante Helene said, shrugging. "The marquis will leave when it pleases him."

Glancing avidly at the meat that Tante Helene was cutting into thin strips, Katrina pursed her lips and reached for the loaf of dark bread. She tore off a healthy chunk and, not waiting for permission, snatched two dripping pieces of meat and wrapped them in a linen. Tante Helene put down her knife and raised her eyebrows in surprise.

"What, Katrina? You plan to eat all of that?"

Katrina's prominent cheekbones flushed with color. "I've not eaten all day," she said, moving out of the smoke-filled kitchen. "And, as you say, the duchess will never notice."

Katrina wandered along the twisting path that led behind the stone church into the thick forest. She glanced around surreptitiously, watching the passersby with interest. None seemed to notice the girl who slipped between the trees and moved soundlessly over the twigs. They were more interested in their own load of grain or flour. Katrina tucked a stray lock of hair beneath her simple peasant's cap and turned to move deeper into the forest. The leaves rustled softly at her passing.

Cool in the dappled shade, Katrina wrapped her arms around herself, wishing she had taken a wrap of some sort, and ruing the loss of her shawl. Tante Helene had only relectantly accepted her story of slipping and falling in the forest, which was the only feasible way to explain the huge, throbbing bruise on her chin. Fortunately, it was the only visible evidence of the previous night's escapades. The other bruises, those on her thighs and arms, were more easily hidden—but would be less easily explained.

Katrina patted the small pouch secured at her waist. The morning's search for herbs had given her an opportunity to find the necessary ingredients for a poultice for the brigand's wound. She hoped he would not need it, but if the wound was as bad as she remembered . . .

She shivered at the memory of last night. The marquis's hateful eyes had haunted her dreams, but periodically a pair of dark, laughing eyes calmed her fears. Had she dreamed the entire night? It hardly seemed real that she was caring for a brigand. But to leave him there, unattended, would be inhuman. By now he could be deep into fever—

She closed her eyes tightly, willing away her apprehensive thoughts. A wounded, feverish man, especially one with the strength she remembered, would indeed be a dangerous one. She clearly remembered the click of his gun as he threatened her. He might shoot, without looking, in fear of being taken captive. Or perhaps the intendant's men had found him, beaten him, taken him to Poitiers for quick sentencing. Katrina winced. He would be broken on the wheel in the open marketplace as a lesson.

She slowed her step as she neared the shed. The intendant's men could be here, waiting to find anyone who dared to help such a traitorous rebel.

Katrina's sharp eyes peered through the thick forest undergrowth, discerning the jerky step of a bird searching for seeds and the quick rustle of a rodent, then she scanned the branches for soldier's boots, for the telltale sagging of branches holding the weight of men. Satisfied she was alone in the clearing, Katrina clutched the food to her breast and moved toward the wooden shed.

"Monsieur, it is I," she said quietly but loud enough for her voice to carry through the mold-eaten wood. She strained her ears for sound. "It is I, Monsieur," she repeated, "Katrina." A bird flitted in the branches, sending a spray of nettles over her. She brushed them from her hair, tilting her head toward the silent shed. Cold dread spread over her body. She sucked in her breath and covered her mouth with her hand.

What if he were dead?

Bracing herself for the worst, she gripped the cold, rusty handle and pulled the door open. It took her eyes a moment to adjust to the darkness within. As she recognized the sleeping shape on the floor, she breathed a sigh and slumped against the damp doorframe. Glancing around, she closed the door behind her and entered the shed.

She had forgotten how big he was. His body filled the length of the shed, his legs curling somewhat to accommodate the space. Hesitantly she bent over him, pushing away the woolen manteau he had drawn to his chin.

His dark hair, tousled from a restless night, shone blue-black in the dim interior. His lashes cast long shadows on his wide cheeks, and even in the light of day, dark shadows played about the deep-set eyes. She traced the beard-bristled edge of his jaw, slowly moving up to the faint laugh lines that radiated from the corners of his eyes.

His shoulders seemed to span the width of the shed, forcing her to kneel close to the wall. This was no ordinary dayworker, no ordinary brigand. His skin stretched over lean, taut muscles; his back was straight and firm. Her fingers drifted from the uncompromising line of his lips down his chin to trace the skin of his exposed throat, then down farther, to brush the light matting of dark hair.

He was the most handsome man she had ever seen.

Katrina abruptly pulled her hand away. *What was she doing?* He was a brigand—a ruthless, violent thief.

Sobered by this thought, she removed his manteau. She gagged as she glimpsed the tattered linen that had served as a bandage, now dry and caked with blood. Her stomach heaving at the sight, she carefully began removing the material.

The wound bled anew as she gently pulled on his leg to release the linen. She threw the offensive material to a corner of the shed and winced. Matted with blood, the wound was impossible to see. Steeling herself for the job to follow, she rose and searched the saddlebag for the flask of brandy, then cursed as she noticed the empty flask near the brigand's hand.

"Foolish man!" she scolded. "Drinking away your only medicine." Shaking her head, she took the empty flask and walked resolutely to the nearby stream.

The grass along the path was soon matted flat by her many crossings. For hours she toiled over the giant brigand, washing his wound until it bled fresh and red. She mixed some of the herbs with water and misty webs she had found resting in the corners of the shed, and then ruthlessly applied the mixture to the angry wound. The brigand stirred weakly.

Katrina brushed a lock of dark hair from his broad forehead, gazing with concern at the gray pallor of his skin. His forehead felt hot beneath her hand. Fever.

She hastily moved back to his leg, gently removing the second poultice, cursing the lack of heat. She dared not build a fire here; the smoke would alert the villagers in minutes. She poured the icy stream water over the wound until the remnants of webbing and herbs flowed free. She placed a hand on his twitching thigh to still his restless movements. With deft strokes, she wrapped clean linen about his leg and tied it firmly in place.

"Well, my brigand," she murmured to herself. "I've done my piece. It's time for you to do yours." As she briefly rested her hand on his forehead, a crease appearing between her brows, the man stirred beneath her cool touch.

Katrina pulled the manteau over the brigand's restless body. His legs kicked out of the covering, pressing hard against the walls of the shed. Frantically, she pulled the manteau over his legs only to find his arms had come free of the woolen warmth. She patiently covered him again and tucked the fine wool beneath his unshaven chin.

The late afternoon light filtered through the ill-fitting lathes of the shed when Katrina closed the door quietly behind her to return to the chateau. Tante Helene expected her for the evening meal, and Katrina would need food, water, and more herbs to tend her restless patient. His wound had broken open again, but she was more afraid of the fever that had taken hold. She bore new bruises as testament of his strength, and she feared his response should his delirium become worse. She wondered if her whispered words of comfort had penetrated his fever-clouded mind.

Katrina scanned the roads carefully on her return to the chateau, noting that no soldiers patrolled its length. She smiled secretly. The marquis did not think the brigand would dare come so close to the duke's chateau, and that misjudgment would save the brigand. She chuckled with the joy of outwitting the marquis.

Tante Helene asked Katrina no questions when she re-entered the crowded kitchen. She sat down with the other girls and ate the watery meat stew and dark bread with little relish, secreting pieces of bread in the sack at her waist and wondering how she could bring meat stew to the shed. The brigand might not be able to eat, but a few drops of broth squeezed through his lips during a moment of semiconsciousness could strengthen him.

"The marquis's arrival has not affected Katrina, though." Marie's whining voice traveled the length of the table. "She spent the day frolicking in the woods."

"Gathering herbs for the marquis's sophisticated tastes," Katrina retorted. "The duchess insisted on fresh herbs, as if, after drinking all the local wines, one could taste the difference!"

"Your tongue will get you in trouble, Katrina," Tante Helene scolded.

Katrina shrugged casually. "I speak the truth."

"You wouldn't be so unconcerned had you seen the marquis this afternoon," Marie said, her voice falling to hushed tones. "He's tall and gnarled like an old oak. His face is slashed on one side and distorted like some kind of evil mask. He would have stopped your tongue quickly, Katrina."

"I doubt it," she replied casually. She knew only too well what the marquis looked like.

"And he stopped every woman servant as she passed, staring at her with those icy eyes. Oooh." Marie shivered dramatically. "His hand felt like a claw on my arm."

"He liked Charlotte the best." Anne smiled briefly at Katrina. "I guess he likes fair-haired women."

Katrina froze at the girl's words.

"He couldn't keep his eyes off Charlotte," Marie admitted reluctantly. "Kept pulling her hair."

"Ugly man," Charlotte said, shaking her head. "He . . . he seemed so evil."

"You are fortunate you didn't go into the chateau, Katrina," Marie persisted, noticing Katrina's sudden pallor. "With your blond hair, he'd have been all over you. Who knows, perhaps he would've taken you in—"

"I'll clean the pots, Tante," Katrina interrupted sharply, rising from the table. "But I'll use the stream, where it is cooler."

Tante Helene's dark eyes searched Katrina's face, then she wordlessly turned and piled the encrusted pans atop one another and handed Katrina the load. Marie's laugh rang in Katrina's ears as she left the steamy kitchen.

Ignoring the pump and basin, Katrina headed for the stream that passed by the chateau. The path was mercifully bare as she hurried down the slope and sank into the damp grass. Marie knew not how deeply her words had cut. There was no doubt: the marquis had been looking for Katrina today among the servants. Katrina decided not to enter the chateau for any reason— not even to sneak into the duke's library—until the marquis had gone his way.

Hours later, when a sliver of moon had risen over the far hills of Poitiers, Katrina slipped out of the kitchens again, an old rust-encrusted pot in her hands. She knew Tante Helene would never notice the loss of such an old pan, and she had far more use for it now.

Under cover of darkness, she moved swiftly from the open land into the protection of the forest. The moon filtered silver-blue through the irregular canopy of leaves, lighting the wandering path and playing among the will-o'-the-wisps that circled heavy trunks. Katrina passed fearlessly among the strange, twisted trees, as light and swift as a sprite. Her step faltered briefly before the dark shed, as if she was frightened of the mortal soul within it.

"Monsieur?" she whispered as she opened the damp door and squinted into the dark interior. The brigand's body moved restlessly upon the ground as she bent beside him.

His hands reached out and clasped her shoulders roughly. Katrina pushed against his chest, but his strength won and he pulled her against the length of his heated body. His eyes flew open and stared wildly at her.

"Easy, Monsieur. It is just I, Katrina. I've come to care for you." A flicker of consciousness lit the ebony depths of his eyes.

Katrina winced. His hands dug unmercifully into her shoulders, and she knew new bruises would mar her skin for weeks. She pressed against his biceps in vain; they only hardened at her touch. His eyes continued to probe hers, and she opened her mouth to plead.

"Monsieur, you must release me if I'm to care for you," she argued, hoping her voice was calm. "I'll be of no use if you break my arms." His eyes flickered briefly before he loosened his hold. Sighing, she pulled away from him, but his arm shot out and caught her again. He pulled her toward him until her face was inches from his.

"My . . . name," he hissed, his throat dry and unused, "is Rafe." He licked his dry lips with a swollen tongue. His eyes closed briefly. Katrina glanced with concern at the beads of sweat that shone on his forehead and upper lip. The night was cool, but the fever burned in him. She reached up and wiped the moisture from his forehead.

"Hush, brigand," she whispered, but his hand tightened on her arm.

"Call me . . . Rafe," he said, his eyes flaring open to stare at her. She sucked in her breath at the demonic light flashing there.

"Rafe, you must lie still. You are wounded and—"

"In the village . . ." he continued laboriously, his head falling back, his breath ragged on her cheek. "Village. Chauncey, my brother . . ." His eyelids fell heavily and he opened his mouth for air. Taking advantage of his loosened grip, Katrina pulled away from him. He stirred briefly, then fell into a restless unconsciousness. Not waiting for another bout of delirium, Katrina snatched the rusted pan and moved swiftly to the stream. Her patient would need much water this night.

Throughout the evening, Rafe tossed violently on the hard ground as his blood heated. Katrina dodged his powerful thrashing arms and legs with difficulty. She pressed her hand against his mouth when he cried out, poured stream water between his lips and over his face, and cooled his burning forehead with damp compresses. In a moment of rare repose, she checked the wound but found no change. His head tossed back and forth as if in battle with some invisible demon. His powerful chest rose and fell in rapid, uneven breaths.

Katrina glanced nervously at the moon as she stepped from the steaming shed. It was far past midnight and the night was quiet, but a restlessness seemed to emanate from the trees. The dry branches creaked in the chilly gusts of wind, and Katrina heard the darting rustle of a small night animal burrowing through the layer of dead leaves covering the ground. The breeze lifted the heavy mass of hair from her tired shoulders, drying the perspiration that gathered on her neck. Her back was stiff from bending over Rafe's prone form. Fatigued, she reached up to massage the ache.

She whirled as she heard her name whispered from the shed. She burst through the door and knelt before the brigand, who thrashed about, and feverishly murmured her name.

" 'Tis I, Rafe. Katrina," she whispered, touching his face.

His eyes opened and struggled to focus on her face. "Cold," he said harshly, his teeth chattering, his arms wrapping around himself. Katrina searched for the much-abused manteau and found it crumpled in a corner. Shaking it out quickly, she pulled the thick wool over the length of his body. His shivers continued, unabated, and she tucked the edges of the wool tightly around him. Her heart chilled as she realized that the fever was near its pitch.

"Cold, Katrina," he hissed through chattering teeth. Katrina cursed the need for secrecy that prevented her from lighting a fire and watched, helpless, as he shivered uncontrollably. She brushed his thick hair with her fingers, her eyes noting his near-blue lips.

Resolutely, Katrina stood up. She knew well the importance

of keeping a fever patient warm. In Katrina's youth, she had nearly died of a fever, and only Tante Helene's warm, near-naked body had saved her from death. Katrina reached behind with trembling hands to unlace her dress, her eyes never leaving the whitened, pain-stiffened features of the brigand.

The ragged fichu she had found unclaimed among the laundry fluttered to the ground. Shivering, Katrina pulled her arms out of her sleeves and let the rough dress fall down her legs and into a heap on the ground. Clad only in a much-mended cambric chemise, Katrina wrapped her arms around her.

And hesitated.

The chill air seeped under her chemise, and her nipples tightened from the cold. She had never willingly been so close to a man, and something inside caused her to hesitate. His body seemed so huge and powerful, even lying helpless on the shed's floor. His arms bulged with muscles; his shoulders seemed wider than she was tall. He could kill her with one unguided sweep of his hand.

She knelt down near him, and a strange warmth lit in her belly as her knees brushed his side. His eyes opened, dazed, to gaze upon her, a flicker of sanity lighting their depths.

Katrina flushed uncontrollably.

"If you . . ." he stuttered, his words thick, "if you are the angel of death . . . I welcome you."

Katrina sighed, realizing he was deep in delirium and would remember none of this if he lived.

If he lived.

Shaking her head free of her own confused thoughts, Katrina pulled off the chemise and quickly lifted the cloak, lowering herself atop his body. His eyes widened and his arms moved instinctively to encircle the beguiling woman. He groaned as the warmth of her body touched him, heating his chilled limbs.

"What strange torture is this?" he mumbled, his hands freely traveling the length of her smooth, curved back. "So much pain . . . and so much pleasure."

Katrina closed her ears to his words, pulling the woolen manteau over their bodies. Her nakedness pressed against the full, hard length of his body, leaving no doubt of the brigand's virility. The ties to his breeches pressed against her lower belly while her breasts were crushed against the hard plates of his chest. As he moved, the fine linen of his shirt rubbed enticingly against her nipples, which were suddenly sensitive to every touch. His hands traveled with warm abandon over her back to rest possessively on the hill of her bare buttocks. Katrina shivered as some strange, unfamiliar fever began boiling in her blood.

"No torture, brig—Rafe," she whispered, her voice betraying her own tumbling emotions. "I'm trying to save your life."

Deaf to her words, he moved his hands up to her sides and pulled her higher on his body, until her face was level with his. Though his body still shook with tremors, his passion-filled eyes belied his sickness.

"Kiss me, *mon ange,* for your kiss must be sweet enough to make men yearn for death." Rafe lifted his head to meet hers, but she pushed away, hiding her face in the hollow of his shoulder. His hands traveled to her head, but he made no move to force her. Instead, he buried his hands in the thick warmth of her hair.

Katrina trembled anew at this gentle attack. His pulse beat wildly in his throat, and unconsciously she pressed her lips against the throbbing, feeling his stubble-roughened cheek press against her forehead. She stirred against him in some instinctive rhythm, her fingers spreading over his unyielding chest. Her legs parted as he shifted his good leg firmly between her own.

She stiffened as he pressed gently against her, and sparks radiated through her body. Her hands tightened involuntarily against the front of his shirt. He captured one hand in his own and brought it to his lips.

"No angel, this," he murmured as his shivering abated. "No, a woman, full and warm."

Katrina struggled with the waves of unfamiliar passion that pulsed through her. His hands continued their restless movement over her bare, tingling flesh. His trembling had lessened, but his skin still felt cold and clammy beneath her own warmth. His head thrashed back and forth as the fever attacked him anew, and his arms tightened unmercifully around her small body. She gasped as his loins pressed intimately against her own. Only the thin wool of his breeches kept him from her. Her eyes closed languidly at the insistent, hot pounding of her blood.

She did not understand what strange spell he had cast upon her, to make her so eager and pliant beside his magnificent body.

Only his fevered state and the periodic bouts of weakness kept him from fully claiming her. She knew that, were he conscious, she would not leave this shed a virgin tonight. His warm, earthy scent and his tender touch sent her head spinning, her blood pounding, her heart aching for something she did not quite understand. Through the night, she accepted his delirious caresses, trembled at his skillful touch. Her body ached as his fever subsided and he fell back into a heavy, deep sleep.

The sun had begun to lighten the eastern sky when Katrina finally pulled her clothes over her trembling body. Rafe's forehead was cool. His fever had nearly passed.

But, as she tucked her fichu into her bodice and over her passion-swollen breasts, she wondered how she was going to cure the fever he had started in her.

Chapter 4

Katrina stumbled wearily into the kitchens, the pails of milk she carried spilling onto her skirts. Tante Helene stared as she entered, her face puckering into a frown at the sight of Katrina's violet-rimmed eyes and pale skin. Katrina placed the milk on the table and sat heavily at the end of the wooden benches.

"It might be time for you to get some sleep," Tante Helene said firmly, hefting the pails to the large vat in the back of the kitchen. "Instead of prowling around at all hours of the night."

Katrina stiffened in her seat. She did not relish the prospect of arguing with Tante, especially when she knew she would be forced to lie again. "The church tocsins have been ringing interminably for weeks now," she explained. "They wake me up."

"You don't have to lie to me, child," Tante said quietly.

"I'm not lying!" Katrina exclaimed, flushing in embarrassment. "Every time a beggar sets foot in the province, the tocsins ring in warning of—brigands." She stumbled over the last word.

Tante Helene sighed and turned her back. From the tilt of the older woman's peppered chignon, Katrina knew she was angry. Katrina shifted uncomfortably in the long silence that stretched between them.

"I have raised you like my own," Tante Helene said, turning suddenly, tossing a half loaf of bread on the table. "I must have my say, even if you won't listen to me." She paused briefly, then rushed on. "Men'll do and say what they will—anything—if they think they can get a girl on her back. They'll even make sweet promises. But mark me—be careful what you give them before your names are in the church book. There are altogether too many bastards in France."

Katrina gasped. "Tante—"

"I'll hear none of it," Tante Helene insisted. "Now come, help me spit this hare."

Speechless, Katrina joined her at the hearth and held the rod while she skewered the skinned hare on its length, then placed it upon the fire.

"Plainer fare," Katrina commented quietly, not willing to set Tante Helene off on another diatribe. "Has the Marquis de Noailles left?"

"Yes. None too soon, either," Tante Helene said quietly, still red-faced from her outburst. "The duchess is furious. The marquis left after the duke went off on one of his ravings. The duchess insists the duke did it on purpose to get rid of the marquis." Her dark eyes sparkled. "Frankly, I think the Duke is less senile than he appears."

"Was he raving about his first wife again?" Katrina asked, her stomach growling at the scent of the meat.

"What else? Apparently the marquis was discussing his preference for fairer women when the duke began reminiscing about his first wife. I think she must have been quite fair, though no one really knows. When the duke remarried, the new duchess fired all the old help and brought us from her own chateau." She handed Katrina a leg of some barnyard fowl, and Katrina bit into it eagerly.

"Well, at least with the marquis gone the chateau will return to normal," Katrina murmured.

Tante Helene glanced at her oddly. "Perhaps," she said. "Why don't you take a nap, Katrina? You look exhausted."

"Perhaps later. I think I'll go for a walk now."

The cool spring air ruffled her skirts as she left the heated kitchen. The low-lying, gray clouds moved over the land while the chickens clucked boisterously in the nearby pen. The weariness of the past days weighed heavily on her shoulders, but the turmoil of her emotions had kept her from enjoying what little sleep she'd had.

The brigand had not yet come to full consciousness. Although his breathing seemed normal, his wound did not fester, and his fever had broken two days ago, Katrina feared this lengthy sleep . . . almost as much as she feared his inevitable awakening.

Would he remember the evening when she lay with him, naked, warming him with her body? Would he remember her response to his roaming hands? She flushed at the memory, and the strange tingling began anew in her belly. Shaking her head, she strode determinedly toward the rear entrance of the chateau. She knew she could not sleep, but a copy of *La Nouvelle Heloise* lay half-read in the upper stories of the duke's library. With all that had happened, she had had no time to finish it. Now with the marquis safely away from the chateau, and the brigand sleeping in some comfort, perhaps she could finish the book. Anything to get her mind off the memory of his probing, warm hands.

She glanced carefully around her as she approached the chateau. It was late afternoon, a time when the liveried servants normally ate dinner, after the duke and duchess had finished theirs. Seeing no one in the courtyard, she bravely pushed open the back door and scurried into the chateau.

Katrina anxiously eyed the gleaming, paneled hallway and pressed against the heavy oak door which led into the back of the duke's library. Her heart pounded as it always did when she made this dangerous trip. If she, an unliveried kitchen maid, were seen inside the chateau, she would be severely chastised. Her place was in the steaming kitchens that were set back behind the courtyard, close to the pens that held goats, chickens, and other fowl. In the main house, all servants had to be liveried in uniforms of dark blue with gold and silver braid.

As she entered the library, Katrina braced herself for the sound of the duke's voice. After his most recent bout of "senility," she doubted he would be working in his library. Hearing no sound, she scuttled to the end of the rows of bookcases and climbed the polished staircase that led to the balcony. The balcony ran on both sides of the huge, gleaming room, yet few books filled the shelves that lined the walls. Most of the leather- and buckram-bound tomes were on the lower floor, with this alcove used to store the excess. According to Tante Helene, the Duke had stopped buying books after the death of his first wife.

Katrina had managed to secret away a few books on the last bookshelf: John Locke, Montesquieu, Rousseau, Voltaire. For years she'd come here to sit on the hardwood floor and absorb those works that Father Hytier forbade her to read, primarily because some authors, such as Voltaire, criticized the Catholic Church.

Just as Katrina settled down with Rousseau, she heard an ominous scraping on the bottom floor.

"Well, gentlemen. Come in here and we'll discuss whatever news you have. It's been months since this room has been graced with good conversation."

Katrina stiffened in recognition of the duke's rasping voice. The door on the lower level closed, and chairs creaked as several individuals took their seats. It was too late to leave now.

"This is a dusty old room, isn't it, René?"

Katrina leaned closer to the cherrywood spokes of the railing, raising her head slightly to see the men. There were two others besides the white, balding head of René, the Duke de Poitiers.

"It is not used often enough, Monsieur de Gourville—"

"Please call me Jean, René."

"Very well, Jean. This room is used only by me, and not often enough. Could you imagine the duchess with her powdered nose in one of these tomes?" As the duke's hand swept out to point to the balcony, Katrina ducked. "Why, she would only ruin them." The men chuckled lightly and Katrina heard the clink of glasses.

"Indeed," Jean said. "This room is far from the duchess's, ah, bright taste."

"But come, Jean. I wish to know the news," the duke insisted. "I have spent nearly a week with the most pompous aristocrat."

"The Marquis de Noailles," Jean said dryly. "I've heard. You should take care, René, for he has much power at Versailles."

"I care little," the duke said vehemently, "for him or Versailles. You know that well." A long silence stretched as he leaned back in his creaking chair. "Well, you had news for me. Out with it."

Jean cleared his throat and shrugged. "It is nothing more than the results of the elections for the *Etats généraux*, Monsieur," Jean said. "The elderly Thibaudeau has been elected as a Poitou representative."

"Thibaudeau?" the duke said. "I approve. He is a good republican."

"Come now, Monsieur," the third man said to the duke. "Surely you do not want a liberal in this blasphemous group? When the king called a meeting of the *Etats généraux*, he only wanted approval for more taxes to get France out of debt. He did not want a bunch of liberal rubble speaking up and disrupting the day-to-day court proceedings!''

"I know very well what the king wanted when he called the *Etats généraux*,'' the duke said succinctly. "But what he will get is an entirely different matter, Monsieur de Verteuil. You must be aware of the bread riots in Paris and in every French province. You must know of the famine that has swept the land this year, the fear of hoarded grain, the fear of brigands—''

"There have been other years far worse,'' Monsieur de Verteuil argued. "The important thing is to get France out of debt. Then those problems will take care of themselves.''

"Spoken like a true aristocrat. I am sure the king agrees with you, but he has called a meeting of the representatives of the people—including the peasantry. The peasants will find problems of famine and grain-hoarding far more important than paying for Marie Antoinette's jewels.''

Katrina leaned close to the railing to hear better. She jumped back suddenly as Monsieur de Verteuil waved a hand toward her, and she pressed against the uncarpeted floor in panic.

"The King will crush any opposition!'' the man insisted.

"Or perhaps the *Etats généraux* will crush the king's opposition,'' the duke said bluntly. The other two men gasped at this notion. "I think you underestimate how desperate the people of France are becoming, *mes amis*. They have faith in King Louis XVI, and many of the peasants believe this meeting of the *Etats généraux* will end taxation, will end forced labor, will end the hunting restrictions, will end all the aristocratic privileges that crush them.''

"Foolish beliefs, then,'' Monsieur de Verteuil said, "for the king has no intention of doing any of those things. He wishes only to force more taxes—perhaps on the nobility—to pay for his and his wife's extravagances.''

"How disappointed he and Marie Antoinette will be, then,'' the duke said calmly, "when the *Etats généraux* unseat him.''

"You speak treason, Monsieur!'' Jean exclaimed, suddenly roused from his observant silence. "The excuse of your senility can go only so far.''

"I am not senile!'' the duke boomed, rising from his seat. Katrina caught her breath and moved back from the railing, but her cry had been heard. The duke's head turned toward the balcony, and for a brief moment their gazes met. Gasping in surprise, he started to say something, but he fainted before a word could be uttered.

Katrina jumped up and swung around, her golden braid trailing. With fleet feet she scurried down the staircase and, while the two guests hovered about the dazed duke, raced through the side door and fled the chateau.

The swiftness of terror carried her to the edge of the forest and into its hidden depths.

Rafe struggled with the gray fog that threatened to suffocate him. His eyelids weighed heavily and it took a great feat of strength to open them in the hazy light. He winced as he tried to move, and knives of pain shot up his leg. But the pain jolted his memory, and with it, his sanity.

Gingerly, he reached down to probe his wounded leg. It was covered with linen, tightly knotted at the top, and the linen felt dry, if not completely clean. There was no putrid scent of rotting flesh—a scent with which he had become familiar while battling the English in America. Though the wound pained him, it did not have the pulsing throb of a more serious injury. He sighed and leaned back against the hard ground.

Calmly, Rafe took stock of his situation. The roof above him was poorly covered, and spots of wetness on his manteau gave evidence of recent rain. He turned his head painfully to survey the shed. It seemed to be a single room, an old one. The earthy scent of rotting wood permeated the air. A rusty, broken scythe leaned against the far wall, and shoots of hardy weeds pressed up between the uneven floorboards. A pile of blood-soaked linens was heaped in a corner; they were undoubtedly stained with his own blood. The sun, bright through the ill-fitting boards, pained his eyes. He squeezed them shut again.

How long had he been unconscious? Vague, clouded memories of cool, white hands and a voice as calming as a murmuring stream invaded his thoughts. A flash of concerned green eyes, the brush of silken hair against his cheek. His brows drew together as more disturbing memories rose from the mist.

He shook his head free from the pain of concentration. Soon enough the memories would rise of their own accord. Now he must concentrate on regaining his strength. He searched the room for sustenance, and found beside him a small pan filled with water. He did not stop to wonder at its freshness.

Rafe lay back against the ground, his thirst quenched and his throat cleared of its dusty dryness. The mist of unconsciousness slowly lifted and he calmly tried to retrace all that had passed.

The raid on the marquis. Damned aristocrat! Rafe should have known the Marquis would not risk carrying such a huge sum of money without guarding it properly. The arrogance of the man! The marquis had hoped to capture the brigands as well as make a safe escape with the blood money he had squeezed from his peasantry. Rafe swore never to underestimate him again.

The little blonde. The glint of lantern light in her hair. What was her name? Katrina. Rafe's lips curved in a slight smile. The full memory of the evening flooded in on him. Their escape, the marquis's surprisingly faulty shot, Katrina's concern over his wound, her gentle ministrations.

An elusive image tugged at his memory. A flash of white skin tinted blue by the moon's glow. A soft warmth pressing against his chest. He once again shook his head free of his jumbled thoughts.

How many days had it been? He reached for the pan of water again and drained it of its contents. He scanned the room for food, but saw none. He would have to wait until the woman who tended him returned.

Was it Katrina who had tended him? The girl he remembered in the forest did not seem to be the woman whose hands soothed his fever, whose husky, lilting voice whispered sanity through his delirium. The woman who tended him . . . the woman who tended him . . .

He closed his eyes as the memory of her lithe, naked body rose full and proud above him. Had he imagined such alabaster beauty? Had he imagined the golden halo that surrounded her head, fell over her shoulders to her hips? Shamelessly she had pulled the blankets from him and pressed her naked body against his. She murmured to him . . . he could not remember her words, but he did remember the smooth satin of her skin and the rounded body that surrounded him with warmth and comfort. A thousand sensuous moments were wrapped in the memory of the angel who had held him.

The angel of death, he had called her. Perhaps she was, and only her reluctance to kiss him kept him alive.

Rafe dismissed such foolish, wandering thoughts. Apparently the delirium was not yet gone. He would soon find out who his nurse was, who had dared to risk her life to save that of a brigand. He vowed to reward her for her bravery, whoever she was. In the meantime, he had to move to relieve the sores that bruised his back and buttocks from what must have been days spent on the hard floor.

His head swam as he lifted himself up on his elbows. He squeezed his eyes shut and breathed deeply before opening them again. The room stopped spinning. He glanced down at himself, noticing the hollow of his abdomen. He had not eaten in days, perhaps weeks. There was no way to tell. He pulled himself higher, but the blood left his head, and he fell back weakly to his elbows.

"Up. Finally." The tart voice came from the doorway, and Rafe threw an arm across his eyes at the glare. "I thought you'd never awaken."

"Close the damned door," he hissed. "You're blinding me."

"I see you've recovered almost completely," she remarked, shutting the door and coming to his side.

Rafe's eyes watered from the pain of the sudden light. He felt the brush of a worn skirt against his side and a cool hand passed over his forehead.

"Your fever is gone, as well," she said in that tantalizing, lilting voice.

He struggled to open his eyes, but red spots obscured his vision. The cool hands moved to his thigh and picked at his linen. He flinched.

"I must see this wound," she insisted, "to make sure it has not festered."

"It is not festering." Rafe laid back and blinked spasmodically. "If it were, I would smell it."

"You're the patient, remember? Be still while I remove this bandage."

Rafe smiled and lifted his head. Her blond hair lay in a haphazard plait down her back, brushing against the ground. Her eyes stared intensely at his wound, but he knew their color: green and clear, like the color of the grapes of Champagne.

"Katrina," he murmured.

She smiled, showing a row of perfect teeth. "You remember my name. From the look of this wound and your astounding memory, you should be well in a few weeks."

"Weeks!" he blurted, rising to his elbows. "How long have I been here?"

Katrina pressed him down. "A fortnight. Don't you remember? You seemed rather lucid every once in a while."

"A fortnight!" he exclaimed, breathing deeply. "My men? Have you heard anything of my men?"

Katrina stared at the brigand and rose, dusting her skirts. "None of the other brigands were caught, if that's what you need to know. The Marquis de Noailles sent out men to search for all of you, and so did the Duke de Poitiers and the intendant." She lifted a winged brow. "All in all, you were a much sought after man for a while, but now the searches have all been called off."

Rafe stared at the girl who stood before him. Her dress, large for her slight body, obscured any curves that lay below. Yet staring up at her from his makeshift bed, he recognized the identity of the soft, enchanting woman who had warmed him that night.

Katrina saw the knowledge in his eyes and bit her lower lip, her face flushing brightly. She turned toward the door. "I will get you water," she said abruptly, ignoring his moan as she swung the door wide, letting the afternoon sun pour through the opening.

She hurried to the stream and plunged her arms up to her elbows in the frigid water to still the hot pulse throbbing through her body. She had hoped fervently that he would remember nothing of that delirious night, but she had seen the memory clear and vivid in his eyes. What would he expect of her, now that he knew she had pressed wantonly against him?

She breathed deeply and busied herself gathering berries and filling the pan with water. Although his wound seemed to be knitting well, she must remember that he still lay ill, far from health. Once he grew strong enough to walk, she would leave him to his own devices. Until then, she had an obligation to this disturbingly attractive man.

When Katrina returned to the shed, her face bore no traces of her earlier shame. Rafe twisted away from the light but turned back to her quickly, watching her movements as she prepared food for him.

"You've been caring for me for a fortnight?" he asked, his stomach growling loudly in the small shed. Katrina smiled at the sound.

"Yes," she answered. "No one else knows of your presence. You have woken at a good time—Tante Helene, my guardian, suspects I have a lover. I cannot keep coming here and staying with you late at night . . . it is too dangerous."

"Aren't you rather young for anyone to think you have a lover?" he asked steadily. "How old are you, *petite?*"

Katrina turned away to break the half loaf of bread she had secreted from the kitchens. "Nearly eighteen."

"With that formless dress and your hair pulled back, you could pass for twelve."

"As is my intent," she retorted. "Men will do things to an eighteen-year-old that they would not do to a twelve-year-old." She shrugged one thin shoulder.

Rafe reached for the bread she handed him and bit into it voraciously. He drank some fresh spring water before taking another bite. Katrina watched him eat, a slow smile spreading across her face.

"Shall I give you a knife to pick your teeth with?" she asked. "You eat like a beast."

"I haven't eaten in days and I'm famished." He nodded toward the small sack at her waist. "Don't you have anything more substantial? Meat, perhaps?"

Katrina shook her head. "I do, but I will not let you have it. You couldn't keep it down." Rafe sank against the back wall of the shed, turning his head to watch her. "I'll let you have some meat tomorrow, but even then only a bit. You're still far from health, brigand."

"Didn't I tell you my name?" he asked wryly.

Katrina glanced at his dark eyes and the smile that tilted his lips. Propped up against the wall, blocking the light behind him, his shoulders seemed wider.

"Yes," she said hesitantly. "You said your name was Rafe."

"Use it, then," he insisted. "I prefer it to 'brigand.' "

"But you are a brigand, after all. Why should you deny your

métier?'' Katrina queried, rising to brush the crumbs from her skirt.

"Would you approve if I called you 'nurse'?" he countered.

She flashed her eyes at him, noticing his smile had widened to show strong, even teeth. "Of course not," she said crossly, "but that is different. I have been calling you 'brigand' for so long, I can hardly call you by any other name. Besides"—she hesitated, sipping from the pan of water—"I need to remind myself of what you are."

"Why, *ma petite?''* he said. "Do you think I will ravish you as soon as my strength returns?" His eyes sparkled.

"Perhaps." Defiantly, she moved by his side to change the linen on his wound. Brutally, she poked his leg up to pull the material from beneath it. He winced but made no sound of pain. She examined the wound with care, tracing the angry, yellow-green bruise.

His breeches had nearly fallen off below the thigh from her constant care. She pushed them down farther to check the full extent of the bruise and gasped as she noticed a scar tracing the inner part of his thigh, nearly down to his knee.

"I see you have experience with severe wounds," Katrina exclaimed. "I suppose that it is a common occurrence in your line of work."

"That wound was a far more honorable one, Katrina," he said, his voice a caress. "I received it under the service of the Marquis de Lafayette, in the American War of Independence."

Katrina's head snapped up in interest. "You were in America?" Her light eyes clouded with questions. "How did you achieve such a fall from grace?"

Rafe's laughter rang weakly through the shed. "I was not always a brigand, *petite,''* he assured her. "Do I have the look of a hardened criminal?"

She bit her lip. He had more the look of a fine, young aristocrat, but she'd be damned before she would tell him that. "I wouldn't know, for I've never known a hardened criminal," she answered and wrapped a new piece of linen around his leg. "Tell me of America." She pressed the linen flat against the dark skin covering his hard thigh. "I know little from what I've read, and I am sure it is all lies."

Rafe glanced down at her, his eyes raised in surprise. "What you've read . . ." he said. "Where did a simple peasant girl find time to learn to read?"

"I am hardly simple, brigand," she spat. "As for learning, the priest that lives not one hundred paces from here took pity on an eager young girl and taught me much more than reading. He taught me Latin, geography, mathematics, and a bit of English. The rest I have learned on my own."

"I have underestimated you, my Katrina," he said, respect in his voice. "I thought you were nothing more than a spirited young wench with an aptitude for healing."

Katrina lifted her chin in faint defiance and saw the gleam of amusement in his eyes. "Now you tease me," she murmured, flushing. She finished his bandage and moved away. His face was drawn in pain, but life glowed in the onyx of his eyes. "I should be going," she said, rising to leave.

He reached out and pulled her down beside him again. Katrina trembled at the warmth of his hand on her wrist.

"You've endangered yourself these past days by taking care of me." His dark eyes rested seriously on her face, all hint of mirth gone. "I will never forget such a debt."

Katrina's gaze clouded with the uncomfortable confusion his touch created. She tried in vain to pull gently from his grasp. "It's nothing—" She stumbled, her face flushing at his intense scrutiny. "I would do the same for anyone in need."

"Nonetheless, you have saved my life, *ma petite.*" He pulled inexorably on her arm until she half lay, half sat beside him, her face inches from his. The heat of his eyes warmed her blood.

"Please . . ." she pleaded breathlessly.

His gaze fell to her full, trembling lips. He leaned toward her, pressing his own lips gently against hers.

It was meant to be a gentle, comforting kiss. But the feel of her soft mouth beneath his, mixed with the hazy memories of the woman who had nearly given herself to him, urged him on to greater passion. Rafe ran his hand over her head, entwining his fingers in her hair. She lifted her hand to his arm in a mockery of resistance.

"Katrina . . ." he said hoarsely, pulling away from her. Her eyes were filled with conflicting emotions and her lips were swollen from his kiss. With a touch of triumph he saw the passion throbbing in her throat. Gently, he released her wrist and pulled away from her.

"I want you to know I will never hurt you," he said, his fingers tracing the soft skin of her palm. "You'll never have anything to fear from me."

Chapter 5

"I thought you'd never return," Rafe said loudly as Katrina swept into the small shed. A half loaf of bread tumbled out of her arms and onto the floor, and in a minute, he had it in his hands.

"It's been only a few hours!" she exclaimed. "Didn't this morning's sausage fill you up?" Rafe's dark eyes traveled intimately over her small frame. Katrina flushed at his expression.

"That morsel may be enough to fill your stomach, *ma petite*, but mine is far larger than yours." Rafe bit ravenously into the bread as she set the meal before him. He studied her hair, bound at the nape of her neck by a single, ragged green ribbon. In the spring sunshine seeping through the boards of the shed, her hair shone like spun gold and polished copper. Absently, he reached out and fingered a strand that flowed over her shoulder.

"Such hair," he said between bites. "Where in God's name did you come by such coloring?"

Katrina smiled shyly and pulled away from his hands. "I don't know," she replied, reaching for a piece of bread before the brigand ate the entire loaf. "Tante Helene found me abandoned in the woods as a babe and took me into her care. We never discovered who my parents were."

"Katrina Dubois," he said. "You are, indeed, a child of the forest. How did you come by such an unusual first name? Was there a note tied around that lovely neck?"

She glanced at him, noting the dark color that stained his cheeks. He sat upright against the back of the shed, his wounded leg straight in front of him. During the past days he had eaten like a starved man, and it hadn't taken long for the brigand to regain a good portion of his strength.

"I was found a few days before the duke's only child was kidnaped. Tante Helene thought it was appropriate to name me after the missing child."

"I didn't know the duke had a child of his own," Rafe said, reaching for another piece of cold meat. "I thought he only had a stepdaughter from his second marriage."

"She is his only child now," Katrina said. "The kidnaped child was never found, and no ransom was ever demanded." She sighed, leaning back against the opposite wall. "It was a great tragedy for the duke, who had lost his first wife only a few months earlier and had just married the current duchess—a genuine shrew. Rumor has it that he married her in his grief only so that his daughter would have a mother."

"It seems that, for an aristocrat, the duke has had his share of sadness," Rafe said, observing the girl with interest.

"Yes, he never recovered from the tragedy," she said, the exhaustion of the past few days weighing heavily on her shoulders. "He started saying and doing crazy things shortly after. He's quite senile now, poor old man." Katrina's unusual, tilted eyes half closed in weariness.

"I've heard those rumors," Rafe said, his interest renewed. "Don't fall asleep on me now, I've had no one to talk to all morning." He tossed a piece of bread upon her lap, and she started awake and stared at him. His eyes twinkled at the dazed expression on her face. She flushed at his intense scrutiny, and readjusted her skirts.

"Well, then, talk and I will listen," she said irritably. "Ungrateful, aren't you? I have hardly had any sleep in weeks and you're poking me awake."

"Poor child," he teased. "But you can't sleep yet. You must tell more about the duke. Here, eat this chicken. You are far too skinny, and perhaps it will keep you awake."

Katrina regarded him with suspicion. Rafe held out a piece of meat, urging her to take it. She reached for it and his fingers curled firmly around her hand. Her gaze fluttered to his, and she quivered at the look in his eyes.

"I—I can hardly eat it," she stuttered, "if you don't release it."

"I know," he said. She looked away, knowing that her cheeks glowed hotly. He laughed and released her. "I just wanted to see you flush," he remarked, his voice not as steady as he wished it to be. "Your face glows like sunshine when you blush."

"Why—why do you want to hear about the duke?" she asked.

"I'm interested in any aristocrat," Rafe answered carefully. His mouth lifted in a half smile. "It's my business to know the activities of all the local aristocrats."

Katrina's eyes flashed hotly and she stood up.

"You will not raid the duke's lands," she said firmly. "Not if you hold any gratitude for me."

Rafe's eyes narrowed. "I had no intention of stealing his money or grain, Katrina. I have already heard of the duke and find no cause for such a raid."

Katrina paced angrily before him. She pulled upon her fichu. "It's warm in here. I'm going to sit outside for a while." She pushed open the shed door and stomped over the sun-warmed grass to a small spot of shade. As she turned to sit, she gasped to see the brigand's tall width leaning against the shed, a lop-sided smile on his face.

"You should not be up!" she exclaimed, running a few steps toward him. "You'll reopen your wound."

"You'll not get away so easily, *ma petite.*" He pushed away from the shed and began limping slowly toward her. Her hands flew to her mouth and she stepped forward, but he held out a hand to stay her.

"No, Katrina," he said. "The only way I will strengthen this leg is by walking upon it."

She resisted the urge to run to his side, instead waiting with bated breath as he crossed the clearing with halting, laborious steps. She noticed the beads of sweat upon his forehead, and his bare chest gleamed with the effort. The linen that bound his upper leg showed no signs of new blood, but Katrina knew that the delicate knitting would not withstand too much strain. When he was a few steps away, she rushed to his side and pressed her hands against his hard chest.

He drew a ragged breath and shook his head free of dizziness as her slight form moved to support him.

"You must sit, Rafe," she said softly, her sweet breath falling upon him. He opened his eyes to glance down at her flawless, near-translucent skin. He had never seen her in the light of day and the sight astounded him. Her eyes glowed with the brightness of emeralds; her hair, tossed in fabulous disarray around her face, shone as blinding as sunlight.

"Only if you will sit with me."

Katrina caught her breath as his finger touched her cheek. His great height cast a shadow upon her as she looked up into his eyes. His hair, ablaze with indigo-blue highlights, surrounded his face like a dark, shimmering cloud. Though the strain of the walk had tightened the skin over his smooth cheekbones, his eyes bore no hint of pain. Instead, they devoured her with an intensity that turned her legs to water.

"Of course," she agreed huskily, supporting him as he bent his good knee and lowered his towering body to the ground. Katrina knelt before him and reached to touch the linen bandage.

"The wound heals well, thanks to you," he said. "Your Tante Helene taught you well."

"She'd be appalled if she knew I'd aided a brigand," she said, caught up in the strange, thick currents that flowed between them. He laughed and the sound vibrated languidly through her blood.

"I should ease your mind, little one." His deep, resonant voice calmed her. "I am not the violent thief you think I am." He leaned easily upon one elbow, toying with a weed.

"I saw differently the night you attacked the marquis's carriage," she replied. "You stole bags of his money—"

"That was not *his* money, Katrina," Rafe corrected. "Those were taxes he levied upon his people, which were not approved by the king. As if all the other taxes weren't enough." A note of anger had crept into his voice.

"What about the burnings, the raids upon the peasantry, the stealing of grain—"

"We've done none of that," Rafe interrupted. "We did burn the marquis's carriage, but only because he killed a village boy by racing carelessly through the marketplace."

"You stole no grain?" Katrina asked, a crease appearing between her brows. "But—but I've heard so many stories . . ."

"That's exactly what they are, *ma petite,*" Rafe said, facing her. "Stories. Nothing but wild rumors. All of France is rife with rumors. The people wonder why so much grain travels the roads of France and yet they still starve. They wonder why the king has allowed French nobles to sell their grain abroad at high prices, while people go hungry in their own fertile land." He shook his head. "I spent nearly ten years in America, Katrina. Ten years fighting with men who wanted nothing but freedom from unfair taxation, the freedom to live the way they wanted!" He ran a hand through his unruly hair, one lock stubbornly springing back over his forehead. "I watched the birth of their constitution and wondered why the people of France still did not rebel against the oppression of the monarchy.

"I returned two years ago. Since then, I've fought against people like the Marquis de Noailles throughout France." He glanced at her widened eyes and smiled briefly. "You see, little one, I'm not the ogre you believe me to be. Our actions have motives behind them: they are not the raids of senseless, violent men. Disappointed?"

Katrina stared at him, seeing the one wall she had built as a defense against his irresistible charm crumble down before her.

"But—but this is treason you speak of!" she stammered. "We—all of us—love King Louis XVI!"

"Ah, yes, I know." He reached out to clasp her cold hand, and his fingers curled around hers naturally. "Despite the king's excesses, and those of the two kings before him, the people of France still have an overwhelming love for him." He shrugged, stroking her fingers. "I have no desire to unseat the king, merely to reform his policies. I hope the meeting of the *Etats généraux* will accomplish that."

"You sound doubtful," she whispered, the caress of his hands distracting her.

"I have heard the king is not willing to listen to the words of the people," Rafe explained, watching with renewed interest the play of light in her hair. "I fear that change will not be easy in this country." He released her hands and reached for her shoulders. Gently, he eased her next to him and laid her head on his lap. She closed her heavy lids, relaxing on the strong pillow of Rafe's good thigh.

"You are weary, *ma belle*," he murmured above her. He untied the ribbon at her nape and combed his fingers through the sun-warmed length of her hair. She sighed contentedly. "Sleep for a while. I will wake you before long."

* * *

Katrina stretched languidly on the soft ground, lifting her arms above her head and arching her back. She squinted against the warm light teasing her eyes and turned away from it, finding herself against a vibrant, living warmth. She drew her brows together in curiosity. Her eyes fluttered open to see Rafe's gaze dance upon her, his mouth twisted in a lopsided smile. She blinked sleepily a few times, wondering why such a devilishly handsome man would look at her in such a way.

"Have a good sleep, my forest sprite?" he asked.

Katrina rolled effortlessly into the heated circle of his body. She glanced up in surprise at the closeness of his face. "Sleep?" she echoed, her eyes falling to his lips. "How long have I been sleeping?"

"Over an hour, *ma petite*," he said, reaching up to brush a lock of hair from her face. He rested his hand on the back of her head. "You looked so innocent, I had not the heart to wake you."

Katrina cursed her heart for pounding so furiously and so loudly. She knew he could hear it, knew he could sense her reaction to his nearness.

"As I watched you sleep, I wondered if such innocence could be real," Rafe murmured, his smile waning. "I have never seen such innocence in a woman as breathtaking as you."

"You're not well yet, I see," she said. "You're still delirious."

"I wondered . . ." he continued, laying her head upon the soft ground and shifting his weight. His shoulders cast a dark shadow over her face. "I wondered if you could be the same woman who has haunted my dreams of the past week. The woman who, during my fever, tossed her clothes aside and pressed against me—"

Katrina touched her fingers to the warmth of his lips, her eyes wide with fear of the words to follow. "Please . . ." she pleaded.

He caught her hand and kissed each pink-tipped finger. "Do not fear me," he said raggedly, moving over her until her head was caged between his elbows. His dark hair fell over his forehead. "Never fear me, my little Katrina."

She closed her eyes as his lips descended upon hers, her body trembling beneath his strength. She could not move even if she wanted to: his body lay nearly atop hers, one leg moving seductively between her own. His lips played over her mouth, pressing gently against her soft lips. He lifted his head, but her lips clung to his, not wanting to break the sweet contact.

"Sweet Katrina . . ." His mouth descended again, and his hands curled in the sun-warmed pillow of her hair, entwining in the silken thickness. Katrina lifted her hands to his sides, running them lightly over the well-developed length. He was so muscular she could hardly reach around to his back, and instead explored the rock-hard strength of his arms.

A gentle wind eased the early spring's heat and ruffled Rafe's hair. Deep in the forest young birds chirped their hunger to rustling leaves, while gray-tailed squirrels burrowed in last year's litter.

Katrina heard none of these familiar forest sounds. Rafe's heart beating strongly beneath her hands, his breath growing ragged against her cheek—these were the only sounds that mattered. His tongue urged her lips open, and he plunged gently into the sweet, unexplored recesses of her mouth. Her body tingled with this intimate probing, and she reached up to brush his soft, short beard. Unconsciously, she arched against him.

Rafe moaned deep in his throat as Katrina pressed against his aching body. Her lips tasted as sweet as spring wine and he drank deeply of the precious draught. Her light hands traveled over him with hesitant curiosity. Boldly, he traced her side with one hand, stopping to rest at her thigh then return again, pausing at the base of her breast.

Katrina's hands tightened on his shoulders as his hand brushed over her swelling bosom. Sparks of fire radiated through her body, swirling to settle in a growing blaze in her abdomen.

"Rafe . . ." Her body surged beneath him, seeking his strength, his warmth, his magic.

She gasped for breath as Rafe turned to taste the delicate tip of her ear, the hollow of her throat, the racing pulse just beneath her skin. The faint wood-spice scent of her filled his senses. His hands ached to feel all of her; his skin burned for her own naked flesh; his lips explored the sweet, sensitive arch of her shoulder.

She moaned beneath his caresses, her bright eyes opening in surprise. Rafe lifted his head to stare into the green pools.

Her breath came swiftly between rose-kissed lips. Katrina stared at the giant man above her, her heart beating hard in her chest. A muscle moved spasmodically in his cheek. As his gaze swept her from her hair to the tips of her bare feet, she shuddered uncontrollably beneath his strength and power.

"You are an innocent, aren't you, little Katrina?"

She blinked at his sudden words. Unconsciously, she nodded. He cursed and rose stiffly off of her.

"It doesn't matter . . ." she whispered, wrapping her arms around her as a chill swept between them.

"Yes, it does," he insisted. "It makes all the difference in the world." He sat upright, his back to her, running a hand through his hair. "I'm only a man, Katrina. I suggest you move as far away from me as you can."

She felt as if he had just thrown her into an icy stream. Katrina sat up abruptly, her face flushing. Her fichu had come out of her bodice and her breasts nearly rose from the edge. With trembling hands she adjusted her clothing and tried in vain to comb the tangles from her hair.

"I—I don't understand . . ." she stuttered, her blood still pounding painfully in her ears. "Have I done something wrong?"

His dark eyes blazing, Rafe glanced back at her disheveled figure, shook his head, and turned away.

"You have done nothing wrong, *petite*. Quite the opposite. *I* forgot that you were an innocent and could not forget that you were a woman. It is that simple."

Katrina stood on shaking legs and moved away from him, entering the shed to gather the linen and other items she had brought with her. When she left the shed, Rafe stood leaning against the wall. She glanced briefly to his thigh and flushed.

"Keep blushing, Katrina," he said. "It will save you from me."

But I don't want to be saved from you! she thought. She looked away from the intensity of his gaze.

"I guess . . . I should be going now," she said. Rafe reached out and grabbed her arm as she passed.

"Look at me, *petite*," he demanded. She lifted confused, clouded eyes to his brutally handsome face.

"You've done too much for me, little one. I am deeply in your debt. The last thing I want to do is rob you of your innocence." Rafe turned from her, his desire awakening anew. "I must leave here as soon as possible. Can you take a message to the village?''

"I will not be in league with brigands," she said.

He lifted a brow in sarcasm. "I thought we had been through all this, Katrina," he said. She shook her head. "Come. It is time for me to leave the protection of this shed. You are in danger as long as I am here." *In more ways than one*, Rafe silently added. "Will you carry a message to my brother in Poitiers? He'll make arrangements to get me out of here."

"You'll be leaving?" she asked softly, her eyes tracing the hard planes of his face.

He looked away. "Yes. I have one more score to finish with the Marquis de Noailles, and then, little one"—he traced the pert uptilt of her nose—"it will be time to leave you in peace."

Poitiers was set on a ridge overlooking fertile plains, most of which were owned by the duke. The spires of Notre Dame La Grande and Notre Dame La Petite rose above the close buildings of the city, ornately stark against the sky. The domes and turrets of the other churches, St. Hilaire and the cathedral of St. Pierre, also contributed to the bumpy, indistinct skyline. But Katrina's gaze lingered on it for only a moment, falling instead to the people that entered the city in long, mobile lines.

She recognized the dirt-stained dress of the *journaliers*, dayworkers whose short spurts of work kept them full in the spring and fall, but hungry in the long months of winter. Several farmers possessively carried their hoards of precious grain, the carts surrounded by the sons and daughters of the family. A hawker burdened with his wares pranced among the people, lifting glittering objects and bottles of vile-smelling liquid for approval. A number of high-spirited horses led a low-slung carriage, which pushed aside the slow-moving lines of people to commandeer the road for itself, the driver yelling loudly to those who dared block his way.

Katrina walked confidently through the city gate and into the narrow cobbled streets, waving off a merchant who raised heads of cabbage for her approval, and the cobbler whose eyes glittered greedily at her approach. The spicy scent of the *épicerie*, mingled with the earthy warmth of the neighboring *boulangerie*, whirled through the air, teasing the passersby. Three colorfully clad acrobats performed monkeylike flips through the courtyard.

The buildings were nestled so closely that the streets were dark except in the height of day. The awnings of the shops threw shade over their wares. A chill seeped through Katrina's thin dress, and she hurried into the open courtyard of St. Pierre, raising her head to the sun and breathing deeply of the city's excitement.

She sobered quickly as she remembered why she was there.

Although Rafe's terse instructions were branded on her mind, Katrina wished she could have delayed this trip a few days more until she had built up her confidence. The printer's shop of which he had spoken could not be far from St. Pierre, and now was the moment of truth.

The memory of Rafe's kisses and her own wanton response suddenly entered her thoughts uninvited. He must have thought her a loose woman for clinging to him so passionately. She could hardly believe her own reaction! She swore she would not let it happen again. Rafe would soon leave her life without a thought, and she did not relish nursing either a baby or a broken heart after his departure.

Katrina could no longer call him brigand. Now that she knew more about him, she could not hold up the image of a thieving, plundering beast to ward against his smoldering glances. He had fought for the Americans, had returned to France with Lafayette and, like Lafayette, now worked for reform in France. He owned a printing press and dealt in the black market of revolutionary pamphlets and books. His cultured voice and his healthy, robust form proclaimed that he was an unusual man: no man that Katrina could dare call her own.

Not that I would want to call him my own, she quickly thought. She tossed her head, squinting against the sun. What woman would want a man who roamed the forests at night, who brandished guns and spent most of his time hiding from soldiers?

The memory of his rock-solid warmth, his gentle, vibrant touch, rushed upon her in full force. She gasped aloud and shook her head vehemently.

He had been so cold since that afternoon. Though they had spoken often in the past week, he kept a good distance from her and rarely met her eyes. He had asked her constantly when she would make the trip to Poitiers until she finally snapped at him in irritation and stormed off to complete the mission. Today he would go without dinner because of his impatience. She brushed a pang of guilt away quickly. He had eaten enough in the past week for two people.

Katrina moved swiftly through the narrow streets, stopping in front of a crumbling wall to decipher the street name. At the end of the shaded alleyway, she noticed a placard and her heart jumped. The printer's shop.

Katrina approached the shop hesitantly, peering into the darkened interior. She tried the handle but found the door securely locked. Frowning, she placed her hands on her hips in frustration.

"May I help you, Mademoiselle?"

Katrina jumped at the deep, resonant voice and turned to the speaker. Unprepared for the sight that greeted her, she gaped rudely in response.

She had rarely seen a man as well-dressed as this one, every stitch perfect on his lean body. His cravat fell in lacy, well-lined rolls; his waistcoat and breeches fit his form like a second skin; his shoes sported bright gold buckles. One foot tapped impatiently beside a shiny cane.

"Mademoiselle?" the man repeated, a bit tersely. A corner of his mouth tilted up in conceit.

"Monsieur . . . I am looking for someone. . . ." Katrina hesitated, watching him carefully.

"Indeed," the man replied. Abruptly, he stopped tapping his foot and peered at her, an astonished recognition in the chocolate-brown depths of his eyes.

"Why, you are the marquis's woman!" he exclaimed, his mouth dropping in surprise.

Katrina started and stepped back from the man. "Excuse me?"

Without the airs, Katrina could tell that he was a young man, not more than five or six years older than herself, but the way he carried himself and the clothes he wore belied that age. Only his eyes and smooth, unlined face gave him away.

"Who are you looking for?" he demanded.

Katrina folded her arms defiantly and tilted her chin. "I am looking for the owner of this shop, Monsieur," she said haughtily, mimicking the aristocratic tones of Father Hytier. "Would you be kind enough to help me find him?"

A twinkle of merriment appeared in his dark eyes, but it died quickly as he stepped away from her, clasping his hands behind his back. "That depends, Mademoiselle. I do know the owner. Why do you want to see him?"

Katrina's eyes sparkled with challenge. This man mocked her, she knew it, but she refused to bend to him. "I have a message for him," she replied, "from his brother." She pulled out a piece of knotted leather that Rafe had given her. The man glanced at it and stiffened.

While she watched in astonishment, the man lifted his arms and made an ungraceful, common leap in the air. He rushed to her side and clutched her shoulders.

"His brother, you say?" he said excitedly. "A message from his brother?"

"Yes, yes."

The man leaned over and placed a sound kiss directly on her lips. Katrina fell back against the wall as he released her to spin around comically in the streets. Just as quickly, he returned to her side.

"Come in, come in," he said breathlessly. "I am Chauncey, I am the man you seek. Please come in!"

Katrina stared at Rafe's half brother in confusion as he brandished a key and opened the shop door, his arm moving in a grand arc as he stepped back to let her in. She heard him laugh behind her before closing the door.

It took a minute for her eyes to adjust to the dimness of the interior. The air was musty and full of the spicy odor of wood dust, but the shop was silent.

"I knew Rafe could not be dead," Chauncey exclaimed, nearly dancing across the shop to pull out a bottle of wine. He liberally poured two glasses and returned to hand Katrina one. She eyed the dark liquid briefly, then turned to him in wonder.

"You are not what I expected Rafe's brother to be," she said bluntly.

His eyes twinkled. "And you are not what I expected his lover to be."

Katrina choked on the wine and coughed loudly. "His lover—"

"Younger than his usual type. Where has he been? Tell me, I must know." He glanced briefly out the shop window. "For a while I thought he was hiding at Rosalie's. But Rosie denied ever seeing him." Chauncey's gaze returned to Katrina, roving intimately over her body. "I will have to tell her she has competition."

"Excuse me!" Katrina exclaimed, her face flushing redder as the man continued his reckless tirade.

"I must say, his taste is improving." He circled around Katrina. "Much more refined than the usual wh—" He stopped himself at the sight of her flashing green eyes. "Excuse me, Mademoiselle."

"No!" Katrina shouted angrily at him. "I am not Rafe's whore, or anyone else's!"

At her outburst, Chauncey's mouth fell open and he nearly spilled his wine upon the fine brocade of his waistcoat. "Well, you certainly do have more spirit than most of them," he admitted wryly, then realized he had angered her further. "I'm sorry! We will speak no more of it!" He refilled his wineglass and moved again to her. Her eyes seemed to spit flames at him.

"Rafe was hurt in the raid—shot in the leg," she said stiffly, her anger smoldering. "He asked me to come and tell you where he is. He needs some things." She reached into her bodice and pulled out a folded parchment.

Chauncey took the paper and opened it, briefly reading the list. His mouth flickered in amusement again when he read the last item: breeches.

"So, he is well now?" he asked, unable to control the smile that spread over his face.

"Yes. His leg is knitting well. It will be sore for some time, but he is lucky he did not lose it."

"Who tended him?"

"I did," Katrina said simply.

Chauncey looked at her in surprise. "Very well, Mademoiselle. Give me directions to his hiding place. I will come to get him tomorrow evening at midnight."

Chapter 6

Rafe blew gently on the small flame, urging it to rise to a heartier blaze. Its yellow tip licked the dry kindling and sparked, spreading over the gathered twigs.

How much like the color of her hair, he mused. Katrina. Katrina of the forest. Wherever he turned he saw her: the color of her eyes in sun-struck elm leaves, her lips in ripening raspberries. Even the soft spring breezes seemed to whisper her name through the boards of the shed. So many feverish, restless nights he had spent on the hard floor, his mind racing with the softness and warmth of this woman he could not have.

He laughed harshly. Not "could not have," but "would not have." Many times he had seen the lights of desire dancing in her eyes, and her kisses made offers he ached to fulfill. He had nearly lost his control once already, but he swore not to do it again. She was an innocent; no matter how passionately she clung to him, no matter how soul-wrenching her kisses, he could not, would not defile her with his base lusts.

She wants you. The thought echoed starkly through his mind. How could a woman's eyes be so clear, so free of guile? She kissed without conceit. She knew nothing of him, yet opened herself to him without hesitation. He had known no one like this forest child, this wood sprite. What magic had she cast over him to make him so enamored?

You want her. He squeezed his eyes shut against the rush of desire. How simple it would be to kiss her, and keep kissing her, until the fires that raged in his blood were extinguished. Take her once—and then realize that she was simply human, not some precious, unusual being. Shake this turbulent craving, this insatiable hunger she had awakened in his soul.

She had saved his life. That winsome fair-faced slip of a woman had risked her life and her virtue to heal him. He would not reward her by defiling her—no matter how much he desired her.

Rafe eased himself to his feet, and limped over to the small pile of tinder he had collected. His leg twinged, and a wry smile spread across his face. That pain would remind him of these days in the woods for many years to come—as if he would need reminding.

He tossed a few branches upon the growing blaze. The hare he had caught a few hours before lay skinned on a soft matting of grass nearby. He bent and carefully lifted the meat, carrying it to his makeshift spit. He would have to cook it fast, before the sun set and the fire became obvious. Although Katrina claimed the search was abandoned, Rafe knew better than to believe the marquis had given up his plans for vengeance.

A wrapped packet flew across his path of vision.

"Your things, Monsieur," Katrina said tartly, sweeping into the small clearing.

"You were quick," he said.

Her cheeks flushed and her eyes sparkled with an unreadable brightness. "As quick as I could be," she said sharply, "with your brother leering through my clothes."

Rafe flashed a white smile. "I should have warned you about him. My brother has always had an eye for . . . ladies."

"Whores, you mean. It seems to be a family trait." She bit her tongue at her own audacity and glanced up at Rafe through thick lashes. He stood casually before her, his shoulders wide and sloping, a smile lightening the swarthiness of his face. "Why did you have to ask for breeches, anyway?"

"Mademoiselle . . ." He gestured to the tattered pair he was wearing. "Do you think I make such a good *sans-culotte* that I should wear my breeches like this?"

A corner of Katrina's mouth quirked. "Well, I must admit— you do not look like a worker, even if one leg of your breeches is cut off." She looked away from his exposed thigh and tried in vain to dredge up the anger that had built up in her on the walk back from Poitiers. But faced with his warm, twinkling eyes, her wrath melted like butter. She sighed and threw up her arms. "I cannot stay cross at you, brigand," she said. "I was prepared to curse you soundly for sending me to Poitiers."

"Certainly Chauncey couldn't have been that bad." He picked up the packet and moved by the fire, wincing slightly as he sat down by the small blaze.

Katrina rushed to his side and grasped his shoulder. "You must be careful, Rafe!" she exclaimed. "Your leg is far from healed."

"My leg needs exercise more than anything now." He glanced at her concerned face. A soft red glow had crept over her wide cheekbones, and her fingers tightened their grip. His heated blood coursed through his veins, but he abruptly tore his gaze away and began untying the stays of the package.

She kneeled by his side, close enough for him to smell the sweet scent that emanated from her thick hair. From the corner of his eye he watched her spread her skirts around her.

"What did Chauncey say to you?" Katrina shrugged in response, and Rafe couldn't help but notice the way her bodice stretched tightly across her breasts.

"He thought I was a—" She stumbled over the word. "He thought you and I were . . ." She avoided Rafe's penetrating gaze and the smile that flickered on his lips. "He thought I was your . . . I was a *petit aventure.*"

"Charming Katrina," Rafe murmured. "What else could Chauncey think when he saw such a beautiful woman?" He noted her embarrassment and said quietly, "Chauncey thought we were lovers."

"You say that so calmly," she said, petulance creeping into her voice. "It must be a common occurrence." She thought about the woman named Rosie whom Chauncey had mentioned.

"I am a man, *petite,*" he said, his eyes leveling on her face. "You should know that well."

Not well enough.

The unspoken thought lingered in the air between them. The sky had darkened early, obscured by rolling gray clouds. Gusts of wind tossed the dry foliage, toyed with Katrina's skirts, and tousled Rafe's unruly hair in wild abandon. Katrina pushed a lock of her own hair from her lips.

"Do I see jealousy in those precious eyes?" Rafe reached over to capture her chin in his hand. He rubbed the soft hollow beneath her cheekbone.

"Perhaps," she whispered as he slid across the ground to her side.

"But you do not know me, *petite.*" He released her chin and traced the arch of her brow. She watched him with bright, liquid eyes.

"I know enough." Her voice seemed to speak of its own accord, not listening to the warnings of her head.

"You only know what I have told you." He dropped his hand. "I could have lied."

She shook her head, closing her eyes briefly. "I believe you," she said simply.

Astonishment flickered over his face. "I wonder at your innocence, little one." His brows drew together in a frown. "Someone may take advantage of it."

She reached over to capture his large hand. "I don't want 'someone,' " she said slowly. "I want . . . you."

His hand tightened on hers. "You don't know what you are saying."

"Yes, I do," she said calmly, surprising herself at the revelation. "Yes, I do."

He captured her shoulders, pulling her beneath the full length of his body. His lips descended upon hers, plundering her mouth, drinking his fill of her sweet breath. She shuddered beneath him as he turned her on her back, pressing her against the ground. Imprisoning her hands in one of his, he stretched her arms above her head, forcing her body to arch achingly against his own burning flesh. His other hand ruthlessly explored the curves and hollows of her body.

Katrina squeezed his hand as waves of need washed through her, over her, around her, settling in turbulent eddies in her abdomen. She tasted his lips, his tongue, his skin, reveling in the warmth of his desire. She tried to free her arms from his grip to feel him, to touch him, to explore this man, this brigand, this love that had burst into her life.

Rafe drew ragged breaths as he released her mouth and explored her long, arched neck. He had meant to frighten her, to terrify her with his passion. He needed to see the light of terror in her eyes—only that would cool the heat of his ardor. But beneath him lay a warm, giving woman. His body ached for her. Instinctively he pressed against her.

"Rafe . . ."

He lifted his head to gaze at her tilted, half-closed eyes, which smoldered as deep and dark as pine.

"Katrina," he whispered. "You were supposed to be frightened of this." He gripped her hands more tightly, sensing that if he released her, he wouldn't be able to stop.

"Frightened?" she asked huskily, her breath brushing against his face. "I am not frightened. Let me go, Rafe. I want—"

"Hush, *mon ange*," he murmured. "You will tempt me beyond control."

"Why control?" she asked. "Am I so ugly in your eyes that you will not take me—"

He drowned her words in a savage kiss. *To take her, as I have taken so many willing women.* How simple it seemed. She wanted him, the undulations of her slim body telling him more than her words. He had spent weeks in the shed, tortured by her slender grace, her tilted eyes, her full lips. Take her.

Take her.

Katrina raised her mouth to his, every fiber of her being aching for this man. His lips raged over her own, lighting new fires against her burning skin. She pressed with all her strength against the prison of his hands and freed herself. Gasping, she wrapped her arms around him, kneading the tightening muscles of his back.

Rafe's control disintegrated beneath her caresses. Mindlessly, he ran his hands over her body, pausing in the most sensitive hollows, the softest curves. Their bodies pressed in perfect fit against each other, only their clothes separating flesh from aching flesh. Rafe captured her tangled skirts, easing the material up over her knees, her trembling thighs. He moved his hand from the material to gently massage the silky skin, wondering at its satin smoothness. Her eyes flew open and she stiffened as he touched her most private place.

Rafe lifted his head to stare at her expression. Two bright spots of color stained her prominent cheekbones. Her lips, swollen with passion from his kisses, trembled beneath his gaze. Her eyes wore the half-dazed fear of a fawn.

In a burst of clarity, he pushed himself away from her, cursed soundly, and moved into the trees. Katrina lay, stiff and cold, listening to his imprecations and the splash of stream water.

Her body pulsed with an unfamiliar need. He had touched her as no man had touched her, and with the age-old woman's fear, she had cringed away from the intimacy. Now she lay, cold and trembling, all her senses tingling with desire.

She bolted upright as she heard his noisy return. Throwing her skirts over her bared legs, she tried valiantly to still her ragged breath. She fumbled with her fichu, keeping her gaze away from his tall, swarthy figure as he crashed through the undergrowth and stopped on the perimeter of the small clearing, motionless. Katrina slowly raised her eyes to his, which still burned with unsated passion.

"I can no longer promise you my protection, Katrina," he said raggedly, his blood pumping anew at the sight of her disheveled, love-touched figure on the flattened grass. "I have tasted your wine and now can think of nothing but its sweetness."

Katrina rose to her feet, a newborn fear burgeoning in her chest. She stepped back from him, though he stood many paces away.

"Keep that fear, *ma petite*," he said. His chest rose and fell in short, deep breaths. "Only the innocence and terror in your eyes will keep me from taking you tonight, and even they are thin armor against my desire."

Katrina bit her lower lip, clutching her loose fichu against her chest. "I have done nothing to deserve your hatred," she murmured, her heart pumping painfully.

"No," he said in a half-strangled voice. "You have done nothing. This is not hatred, Katrina. This is the blinding need of a man for a woman. You have bewitched me despite yourself, little one. I will go mad if I must watch you another day without taking you."

Katrina heaved a long, heavy sigh. She backed away from the clearing, nearing the protection of the trees.

"Go, sweet Kat," he whispered. "Return to the safety of the chateau kitchens. Forget you ever knew me."

"Forget?" she cried.

"Do not come back here," he warned as he saw the light of

fear dim in her emerald eyes. "If you do, I'll take no responsibility for my actions."

She turned and fled soundlessly into the forest.

For hours Katrina wandered aimlessly along overgrown paths. She could not yet return to the chateau to face Tante Helene and the chores she knew by rote. Her body still throbbed for Rafe.

The first drops of rain splattered on her face. She thanked God for the wetness of the rain, and her tears fell freely, running down her cheeks to drip off her chin into the cold ground. A crack of thunder far off beyond the hills brought her attention to the sky, and she realized that this was far from an ordinary storm.

The rain blurred her vision. The undulating, black-edged waves of clouds swept low to the ground. It was an angry storm. If she didn't get home soon, she would be soaked and in danger of being struck by lightning.

Forget you ever knew me. His voice echoed in her head, and as if sensing her tumultuous emotions, the thunder cracked closer, bringing her to her knees. She cried out, pressing her hands against her ears. How could she forget she had ever known him? He had anchored himself into her soul, and to yank him out would mean to yank out part of her heart.

I love him!

Sheets of water poured onto the land, soaking the young woman who lay pressed against the hard earth. The trees creaked their resistance as the air whistled roughly through them, singing strange songs. The last of the dry leaves swirled through the maze of trunks. Katrina lifted herself stiffly from the ground.

I love him. The words echoed through her head, growing in volume until they drowned out all sounds of the forest that had come alive in the sizzling air. How could she not have known before? She lifted her face to the blackened sky, her long hair darkening as the sky baptized her. The heavens opened up on her, shining down on her face, as the lightning ripped silver seams through the sky. She laughed as the rain battered her smooth skin.

What did his grand ideas of protecting her matter? He did not know of her love. She must have something from him, something that she could treasure even if their paths never crossed again.

What better than the memory of their lovemaking? He would not—could not—refuse her if he understood.

She rose to her feet, heedless of the water soaking through her clothes, stealing the heat from her body. She shivered as a cold gust flew through her.

He will not know of my love, she thought desperately. *He must not, for then he will make love to me out of pity. No pity. He must make love to me as a man makes love to a woman he desires—nothing more, nothing less.*

Swirling in the deluge, Katrina laughed, her face lifted to the skies. A bolt of lightning blinded her for a moment, and she danced under it, heedless of the long length of leg exposed to the forest's eyes.

Moments later, she burst through the shed door and stood silhouetted in its opening, the rain water soaking her skin and dripping down her ankles. The sky was dark as pitch and she squinted into the shed, searching for a sign of movement.

Her heart sank. He was gone.

Suddenly rough hands gripped her arms, dragging her into the darkness.

"I told you to stay away." Hard lips descended on hers and she gasped, the rain water pasting their skin together. His hands lifted her heavy mass of hair, wringing the water from its length. It splashed on the floor, spraying her bare feet. "You're soaked," he said, a husky edge to his voice.

Katrina peered at him, wishing she could see his expression in the darkness. His hands were all over her, pulling her dripping fichu from her chest, deftly unlacing her dress. In moments his skilled hands had stripped her down to her corset and chemise. Instinctively, she wrapped her arms around herself, feeling very white and exposed. Yet she still could not make out his features.

Thunder shook the timbers of the small shed; lightning lit the countryside and flashed through the slats. Katrina gaped at Rafe. His face, all light and shadow, had drawn brows and straight, hard lips. His square chin was clean-shaven, and lights danced in his hair.

He stared back at her, at her exposed body. The chemise clung to her every curve, bunching seductively around the hardened peaks of her nipples, which were darkened by the cold. The blond mound of her secret place was molded in a silken curve.

He stepped over to her. Their bodies touched, and for a moment she felt fear. She moaned, her hands moving to push him away.

"It's too late for that, *petite*," he rasped, his lips softly brushing against her earlobe. "You would have been safer in the storm." His mouth descended on hers again, his tongue ruthlessly parting her lips and plunging into her. Effortlessly he lifted her up into his arms, one hand caressing the firm roundness of her buttocks while another supported her back, the length of her hair laying heavy against it. Katrina lost all sense of balance, her head falling at the sweet onslaught of his kisses. He was warming her body from the inside out. Her thighs trembled as he placed her gently on the fine wool of his manteau. He covered her small body with his own long, lean one.

Thighs against thighs, hips against hips, muscle-rippled abdomen against soft, flat abdomen. Round breasts pressed under the armor plates of his chest, lips crushed beneath his demanding kiss. Katrina gasped under his weight, craving it, needing it, and her arms lifted slowly to pull him closer to her aching body, spanning his muscled back. She felt his hardness against her thigh and her heart leaped.

His body slipped off hers. Katrina moaned as cold air chilled her body to a taut hardness. He fumbled with the ties to her corset. The warmth of his fingers brushing against her breasts sent strange sparks of pleasure through her, and she clutched his hand, pressing it upon her.

Lightning again revealed his face. His black eyes were fixed on her, blazing with an unearthly light. The thunder boomed, shaking the rusting scythes leaning against the far wall. Rafe cupped her breast, his fingers digging into the soft flesh. The white column of her throat strained against the rivers of pleasure that flowed all the way to the taut arches of her feet.

Rafe stared at her, drunk with passion. Her hair smelled as sweet as cinnamon, and the heady aroma sent his head spinning. She had swept in here like the storm itself, her body molded against the silver-lit sky, her eyes filled with yearning. He could no more have resisted her than he could have stopped breathing.

He cupped her breast through the gossamer-thin chemise, his lips lowering onto the waiting nipple.

Katrina gasped aloud at the warmth of his mouth. A tight coil wound in her abdomen, and she reached for Rafe's arms, pulling his body onto hers. She vaguely felt his hands rip through the wet chemise, his lips following in their wake; red-hot whirlwinds of pleasure raced over her trembling skin. His lips captured her breast again, and she ran her hands through the silky thickness of his hair.

Blind with need, she pulled at his linen shirt, needing to feel the heat of his skin on hers, needing to trace the muscled hardness of his body. She struggled with it until he lifted himself up, moving away from her to deftly pull it from his chest. Just as quickly he doffed his breeches and stood before her in the darkness, gazing down at her soft white body.

He waited as a bolt of silver lightning sent its glint through the open slits of the shed. The thunder subsided for a moment, as if listening to their heartbeats.

Katrina shivered against the manteau, waiting for him. She lifted herself on her elbows to see him, half fearing in her confused, dizzy passion that perhaps now he would suddenly leave her.

The smoky light etched his motionless body into stony planes. His arms were boldly crossed in front of his chest. She fell back against the manteau as the statue moved toward her, each sinew flexing in perfect confluence.

Rafe stared at the alabaster angel who lay against the dark cloak, her golden hair about her shoulders. Even in this darkness, he could clearly discern the green of her eyes and the darkened, dusky-rose nipples. Her lean, supple body arched against the manteau, making his blood surge. He would have her.

His weight fell roughly upon her, his hand caressing her intimately. Mindlessly, her mouth opened under his as her uninhibited hands touched his chest, then moved to press him closer. An ache began deep within her, and she strained her hips against him. Sensing her need, Rafe reached down and spread his hand over her silkiness.

Her partly dried hair tossed over the ground and she squeezed her eyes shut against the intensity of her own passion. Groaning, Rafe claimed her mouth again.

His lips fell heatedly on hers, and his weight shifted over her, parting her thighs with a soft nudge of his knee. She gasped as he pressed against her inner thighs, moving higher to gently probe her. Instinctively, she bent her knees and arched up to him.

But he did not move.

Rafe lifted his head from the hollow of her neck and stared down at her. She squinted, trying to read his expression in the darkness.

"Rafe . . ."

"Katrina, *ma petite,*" he said in a constrained whisper. His arms stiffened along her sides. "Katrina, there will be some pain. . . ."

She was not listening but clinging to him, stretching the fine column of her neck for her lips to meet his.

Her silky skin rubbed against his hips. He had waited long enough. He could wait no longer.

As the pain shot through her body, her eyes widened, accusing eyes that riveted onto his face. Her hands pushed on his chest in desperation. "Rafe, you hurt—please, let me go!"

He turned a deaf ear, his hands clutching her sides, his arms tense. Only the tightening of a muscle in his jaw showed his restraint.

Slowly the pain subsided, and with it Katrina's resistance. She lay motionless on the manteau as Rafe turned his face to her. One hand moved tenderly to her forehead, brushing aside a wayward curl.

"It hurts only the first time, *petite,*" he explained softly, his fingers soft on her face. He wiped away a tear that had slipped from under her lashes, and he kissed her forehead gently.

Katrina gasped as he moved in her, and the movement sent charring shots of pleasure through her body. He watched the lights of her passion darken her eyes. Groaning, he pressed into her again, feeling the velvety sheath contract against him.

What was he doing to her, this dark man whose hands could caress her into insanity? He was sending spirals of shivering pleasure whirling through her, ravaging her mind into nothingness. She clung to him, pushed against him, the pain already long gone and forgotten. She gasped as the sparks of her own explosion sprinkled over her body, then she listened with delight to the groans that slipped through his lips.

Unable to hold himself any longer, Rafe stiffened against her, wondering even at this peak how he was ever, ever going to get this woman out of his mind, how he was ever, ever going to forget her uninhibited passion.

Chapter 7

Droplets of cold rain water fell from the roof of the shed and slipped onto Katrina's bare skin, making her shiver as one drop traced a path between her breasts and over her ribs. She turned and curled in Rafe's protective warmth.

"Mon ange," he whispered, pulling her closer. She fit against his body perfectly. "Are you still in pain?"

Katrina nuzzled in the soft hair of his chest, not wanting to break the peaceful silence that had settled around them. The storm had subsided, and the only sound in the forest was the constant, erratic patter of rain water falling from the trees.

"No . . ." she whispered, pressing closer to him. "No pain."

Rafe ran his fingers carefully through her tangled hair. He lifted a strand and held it up to the faint starlight seeping through the cracks in the shed. It shimmered like a gold ring around his finger.

"For your sake, little one, I wish this had not happened," he said, his voice barely audible.

She lifted her head from his chest, staring into his dark, unreadable eyes. Boldly, she reached to trace the hard path of his smooth jaw.

"Perhaps Chauncey will be delayed by the storm," she said huskily, ignoring his words. "It cannot be midnight yet."

Rafe sucked in a ragged breath. In the dim light she lifted her smooth face to his, her lips parting in open invitation. He felt a familiar stirring in his loins again, and he wrapped his arms around her.

Temptress. Woman of nature. Daughter of Eve. How quickly she learned the wiles of her gender.

A low whistle pierced the stillness of the night air. Rafe stiffened and pushed Katrina gently away.

"What is it?" she whispered, as he rolled onto his back and rose on his elbows.

The whistle came again, this time longer.

" 'Tis Chauncey, Katrina," he said. "It would be best for you to dress."

He stood up, unabashed at his own nakedness. He searched the shed for his breeches, knocking over a scythe in the process. Katrina could not avert her eyes from the magnificence of his frame.

"Our clothes seem to be quite entangled." He lifted up his breeches, which were knotted in her corset. After separating them, he tossed her the corset and picked up her filmy chemise, which he'd ripped in the heat of passion. His lips twitched. "I will have to send you a new one," he murmured. "This one is not worthy of you."

"You can't . . ." Katrina interrupted, suddenly embarrassed of her nakedness. She reached for the chemise and pressed it against her body. "Tante Helene would think the worst."

Rafe stared at Katrina's bent head for a moment, a strange expression flitting over his face. The whistle came again, more closely, and he pulled his breeches over his muscled thighs.

"Stay here until I call for you." He moved to her side and kissed her, then stepped warily out into the darkness. He fingered the handle of his gun, grateful that weeks ago, when she had first brought him to the shed, Katrina had had enough composure to remove the saddlebag on Rebel before sending the horse into the darkness. Weeks ago? It seemed more like months. How quickly one's life could change.

"Risen from the dead, Rafe? You have quite a habit of doing that, you know," Chauncey said, emerging abruptly on horseback from the woods. "Sorry I'm late. The storm kept us in Poitiers, and for a while I thought I'd have to wait till morning."

"I don't regret your tardiness, Chauncey," Rafe said, his eyes sparkling. "And it's good to see you have suffered no ill effects from the raid, even better to see you have recovered Rebel." He stepped toward the mare to stroke her nose.

A second horseman moved into the clearing, and Rafe raised his gun.

"Whoa, Rafe," Chauncey said, holding up his hand. "I brought Renauldo." A slight smile flickered around his lips. "It's not safe for a gentleman to ride at night, you know. Brigands and all."

"Did you bring an extra horse?" Rafe asked.

Chauncey shook his head. "Too suspicious. You will have Rebel, here, and I shall ride with Renauldo." Chauncey eyed his half brother carefully. "I see you have recovered quite well."

"I had a capable nurse," Rafe said briefly.

Chauncey's eyes flickered. "I know. I've seen her." He smiled. "Magnificent little woman, though I thought her a bit young for your tastes. A mite too innocent, as well, or have you acquired a taste for deflowering young girls, *mon frère?*"

"You have a rattling tongue, dear brother," Rafe said sharply. "I suggest you still it before I tear it from your head."

"Cursing me so soon, Rafe?" Chauncey said, his eyebrows lifting in surprise. "Why are you in such a foul mood this night?"

"Your things, Monsieur," Katrina said tartly, moving out of the shed. Chauncey turned wide eyes toward her.

Katrina lifted the saddlebag and Rafe's linen shirt. Although her dress was damp, it was unmussed and her fichu fell in acceptable folds over her chest. Only her hair, curled and riotous from the evening, gave any indication of impropriety. Her eyes sparkled brightly as they rested on Chauncey.

"Sacré bleu!" he exclaimed, staring at the vision in the doorway. He shifted in his saddle. "Good evening, Mademoiselle. I must say the starlight complements you."

Rafe approached Katrina and took his belongings. His body towered over her, his powerful chest blocking her from the eyes of his men. Chauncey's haphazard comments had struck home. Despite all of his noble intentions, Rafe had deflowered a young woman this evening. Now his brother's frivolous banter threatened to cheapen the act, and Rafe could see the pain flickering in Katrina's wide eyes. Tenderly, he touched the curls of her hair.

"I could do nothing with it," she said, shrugging. "It is hopelessly entangled."

As I am with you, little one, Rafe thought, pressing his hand against her cheek. He watched her eyes fill with tears until the drops spilled onto her smooth cheek.

"Don't cry, *ma petite*," Rafe said, wiping the tears with the back of his hand. His heart ached at the fall of every pure, glistening drop. As he studied her, an idea unfolded. A wonderful idea. "When have we planned the next raid, Chauncey?"

Chauncey glanced around and moved closer. His eyes flickered in curiosity toward the girl. "For one week from tonight."

Renauldo kicked the horse into the small circle. "Not in front of the girl," he said harshly. "She could be a traitor."

Rafe's back stiffened at these words. Katrina touched him, but he did not feel her caress. Renauldo straightened in his saddle as Rafe's eyes bored unmercifully into him. "This woman has saved my life," Rafe said. "You will never speak that way again."

Renauldo's horse pranced back at the warning in Rafe's voice. "Yes, monsieur," Renauldo said meekly, moving into the darkness, but his eyes flickered rebelliously beneath the tricorn.

"When is the raid, Chauncey?" Rafe asked.

"It's set for ten-thirty."

"Then we should be finished by midnight."

"If nothing goes wrong."

Rafe turned to Katrina, whose eyes brimmed with questions. He touched her cheek again, then dropped his hand. "After the raid, *petite*, we go to Paris," he whispered. "I have little to offer you but my protection."

"Protection from what?"

He flashed a quick smile. "From everyone but me," he murmured. "For if you choose to come, you will never be safe from me." Her eyes widened and she opened her lips to speak, but Rafe silenced her with one finger. "Hush, Katrina. Do not give me an answer tonight." He dropped his hand from the softness of her lips. "I have done you enough injustice for one night. You must think on this proposal before you choose. I will be waiting at the small copse of chestnuts by the church at midnight, one week from tonight." He sighed raggedly. "Then, *ma petite*, you will give me your answer."

Katrina had made her decision the moment Rafe gently touched her lips in good-bye. Now, a week later, she would soon leave the protection of the Duke de Poitiers's chateau and meet her brigand lover by the church. The days had passed so slowly she had been sure she would die before this night came. But here it was, and the brass clock chimed the eleventh hour as she sat in the balcony of the duke's library.

She had considered the darker possibilities. Rafe had made no offer of marriage, no promise of fidelity. He had vowed only to protect her from other men. Undoubtedly, children would come of their illicit union. Would Rafe cast her aside as she grew heavy with child? Or would he embrace both her and the babe, and wonder at the life they had produced? She blocked the questions from her mind for the hundredth time, forcing herself to think only of the tenderness in his eyes as he asked her to run away with him.

Something deep inside her told her he would never abandon her once she went to him. She smiled in the darkness at her own foolishness. Was there really any other option than going with Rafe? How could she live here and grow old in the kitchens with Tante Helene and never wander outside her own small village? Since childhood she had known there was more to life than this drudgery. That knowledge had driven her to this library, to Father Hytier's teachings, to the darkness of the forest.

And she loved Rafe, this man who had swept into her life. She couldn't live without him.

She rose, her skirts swishing quietly around her legs. Impulsively, she undid the tight plait that fell down her back. Her hair flowed around her like a halo.

She jumped as she heard a hiss. Glancing furtively into the darkness, she watched as a small, bent shadow detached itself from the bookshelves.

"Oh, Clarisse—don't go!" he pleaded, his arms reaching out for Katrina. Her skin turned to ice as she noted the rich velvet waistcoat and breeches, the glitter of a gold watch swinging from his chest. This man was the Duke de Poitiers! She glanced around for escape.

"No, don't leave, Clarisse. Please, I beg you. You may be nothing but an apparition of my madness, but please, Clarisse, don't leave, not yet—"

"Monsieur," Katrina began tentatively, holding a hand out to ward off his approach.

He groaned. "A voice! Thank God my prayers have been answered! Speak to me, Clarisse, tell me of your love."

"Monsieur, please, there is some mistake—"

"For years I have caught glimpses of you, Clarisse, only glimpses, but often you would be up here, watching me. Don't torture me, my sweet love. Take me with you. I am not alive here without you—"

"Monsieur, please! Stop—" A cold draft stung her skin and she stared desperately at the approaching man.

"You are more beautiful than I remember, Clarisse. So perfectly exquisite." The duke stopped abruptly as he grasped Katrina's arm. His gaze widened and fell upon the warm flesh trembling under his hand.

"I am no apparition, Monsieur."

"My God!" the duke exclaimed, releasing her and crossing himself. "My God." He fell on his knees, bowing his head before her.

"Please, Monsieur. I am not Clarisse, I am only one of your servant girls. Please lift your head and look at me again. You will see that I am not your . . . your former wife." The duke started as Katrina placed a hand on his thin, bowed shoulders.

"Don't mock me. You are the very image of Clarisse. I will not be mocked!" He stared defiantly into her eyes.

Katrina shrunk back, wishing she could vanish into the air, as he expected. The duke's blue eyes were wide and feverish, and she feared he had gone mad.

"I will not be mocked!" he repeated, rising to his feet and staring hard at her. "If you are some demon come to drive me to insanity, I will not take it. Begone if you are not the spirit of my dear wife!" Katrina gathered her skirts and rushed toward the stairs, but the duke's arm restrained her, knocking the wind out of her.

"Indeed, you are flesh and blood." He pulled her around before him. "Why are you here? Who has sent you? Why do you torture me?"

"Monsieur, please . . ." Katrina wished he would loosen his clawlike grip and turn the mad light of his eyes off her face, "I have been living in the servants' quarters all my life; I work in the kitchens—"

"Who is your mother, your father?"

"I have none, Monsieur."

"Who were they, then? Stop playing with an old man!" The duke's face reddened dangerously.

Katrina licked her lips, turning away from him. "I don't know Monsieur. I was abandoned as a babe. Tante Helene—one of your cooks—found me and took me in." She pulled gently on her arm. "Please, Monsieur, I am not your Clarisse."

"Fie! If you are not my Clarisse, then you are her double. Come." Without ado, the duke dragged Katrina past the bookshelves toward the door.

"Monsieur, please, I am not supposed to be here, and I promise I will never disturb you again."

"You will see that you are Clarisse—or a good imitation. And, if nothing else, I will prove that I have not lost my mind."

The duke dragged her through the door to the second floor of the house. Katrina had only a moment to observe the dark, rich wood paneling and the large portraits hanging between the rooms before the Duke pulled her through one of the heavily carved doors and into the rich opulence of his bedroom.

"Look." Moving toward the mantel, the duke pulled off a velvet cover hanging over a painting above the mantelpiece. Katrina gasped as the folds slipped away in a cloud of dust.

Was it a mirror? It could not be. . . .

She stared into painted green eyes in a fair face, surrounded by hair the same fiery gold as her own. Yes, the woman's cheeks and chin were rounder, her forehead lower and her body fuller, but there was no doubting the resemblance between Katrina and the painting. They could be sisters. Katrina gazed, incredulous, while the duke scrutinized her face.

"That can't be. . . ." she whispered, her hand rising to quell the tension in her stomach.

"It is who you think it is," the duke said quietly. "That is Clarisse. My first wife, and my only love. She died about eighteen years ago in childbirth." The duke approached her and she turned to stare wide-eyed into his wrinkled face. His eyes were narrow and quizzical now. "The babe, a daughter, was kidnaped several months later, after I married my present wife. We never did find her."

Katrina sank slowly on the edge of a cushioned seat, her legs giving way beneath her. "I don't understand this. It must be merely a coincidence."

"Don't be ridiculous. Look at that portrait!" The duke's arm swept up to the painting. "Now, is there anyone who can verify your story, who can tell me that you were found as a babe in the woods?"

"Of course." Katrina hesitated. Tante Helene would find out sooner or later that she had been sneaking around the manor, and she would be furious.

"Why are you waiting? Come now, who can verify your story?"

"Tante Helene."

Tante Helene bowed her head as a liveried servant led her into the duke's bedroom. Her eyes widened as she stared up at the duke, but she flashed an angry glare at Katrina sitting nearby. Tante squinted a bit, as if the gilt-bordered room was too bright for her eyes.

"Tante Helene?" the duke asked.

She dipped a clumsy curtsy, nodding her head.

"Who is this girl?" He gestured toward Katrina.

"She's in trouble? I vow, Monsieur, she didn't mean to—she's a good child. It's just that she's curious and always poking her head where it doesn't belong—"

"Hush!" the duke said sharply. "Just tell me who she is." His foot, encased in fine leather, started a nervous *rat-tat* on the floor.

"Her name is Katrina, Monsieur. I—I have taken care of her all her life."

"Katrina?" he whispered, his face crunched in intensity. "That . . . that was my child's name." His eyes lit anew on Katrina. "My kidnaped daughter's name." His gray hair was disordered, and the bald spot shone red atop his head, as if he had spent too much time hatless in the sun. He stared more closely at Katrina's face.

"I named her after your child, Monsieur," Tante said proudly. "I found her on the forest floor in the dead of winter, bawling her poor eyes out. A few days later your babe was kidnaped. I thought it appropriate to call this nameless child after the missing babe."

"You found Katrina a few days *before* the kidnaping?" the duke asked, his voice falling. When Tante Helene nodded in agreement, a puzzled frown deepened in his forehead. "Are you quite sure?"

"Quite sure," Tante said vigorously. "If—if I had found the babe after the kidnaping, I surely would have brought her to you, Monsieur. You were mourning so for the child. But I am sorry. I found this babe nearly a week before the kidnaping."

The duke turned back to Katrina. "It seems you were telling the truth. All these years under my roof and only now have I spoken to you." Slowly he sank to the edge of the bed, leaning on his cane for support. "It cannot be a coincidence. You could not be a relative of Clarisse's family; she had no sisters or brothers, and she came from far more northern climes. I had hoped . . ." He shook his head wearily. Katrina rose to leave, her fingers fiddling with the rough folds of her skirt.

This was too much—the duke's dragging her about his house, babbling about how much she looked like his late wife, then showing her a picture that could have been a painting of herself. Katrina's head was pounding painfully. Just a coincidence, that is all. But so eerie, and on such a night! She glanced furtively around the room and gasped as she caught sight of a gilded clock. It was near midnight!

"Monsieur, it is late. I am sorry for the fright. I promise—"

"No, no, you cannot leave just yet. You are obviously not my first wife, and apparently not my lost daughter. Nonetheless, I must show you to the duchess to prove that I am not losing my mind. She, too, will see the uncanny resemblance."

Katrina sighed, closing her eyes. *No! Please, no more. Let me leave this madness.* The Duke pulled a tassled cord near his bed and a young liveried servant came immediately to the door. As they awaited the duchess, the duke stared pensively at Katrina.

Katrina ignored Tante Helene's stern gaze. Her own eyes wandered over the room, centering on the thick canopy bed draped in royal blue and trimmed in golden braid. Every piece of furniture was lined in gold, with sculptured golden cherubs and clawlike feet, colored porcelain insets and smooth marbled exteriors. She avoided looking at the portrait that stared down at her over the marble fireplace, and turned her attention to the duke instead. He was much smaller than she had thought, seeing him only from atop the balcony.

He was observing her with just as much curiosity. His blue

eyes sparkled in the pasty, wrinkled face. His graying hair had
become more disheveled as he ran distracted fingers through it.

"Helene, exactly when did you find Katrina?"

Tante quickly turned her head away from a critical examination of the well-padded chairs to her own work-darkened hands.
"It was near eighteen years ago, Monsieur."

"Exact date—month, day?"

"Why . . . well, I think it was about December . . . seventh,
no, eighth. Yes, Monsieur. The eighth. Your babe was kidnaped
on the twelfth. None of us could forget that."

"Four full days before my own child disappeared," he muttered. Katrina looked up to find his gaze locked on her. "Far
too much of a coincidence."

"What morbid . . . please, Monsieur, please stop." Katrina
bit her lip at her audacity. *"Pardon,* my lord, but please, this is
nothing but a strange coincidence. Nothing, nothing more." She
spread her hands before her, imploring the duke to listen to her.
"I am naught but a servant girl; I have known nothing else. I
certainly cannot be your child. If I had been found after your
child disappeared, I would certainly have been brought to you—"

Katrina bit her lip as the Duchess de Poitiers swept into the
bedroom in a wave of perfume, her face flaking with powder and
rouge, her dress a shimmering pink satin gown, with lace and
ribbons that seemed to drip from every hem. She turned insulted
eyes toward the duke, ignoring all others in the room, waving
an ivory-handled fan before her face.

"What do you mean by summoning me to your bedchamber
at such an outrageous time of—" Her mouth fell slack as she
caught sight of Katrina. Swooning, the duchess fell in a lump of
pale pink satin, her wig twisting as she neared the ground.

"See to the duchess," the duke said dully, and servants soon
surrounded her prone figure. The door was wide open, and from
the number of servants milling around, Katrina knew the news
would spread all over the manor in minutes.

"Such dramatics," Katrina heard the duke mutter, and she
suppressed an involuntary smile. After much pampering and attention, the duchess was slowly helped up by several men. Her
eyes remained fixed on Katrina, her hand to her chest.

"What—what is this, René, what have you done? Why are you
torturing me?"

"I am not torturing you, Madame, I am only proving to you I have not lost my mind. I have discovered tonight that this servant girl has been living under this roof for nearly eighteen years, and I have never fully seen her until tonight. Of course, I have caught glimpses of her, enough to make me crazy. Since you fired all the servants who served Clarisse, you are the only one in this chateau who remembers my first wife. Does she not look like Clarisse, Madame?"

The duchess took a deep breath and lifted her open fan to her face, which was pale beneath the rice powder. Katrina watched her warily as she approached. Stopping several yards before her, the duchess's gaze flickered over her. Katrina held her breath as their eyes locked. Hostility glared from every line of the duchess's well-powdered face, and she wrinkled her nose in disgust.

"She has the same hair color, René, but that is all. Why, she is only a stick, and her eyes are too big. She looks like a cat and smells much worse."

Katrina's chin tilted defiantly at the duchess, who gasped and stepped back.

"Now she certainly looks like Clarisse," the duke said hoarsely.

"But she is not. That's macabre." Turning her well-padded backside toward Katrina, the duchess moved away.

"The strangest coincidence," the duke said evenly, his eyes fixed on his wife. "She does not know her parents. She was found in the forest as a babe, by this good servant." He gestured to Tante Helene. "And, since my own child was kidnaped a few days later, Helene named this child Katrina."

The duchess stopped her regal walk to the chamber door and turned narrowed eyes onto the duke. "When—when was she found?" she asked carefully.

The duke glanced at Tante Helene, whose face had flushed hotly from the attention. "A few days before my daughter disappeared," he repeated.

The room fell strangely silent; even the servants milling outside the open door stilled to alert stiffness. The lady's-maid who had accompanied the duchess into the bedchamber stared at her mistress with alarming intensity. The duchess's face flushed beneath her powder. From her seat halfway across the room, Katrina watched the duchess's eyes glitter with a strange, mysterious light.

"How many days before your daughter disappeared?" The duchess's voice quivered high and taut in the silence.

"Four days, Madame. Do you know something you're not telling?"

Abruptly the duchess turned, and the servants leaning into the room from the hall jumped back at her stare. Waving her be-ringed hand, she ordered a liveried servant to close the bedroom door.

The duchess turned to stare at her husband, her eyes bright in sunken folds of skin. Her lips tightened into a painted line. When she spoke, the words came from her lips reluctantly, as if they were choked out of her one by one.

"I always meant to tell you this when you were in good health again, but after your daughter was kidnaped you never seemed quite yourself." The duchess looked away from him as his gaze intensified.

"Beautrice . . ." The word held suspicion, venom, and anger.

"Not a word, René, until I am done. Grant me that." She took a deep breath, her bosom nearly rising out of her low-cut dress. "When I married you, you were still in mourning for Clarisse. She had died only several months before our wedding. I knew that when we married; it did not matter to me. I knew the match was good, for both of us, and for your newborn babe."

"You knew I was rich."

"Yes," the duchess responded, arching a darkened brow. "Come now, René. You were quite lucid when you proposed. I think you said something like, 'Marry me. I will pay your debts and keep you clothed. You will raise my daughter as an aristocrat.' That was the bargain, wasn't it?" She pulled upon her handkerchief and plunged on. "I did raise your daughter, for several weeks. It was winter. You had taken ill—quite ill. The doctor told me he did not know if you would live. When your daughter was kidnaped—"

"When *was* my daughter kidnaped, Beautrice? Was it on the twelfth, as you told me—"

"We did not want to upset you. You were deathly ill. We kept the news from you, hoping we would hear from the kidnapers and pay ransom before you discovered her disappearance."

"Beautrice. When was she kidnaped?"

The duchess straightened her back and glanced at her lady's-maid. "The seventh of December. Perhaps the eighth."

"It was the seventh, Madame," the lady's-maid interjected. She cowered when the duchess glared at her.

"Yes. It was the seventh," the duchess confirmed. Her gaze moved slowly to Katrina, who shivered at the icy blue stare.

I don't believe this, Katrina thought, her eyes closing. *I am caught in this room with a madman. It must be a nightmare, and I will waken soon, waken in Rafe's arms.* She glanced quickly up to the clock. Midnight! Rafe would be waiting in the copse for her, waiting for her to come to him. . . .

The duke rose to his feet in anger. "You mean to say that the babe had disappeared, and you held your tongues for *days?* All of you? All the house servants as well as my own wife?"

"Not all the house servants—only a few. We were concerned for your health, René." The duchess refused to meet his gaze.

"You lying . . . I knew long ago I should never have married you, but I never expected . . . I never expected—"

"Monsieur! You forget yourself!" the duchess exclaimed. "The child had been missing for days, we were sure she was dead." Her husband approached her slowly but stopped himself, knotting his hands into fists. "Your physician, as well, thought we should keep the news from you as long as we could. He thought you would die from the shock—"

"Monsieur . . ." Katrina hardly recognized her own voice, but he turned to her immediately. "Monsieur, I don't understand . . ."

He took her hands. "You, my child, may be my daughter. The daughter of Clarisse."

Katrina's head spun and she grasped his old, withered hands.

"That is hardly likely," the duchess said, quickly regaining her equilibrium at the sight of the duke holding Katrina's hands. "There is no proof. She's nothing but a servant girl."

" 'Tis proof enough for me," the duke said firmly.

Katrina stared into the warmth of his blue eyes. Her father. Was it an illusion or did his nose seem to be the same shape as hers above the white, scraggly mustache?

"Not enough for me, or for anyone else of import, René!" the duchess said, her voice quickly becoming shrill. "You have lost your senses. Don't let this woman wheedle her way into your wealth! Can't you see what is happening?''

"It is proof enough for me," he said again, reaching to tilt Katrina's face up. "Look at that resemblance." He gazed over her head toward the painting. "She is the very image of her mother."

"Coincidence! She was probably sent by some jealous aristocrat who knows of your, ah, illness and wants to take advantage of you—"

"Enough, Madame! This is my daughter." Once again, the duke's eyes settled brightly on Katrina. "I will hold a ball for her, introduce her to society. That will convince all your highborn friends of her identity. One look at her and at that painting, and all doubts will be erased. As of this night, she becomes a part of this household. I will hear no more of it."

"Monsieur!" Katrina gasped. "I am not . . . I cannot be . . ." She stuttered to a stop, confused by the sudden turn of events. "I am naught but a servant. A kitchen servant."

"Hush!" he admonished.

"Monsieur . . ." she repeated weakly, lifting her hands to her throbbing temples.

The duke grasped her shoulders. "My daughter!" he exclaimed, his eyes watering. His face seemed unused to the tentative smile, and new lines fanned from his eyes. Katrina reached for his hands, squeezing her own eyes shut as the warmth of his grip spread over her icy fingers.

In the darkness of the silent library, the chimes on the ancient gilt-bronze clock rang once, then echoed back into silence.

Chapter 8

"Mesdames and Messieurs, it is my greatest pleasure to introduce to you my daughter, Katrina d'Hausseville de Poitiers."

Katrina started. In the two months since the duke had found her in his library, she had never heard her full name—her real name—spoken aloud. She wanted to correct him—*No, I'm Katrina Dubois*—but that was unspeakable; not while two hundred pairs of aristocratic eyes stared at her.

She sank into the curtsy she had practiced until her knees ached. The panniers the duchess had forced her to wear spread nearly two feet on each side of her hips and made the curtsy fiendishly difficult, but Katrina was determined to perform it smoothly. She could feel the perspiration on her palms dampening the blue-green satin of her gown.

As she rose, she dared to lift her gaze to the ballroom. The whole room glittered—from the polished floor to the chandeliers to the brass buttons on the blue and silver livery. A blanket of silence had fallen over the room.

Her body stiffened in terror.

She was not sneaking into the woods to aid an outlaw, nor was she stealing into the chateau to borrow some of the duke's books. All of that she had done without fear. Now, looking upon the shimmering crowd of aristocrats, she felt more afraid than ever before.

"Ah, my darling Katrina. You are trembling like a doe."

As her head jerked toward the duke, the jewels dangling from her ears brushed her neck. Her father smiled benevolently down at her. *How familiar your smile has become, mon père,* she thought.

"Come now, Katrina. Where is the girl who said last night, 'I am going to have a marvelous time at my ball tomorrow night, no matter what"?''

"She is quivering inside this stifling corset, Papa," Katrina whispered, "and she is wondering why she agreed to this fanfare."

"I did not give you a choice, my child. You are my daughter and I wanted to show you to the world." The duke took her arm firmly and led her inside the ballroom. "Besides, I do not want those endless lessons to go to waste. You have said I am an exceptional teacher. Now you must prove it."

A hundred lessons flashed through her mind. How to curtsy, how to walk, how to talk, whom to talk with, and whom to avoid. What to talk about, when to talk about it, and for how long. What to eat, or rather, what not to eat, for it was the fashion for young ladies to pick, never to chew. How to waltz and dance the minuet. She had laughed with Papa as she stepped lightly upon his toes, but there would be no such laughter tonight.

Fear raced through her body as they walked into the center of the ballroom. The scent of a thousand perfumes assaulted her nose. She tilted her chin high as the wigged and powdered assembly examined her from the tip of her coiffure down to each fold of her gown. She knew she had no need of *maquillage;* her face flushed as pink as if she were standing before the kitchen's hearth.

Oh, Tante Helene! How I wish I could be in my simple serge, sharing supper with you in the kitchens!

Katrina lifted her gaze to the guests. Their eyes glittered with strange, avid lights. She could feel their scrutiny all over her body: on her hands, her waist, her breasts, her blue-green silk slippers.

What do they expect? she wondered. *Do they expect a painted street whore? They look at me as if they are wagering to buy.* Katrina felt a small surge of anger below her terror.

"You must relax, Katrina," the duke whispered. "Come, you never walked so stiffly with me across this parquet floor."

"I was never trussed up so tightly, Papa. Nor did I have so many people watching." Her lips tightened. "The duchess is looking at me as if she is waiting for me to trip on the lace of my petticoats."

As the duchess met Katrina's gaze, she detached herself from a group of women and moved toward them. Her ample bosom was almost totally exposed above pale pink silk. Katrina raised her chin still higher as she approached. The duchess's faded blue eyes raked

Katrina's figure and rested on her unpowdered hair. Her mouth twitched downward in disapproval.

Since the first night of Katrina's discovery, the duchess had made it clear that she did not approve of her presence. Katrina suspected the duchess feared for her own daughter's prospects. Florence was as uncivil as her mother, but far more quiet. With another girl of marriageable age in the chateau, it would be difficult to find a good match for a girl as plain as Florence. Katrina sighed. *If the duchess only knew that there is only one man I want, only one man I will ever marry, if he still lives. . . .*

She shook her head. *I cannot think of him now, not here, where the world watches me.* The precariously perched golden curls on top of her coiffure bounced. The duchess cast another disapproving look at the riotously brilliant tresses and leaned forward to brush her cheek against Katrina's, her rice powder flaking onto the young woman's smooth skin.

The duke pulled a square of white linen from his waistcoat and boldly wiped the powder from Katrina's face.

"Welcome, my dear," the duchess said thickly, clutching Katrina's hands in her own.

Katrina controlled the urge to pull her hands away. *"Merci."* She did not mask the hostility in her own eyes; the duchess certainly did not bother to mask hers. Their enmity charged the air.

Before I came to this chateau, I never had an enemy, Katrina thought as the duchess moved away. *But, before now, neither did I have a father. Bitterest hate and sweetest love.*

Florence moved to Katrina and brushed the air beside her cheeks, not deigning to touch her. Florence's face flaked with rouge and powder, and her lower lip curled downward in a petulant pout. The white muslin dress spread in flounces around her shoulders and bosom. It was far too soft and pale for Florence's heavy, dark looks.

The formal greetings from her new family finished, the duke took her arm again. "It is time for introductions. Shall we?"

Gratefully, Katrina turned away from the hostile women.

The duke had not been teasing when he said it was a large ball. The crowd filled the room and spilled out into the foyer. A space had been cleared before the orchestra for dancing, but now it was full of beribboned aristocrats eating the delicate hors d'oeuvres carried about on silver trays by liveried servants, and drinking wine from crystal goblets that rang when they knocked together.

Katrina heard the murmur of lowered voices as she was introduced to each group of people, and felt the bold stares on her skin like the whisper of a hundred eyelashes brushing the edges of her bodice. How long must she endure this scrutiny? Feeling like a pedigreed dog paraded about the village on a leash, she half expected one of the men to reach out and check the size and shape of her breasts.

Katrina had felt shamefully exposed when she left her room that evening, but looking over the exposed flesh of the aristocrats, her fears were calmed. The Parisian milliner had trussed her up in a corset and magically produced a cleavage from her thin body, which she had thought would be covered by her dress. Only tonight, when she had finally tried on the finished silk gown, had she seen how low the bodice dipped between her breasts. The blond lace that trimmed the edge did little to hide her bosom, but she could see here that most of the women wore dresses with equally scandalous décolletage.

How far from the simple cottons in which I was raised, Katrina thought, her mind wandering during the endless introductions to barons and marquis, viscounts and bishops. She sighed quietly. She did not miss living in the kitchens, not really. There was too much she enjoyed here, in the chateau: lessons, riding horses, eating rich jams on white bread with Papa on mornings before mass. There was only one person she truly missed from her previous life, but he was lost to her forever.

"Papa, when will this be over?" she whispered urgently between groups.

"Very soon, Kat, but keep smiling. They are all watching you now, though once they see you are flawless, as I see you, they will turn their attention back to more sordid matters." He squeezed her hand. "Ah, Marquis. How could I miss you?"

"I have only just arrived." The deep voice struck a discordant note in Katrina's memory. Her head jerked up as the man's slate-gray eyes assaulted her.

"Katrina, this is the Marquis de Noailles. Monsieur le Marquis, it is my pleasure to introduce my daughter, Mademoiselle Katrina de Poitiers."

The marquis's eyes remained fixed on her. A slow smile distorted his face, and one eyebrow rose in recognition as he bent over her clammy hands. His tongue flickered over her fingers, and she pulled her hand away abruptly, curtsying to avoid arousing suspicion.

The blood left her face. The scar over his left eye seemed less pronounced than she remembered, but his brawny physique and sharp face were those of the man who had tried to rape her. He exuded a sardonic aura, an evil that seemed to seep from his black, well-cut clothes. She dared not lift her eyes to his again.

"Charming girl, René. She will receive many offers."

His voice grated against her ears, and Katrina wished she could be anywhere but under the hawklike regard of this man.

"Hopefully not too soon. I have had precious little time with her as it is. Now, if you will excuse us."

Katrina breathed an audible sigh of relief as they moved away from him.

"Are you quite all right, child? You paled when you saw the marquis."

"I—I am fine, Papa. It's just . . ."

"He is quite sinful-looking, isn't he?"

"He's a demon," Katrina said sharply, her thoughts swirling. She should have known he would be here; of course, he would be here! He was one of the nearest aristocrats in the province.

"My wife seems quite taken with him," the duke mused, oblivious to Katrina's agitation. "She spends much time with him and his sister at their chateau. Well, there is no accounting for taste in that woman."

"She married you, Papa, didn't she? That shows some taste," Katrina teased, trying to shake the disturbing effect of the marquis's presence.

"She married me for money, my dear, there is no doubt about that. But enough of this. Shall we start the dancing?" The duke signaled to the orchestra to begin a minuet, and Katrina focused her full attention on her father. He looked wonderful tonight, his lacy cravat ruffling in a draft, his regalia glittering with gold embroidered threads.

After only two months, Katrina felt as if she had known the duke all her life. He had opened his arms, his house, his wealth, and his heart to her without hesitation, and when the duchess's vicious tongue hurt her one too many times, Katrina found comfort in the duke's shining faith.

She smiled unselfconsciously as they danced. The marquis could not hurt her here, in her father's house. No one could truly hurt her as long as the duke's love was constant. Katrina swore to herself to make him proud of her.

When the music stopped, she sank into a deep curtsy. The duke took her hands in his. "Now, Katrina, I must sit. I am quite winded." Beads of perspiration had formed on his forehead. "I think you have passed scrutiny quite well. Enjoy this night, my daughter." He turned to guide her to her waiting partner.

Katrina stiffened for a moment, fearing that her next partner would be the marquis. She sighed in relief when she greeted a young man, tall and blond with dancing blue eyes.

How he could dance! He had none of the heavy, regal stateliness of her father, but a light, bantering step. He flirted as he danced, teasing her with light touches on her hand, elbow, and waist. Katrina carefully avoided other caresses, fearing the gossip of the eagle-eyed matrons watching across the room. She curtsied when the dance ended, and Jason de Niort—as he proudly reminded her—demanded the next.

"I am sorry, Ja—Monsieur, but I am already promised for the third." As if on cue, a dark gentleman stepped promptly to her elbow, claiming his turn.

Katrina whirled around the ballroom, reveling in the newfound joy of dancing. None of the duke's ponderous lessons had hinted at such fun! She felt now as she did when she rode the duke's horses: free, unfettered. She smiled rapturously into her partner's face. The marquis seemed to have left; she could not feel his heavy, sardonic presence. Whirling around the ballroom, she did not encounter his icy gray gaze. She shook her head. The marquis could not touch her. She would not think about him.

She closed her eyes briefly as she twirled away from her partner. Memories she was trying so hard to suppress assaulted her. Not only memories of the terrible night the marquis had attacked her, but sweet memories of the weeks that had followed, thoughts of the man she had struggled for two months to forget.

Rafe.

As his name echoed in her head, her heart lurched beneath her clothes. She stopped in mid-twirl and clutched her bosom.

Her partner stopped beside her and gazed into her eyes. "Are you quite all right, Mademoiselle?"

Katrina stared at him blankly. "Yes. Yes. I just need some air."

"Would you like me to get you something?"

"Water. Could you get me some water?" Katrina stumbled toward one of the windows that opened onto the garden.

The heat of the room closed in on her. She felt as if she were choking on the stench of rich perfume. She walked through the open window into the semidarkness. In the garden she heard a young woman's laugh, then silence again. Glimmers of jewels and the flash of a pale dress fluttered about the pathways. It seemed that here, the formality was dropped and lovers gave in, at least a little, to their desires.

The cool night air caressed her skin, lifting the curls softly off her neck. She sighed deeply, finding her breath again.

How could she forget? There were times, brief moments, such as when she spurred one of the duke's horses to breakneck speed, that she could forget him. But they were only moments, and as soon as the mare's panting had slowed, Rafe's image would rise in her mind again as brutally clear as before. Why could she not erase his black eyes from her mind? Why did his hands and lips still torment her in the darkness of the night?

Katrina closed her eyes. The night the duke had found her in the library, she had been forced to stay up with him all night. He would not let her leave his sight—as if afraid she would disappear should he let her go. The duke was right, in a sense, for if he had released her that night, she would have run to the copse of chestnuts by the church and allowed Rafe to take her away with him to Paris.

Katrina blinked back the tears that stung her eyes. A messenger had come to the chateau that next morning, while the duke was still bombarding her with endless questions. The Marquis de Noailles had sent news that he had ambushed a band of brigands on his lands the previous night and killed three of them.

Rafe had planned a raid on the marquis's lands that same night. There was no doubt—the brigands the marquis had killed were part of Rafe's retinue. No word came from Rafe, and yet, he must be alive. . . .

She refused to believe he was dead. Surely, she would know, in her heart, if he were dead. But why, then, had he not tried to contact her?

Katrina buried her head in her smooth, white hands. *What did it matter?* she asked herself for the thousandth time. *Perhaps it is better this way.* Slowly, she lifted her head, blinking back the tears that threatened to stain her cheeks. After all, she was no longer Katrina Dubois, kitchen servant. She was now Katrina d'Hausseville de Poitiers, the sole daughter of the Duke de Poitiers. Her son, if she ever bore one, would inherit all the duke's lands and titles. She had chosen her lot, willingly or not. If Rafe ever returned, Katrina would be forced to choose between the man she loved and the father she had just found. Perhaps it was better that she did not have to make the choice.

Oh, but if he could see me tonight, dressed like a queen. She closed her eyes, allowing the memories to wash over her. . . .

His hands had been so sure as they stripped her sodden clothes from her trembling body, so warm in their subsequent onslaught. Had there ever been any doubt that they would make love? How could she resist him, his tall body so wide and strong underneath his rough-hewn clothes? When he kissed her, she swore he was drawing her very soul from her body.

She had had no will to resist.

Where are you, Rafe? Where are you tonight when I look worthy of your touch? Was he alive? Had he forgotten her already, forgotten the night when the wind whipped away their will, merging their hearts, their bodies. *Am I nothing but a blurry memory—*

"Katrina? Are you all right?" The duke's voice broke into her reverie, and she turned to face him. Once more she was back at the chateau, at her own ball, and the breezes that lifted her curls were far more gentle than the touch she was remembering.

"I am quite all right, Papa." She smiled at him. "I just needed some air."

"Your presence was missed. Need I tell you that you are quite a success? Three young men have already asked permission to call on you."

She blushed. *If only one of them could be Rafe. . . .* "They say the most outrageous things, Papa. I have never heard such compliments!"

"Ah, Katrina." The duke regarded her fondly. A few strands of white hair had fallen from beneath his silvery wig, and he reached up to scratch beneath it. "You will hear many more such compliments in the months to come. I just hope . . ."

"What, Papa?" Katrina placed her hand on the rich green velvet of his embroidered waistcoat. Sadness passed over the soft, well-lined face, but he lifted his chin as if to fight it off.

"I hope, my dear daughter, that you do not leave me too soon for one of these noblemen." He gestured over his shoulder to the noise of the ballroom. "You have charmed so many eligible men. I am afraid you will fall in love with one of them—"

"Don't worry, Papa," she interrupted. "I do not plan to marry for some time . . . if that is what you want."

"The ways of the heart are mysterious. But you are too young yet to understand."

I understand, Papa. Oh, how I understand!

"I fear our time together will be short," he continued. The duke pulled away from her and tapped his cane on the stones of the garden. His colorless lips tightened with sudden ferocity. "How I wish I had raised you from birth."

Katrina bit her lip. Although she felt the same way, she also knew that if the duke had raised her, she never would have met Rafe and never would have known his love. . . .

"Perhaps we should get back, Papa."

"Yes. Your men will be anxiously waiting for your return, I am sure." His scowl dissolved into a grin. "You are very much like your mother, Katrina. Collecting hearts like jewels."

She rolled her eyes, glad that his melancholy mood had passed and left him his usual, happy self. "Really, Papa! I would not know what to do with a heart if I caught it!"

"You'll find out."

They had only just stepped into the ballroom when a young man moved jauntily to their side.

"May I have this dance, Mademoiselle?" He bowed to the duke and reached for Katrina's hand.

"Certainly, Monsieur d'Epinay," she said quietly, suppressing a laugh. D'Epinay smiled in delight that she remembered his name. *If he only knew how I remembered his name,* Katrina thought, staring momentarily at the skin-tight, dove-white breeches and the ornate shoe buckles that had moved her to hilarity when she first met him.

She smiled and whispered small thank-yous as the man gushed sticky compliments. Katrina quickly grew bored with him and his jerky dancing, hoping it would end soon so she could rest with her father. The matrons on the other side of the room were still watching her with unnerving intensity—she could not bear it! There must be no more balls after this one. Life in the chateau would be pleasant, if it were only she and the duke. She did not need these other aristocrats. She needed only Papa.

The music stopped and a hush fell over the crowd. Soon, a buzzing started in the foyer and traveled quickly through the dancers.

''What is happening?'' she asked d'Epinay, whose eyes had never left her low-cut *décolleté*.

''I believe a guest has arrived rather late,'' he said petulantly. ''It must be an important one, or . . . an unusual one.''

''Mesdames and Messieurs,'' the valet boomed out, and Katrina strained to see over the heads of the crowd in front of her. ''Monsieur de Libourne.''

''Ah,'' d'Epinay murmured as the crowd gasped. ''A scandalous guest. The Duke de Libourne has only recently recognized this man as his, ah, illegitimate son.'' He blushed a bit. ''According to recent gossip, the duke has made him heir to his entire estate.''

Katrina was not listening.

On the steps that led down into the ballroom stood the man who had haunted her dreams, the man who had awakened her into womanhood in the darkness of a spring night.

And he was staring at her with black, stormy eyes.

Chapter 9

Traitoress! Rafe's mind screamed.

How could she stand there like a flame in darkness, her eyes like warm jewels glowing with . . . could it be joy? Yes, even now in the heat of her own guilt, she could light her cold heart and feign joy at his arrival.

Rafe gazed at Katrina's satin-clad figure, stared recklessly at her upthrust bosom. He must remember she was tainted—tainted with good men's blood. What a price she had received for her work! With a few whispered words, she had become the pampered daughter of the Duke de Poitiers. Rafe hadn't realized how well the Marquis de Noailles rewarded his spies, for if he had, he never would have trusted the wench.

Rafe's mouth quirked slightly. How innocent she still seemed! How like the waif he had ravished. *Innocent! She's as innocent as Satan's own demons, smiling sweetly into my face while she listens, thirsty for news, eager to be the Judas of all French patriots.*

But even now, glaring at her so transparent face, he had doubts. . . .

Still there could be no doubt. Katrina was the only person outside of his men who had known about the operation. And that disastrous raid had cost the lives of three men, one of them Renauldo, who had warned Rafe repeatedly of the danger of trusting her. Someone had informed the Marquis de Noailles of the time and place of the raid. It could be no one but Katrina.

It had all fallen into place. Her appearance the night Rafe was wounded had been strange enough. Combined with the marquis's faulty aim, Katrina's extraordinary skill with healing, and Rafe's

103

undiscovered presence so close to the chateau of the Duke de Poitiers, there could be little doubt that the marquis had planned it all.

Rafe had been outwitted by the marquis's cunning, with the help of a green-eyed witch. Her "sudden" discovery as the daughter of the allegedly senile Duke de Poitiers, and her failure to appear in the copse on that fateful night had finally convinced Rafe of her guilt. She had made a pact with the devil, selling her soul for the chance to be an aristocrat. She could look as innocent as she liked, but Rafe could see through her veneer to her empty, blood-stained soul.

His gaze raked the ballroom, ignoring the curious stares and whispers behind fluttering fans. His presence usually evoked such a response. Every aristocrat loved a bit of spice added to their soirées, and the bastard son of a duke proved to be a healthy portion.

Katrina valiantly tried to stop her flushing face from breaking into smiles. He was alive! He had come back for her! She clutched the cool satin of her voluminous skirts to stop the trembling of her hands. From across the ballroom she could feel the heat of his eyes on her, yet he only stood and stared.

He was alive!

What was he doing here? How did he dare come under a false name? Certainly he realized someone in this room might know this son of the Duke de Libourne and might expose Rafe as an impostor. How could he take such a chance, risk his own life, just to come to this ball? Her cheeks heated again. Why else? He had come to see her, to take her away with him.

Her heart hammered as he approached, his white breeches molded to the familiar length of thigh. The room quieted to an annoying buzz, but Katrina was conscious only of the tall, dark form that approached her purposefully. She sank into a deep curtsy—too deep—and a gasp crossed the room. She cared not what the matrons were thinking; all she cared was that her love had returned to her. Her eyes focused on his feet as they came into her vision, planted firmly apart.

"You may rise, Katrina. I have seen enough of your bosom," he said in a low voice. "In fact, I know it . . . intimately."

Her breath hissed through her teeth as she met his cold eyes. His face was set in ruthless lines that softened not one bit as she gazed upon him. His cheeks seemed leaner beneath the high cheekbones, his eyes as flat and hard as polished onyx.

"Monsieur . . ." She cursed her own husky voice. As he stared at her face and body with brutal intimacy, her heart thumped slow and hard in her chest.

"Shall we dance, Mademoiselle?" he asked. Katrina winced at the pressure of his hand as it closed over her upper arm and pulled her onto the floor. "A waltz!" he ordered to the orchestra before he turned to imprison her in his arms.

There was nothing Katrina could do but allow him to lead her across the floor in front of the guests, his hand spread intimately over the base of her spine, pressing her abdomen into his. Her heart beat erratically and she was having difficulty breathing, yet Rafe continued his quick pace, leading her mercilessly among the few other couples brave enough to waltz. His jaw was stiff, the cleft in his chin deeper than she had remembered.

"Rafe, what—"

"Quiet, Katrina. Enjoy the dance." His lips cut into a thin smile. "Isn't this what you wanted? To be waltzed about by an aristocrat?"

"What I wanted?" She glanced around the room. "Rafe, don't you realize the Marquis de Noailles is here—" In vain, Katrina tried to push away from his grip. Rafe swirled her around, making her hair fly into her face.

"Stop acting the innocent, Katrina. Don't worry about the Marquis de Noailles. I will not hurt him tonight."

Her brows drew together. She glared at the planes of his fine-boned face and caught her breath anew at the flames in his eyes, the dark sweep of hair that fell over his forehead. Though his arms were like iron bars, she already felt a strange excitement at his touch. The thews and sinews of his body flexed intimately against hers, and memories of their night together rose in her mind.

"What are you talking about?" she uttered, trying to regain her composure. "Why in the world would I worry about the marquis? I am worried about you—"

A dry laugh twisted his lips. "Now we both know you are lying."

Katrina's mouth dropped and she pushed against his chest. Coldness washed over her body. "What's wrong with you?" she demanded, confused at the harshness in his voice, the hatred in his eyes. "Could you really be so angry because I couldn't meet you that night? Certainly you know why I was unable—you see that here, tonight—'' He pulled her so hard against him that she gasped for air.

"Lies!" he exclaimed. "Don't you realize I know very well what happened that night?''

"Rafe, you're hurting me!'' She again pushed against his unyielding chest.

His eyes blazed hotly upon her flushed face. "This is nothing compared with what you did to Renauldo, Katrina,'' he said quickly. Confusion flooded her expression. "Oh, very good. Confusion, innocence. You have mastered the art. I suggest you be quiet and smile. Your guests are beginning to stare. We will discuss it at length . . . later.''

The room whirled with colors, and Rafe was at the center of it. Katrina grasped his arms, desperately trying to quell the dizziness and confusion that muddled her thoughts. She dared not look into his face, but her eyes were drawn to it nonetheless, lost in the thick blue lights of his hair, in the firm jaw lifted so proudly above the lacy cravat. What in God's name was he talking about? What did Renauldo have to do with it? And why were his hands biting into her so violently? The mellifluous strains of the waltz flowed through their bodies, drawing Katrina's nerves tighter and tighter until she swore she would snap in two from the strain.

The dance ended abruptly. Rafe drew Katrina to a sudden halt, her dress rising high enough to show a length of slim, silk-clad calf. He did not release her arms from his binding grip, and it seemed minutes before his hand eased its pressure from the small of her back.

"Rafe . . . please,'' she whispered, the faces and forms of the other guests finally taking shape beyond his tall form. Her hands spread over the smooth linen of his shirt exposed above his waistcoat.

"Please what, Katrina?'' he asked, his eyes narrowing dangerously.

"Let . . . let me go, Rafe. They're staring.''

"We're not finished yet, Katrina.'' Turning on his heel, he walked away from her, the satin-clad crowds parting at his approach.

Absently, Katrina took the proffered hand of an elderly man who smiled gently down at her. His step was heavy, mercifully different from Rafe's overpowering vitality. Mindlessly, she returned the man's smile, her lips moving in the expected responses. But her gaze searched for another figure over his wigged head.

Where could he have gone? she thought, catching her lower lip between her teeth. She drew her brows together, marring the clean line of her forehead. What in the world was he so angry about? She forced her face to relax again as her partner commented on her distraction.

"I am sorry, Monsieur, it's just that . . ." She shrugged gently. "It's just that it has been such a long ball and I have danced so much."

"Certainly you could dance one more, with an . . . old friend." The voice that came from over her left shoulder made her nape prickle.

Regretfully, her partner backed away and bowed. "I leave her to your hands, Monsieur de Noailles. Mademoiselle, it was my pleasure."

Katrina dared not turn around.

"What is the matter, *lapin?* Have you forgotten me already?" The marquis's voice rose cold in the warm buzz of the ballroom.

"How could I forget you, Monsieur? I have spent many sleepless nights as your face appeared in my nightmares." She turned slowly, her back ramrod-straight, to face her nemesis. "I had not thought you would dare to come here."

"I must admit, your presence was a surprise. The duchess did not do you justice when she described you to me. Indeed, if she had given me an accurate description, I might have guessed that the new heiress to the lands of Poitiers was also the fine young girl I once ensnared while she was frolicking in the woods." He smiled, the skin around the scar distorting his face. "I came out of curiosity and was greatly rewarded."

"You should leave now," she said angrily. "Unless, of course, you intend to expose me to this crowd and ruin what reputation I may have." Her voice shook slightly, but she did not let her eyes waver from the marquis's.

He threw back his head and laughed. "Why would I do that, *lapin?* That would defeat my purpose. You see, I think perhaps we are destined for each other, my dear Katrina. We have been thrown into each other's path one time too many. . . . No, I will do nothing to mar your reputation. You need not fear for that."

"I suppose you believe I should thank you."

"That would be a beginning," he whispered. "But you could thank me simply by dancing—"

Katrina opened her mouth to protest, but his hand was already on her, pulling her into the crowd. She shrank away from his touch, but before she could completely extricate herself, he deftly whisked her onto the floor in a minuet.

"Why do you insist on tormenting me?" she said through clenched teeth.

"I should ask you that question, *lapin*. You torture me by your very existence. I have thought of you more than I usually think about a wench. I am also quite curious, Katrina—"

"Mademoiselle, if you please," she corrected. The dance required that they part, and Katrina smiled stiffly. She knew she should be careful, that she should not taunt this evil man, but her insides were aflame. Where was Rafe? Why did he not come and help her? Only he knew the harm the marquis meant for her. Her eyes searched the length of the heated ballroom.

"I am curious, Katrina." The marquis recaptured her hand, engulfing it in his own. "I noticed that your savior from that most unfortunate night—"

"The night you almost raped me?"

"Please, Katrina. The night I mistook you for a woman of lesser virtue," he corrected. "The man that saved you—he is here as the Duke de Libourne's son. I wonder, could there be something more to this peculiar meeting?"

"Don't be ridiculous," she snapped. "That could not possibly be the man who saved me that night."

"Indeed, Katrina, it is. I would not forget the man who tore such a prize from me. Even though he wore a linen mask that night, there are few men of such height and with eyes so black, *lapin.*"

"I would think I could not forget that face, either, Monsieur. Indeed, the son of Libourne could not be my savior. The man who saved me that night was not an aristocrat. He was no more than a highwayman."

"I see you are protecting him, *lapin.*" The hand that held hers tightened cruelly. "Did he enjoy the sweets that he stole from me that night?"

"How dare you—"

"He did, then. I should have known." The marquis sucked in

his cheeks, his gray gaze moving slowly over the room. "He shall pay for that, as well."

The music required that they separate again, and Katrina closed her eyes against her fear. The marquis knew who Rafe was, and now he planned to seek revenge. She must warn Rafe tonight. Eagerly she searched the room again, ignoring the insistent pull of her partner.

Where was Rafe? She had not seen him during the dance. She had caught only glimpses of his dark head or the width of his shoulders, then he was lost from view. As the interminable minuet finally concluded, Katrina left the marquis's grip only to be swept up into another man's arms, and then another's after that. She hardly spoke to her partners now, and finally refused a dance with the excuse of finding her father.

"Papa!" she said, catching sight of her father's gold-edged waistcoat.

He turned to her with a small smile. "There you are. I thought you would never leave the floor, with so many men waiting for your hand." He leaned down to brush her cheek. "Are you enjoying yourself?"

"I'm so exhausted from all the dancing, Papa, and glad you're here to deter those men." She took his arm.

"Didn't I tell you that you're absolutely ravishing? And I'm not the only one with eyes, Katrina. Why, when you were out there with Libourne, every eye in the room was turned your way."

"The duchess will scream about that tomorrow," Katrina said. "I can just hear it now: 'She danced a waltz—a waltz, mind you— with a strange man, and an illegitimate one at that.' "

"Hush, child. While I'm here she can do you no harm. Now, I must have a word with the intendant; he just got back from Paris and has news about the meeting of the *Etats généraux*. Look, there's Libourne now. I saw the way you looked at him, child. Go speak with him."

Katrina stared numbly at Rafe, but her feet would not move. His attention was fully taken by a robust, heavily powdered woman whose fan periodically tapped his strong arm. The woman's breasts seemed to swell out of her bodice and pout into Rafe's smiling face.

"Papa, he is quite busy," Katrina said petulantly. But he had gone, accompanied by an animated guest. She glanced around the room, suddenly realizing that she was alone. The music attracted most of the guests, and she gloried for a moment in their satin, silk, and velvet-clad backs. Another glance toward Rafe revealed that he was quite involved with the tart, his white smile flashing against his dark, smooth skin.

"Very well, then," Katrina muttered, her heart lurching despite herself. "Take your joy in her." She lifted her skirts and scurried out through the ballroom door. The dimly lit foyer and hallway on either side of the central staircase were filled with low, husky laughs and coupled shadows. Wanting only to flee the perfume-filled house and breathe the fresh air, Katrina dodged the figures, ignoring the exclamations and flashes of linen handkerchiefs that rose to hide the faces of the gossiping women.

As she leaned heavily on the door, a gust of cool air burst through from the garden. The moon was only half full, but it shone brightly over the dark land. Eager to get far away from the sound and smells of the ball, she wandered into the mazelike depths of the garden. Wisteria vines covered the trellises that bordered each pathway, the blooms full, the scent heady. She inhaled deeply of the dark night air and picked a dew-covered branch of white blossoms, pressing the petals against her skin. The garden seemed empty, which surprised her. Certainly this would be a better place for a romantic tête-à-tête than the nooks and corners of the chateau. If only Rafe were here to—

"White flowers, *petite?*" The familiar voice came from behind a trellis. Rafe moved away from the thatching and approached her, his dark eyes examining her face.

"How—how did you find me?" she asked.

He leaned casually against the trellis, the red end of his cheroot glowing. "I thought you were trying to lure me out here, my dear Katrina," he murmured. "Where is the marquis? Certainly he's here to take me away."

Her brows drew angrily together. Despite the effect he had on her, she calmed her heart and raised her hands to her hips. "What foolishness!" she snapped. "I had no intention of luring you anywhere, certainly not into the marquis's hands. Quite the opposite. The marquis has figured out your true identity." She moved a step backward, disturbed by the aura of repressed passion that exuded from his body. "I wanted to tell you, but you were so intent on flirting with some bit of fluff that I had no chance."

"Now you play the jealous lover," he said sarcastically. "It does not suit you, Katrina. Though I must say you are a far better actress than I thought.''

She tilted her head, trying to read the unfathomable depths of his eyes, and sighed heavily, tired of the evening, tired of the surprises that had so suddenly been thrown at her. She turned her back to him.

"Rafe," she began softly, "I do not understand your anger. You must know by now that the night I was to meet you was the night the duke discovered I was his daughter. It all happened very late, and by then, you were far gone—'' Katrina choked a bit, then composed herself. "I don't understand your anger. I have done nothing but yearn for you—'' She heard his step behind her and whirled to face him. He reached out angrily and dragged her body against his, his hands hard on her shoulders.

"You don't understand my anger, Katrina?'' he said harshly. "I will explain it to you.'' He paused. "Don't you fear me?'' he asked incredulously. "Didn't you fear I would stab you as we danced, or even shoot you here in this garden after all you have done?''

"Stop!'' she exclaimed, pressing against him. "Fear you? I don't fear you!'' she insisted, but felt a seed of fear burgeoning in her breast, nonetheless.

"Then you are a bolder harlot than I thought,'' he snapped.

Her breathing quickened under his insult. His gaze boldly raked her bodice, resting on the necklace her father had given her earlier that evening. "Did the marquis give those emeralds to you? I must admit the man has an eye for women. He's set you up quite well.''

"The marquis? What does he have to do with it?''

"Allow me to help you 'remember,' *petite*.'' With an effortless flick of his arm, Rafe pushed her away. She stumbled against vines that caught at her hair and dress. Her bodice slipped a bit lower as she struggled to extricate herself and his eyes moved over her bosom boldly.

"The night you were going to meet me, the night of the raid on the Marquis de Noailles's chateau—do you remember that night, Katrina?''

"Of course I remember.''

"On that fateful night, my dear,'' Rafe continued, "the marquis and his men waited for us. He knew of our raid. We did not come within one hundred feet of the stables before musket fire burst from all sides; men appeared out of cracks in the walls and ran toward us with murder in their eyes.'' He watched her face carefully. ''We were surrounded by a pack of paid killers. I won't offend your tender ears with the details, Katrina, but three men died that night. Renauldo was one of them.''

Katrina lifted a trembling hand to her mouth, and lowered her eyes. ''I had heard that three were killed. I feared one of them was—''

''Before the raid,'' he interrupted, ''Renauldo had suggested that you would betray us. I nearly killed him for slandering you, until I heard the musket fire and saw one of our men fall under his own horse's hooves. I had not dared to think those sweet lips of yours could betray as well as bewitch. But as another of my men was killed, and Renauldo was dragged away by a score of others, never to be seen again, I knew that it could only be you.''

''No!'' she exclaimed, ''Rafe, how can you—''

''I will tell you how I can believe this. When we retreated and raced to this copse, I still had a foolish hope. I hoped beyond words that you would be hidden in those trees and would convince me of your innocence.''

''I would have, if—''

''*If!*'' He laughed brutally. ''If what, Katrina? If the marquis had not made you a better offer?''

''Stop!'' she cried, moving toward him, raising her hand to still the flow of hateful, horrid words. He snatched her hand in his and bent it away from him until she cringed. He released her and shook her violently, causing a single golden curl to fall from the mass on her head and brush over one naked shoulder.

''You were not there, Katrina. You weren't there at midnight, or at one o'clock. We waited—risking our lives—for one hour. But I never did see you race down that hill toward me.''

''The duke would not let me out of his sight. We had only just—''

''You're a lying traitor,'' he retorted, stilling the urge to shake her until her teeth rattled in her head. His hurt throbbed painfully below his anger. ''Two days later I heard people gossiping that a young woman had been discovered, the Duke de Poitiers's daughter, on the same night you were to meet me. They said she was fair, her hair the color of a summer sunset. And her name was Katrina.'' His hands tightened, bruising the fair skin of her shoulders. ''What could I think?''

"No . . ." Tears pricked her eyes. She tried to find words to unknit the fabric of lies that enveloped her.

"I don't know how the marquis managed it, but he made the duke believe that you, a mere kitchen maid, were his long-lost daughter. Now you have not only wealth, but also position. What a fine reward for a traitor."

"Hush!" she exclaimed, a knot of anger growing in her chest. She knocked his hands from her, cursing the tears that threatened to spill onto her cheeks. "I am no traitor. And I *am* the duke's daughter. It was more of a shock to me than it must have been to you, but you must understand, I did not betray you—"

"You needn't continue, Katrina. It's all very clear to me now. The staged rape with the marquis, taking care of me in the shed so the marquis could get the whole band, not just the ringleader. All for what? The chance to be a duchess." He lifted a hand to a golden tress that had come loose of the pins and caressed it. "Do you feel any remorse for fooling that poor old man? I doubt it. A woman with as many sins on her soul as you—"

"Stop it!" Katrina cried, raising her hands to his lips, letting the tears fall unchecked down her face. "How could you believe—"

"And you played such a convincing innocent," he continued softly, relentlessly. "I must admit I was quite taken in." The hands that had loosened on her shoulders wound tightly around her body, pressing her obscenely close to him. His lips fell to hers, crushing her. He pressed her body against the trellis until every lathe dug into her skin. Katrina lay against it, her tears flowing freely. She stared into the hatred-filled depths of his ebony eyes. She could not struggle; she could not fight. He hated her and the pain made her limp. Brutally, his rough hands moved over her corseted body, and she squeezed her eyes shut against his onslaught.

Abruptly, he released her, stepping back. "What, Katrina? No passion? What happened to the passion we shared that night?"

She opened dull eyes to stare at him. "That was very real, Rafe," she murmured. "That, like everything else, was true." She winced as he laughed.

"I wonder if anything we shared was true," he said huskily. He turned away, gracing her with his straight profile.

Her heart aching at the words that tore them apart, Katrina

watched his face in the silver light, hope rising in her breast as she saw doubt flutter over his hard features. How could he believe such lies? How could he believe, above all, that the night in the shed was anything but real? She closed her eyes against the memory, not wishing to taint it with the events of this night.

There was a way of convincing him of her emotions. If she could kiss him, kiss him the way they had kissed that night . . . if she could show him how much she loved him . . .

Katrina moved silently in front of him. He lowered his chin to look down at her through thick-lashed eyes. His face was stony.

She struggled with words. What could she say that would convince him of her innocence? There was nothing. As she stood below him like a servant before a lord, his eyes grew harder and harder.

Tentatively, she lifted a hand to his chest, exploring anew the hard peaks and valleys of his body. She reached higher, tracing his strong collarbone and touching his smooth chin. Her other hand followed the same path, until both hands rested on his face. Still he did not move, watching her with curious, emotionless eyes.

She moved closer and entwined her hands behind his neck. Her face flushed as their bodies moved slightly against each other.

"Kiss me, Rafe," she murmured. "Kiss me like you used to. No anger."

He stared intensely into her eyes for a moment, not moving, probing her mind for its secrets. She nudged his neck again, urging him down to meet her lips. The hateful light in his eyes flickered and he lowered his head to her own.

Their lips trembled against one another at the soft contact. Katrina ached at the sweetness of the touch, her mind washing over with the memory of their lovemaking. Mindlessly she pressed against him again, running her hand through his thick hair. He pulled away a bit, his eyes raking her moonlit face.

"Rafe . . ." she murmured, brushing a dark lock off his forehead. He made no protest. "Look into my eyes and tell me I am a traitor."

His eyes continued to probe her face, wandering over the cat's-eyes that shone so brightly in the night; the sharp, pointed chin and cheekbones; the hollows of her throat. Her lips parted in hope as his gaze again returned to them, followed by his lips.

She moaned in a half-strangled cry of joy as his arms moved around her and his lips gently took her own. She nearly swooned from the aroma of the faint cologne rising from his lacy cravat. The rough surface of his tongue flickered over her lips.

Ah, Katrina . . . Rafe felt his heart melt with her kiss. *Perhaps I am wrong. Perhaps you really are as innocent as you seem. How I missed—*

"What was that?" He lifted his head abruptly and tightened his grip.

Katrina's eyes fluttered open in confusion. "What?" she asked. "What's the matter?" Rafe's head cocked toward the manor and he pushed her roughly against the trellis, moving to cover her. She tried to cry out, but his hand clamped firmly over her lips.

"You wench!" Suddenly soft footsteps could be heard moving through the garden. "You knew I would follow you out here. You sent the marquis to catch me, didn't you?" His eyes blazed into hers, which were widening in confusion. He pushed her away, his lips curling in disgust. "And to think for a moment I believed your artful lies; that I was almost lost again in the feel of your kiss."

"You're a fool!" Katrina gasped. "I'm no traitor. I don't know who is here—"

"Stop, Katrina. It's time for me to leave. I came here hoping to see guilt in your eyes, perhaps some remorse in your soul."

"Stop it!" she said, her tears beginning anew. "Stop torturing me. I have no sins on my soul." She sobbed quietly against the trellis. "I'm paying now for someone else's."

He was gone. The leaves rustled at his departure, as if a slight breeze had started and just as suddenly died. Katrina dared not look after him, but leaned back against the trellis, her eyes seeking answers in the stars. He was gone now, and she knew he had left her for good. His hatred lingered in the air like the smoke of his cheroot which still burned on the flagstones. She turned her attention to it while the red embers flickered faintly.

"Katrina. What a surprise."

She did not need to lift her eyes to know it was the marquis. His heavy cologne had preceded him.

"What evil brings you out tonight?"

"We thought we heard a scream out here, Katrina. I brought some of my men to help eliminate any of the peasant swine that may have crawled in." The marquis moved closer to the cheroot, staring down at it with interest. "These are dangerous times, Katrina. You should not be out here alone." He lifted his head and looked at her. One hand fell to his hip, parting his rich velvet waistcoat to reveal the glitter of his watchchain. "Are you sure you're all right?" he persisted. "You look exhausted."

She rolled the single curl that had fallen over her shoulder and tucked it into her coiffure. "I am fine, Monsieur," she said dully. "Fine."

"Perhaps you should come into the house. It's getting cool. I wouldn't want you catching a chill." He directed two of his men down darkened paths.

"What does it matter to you if I catch cold?" she said bitterly, moving away from the trellis.

"Why, Katrina, haven't you realized that yet?" He lifted a booted foot and planted it firmly on the glowing stick of tobacco. "You are going to be my wife."

Katrina numbly watched as a few lingering curls of smoke rose from Rafe's cheroot, now black and lifeless against the sandy stones.

Chapter 10

"She has ruined everything, everything. Why, my friends have practically stopped inviting us to their homes! And what is poor Florence going to do now? Monsieur Edmond de Chatillon has stopped calling—"

"He still calls, Madame, but now he calls for Katrina," the Duke corrected calmly, sipping his coffee. His eyes twinkled over the bone-white rim at Katrina, who suppressed a smile.

"At each ball she makes a scandal of herself," the duchess continued, ignoring the duke's comment. "Why, two nights ago, at the Robillons', she dared to march away from the Marquis de Noailles without so much as a curtsy!" The duchess glared at her husband.

The duke lifted amused eyes to Katrina. "You certainly have made a mark, my dear."

A mark, indeed, Katrina thought. *An indelible mark that the marquis refuses to erase from his thoughts.*

"Does she realize," continued the duchess, "that if word of such an affront gets back to the king, we could be stripped of our nobility?"

The duke sat back in his chair, his gaze resting on the duchess's white-powdered face before quickly moving away from her ridiculous form. "I doubt that, Madame. The king has more weighty matters of state on his mind than stripping me of my estates because my daughter refused to curtsy to the biggest ruffian in the province."

"Is there news from Paris, Papa?" Katrina asked, eager to change the subject.

The duchess eyed her warily, obviously annoyed at the sudden shift in conversation. "The king takes an offense very dearly," she announced, still speaking as if Katrina weren't there. "If he heard of the Marquis de Noailles's treatment at the hands of your daughter, the results could be disastrous."

"I think you exaggerate, Beautrice."

"Exaggerate? The . . . your daughter offends the richest and most powerful man in the province, and you say I exaggerate the king's response?" Her gelatinous breasts wiggled beneath her low-cut bodice.

"There are plenty of others—"

"Oh, yes. Too many others! She leads them on shamelessly. When will you see, Katrina, that they only want our money?"

Katrina quirked an eyebrow at her but said nothing.

"They all know that the duke has been foolish enough to make your progeny the heirs to all his estates."

The duke's smile left his face. "I think Katrina can find a rich husband with her own charms, Beautrice." His voice was steady. "And I think it would be best if you returned upstairs and left us alone."

The duchess gasped in outrage and, lifting her multiple chins, stalked angrily from the room.

"Don't take her to heart, child," the duke said, "She is only worrying about her own daughter. Take pity on poor Florence, instead. She is hardly fair enough to find a man on her own; besides, after being under her mother's care for so many years, it's a wonder she can hear, never mind speak. Beautrice never stops."

"Florence has had plenty of opportunities to meet eligible men. There are at least ten coming this afternoon; I will barely have a chance to speak with them all before the afternoon is over." Katrina frowned slightly. *So many men, but not the man I want. At least their glances and their flirtation take my mind off him.*

"Ah, but, Katrina, you forget your own charm. They have eyes only for your fair face. Florence fades into the background."

Katrina blushed, reaching over the linen tablecloth to touch his hand. "You will fill me with conceit, Papa."

"If you don't have it by now, Katrina, you never will. I have heard some of the outrageous compliments that have been whispered to you,'' he said. "What are your plans today?"

"The callers will start arriving around noon. I had hoped to ride a bit before then." *Ride, let the wind blow through my hair and clear my head of all thought.*

The duke leaned back in his chair, his eyes resting on his daughter. "Will Jason de Niort be there?"

Katrina shrugged. There had been so many suitors in the past months. "Frankly, Papa, I am not quite sure which of my frequent callers is Jason de Niort."

"He has asked for your hand in marriage, Katrina."

Her silver fork clattered loudly against the dish. "When? I didn't know, father," she said, trying to remember who out of the blur of faces was Jason de Niort. She felt somehow ashamed. She vaguely remembered spending an evening with a tall, blond man gazing into her eyes. Was that Jason de Niort? Yes, she had flirted, but she had not expected he would ask for her hand!

"If you would like to marry him, Kat, I will see that you are amply provided for," the duke said sadly. "Although I had hoped you would be with me for a few years before a man took you away."

Katrina looked at the duke and started. His skin had reddened to a dark hue. Alarmed, she reached across the table to soothe him. "Father," she said, concern in her voice. "Are you quite all right?"

"Yes, my daughter. I have eaten too much this morning, nothing else." He pressed his stomach and smiled gently.

He worries about me, Katrina thought. *He is afraid I will leave him.*

"I have no desire to marry yet, Papa."

"Shall I tell Monsieur de Niort, then?"

"No, father. I will, the next time he calls."

Katrina rose early the next morning and donned her dark blue riding habit. Accustomed to her handmaid's aid with the hooks and laces, she dressed alone with difficulty. After quietly sneaking down the hall and stairs, she left the manor to greet the soft early morning. The yard was empty; not even the stableboys were up and about so early. Silently Katrina entered the musty stables, searching the rows of stalls for her favorite horse, Pegasus.

He wasn't hard to find. Pegasus tossed his head defiantly as she approached, the only horse with any energy so early in the day. His moist nostrils flared at the faint perfume still clinging to her hair from the previous night's ball. Katrina deftly saddled the steed and led him out of the dark stables into the rose-lit stableyard, where she scratched his nose until he was calm enough for her to mount.

Pegasus's hooves padded restlessly in the stableyard as Katrina eased onto him, her skirts rustling as she adjusted herself to the saddle. A light breeze sent tender morning scents flooding over her, causing Pegasus to wave his head and neigh loudly.

"Shhh," Katrina commanded, bending low over his neck. "Someone will hear us." Nudging him gently, she led him toward the open road.

She had not bothered to pin her hair up. As Pegasus reached the open road, shielded from the manor by a row of trees, he lunged forward in a reckless run. She let the wind flow through her hair and empty her head of the thoughts that had plagued her day and night for months. She made no attempt to slow Pegasus, exhilarated by his body moving so hard and swift beneath her.

The day laborers were awake, working in the fields, taking advantage of the early morning's coolness. A few straightened to watch Katrina fly by on her muscular black steed. It was not the first time they had seen her. Katrina had made this trip often in the past month.

Tired after a few miles, Pegasus slowed first to a canter and then to a walk. Katrina leaned heavily against his neck, trying to catch her breath. Sweat matted her hair against her face, and her arms and thighs ached from exertion, as if she had run the distance herself.

She knew the duke would not approve of these rides, but she went anyway. Riding calmed her and cleared her head. The situation in the chateau had become unbearable. The duchess raged at every opportunity, and the duke took his meals in his room now, unwilling to listen to her caustic words.

Katrina chewed her lower lip in thought. If she married Jason de Niort, she could leave the duchess's hate behind her. The duchess would be furious at the duke for giving Katrina the huge dowry he promised, and the thought of returning some unhappiness to the woman gave Katrina satisfaction.

To marry Jason de Niort, and forget all that happened with Rafe. She threw her head back to soak in the heat of the sun. *Forget.* How could she ever forget? She still loved him, despite his hatred. Could this mere boy, Jason de Niort, help her forget the man she loved?

Katrina sighed. She knew she would not marry him. Yes, marrying him would anger the duchess; and marrying him might help her forget Rafe; but, above all, marrying him would take her away from Papa, and they had not yet been together for a summer.

Shaking her head, Katrina pulled Pegasus around and headed back for the manor. Today Monsieur de Niort would be calling, and she had to prepare herself to reject his proposal.

Pegasus walked slowly on the uneven road. Katrina did not object. She waved to a few workers as she passed by again, and they returned her greeting, stiffly straightening their bowed, thin backs. A dusky rose streaked the eastern sky, framing the straight, tall walls of the chateau.

As she heard the rumble of wheels behind her, Katrina twisted in the saddle to see a carriage a half-league back. The driver whipped his horses into a run, and the carriage gained on her. Katrina covered her hair with her hood, hoping the passengers would think her only a bourgeois out for a brief ride.

The carriage overtook her quickly. Much to Katrina's chagrin, it slowed next to her. She turned, grimacing as she recognized the eagle-decorated crest of the Marquis de Noailles. She always dreaded when this carriage pulled in before the duke's chateau. Why couldn't the marquis understand that she wanted nothing to do with him? She suppressed a laugh of scorn. As if her feelings had any effect on him.

A ringed hand pulled the leather blinds away from the window. The marquis smiled out at her.

"Good morning, Katrina. You are out terribly early, aren't you?" The scar over his eyes was especially noticeable in the early morning sun, white and stark against his dark skin.

"I could say the same for you, Monsieur," Katrina said politely. "I thought only birds and peasants were out this time of the morning."

He frowned at the implication. "Your cheeks are flushed, *lapin.*"

"That is what happens when I ride."

"And your hair is undone, and,"—he looked around her—"you are unattended. It seems to me that this little trip of yours was of an amorous nature, no?"

"And what if it was, Monsieur?" she drawled, leaning a bit to stare down into his leathery face.

His smile faded and a muscle twitched in his jaw. "Do not bait me."

"Do not threaten me," Katrina retorted. She nudged Pegasus into a gallop and raced away from the carriage. The marquis's horses increased their speed, but they could not catch up with a strong steed carrying a light load. She turned back, laughing, to look at the receding carriage.

The marquis was staring at her, his gray eyes burning as if with the fires of hell.

It was barely ten o'clock that morning when a servant knocked to announce the arrival of the first caller.

"They are exceptionally early today," teased Katrina's lady's maid, Zelda, as she wrapped the last curl into place and brushed the hanging locks into fiery gold.

Katrina flashed reproachful eyes at her. "Please, Zelda. I will not enjoy the next hour or so. I have never rejected a suitor before, and I daresay this man has never been rejected."

She moved toward the high windows. The sun was now full and high, turning the room into a golden-pink confection. She watched the workers slowly moving through the growing stalks and lower vines of the fields. Briefly the memory of Tante Helene's smile flashed through her head. Undoubtedly, Tante would now be preparing the workmen's meals, her sleeves rolled above her rough, reddened elbows, bawling out orders to the giggling maids whose primary concern would be distracting the men from their work. Katrina sighed. Those had been simple times.

Simple times are gone, Katrina thought. The one time she had tried to visit Tante Helene in the kitchens, the woman had hustled her out unceremoniously and told her never to return. "You don't belong here anymore, Kat," she had said. "Your place is in the chateau."

"You look charming today, Mademoiselle," Zelda said, bringing her out of her reverie. The contrast of Katrina's yellow muslin against her peach-tinted skin and golden hair made her look like a ray of sunshine.

"Thank you, Zelda. I need the confidence this dress brings me." She sighed, turning away from the sunlit fields. "There is no use dallying."

Katrina hesitated at the top of the wide stairs, breathing deeply to summon the cool, unruffled calmness she had learned to project since her ball, since Rafe's harsh, biting words had broken her heart into a hundred pieces and left her hollow and empty.

But no veneer of coolness could prevent her from showing the shock in her face as she reached the foot of the stairs. For it was not Monsieur de Niort who called so early in the day, but the Marquis de Noailles. His eyes still held the shadows of his anger from their earlier encounter.

"It is so good to see you again, Mademoiselle. You look surprised. Didn't the servant tell you who was calling?"

"No, he did not," she said bluntly, knowing he had paid the servant not to tell her. "If he had, I would have complained of a headache."

"I know," the marquis replied. "Now, shall we go into the parlor where it is more comfortable?" He motioned to his left, where the doors were wide open to the blue and white room.

Katrina hesitated, but not knowing what else to do, she brushed by the marquis's dark form and entered the parlor. She sat on the one blue-padded chair. The marquis smiled wryly and sat on the couch opposite. Leaning against the flowered print, he watched her through slitted eyes.

"Monsieur, really. If you have nothing to say, I see no reason for your presence here."

"I will say quite a bit, *lapin,*" he began. "I get tired of sitting among a dozen panting dogs every afternoon for the simple pleasure of seeing you. I have allowed you your weeks of pleasure. Now it is time for you to become seriously attached to one man, *lapin.*"

"And who might that one man be, Monsieur?" she retorted uneasily, suddenly quite aware that they were alone.

"Me, of course."

"Let us shorten this meeting, Monsieur," Katrina said angrily. "I will not be insulted if you decide to leave a bit earlier than convention allows."

"Would you prefer me to tell you that your hair is thick and silky and that I would love to feel it brushing my chest—"

"Monsieur, please!"

"Or I could tell you that I see the need in those innocent eyes of yours, how you beg to be kissed—"

"Marquis!" Katrina moved away from his soft-spoken drone. Desperately she searched the doorway for help.

"I could also tell you that I know by the way you move that you are not innocent to a man's touch. . . ."

"I have heard quite enough, Marquis," she said firmly, her lips tightening.

"No, it is not enough, my *lapin,*" he murmured, going toward her. He reached for her arm and pulled her toward the couch, away from the gaping doors. She struggled against his strength. "Relax, Katrina. I want you to sit and hear what I am about to say."

She pulled her arm from his grip and moved to the end of the couch. "I have no interest in anything you have to say."

"Oh, but you will," the marquis assured her. "I told you once, not so long ago, that I would make you mine. Don't look so shocked. I always get what I want, one way or another."

Katrina turned from him, lifting her chin haughtily. "I am not a piece of merchandise, Marquis. I cannot be bought."

"Don't be a fool. I have decided that I want you as a wife or a mistress, it is all the same to me. But for your sake, I think you should prefer the position of a wife. It is more respectable here in the country, although in Paris it matters little."

Her face reddened in fury. "How dare you—" she sputtered, bracing herself against the couch. "How dare you come into my father's house and say such things! I will not be your wife or your mistress. You are no more than a seducer—a murderer! And you are wrong if you think you can force me—"

"I would rather not use force, *lapin.*" His voice was calm, but Katrina heard the threat in it.

She tightened her mouth and rose to dismiss him. "I am not a peasant girl any longer. I am the daughter of the Duke de Poitiers—"

"Sit down," he commanded.

Katrina bit her lip and remained standing.

He rose slowly, his nostrils flaring at her disobedience. "I said sit down." He moved toward her, thin and taut and dressed, as always, in hideous, ghastly black. His eyes, those cursed gray eyes, stared into hers, and she felt as if she were choking.

"I thought I heard voices." The duke was standing at the entrance to the parlor, eyeing them curiously. Katrina's face was pale. The marquis looked like a vulture about to swoop down on new, fresh prey. "When did you arrive, Marquis?" the duke asked suspiciously. "I did not hear anyone arrive."

"My carriage is well-oiled and silent, Monsieur," he said smoothly. "I have only just arrived."

"Good morning, Papa. Will you stay with us for a while?"

"Of course. There should be someone here, Katrina. You know that."

"Yes, Father. I don't know where the servants are, or the duchess, or anyone for that matter. I have only just come down."

"Very well, then. But please, don't let this happen again." The duke's gaze moved to the marquis, who remained silent. "Marquis, since you are a gentleman, I am sure you also will not allow a reoccurrence."

The marquis smiled and bowed slightly.

"I understand you have spent time in Paris?" the duke began, easing down on the couch with Katrina's help. His face was exceptionally florid today, and his daughter's brows drew together in worry.

"Versailles, actually," the marquis corrected. "The situation in Paris is abominable. I spent a day there, just one day, and that was too much."

"What was wrong?" the duke asked.

"The riots have been getting worse," the marquis noted, unfolding a scented linen to wipe perspiration from his brow.

"Bread riots?" Katrina asked.

"I have no idea. Parisians are always rioting for one thing or another. It has gotten worse since that meeting began, that . . ."

"The *Etats généraux*," the duke filled in, his brows drawing together.

"Yes, that's it. I was in a café in the Palais Royal, and it took my servant over two hours to get from the milliner's to my banker's office, and they are located only a few streets from the Palais. Crowds of vermin had attacked the customs posts, overturning wagons, making bothersome riots in the streets. I returned to Versailles immediately thereafter.''

"Perhaps your servant would have gotten to you faster if he had abandoned the hackney and walked,'' Katrina suggested innocently.

"Have you ever seen the streets of Paris, Mademoiselle? A man would ruin his finery in the ooze that coats the stones. Besides, as a servant bearing my livery, he would not be seen walking through the streets like a common grocer.'' The marquis returned the linen to his waistcoat after folding it in neat quarters.

"If you have been to Versailles, then you must have heard rumors that the king is going to dismiss the financial minister,'' the duke prompted, leaning forward.

"Yes, I would say that Necker has fallen into some disfavor in the court. Too many demands about tightening the royal couple's purse. Imagine, forcing good King Louis and the beauteous Marie Antoinette to worry about money. What ridiculous drivel!''

"But, Papa, you told me that the people and the *Etats généraux* support Necker,'' Katrina remarked.

"That is the general rumor.''

"Well, then, if the king dismisses Necker, that ought to cause quite a stir in Paris. You would think the king would avoid that.''

The marquis lifted a dark brow and gazed at her with translucent eyes. "I hear a hint of sympathy, Mademoiselle. Do you care so much for the scum who riot in the streets?''

"You forget, Monsieur, that I was once a peasant.''

"No, Mademoiselle, you were born an aristocrat. True, you lived in trying circumstances for some time, but you were never a peasant.'' His winged brows drew together in disgust over the word *peasant*.

If you only knew how much a peasant I was, Marquis, she thought, her lips tightening. *If you only knew that I harbored—and loved—the very rebel who led so many raids on your own lands.*

Seeming to sense her tension, the duke launched into a discussion of his lands, of which the marquis had no interest. Katrina sat silently, her hands pulling on the yellow muslin of her skirt, anxiously waiting for the marquis's departure.

Finally, he rose to visit the duchess, who was still abed, yet expressed her willingness to entertain him in her apartments. "I shall call on you again, Katrina," he whispered over her stiff hand.

"It will be too soon."

The duke waited until he had left the room. "Now tell me, Kat. What was all that about?"

"The servant did not tell me who had called; I thought it was Monsieur de Niort. He was the only one I expected so early. When I descended, there was only the marquis, with no servants, no chaperone in sight. He . . . frightens me, Papa."

"I can see that. I never did like him. He places far too much importance on his own appearance and, from all reports, is quite brutal to his servants. But then again, that is nothing unusual."

"It would give me great pleasure if he never called. Yet no matter how rude I am, he keeps returning."

"Persistent devil." The duke pulled on his waistcoat, his face crumpled in concentration.

"Devil is the proper word," she murmured.

The duke reached out and captured her hand. "You have nothing to fear from him, my child," he said. "Not for as long as I live."

Katrina smiled at him, moving to kiss the soft, thin skin of his cheek. "Thank you, Papa. I am quite tired. I think I will nap for a while."

After kissing him on the other cheek, she wearily climbed the stairs to her room. It was too early for so much activity. She had had to face the marquis twice today, and the ordeal with Monsieur de Niort still stood ahead.

The heat of the July day invaded the manor, making Katrina's dress stick to her skin and forming drops of perspiration on her upper lip. She hastened to her room, looking forward to stripping down to her fine cambric chemise. She pushed the door open and closed it firmly behind her. Leaning against it, she closed her eyes in relief.

"Finally. We are alone."

The soft voice forced Katrina's eyes open, and she stared at the marquis, a dark swath against the vibrant pink and red hues of her bed. His smile was a slit on his face, the hollows of his cheeks deep and dark. Her skin turned to ice.

"What are you doing here? Leave now or I will call someone to remove you forcefully!"

"And create a scandal? Is that what you want? Why, then I would have to marry you, wouldn't I?"

Katrina froze, and watched him as he smiled from the end of her bed. "What do you want?"

"I thought I explained that quite clearly in the parlor." He rose, moving toward her. Her hand shot out, but he caught it. In terror, she felt the strength of his grip. His lips bit down on hers, forcing her head back until she swore her neck would break. "How many others have done this, Katrina?" he asked, lifting his head. "I know you are not innocent. Just this morning you were on some kind of tryst. Who is it? That weak, doe-eyed Niort boy? Really, Kat, isn't he a little young and soft for you? Don't you want a man who can relieve that burning inside you?"

Katrina kicked wildly, but her efforts were hampered by her skirts. She pushed against his chest, trying to get away from his hot breath, his possessive, wandering hands.

"You were saved once, *lapin*. It won't happen again." He wrestled her arms behind her back and locked them in his large, bony hand. His other hand meandered over her shoulders, arms, breasts, stomach. She ached to cry out, to stop his disgusting touch. His nearness was making her nauseous.

"Why don't you cry out and end it, *lapin?* Either way I will have you, or ruin your reputation so no one else will. Understand? I want you, therefore you are mine." His lips formed the word *mine* and rested on it, savoring the sound. "You are a fine piece," he continued, excited by her nearness. "A little thin, perhaps, but your breasts are full and firm." He squeezed her breast hard, twisting it, and smiled when she winced. "You should be happy I am offering marriage. Another man might just take you and leave. But I think you will be interesting enough in bed to satisfy me for a while. And you certainly would make a good showpiece at Versailles. Just think, *lapin*. Marry me and you will see Versailles. You will have a salon of your own, and I will visit you every night and slake your passion until you scream for me to stop."

"*No!*" She could not stand his roaming hands, his intimate touch. He pulled off her fichu and reached inside her bodice to rub her nipples. His lips descended on hers again, bruising them and cutting off her breath.

Suddenly she heard footsteps pounding heavily on the stairs, and the door burst open. The duke ran into the room, his eyes blazing. He raised his cane high above his head.

"Pity you arrived so soon, Monsieur," the marquis drawled. "We were just getting involved."

The duke's face darkened until it was almost purple with anger. He lunged for the marquis, lifting his cane higher. The marquis threw Katrina onto the floor and easily warded off the duke's blows. Katrina screamed for help, rising and running from the marquis. She turned to her father, who lay prone against the red carpet.

"Papa!"

Something was wrong. She fell to her knees at his side. One side of his face was distorted, twitching uncontrollably. His blue eyes blazed up at her, glazing over. He slumped heavily against her.

"Papa, what is wrong?" She gasped, shaking him. "Papa . . . Papa!"

Chapter 11

The morning wind brushed gently over the silent land as René d'Hausseville de Poitiers was laid to rest behind Father Hytier's church. The churchyard held men and women of all classes: the tenants of the duke's lands, the *journaliers* employed in the harvest season, a few servants, and the villagers whose businesses had relied on his patronage. Closer to the burial site huddled family members, the local nobles, and the few aristocrats that had come from afar to attend the funeral.

Katrina stood in the center, a tiny figure swathed in a voluminous black cloak, her pale face vivid against the dark velvet. The duchess and her daughter stood stiffly nearby, the rice powder caking their faces and glowing pasty gray in the dawn mist. Father Hytier hovered over the open grave and read the Latin prayers in a low, hushed voice.

Katrina stared mutely at the mahogany coffin gleaming at the bottom of the pit. She swayed slightly, as if buffeted by the wind. The Latin droning in her ears settled her into a dreary, dazed state.

I loved you, Papa. She blinked her dry eyes. Her heart hung heavy and hard in her aching body.

The wind blew the hood off her head, whipping strands of her loose hair across her face. The air smelled of rich humus, cut grass, and heavy rain. Dark clouds rumbled over the distant hills of Poitiers. The forest rustled restlessly behind her, thick boughs heavy with greenery brushing against their brothers. Father Hytier continued his mellifluous drone, and Katrina became acutely aware of the verdant land stretching beyond the church, the pristine whiteness of the roses placed upon her father's casket.

She used to play in this graveyard as a child. She had danced among the tombstones, placing single daisies and bunches of lilies of the valley upon each grave. All that time wasted, when her Papa had lived only a short distance away, mourning for her just as she ached, unknowingly, for him.

Katrina stiffened beneath the folds of the enormous cloak. Her father's life had been slashed so pitifully short by a man's insatiable lust.

Murderer! The marquis had killed Papa as surely as if he had held a sword and plunged it through his heart. If it were not for the marquis's scheme to force Katrina into marriage, Papa would still be by her side.

Katrina lifted her head to face the wind, her hair flying recklessly around her. She vowed that if she ever saw the marquis again, she would have her vengeance.

"Amen." Father Hytier made the sign of the cross over the grave.

The gravediggers began shoveling the chalky soil into the ditch, each clod making a hollow thump on the casket until mercifully the sound was muffled. Katrina could no longer look into the grave, but something made her stay by its side, listening to the rhythmic shoveling until the gravediggers made the last, final pat upon the humus and left the site. Slowly the people wandered from the churchyard. The sound of their quiet murmuring annoyed her, like the persistent buzzing of an insect.

Father Hytier stopped by her side. His hand shook upon his gnarled cane, but Katrina knew the power of the old priest's spirit. While she was growing up, he had been like the father she had never had. She placed a white hand on the priest's rough woolen cloak. The strength of his presence flowed in and around her but somehow could not comfort her.

"I'm glad we could bury him in the morning," she remarked. "He always liked mornings best."

"I was told the duke rode through the fields then, after he found you," Father Hytier said. "He had not done that since his first wife died. You were a great joy to him in his final days, Kat."

"And he to me." Katrina espied an aristocratic couple heading in her direction, black feathers waving in the woman's pert hat. Panic touched her with cold fingers. "Oh, Father, I cannot bear to listen to their words of sympathy. Please, take me from here." She leaned against his small, bent frame. He supported her, leading her toward a tree.

"There. Lean against the trunk. They will think you have fainted." He looked surreptitiously behind him, his eyes squinting against the light. "You know you are going to have to listen to their condolences all week."

"I know, Father, but I just can't bear it now." She looked back at the grave, and for a moment she imagined that it was bulging with life and warmth—the soul of Papa himself straining to leave the confines of the earth.

Her knees weakened and for a moment she feared she would faint. Father Hytier touched her shoulder and shook her gently. She closed her eyes and placed an icy hand upon her brow.

"I think I'd better return to the chateau," she said weakly. "I do not feel very well."

Katrina moved slowly through the graveyard toward the chateau, holding Father Hytier's arm. The five-day vigil began to take a toll on her body. She could feel a tremble invading her limbs. Sadness surged through her anew, starting deep in her abdomen and rushing through her body to rest taut and thick in her throat. She choked, stopping in the paved road as her knees weakened beneath her. She tightened her grip on Father Hytier's scratchy robes.

"I'm fainting like a pasty-faced highborn, aren't I?" she remarked, the remnants of a country drawl clinging to her words.

"Not so bad as that, Katrina. Come, the sooner we are inside, the sooner you can sit and rest. The duchess will take care of everything."

The duchess. Katrina's heart thumped painfully. Moments after the duke's death she had run into the room, screaming like a fighting hen, cursing in words Katrina had heard only in the back alleys of Poitiers when the fair was held in the village. The woman's hatred was a physical, palpable thing that followed Katrina through every hall of the chateau. But the duchess had shown extraordinary composure when arranging the details of the funeral, as well as the running of the chateau. Katrina had not had enough strength to do anything but remain in a stunned daze at the loss of Papa, and had even missed the reading of the will.

"Will you come with me, Father?" Katrina knew his legs

ached already from the short walk, but she needed his strength beside her. He nodded his assent.

Conversation stopped in mid-sentence when she entered the stone portal. Katrina felt as if she were at her own ball again, undergoing the same intimate scrutiny. She lifted her chin from the velvet cloak, swallowing the anger that started in her heart, and wished suddenly that she had worn a black lace veil, despite her youth. Why should these aristocrats gaze upon her grief? Snippets of conversation drifted across the old, echoing room to linger painfully in her ears.

"Why, the girl is as pale as a little ghost."

"And so thin! I'm sure she hasn't eaten in days."

"They say she fainted down by the grave."

"Indeed, she is the daughter of Clarisse—a consummate actress. I can almost see *tears* on her face."

"I hear her stepmother is going to throw her out of the house."

"The duchess certainly has the look of victory smeared like cream on her face."

"But the late duke doted on the child so much. She will become quite rich, I wager. I will have to start courting her as soon as she's out of mourning. A wench with such a dowry as the estate of Poitiers is worth marrying, despite her upbringing."

"There was some scandal attached to the duke's death."

"Someone said the duke caught her with a lover when he walked into her room."

"Yes, I heard she was with some aristocrat. Everyone viciously denies it, though. Even the duchess."

"Why would she perpetuate such a story? It would ruin the family!"

"And her own daughter's chances for marriage. . . ."

The aroma of rich mutton wafted over Katrina as she passed the banquet table. Her stomach churned at the scent.

Father Hytier sank into a wooden chair not far from the table. "Go, child. Greet the mourners. I will rest here awhile."

Greet the mourners! Katrina glanced around. She did not care for any of these people: they were the duchess's allies. She noticed a few of her daily callers dressed in somber black lounging around the room, and quickly looked away. She could not muster the idle banter that had kept her entertained during those painful days after Rafe had left.

She closed her eyes. *Rafe.* How she needed him now. Not the Rafe who had cursed her at her ball, but the Rafe of old, who had loved her in the coolness of spring. Her heart fluttered, and she knew that the only one who could ease the loneliness in her heart was Rafe. *If only he loved me still.*

The first of the mourners approached her, and she took a deep breath, drawing a mask of coolness over her face. *At least I have learned something from my brief time with Papa,* she thought. *I have learned that politeness can be donned as easily as a wig or dress.*

She felt awkward in this chateau, greeting strangers. She had hardly gotten used to being an aristocrat, and now the sole reason for that existence was dead. She felt as if she should leave here and return to the kitchens, where she belonged.

You are my daughter, Katrina. Never forget that.

Katrina started, as if her father had whispered his words into her ear. The sweet, well-remembered voice echoed in her head. She closed her eyes. *Yes, Papa. I am your daughter.*

After speaking with as many people as she could bear, she turned from her guests and walked purposefully to Father Hytier, who lifted his head at her approach. "Father, I am quite weary. I'm going to retire for the day. Shall I have the carriage sent around for you?"

"Thank you, my child." His gnarled hand shot out with surprising quickness. He gripped her arm. "Katrina, I want you to remember something." He paused. "You will always have sanctuary in my church."

How perceptive you are, dear Father Hytier. "Thank you. I shall remember that."

Katrina walked up the gleaming staircase and turned toward the east wing. She entered her room—her mother's old room—rich with dark, polished mahogany and maroon lacquer. A cool breeze pushed the gossamer drapings of her bed as she opened a window. Listlessly, she sat on the corner of the bed and stared over the fields.

The day passed faster than expected. Several mourners knocked tentatively at her door to express their sympathies, and Katrina's heart warmed. These were not the aristocrats who came only to drink the duke's wine and share gossip with the duchess.

These were the local bourgeois: the duke's lawyer, his tenants, the people who would feel the effects of his loss most deeply. She was surprised that Tante Helene had not sought her company, but assumed she was too busy cooking for the guests to get away from the kitchens.

A servant brought a platter of food, but Katrina left it on the table, untouched. She listened to the jangle of horses' harnesses as the first guests began to leave, and felt relief. She needed silence for her grief.

Papa, gone already. They had known each other only for a few months. A few months with Papa out of nearly eighteen years alone, and then he had been taken away. Now, indeed, she was more alone than ever before.

She did not light any tapers even when the sun showed its last arc over the swell of the far hills, but sat in the darkness for hours, watching the stars pull off dark covers to twinkle in the indigo sky. She watched as the last carriages pulled into the night, their amber lights flickering beneath the trees. The night wind blew through the darkened room, catching beneath heavy drapes and teasing the gold-trimmed edges.

"You knew, didn't you?"

The voice was deep and gritty, and Katrina's neck prickled in terror as she wondered if the voice came from this earth or another. She turned to discern the duchess's wide panniers in a shadowy corner of the room.

"You knew he had altered his will before his death," the older woman said, moving deeper into the room. Her hatred grated harshly in Katrina's ears, and her presence intruded brutally into Katrina's soft reverie.

"Papa told me that some time ago. He made no secret of it."

"Then, you arranged that scene with the marquis to kill your father," the duchess persisted, tugging at her wide blue satin skirts.

"How dare you accuse me of killing Papa!" Katrina retorted. "And since when am I in concert with the marquis, Duchess?"

"You are clever, Katrina. Very clever, indeed. I only wish—" She cut herself off, swirling sharply in a whirl of satin. The stiff petticoats rustled angrily against one another.

"That I had never been found?" Katrina finished. Disgusted, she turned her back to the duchess. She closed her eyes and wished the duchess away, knowing well enough that the woman would stay until she said what she came to say. Katrina lifted her chin to the soft night breezes. She swore she would lock her door from now on. The duchess would not intrude into her sadness anymore.

The duchess popped open her iridescent fan and waved it in front of her bosom. "Your mother was an actress. I see she has left some of her blood in you. You may think you convinced the *haut monde* of your sadness, but no one truly believes you mourn the duke."

"You will not speak of my mother or my father in my presence. I will not stand for it." Katrina's voice trembled. The duchess laughed quietly and caressed her fan. She walked leisurely to the window on the opposite side of the bed, tracing the embroidery on the coverlet with a white hand. Katrina nearly choked on the overpowering lilac scent of her perfume.

"I will do whatever I damned well please," the duchess said clearly. Katrina noticed the determined tilt of the woman's chin, rising under folds of fat. "You missed the reading of the will, Katrina, and I wager there was a thing or two that the duke did not tell you."

Katrina stared at her calmly, observing the rich satin of her dress, the stiff blond *point d'anglaise* lace of her bodice, the diamonds that sparkled on her neck. Quite inappropriate attire for a woman in mourning. Katrina wondered why she had not noticed before.

"I trust the duke's judgment implicitly." Katrina forced herself to stare back into the duchess's slitted eyes, which sparkled with a curious vivacity.

"The duke left you everything, Katrina. *Everything.* Your son, if you ever have a legitimate one, will inherit the duke's entire estate, from these wretched lands to the duke's fleet of ships off St. Nazaire."

Katrina's eyes widened, and for a moment she gazed out the windows at the fertile fields below. "Papa told me he would make my sons his heirs, but I never realized exactly what that would mean." Katrina shrugged. She would not tell the duchess that she would gladly give up all her wealth to have her father back.

"He left Florence and me with a pittance," the duchess declared angrily. "A miserly yearly allowance that would not keep us in stockings." Katrina glanced at the duchess's wide skirts and wondered if she knew that most of the French people did not own shoes, never mind silk stockings.

"Perhaps the duke wanted me to supplement your allowance." Though the thought of giving the duchess and her dreadful daughter anything appalled Katrina, she knew that the gesture might lighten the aura of hatred that had taken root in the ancient stones of the chateau.

The duchess flashed spiteful eyes at Katrina and clicked her fan shut. "Don't be so quick, Katrina. The duke left you all of his wealth, but you cannot touch one sou until you are twenty-one." The duchess smiled briefly, watching Katrina's face. "How old are you now? Nearly eighteen, aren't you?" She tilted her head and a faint puff of powder rose around her. "Three years under my auspices."

Katrina's stomach knotted at the icy glare coming from the woman's faded eyes.

"The duke did not expect to pass on so quickly," the duchess explained, a cavernous grin distorting her face. "He left no instructions in case he died before you were of legal age. Since there is no male issue, I am now your legal guardian."

"He could not have—" Katrina whispered, her throat constricting. "For he would never have done such a thing, knowing what a shrew he married!"

"You can do nothing—not come, not go, not marry, not walk, not ride that satanic horse—nothing without my permission." The duchess lost her tight, bitter self-control. Her eyes blazed from sunken, powdered sockets, and her painted lips twisted obscenely. "Is that understood? *Nothing.*"

"Get out of here." Katrina masked her overwhelming fear and shock and moved around the bed to face the haughty duchess, whose eyes were aflame with hatred.

The duchess lifted a frail, blue-lined hand to hit her, but Katrina caught it easily and pushed it away. Instinctively, she lifted her own hand, feeling a shameful rush of joy as she did so.

"Go ahead, Katrina, hit me. Hitting a parent is enough for me to get a *lettre de cachet* and put you away for a long time. A very long time. In fact, I don't even need that as an excuse. I could call for one now. But I think I may have a little use for you yet." As Katrina's arm lowered in defeat, the duchess straightened her ponderous bosom and lifted her jowls, a light of triumph gleaming in her eyes.

"You do not have the authority with the king to do such a thing," Katrina murmured. Certainly, one would need to have the king's ear to call for such a *lettre*.

"Perhaps not, but I have friends who do."

The image of the marquis sprang into Katrina's head.

"Ah," the duchess said, moving away from the younger woman. "You are not as good an actress as I thought. I saw the fear in your eyes."

"Not fear," Katrina remarked. "Hatred."

"Hatred, Katrina? You do not know the meaning of the word. When I married your father, he was a rich widower ailing from a broken heart; his whorish wife, Clarisse, had died giving birth to a baby girl. He married me for one reason only: to be a mother to his child. I had a girl of my own to keep his child company, and I convinced him it was for the best." The duchess laughed shortly. "Foolish man. But, lucky for me, I found myself a duke and became a duchess."

"A duchess, indeed," Katrina said sarcastically.

"Yes, a duchess," the older woman repeated. "I had married once for love; a poor, gambling baron. All he gave me was a pile of debts and a babe before the year was out. And then he died in a duel, protecting a whore's honor. What else was I to do? The duke had lost his wife, his child was motherless, and he was rich." The duchess's thin lips curled. "Easy prey."

"And you sold yourself for money, like any common whore."

"You will learn better than to say such things."

"Never."

The duchess moved toward her, then stopped herself. "I wish to God that wolves had gotten to you," she hissed.

Katrina's eyes widened. "What are you saying?" Cold fingers of dread closed tightly over her heart.

"Oh, come now. You don't really believe that kidnaping story I told everyone, do you, Katrina?"

"What are you saying?" Katrina repeated, her heart thumping unevenly.

"I couldn't have the duke leaving all his money to his only daughter, the daughter of his actress-whore," the duchess ex-

plained joyfully, her eyes riveted on Katrina's flushed face. The
story burst out of her forcefully. "I had my own daughter and
my own welfare to look out for. I did the most convenient thing:
got rid of you, his first daughter."

"You . . ."

"Yes, Katrina. I considered killing you in the crib, but there
were always others around and I did not have the stomach for it.
So I paid one of the maids to take you away into the forest and
do it herself. Several days later, I raised the alarm. I had hoped
to find your mangled body somewhere in the woods, but it was
nowhere to be found. So I took care of the maid, as well." The
duchess's smile faded a bit. "I should have made sure I found
your body. I never thought you would surface again, especially
in this chateau."

Katrina lunged for her, but the duchess moved away.

"Beware how you treat me, Katrina," the duchess threatened,
holding her fan out against the young woman's flaring eyes.

"You tried to murder a babe to secure the duke's fortune for
yourself?"

"Yes!" the duchess shouted, her chest heaving. "I was sick
of being poor! I wanted more than the title; I wanted the money."
She lifted her head haughtily. "Unfortunately, you returned to
our lives. I told the duke the 'truth' about your disappearance
only because your presence caught me so off guard that it was
obvious I knew more than I was telling. Luckily, everyone believed my story and didn't examine it too closely. Now I must
find a way of dealing with you without raising suspicion." She
stared down her pinched nose at Katrina.

"Murderess," Katrina bit, stepping away from her. "You are
nothing but a cold-blooded murderess."

"It would behoove you to remember that, stepdaughter."

"Don't call me that vile name."

"Very well, *whore*—whether you like it or not, I have control
over the estates for the next three years. And that includes everything and everyone on it. That includes you." She leaned
back on her heels leisurely, a catlike smile spreading over her
heavily lined face. "If you haven't noticed, I've fired most of
the old servants and hired new ones. They'll do anything I say."

"I don't believe you," Katrina replied, a cold dread settling in her stomach. "Moreover, I cannot believe that Papa married you. He certainly was blind with grief."

"And I have had enough of your mouth, you disrespectful slut! Things are going to change around here for you. Unfortunately, I cannot kick you out. The duke made sure of that. So we are stuck here in the same chateau and I am your guardian." She reached out a gnarled hand.

"Don't touch me, old woman," Katrina warned.

The duchess's eyes bulged at the insult, and her hand swung out to hit Katrina squarely on the jaw. Recovering, Katrina lunged for the duchess's stomach. The older woman screamed and tried to swing back, but her hands hit only air as Katrina quickly evaded her blows.

Two liveried servants rushed in and held Katrina, who struggled in her captors' grasp. The duchess's red face rose to hers, and Katrina felt the impact of the rage in the ice-blue eyes.

"You have just sealed your fate."

"I want to see what I am buying before I buy it, Madame," said the marquis, leaning indolently against the marble fireplace. His gray waistcoat cut deeply to his hips, emphasizing his powerful, barrellike chest. His legs jutted against the close-fitting dove-white breeches.

The duchess's eyes darted to the floor. "She has not been feeling well; she has hardly eaten in weeks," she insisted, waving her hand before her and moving to the other side of the parlor. She tapped her fan nervously against the blue and white striped couch. "Why don't you come back in a few weeks when she has recovered from this illness? Then we will display her to you like a ripe peach."

"That will not do," the marquis said swiftly. "If you want me to sign this contract, I must see her today." He moved slowly toward the duke's desk, fingering the pages still wet with ink. The duchess moved nervously toward him, clutching her thick satin skirts.

"Very well, very well," she said quickly. "Sign the contract, and then I will take you to her."

"No," he corrected. "Take me to her and then, perhaps, I will sign the contract." He lost the look of a benign courtier and glared with ill-concealed irritation at the duchess's plump figure encased in her customary pink satin. "I begin to suspect that the wench is, er, *enceinte?*"

"Nothing of the sort!"

"Very well, then. I will see her." The marquis turned his back in dismissal.

An hour later the duchess descended to the parlor to fetch the marquis. Her fan waved quickly before her face, and she opened and closed it with precise, distinct snaps.

"I warn you that she's a bit thin and wan. She hardly eats anymore since the duke's death, and she does nothing but stay in her room all day, so she is short of breath and in ill health. She won't receive any callers—"

"I have heard no one has seen her since the funeral. If I had not been tied up at Versailles with the king with this irritating business of the rioting Parisians, I would have come sooner and escorted her out."

"Why . . . why, yes. But it would have done no good," the duchess added nervously, snapping her fan open again. "She has refused to leave her room."

"Quite curious. One would suppose someone of Katrina's youth and constitution would have recovered by now, don't you think, Madame?" He quirked an eyebrow. The rice powder on the duchess's face barely hid the beading of perspiration gathering on her forehead. "You seem to be quite out of mourning."

She glanced down at the rose satin dress, the layers of lace that dripped from her elbows, and the tiny pearls that edged her bodice. "Well—"

"It has been over a month now. And Katrina hasn't ridden? She loved to ride. Isn't that unusual, Madame?"

The duchess adroitly avoided the question, swirling stiffly and leading the marquis up the stairs, through the hall, to Katrina's heavy oak door.

"Ah, here we are. Now, Monsieur, please do not upset her."

The marquis laughed shortly. "Ah, the doting stepmother. Really, Beautrice."

The duchess entered the room without knocking, the marquis only a step behind her.

Although prepared for some difference in Katrina, the marquis was not prepared for the specter who faced him. The bones of Katrina's chest protruded under the thin veiling of her cambric fichu. Deep hollows sank under her cheekbones, in her neck, on the insides of her wrists. Her eyes stared dull and colorless at him.

He turned icy eyes to the duchess, who flicked open her fan again and turned her face away.

"Katrina, rise for the marquis," she said disdainfully.

Katrina braced the armrests of her chair and slowly straightened herself. Overwhelmed, she gripped her head and fell back onto the seat. The marquis moved to her in two steps and grabbed her quickly by the waist, encircling it easily with one arm. With one thrust he swept the girl into his arms and deposited her on the bed.

"Get water. And cool clothes. And brandy. Now."

A few servants scurried quickly out the door. A young woman moved to Katrina's side and brushed her hair away from her forehead.

"Tell me," the marquis began, addressing the servant girl, "what has Katrina been eating?"

The girl raised frightened eyes to the marquis and then hazarded a sidelong glance at the duchess. She rubbed a livid yellow and green bruise on her arm.

"Why, Marquis," the duchess said in a high, whining voice. "I told you she wasn't eating. She won't eat a thing—"

"Shut up, Beautrice," the marquis said through gritted teeth, then turned his attention back to the girl. "The duchess will not hurt you," he assured her. "Tell me what she has been eating."

"Well, sir," she began, considering the dark, gray-eyed man who loomed possessively over Katrina's tiny form. "She's been eating bread and . . . and water."

"Look at me," the marquis demanded, drawing her eyes away from the gesturing figure of the duchess. "What else?"

"That is all, Monsieur." The servant hesitated a moment, then added, "That is all she has been served."

The duchess gasped again and the fan clicked shut. "Lies. Damned lies. That's all servants do is lie—"

"Shut up." The marquis rose from Katrina's side and moved toward the duchess. "I will discuss all of this with you in the study." She bit her bottom lip and swished out of the room. The servant released an audible sigh at her departure.

"Oh, Monsieur, I do not know who you are, but you must do

something for her or she'll never live through the week. That woman has been serving her bread and water for weeks now, and the poor thing is just wasting away. I've tried to slip her meats and vegetables, but I was caught once.'' She took a deep breath. ''I don't know who to turn to, and now I'm imprisoned in this house myself—''

''How did this all happen?'' the marquis asked, stopping the flow of the girl's words.

''Oh, she has been kept in this room since the funeral, Monsieur, and one day she was even whipped for saying something to the duchess—''

''She was whipped?'' The marquis roughly pushed Katrina over and ripped the back of her dress. His lips tightened as he realized she wore no corset, and the smallness of her waist was starvation induced. He could count the vertebrae of her spine. His brows drew together in anger as he examined the red welts and thin scars indicative of a whipping. ''Has she been here since the whipping?'' he demanded.

''Yes. Roget has been guarding her.''

''Who the hell is Roget?''

''He is the man that whipped her. The duchess hired him to oversee the dayworkers.''

The marquis's lips drew in an angry, taut line. ''After the whipping, the duchess began starving her?''

''Yes, sir.'' She bit her lip nervously.

He glanced down again at Katrina, whose eyes were open and vacuous, then he turned and walked firmly out the door and down the stairs.

''I have a mind to send you to the Bastille!'' he barked when he came upon the duchess. ''Were it not now in the hands of the damned *Etats généraux*, I might have.''

She gasped. ''You—you, of all people, believe the lies of a greedy, selfish servant over my word?''

''I believe what I see, Madame. And I see a girl who is being starved to death.'' He straightened. ''You are a fool.''

''Marquis!'' she exclaimed, clutching her ample cleavage and sinking into a chair.

''I want her fed back to health again.'' He stared at the old woman with icy eyes. ''And I want no more whippings. Oh, don't bother denying it, old woman. I saw the marks on her back.

Fortunately, the woman who tended her had some skill, otherwise I would think twice about taking a woman so disfigured.'' The marquis turned away, disgusted.

"Her maid, the one I was speaking to," he continued. "I don't want her touched. She leaves with Katrina. I will return in three weeks. If anything is even slightly amiss, I rip up this contract. Do you understand?'' He bent over the papers and signed his name in swift, angry strokes. He glanced up one more time at the duchess.

"Mind you, I will see her before the wedding. If I am to marry this wench and return her entire dowry to you, I want to make sure that she is well worth it.'' He turned to take his leave. "This will be the most expensive woman I have ever had.''

Katrina did not have the strength to fight the marquis's seering eyes and possessive hands the day the duchess had brought him up to see her. She had listened to his voice over her, speaking in authorative tones to her maid, and had tried to express her anger and hatred through her eyes, but she did not have the strength.

After his visit, the days lightened. Her lady's-maid, Manon, sported a smug confidence, and the sundry servants who entered her chamber periodically displayed frequent smiles and a quickness of step. Perhaps it was just the food, thought Katrina, gazing at the clear, aromatic soup before her.

She did not mind the long, sedate days in bed. Her strength was returning, bit by bit. She wondered vaguely at the sudden change. She knew it had to do with the marquis, but feared examining her turn in fortune too closely. The duchess's future plans for her were not a subject on which Katrina cared to dwell.

She dreamed often of her youth, the warmth of the kitchen, the security of Tante Helene's skirts. How quickly all had been turned inside out. Tante Helene, thrown out of the kitchens, was probably in Poitiers earning her keep by sewing. Rafe's old promises sang in Katrina's ears again, and she often wondered why she hadn't followed him out into the night, instead of staying here where she had been truly happy only a few times. But the duke's warm eyes sparkled in her memory, and she knew the answer to those questions.

As the soups gave way to tender vegetables in cream sauces

and breads thick and warm, Katrina's strength returned. She sat up in bed and asked the questions that had been plaguing her over the last week.

"It's good to see you up!" Manon exclaimed.

"Thanks, Manon. I'm feeling quite well today."

"Well, it's about time. The Marquis de Noailles will be calling to get another look at you in a week or so."

"What?" she exclaimed. "Why?"

"Well, I'm not sure," Manon said evasively. "Probably just to check up on your health, that's all. You do remember when he came last time, don't you?"

"Vaguely."

"He saved your life, Mademoiselle. I've never seen anyone yell at the duchess like he did—in front of servants, no less!" She giggled. "Here, eat your bread."

"What did he say to her?" Katrina asked hesitantly, reaching for the doughy roll.

"Just to shut up," Manon giggled. "Then he asked all these questions about you. What eyes! They look right through you. I tell you, I was so scared—"

"What did he ask?" Katrina persisted.

"He just asked what had happened to you, and I told him absolutely everything. He was in a rage, I tell you. He stood up—"

"Manon."

"Well, anyway. He went downstairs and yelled at the duchess for a while in the study. Then he stormed out, but the duchess seemed pretty pleased with herself. Since then she's kept to her room, real quiet, and she hasn't beaten anyone, either. I don't know what the marquis said, but it sure shut her up."

"I wonder what he's up to?" Katrina murmured. "I don't trust that woman or that man."

"Well, no one trusts the duchess," Manon agreed, "but I'm sure you can trust that man. He looked at you like you were his own wife."

"Don't say that!" Katrina exclaimed, nearly upsetting her dinner. "He probably stared at me as if I were a piece of his property that was marred."

"He had the look of a man in love, Mademoiselle," Manon said hesitantly, lowering her head.

Katrina looked at her incredulously and managed a gritty laugh. "You are wrong. That man nearly raped me last spring when he thought I was 'only' a servant, and since then has never ceased insulting me. He is a vile, evil man. Probably worse than the duchess." The anger flushed over Katrina in waves. "As far as I am concerned, he was the cause of my father's death. He has made sure I am taken care of because he does not want his property disfigured. Can you understand that?" She leaned back against the pillows. "The bastard."

Manon stood up, taking the empty tray from Katrina's lap. She shrugged her shoulders beneath the loose bodice. "I meant no offense, Mademoiselle." She turned and left the room.

"I wonder what the duchess is planning," Katrina murmured to herself, fearing that the marquis played a larger role than she liked. She steeled herself with determination. She was no longer going to be a pawn for that woman, or anyone else, for that matter. She fingered the knife she had slipped under the covers while Manon's back was turned. She would need it soon, she was sure.

Katrina did not have to wait long to discover the duchess's schemes. Later that day she entered the room, perfume first, critically scanning the girl on the bed.

"You are looking better," the duchess said, as if to herself.

Katrina lifted an eyebrow. "And you, Madame, are as hideous as always."

The duchess's lips turned as white as her face. "And I see you have your spirit back. That is good. He will be pleased."

"Who will be pleased, Madame?" Katrina asked haughtily.

"Why, the marquis, of course. Your fiancé." The duchess smiled tightly as Katrina's face paled. "The wedding is in two weeks. It caused quite a stir when the announcement was read last week."

"What are you talking about?" Katrina said hotly. "I never consented to any such union."

"Nobody asked you, Katrina. Surely you would not pass up such a match?" the duchess hissed. "He is a marquis! And a rich one, as well. I am sure that, if you are . . . good to him, he will introduce you at Versailles." She laughed, the lines on her face moving wildly.

"I will not marry the marquis."

"Oh, yes you will. Don't worry. Despite his age, they say he is quite lively in the bedroom." She smiled. "The two of you should get along quite well. And if he bores you, well, there's always Jason de Niort. You could take him on as a lover. If he will have you." The duchess turned away from the bed, moving slowly to the door. "Poor boy. He was quite upset when he heard the news. But he'll accept it when he sees you married."

"What are you going to do, drag me to the altar?" Katrina asked daringly, her voice rich with contempt.

"I don't think that will be necessary," the duchess responded idly, examining the room. "You see, you do have a choice. Either be the marquis's wife, or be his slut." She smiled.

Ice flowed down Katrina's back as she stared at the empty blue eyes of the duchess. Her own eyes narrowed in hatred. "What do you mean?" she said softly.

The duchess moved languidly around the room, examining the porcelain insets of Katrina's writing table, running blue-veined hands over the gilt edges. "It is very simple, Katrina," she said. "If you don't marry him, he will take you as his mistress. With my consent."

"You are bluffing."

"You should know by now that I never bluff." Her usually faded blue eyes blazed in their sunken sockets, and Katrina knew that nothing was beyond the pandering greed of this base woman.

Katrina did not answer her, raising her chin defiantly. A sudden thought made her smile. "Marrying the marquis would make me a very powerful woman, would it not?"

The duchess's eyes flickered. "Not necessarily—"

"It may earn me the favor of, say, the king himself." Katrina looked toward the ceiling, addressing no one in particular.

"You overestimate your whorish—"

"I could do a lot of things then that would seriously hurt those people who have crossed me." She looked evenly at the duchess. "Indeed, Madame," Katrina said, dismissing her. "You may have done me a favor."

Katrina had no intention of marrying the marquis. But the question remained: how was she going to escape without being captured? As the day of the wedding drew nearer, her panic grew stronger. She squirreled away supplies: salted meats, cheeses, hard rolls. She fabricated a makeshift bag small enough to wrap around her waist and hide in the folds of her petticoats. She hid what few louis she had in the bag and shoved it under her bed with her other supplies and the knife. But still no plan came to her, and the marquis's arrival was imminent.

He entered the room one day as silently as a stalking cat. Looking into the gray eyes, Katrina froze as she always did. She was standing on a stool in her corset and chemise, white satin draped over her shoulder, while a dressmaker measured her in preparation for the wedding day. As if sensing that her presence was unwanted by the man, the dressmaker rose stiffly, curtsied, and left. Without a word, the marquis ambled toward Katrina.

His eyes roamed over her figure, stopping to rest on the curve of her uptilted breasts above the whalebone corset.

"You are looking . . . healthier, Katrina," he said simply, a wry smile on his face.

"Do you approve of your new acquisition, Monsieur?"

"Very much, Katrina. So the duchess dared to tell you before the day of the wedding, and you have not tried to escape? What is she holding over your head?"

"Out of curiosity, Monsieur," Katrina asked, ignoring the marquis's words, "how much did you pay for me?"

"Quite a bit, *lapin*. But it is not polite to speak of such things. You will learn that." He reached up to brush his hand across her thinly veiled nipple. She flinched. "You will also have to learn to stop that, Katrina. You will like my bed."

"You cannot make me like what disgusts me, Marquis. You may have bought my body, but you have not bought my soul."

A cloud passed over his eyes, and his jaw set in anger. "You speak idle words, Katrina," he murmured dangerously.

"They are not idle. How does it feel, Marquis, to know that you will not have what you really want, just the shell it is in?"

His arms shot out, pulling her forcefully against his body. "You push too far, *lapin*." His teeth bit down hard on her lips, and Katrina gasped as his arms tightened the breath out of her. He lifted his head. "Now I will ensure that you marry me. Or suffer the consequences."

He tore the chemise from her breasts, exposing them to his hard, thick-boned hands. Katrina cried out, pushing frantically at his chest. He carried her with one arm and threw her violently on the bed.

"You will rape me, then?" she gasped. "Rape me like any other peasant girl you may find on the roads?"

The marquis stopped fumbling with his cravat to stare at her, brows drawn.

Katrina leaned up, sensing her advantage. "That's right, Marquis," she spat. "You will get some kind of pleasure, I suppose, out of forcing a woman to your bidding." Her breasts heaved through the clinging ends of the chemise.

The marquis stared at her, then calmly retied his cravat. "It seems I have lost control," he said calmly, turning from her and walking toward the door. "I give you my most humble apologies."

"Apologies!" she cried. "An apology from the great Marquis de Noailles?"

"The next time, my dear Katrina," he said, turning to her at the door, "you will come to my bed of your own free will."

"Never!"

On the morning of her wedding day, Katrina scrubbed herself in a hot bath, washed her hair, and reveled in the scented water of the shoe-shaped copper bath. She knew it would be some time before she felt such luxuries again. The rest of the day she would have to be tensely alert, searching for an opportunity to run.

A plan unfolded as she stretched in the large tub. She knew she would be surrounded by servants all morning and would not be free of them until the ride to the church, which was to take place with only the duchess and, of course, the driver.

Katrina had no doubt that she could subdue the duchess with sudden attack. But the driver. How was she going to stop him?

Her mind mulled over the possibilities all morning and most of the afternoon, shocking herself at some of the ideas. The presence of the knife began to disturb her.

Meanwhile, swarms of women flocked around her, one combing the slick length of her hair; one heating the irons; one sewing the last-minute adjustments to her wedding dress. A maid laced the corset, put the old-fashioned stomacher carefully into the satin bodice, then arranged the layers of laced skirts studded with pearls. The marquis had spared no expense on her trousseau.

Every piece was perfect, but Katrina hated the stiff, unyielding clothes. The panniers on her wedding gown were twice as wide as those she usually wore, and dragged upon her slight form. Suddenly, she knew where she was going to hide her supplies.

The servants crooned and cooed around Katrina, but her mind was elsewhere, oblivious to the smooth satin, the delicate point lace, and the intricate curls in her hair.

"Please, please . . ." Katrina said, holding her hands up away from her. "Could I have a moment alone?" Among murmurs and comforting pats, the women left her one by one, until Katrina, touching her head in pain, was free of their incessant chatter.

It took her moments to tie the bag of coins around her waist, under her skirts. She attached the packets of food under each pannier, trying to weigh them evenly. Then she pulled out an old green dress. The one she wore the night she and Rafe . . .

But there was no time for these thoughts. She wrapped the dress tightly around one leg, securing it with another set of corset laces, then walked to and fro before the mirror, looking for telltale signs of the baggage. One leg loomed larger than the other, one pannier a bit lower, but only someone with the most critical eye would notice. Finally, she retrieved the knife and slipped it between her breasts, hiding it under her flat stomacher. The blade lay cold against her flesh.

When the women returned, Katrina was sitting sedately on her bed, staring out into the fields. It was a bright August day, and the sun burned through the high window.

But Katrina's hands were icy.

The duchess had only glanced at Katrina as she walked down the stone stairs of the chateau into the carriage, and the young woman's appearance seemed to meet with her approval. Katrina watched her, wondering exactly how the duchess would react if she knew what Katrina was planning. The trip would take over three hours, for the marquis had insisted on having the wedding in a large cathedral near his ancient marquisate. She wanted to make sure that they were in a secluded, wooded area before she began—the forward riders far ahead, and the rear guards far behind.

Katrina opened the shutters briefly to take one last look at the manor. It stood upon its knoll, surrounded by trees, cold and isolated, the walls gray and forbidding.

"Close that shutter, Katrina. You are ruining my hair," the duchess snapped.

"Come and close it yourself, old woman."

The duchess flushed, then leaned over Katrina and reached for the shutter.

"Do not move, Madame." The cold knife traced the folds of the duchess's throat.

The duchess's eyes widened in terror. "What—what are you doing?"

"Shut up, old woman." Katrina closed the window with one hand, blocking them from the sight of any of the riders. "Shut up and turn around."

The duchess rigidly twisted her back to Katrina, her face paling. "You cannot possibly think—" she began nervously, bracing herself against the jolting of the carriage. "If I am hurt, every noble in this province will be out to find you. And there are rear guards not five minutes away."

Katrina laughed, pulling corset strings out of one of her hidden bags. "I have not quite yet decided whether I will disfigure you or just kill you outright," she said. "Either way, I suspect 'every noble in the province' will be glad you are gone, not to mention most of the peasantry. From what I have heard, I would be doing them all a great service." Nimbly, she tied the duchess's arms against her sides and her hands behind her back. "Maybe, if you are quiet, I will let you live." She turned the duchess around and pushed her against the seat, making her wince at the pinch of her tight corset. Grabbing a handkerchief, Katrina roughly shoved it into the duchess's mouth and tied it in the back of her head.

The whole scene took only seconds, and Katrina sat back, surprised at how easy it all was. Terrified, the duchess eyed the knife, flinching as the sun glinted off its sharp edge. Katrina complacently opened the blinds. With the duchess trussed, she knew she could wait until the moment was perfect before subduing the carriage driver.

An hour passed. Two. The land had more hills now, but it was still too open for her purposes. Katrina leaned out, staring toward the south in search of the rear guards. They could not be

seen from her vantage point, and she hoped they had been delayed. Every extra minute she had was precious. She looked
forward, smiling slightly as a forest loomed darkly ahead. It
would not be long now.

"Driver! Driver! *Madame la Duchesse* is very ill!" Katrina
cried as the darkness of the forest closed in on them. "Please,
stop the carriage." The man poked his head around the side of
the carriage to see the bride, hair and veils flying, screaming for
him to stop the carriage.

Katrina gasped. It was Roget, the man who had whipped her
and who was the duchess's chief henchman. No corset-strings
were going to hold him captive for any length of time. She would
have to incapacitate him for a while.

The carriage jolted to a halt. Frantically, Katrina searched the
carriage for a weapon. Her glance fell on the duchess's gold-
handled cane, the heavy top thick with the burnished metal.
Grabbing the cane, she stepped out of the carriage, hiding it in
the folds of her gown. She descended the stairs, breathing deeply
so her breasts pressed provocatively against the stomacher.

"Oh, Roget," she said coyly. "Please, the duchess is very ill.
Could you make sure she is all right?"

"I don't know nothing about treating a lady," he said gruffly,
eyeing the pink-tinted mounds of breasts rising temptingly from
the bride's bodice.

"Well, you must know more than I." Katrina felt drops of
sweat on her upper lip. She licked them quickly, drawing Roget's
eyes to the movement. "Please, would you check on her? Roget?" she prompted.

"Very well." He bent to enter the carriage.

Katrina brought her arm back, tight on the cane, then threw
all her weight into it, guiding the heavy end to his head, where
it made contact with a magnificent crack. Katrina watched in
horror, wondering if she had killed him, as blood began to flow.
The tall, brawny Roget fell slowly to the dirt, clutching his head.

He did not move.

Katrina quickly changed out of her wedding gown, throwing
the fine satin carelessly on the ground. Pulling on her old dress,
she sighed as the soft linen molded to her curves. Gleefully, she
pulled the pins out of her hair, scattering them all over the
ground. Her hair fell in heavy waves around her face. After put-

ting all her supplies into the largest bag, she unhooked the best of the two roans and energetically lifted herself astride. As she cantered around to where Roget was lying, the duchess stared white-faced at the young woman.

Tossing her head in triumph, Katrina took a deep breath, then laughed loudly. She kicked the horse toward the open road.

Freedom!

Chapter 12

The young woman dragged her eyes over Katrina's ragged figure, resting for a moment on the mud caking the hem of her pea-green dress. The same mud coated the streets of Paris and exuded an unbearable stench, fetid even in the coolness of early autumn.

"Sorry. We do not have a position for you," the woman said, clutching her rustling skirts and turning her back to Katrina.

"I would like to see the owner of the shop, *s'il vous plait.*" Katrina dropped the peasant drawl that had colored her speech since leaving Poitiers and answered the insolent milliner in impeccable Parisian French. Despite herself, the young woman moved mutely away to find her superior. Katrina blithely ignored the stares of the curious women grouped in the rear of the shop, and settled back on her callused heels to wait.

Would she ever find a post? For two weeks she had searched every milliner's shop in Paris, it seemed, and now she stood in the Palais Royal itself, hoping that one of the wealthier shops would take in a fairly inexperienced sewer. The satchel of coins she had taken on her flight had been depleted quickly on food and lodging and public coaches. Katrina closed her heavy eyes. If she did not find a position soon, she would be kicked out of her lodging—horrible as it was—and find herself in the stinking, slime-covered streets of Paris without shelter or food.

Katrina suppressed a curt laugh. She should consider herself fortunate. She had successfully escaped the bony grasp of the Marquis de Noailles, and she knew there were few alive who could boast the same. Despite the endless days of walking—from where she had abandoned the horse outside of Poitiers, to Tours, to Orleans, and finally to Paris—the trip was well worth it. Although the population of Paris swelled with seasonal workers returning from harvest, she had been able to find lodging in St. Denis. That search had added more calluses upon her calluses. Now her feet were so hardened she could not feel the poke of the unevenly cobbled streets.

The young woman returned, defiant, her hands on her ample panniers. "I am sorry, there are no positions here and the owner is too busy to see you. I will show you out."

A bedecked aristocrat burst from another room, her satin shimmering and rustling in the breeze of her movement. A flock of milliners fluttered around the woman, dangling ribbons before her eyes, pushing the feathers of her hat into cocky angles, and placing bunches of fruit and feathered birds on its rim. An older woman watched contentedly, murmuring to the aristocrat.

Katrina's eyes brightened. "I would like to see the owner first," she said loudly. "I can wait."

The young woman flushed angrily. "Well you cannot wait here."

"Why not?"

"Because you're attracting attention," she said quickly. "This is a respectable shop. Not just anyone can wander in here—"

"One minute, Violet." The husky voice came from the older woman who, moments ago, had been attending the aristocrat. The woman's rich gown rustled loudly as she crossed the shop. Her gaze raked over Katrina quickly. "What does she want?"

"She's looking for work, Madame," Violet said. "I told her nothing was available. With all the aristocrats fleeing the city, we hardly have enough work for us—"

The older woman glanced sharply at Violet, who held her tongue. The woman turned to Katrina and squinted at her through painted lids. Her lips twitched at the pert hat pinned to Katrina's hair.

"What is your name, child?"

"Katherine Dubois, Madame." She curtsied a bit, lowering her eyes respectfully. She had used the pseudonym many times in her travels. She could not risk the duchess or the marquis finding her and taking her back to the manor.

The owner scrutinized Katrina's face. "Have you any experience?"

"Only at home, Madame."

"And where is that?"

Katrina stiffened slightly. "I am from Poitou, Madame. I worked for a small house in the country."

"The name?"

"You would not know, Madame," Katrina said quickly. "They never attended the court of Versailles."

The woman's eyes twinkled with mirth. "Then you are right, Mademoiselle. *Ces gens, je ne les connais pas,*" she replied, quoting the common phrase for noblemen who did not grace the king's court. "I think I like you. Your dress is little more than a rag, but your accessories are well done." She motioned toward the plain, pert hat that rested atop Katrina's simple coiffure. Lace trimmed Katrina's bodice and hung from her sleeves, and a muslin fichu provided modesty. "You may work in back until you have enough money saved to buy a decent dress. Then we will see about putting you up front."

Violet whirled angrily to face the owner.

"Violet!" the owner said reproachfully before she had a chance to speak. "Just look at her. Underneath that rag is a wonderful body, albeit thin. And those eyes must have conquered more than one country boy." She smiled at Katrina's embarrassed expression. "My name is Madame Bertrier," she continued. "Violet, show her her place and get her started, and you will remember that our business is doing quite well. Though many of the city's aristocrats have fled Paris, the influx of the wives of the National Assembly have more than made up for the loss. I will hear no more such talk." Madame Bertrier trailed away, her skirts swishing, her perfume following in her wake.

Violet turned slowly and led Katrina to the group of milliners gathered in the back of the shop, their heads lowered over their work. "This," she began, her nose wrinkling as her eyes traveled over Katrina, "is Katherine. Lucille, show her what to do." With an audible sniff, Violet marched away from the group.

"Now, don't you mind Violet," one of the girls ventured. "She's all uppity because she's just found a generous lover."

"Sit," another woman said curtly. "There's some sewing to do, still. I'm Lucille."

Katrina smiled shyly into her dark sharp-boned face. Lucille's black hair sprang coarsely from a roll lying at the nape of her neck. Her peasant's cap was yellowed with age and failed to contain the riotous sprigs of hair that poked from its edges.

Lucille flashed a humorless smile and pointed to each of the women. "This is Anne, Yvette, Emilie, Flora, and Grace. Now, come. Here, take this bonnet and sew this rim. Very tiny stitches."

Katrina sank into the hard wooden chair. She could not believe her fortune. Grasping the pin and thread that had been given to her, she examined the bonnet and sewed with quick, rapid jerks.

"You are new to Paris, Katherine?" Yvette, the largest woman, asked smiling. She had the look of a cat who would rather be lying, belly up, in the sun.

"Yes," Katrina replied. "I am from a small village in Poitou."

"And what brings you to Paris?" Anne asked, her cheeks full and round.

"My—my family died in a fire," Katrina replied hesitantly. "I had to find work."

"You're lucky to find a position," Lucille noted, nodding over the bonnet she grasped firmly in one hand. "There's not much work in Paris these days."

"Even for milliners," Grace added, her heavy-lidded eyes rising slowly to Katrina's. "Two months ago we had more work than we could possibly handle. But since we took the Bastille, all the aristocrats have been fleeing." She lifted pin-pricked fingers. "And so has our work."

"Madame Bertrier seems to think otherwise," Katrina commented. "She warned Violet against such talk when she hired me."

Lucille's eyes narrowed slowly on Katrina's face. "You have the face of an aristocrat, Katherine," she said quietly. "That is what got you this position."

Katrina stifled her surprise at Lucille's sharp-eyed observance. "How wrong you are. I was brought up in kitchens." She bent deeper over the bonnet. "I daresay there's nary one aristocrat in all of France who has ever scoured a pot."

Yvette cackled loudly.

"Well, then, your mother or grandmother was raped by the local aristocrat," Lucille said haughtily. "That's how it usually works."

"Oh, Lucille, you'll offend her!" Anne exclaimed.

"Are you a member of the *tiers état?*" Lucille asked swiftly.

Katrina lifted her chin and pulled upon a green cockade pinned to her bodice. *"Bien sûr."* In her few weeks in Paris, she had learned one elemental rule of survival: be a revolutionary, or else you might be arrested and carried off to some dreadful prison. Katrina had taken to wearing a green cockade to advertise her political bent. As she faced these women, she felt a small surge of pride.

"Good." Lucille reached over, covering Katrina's hand with her own bony one. "I see the anger in your eyes, Katherine. I see that you, too, hate the aristocracy."

"There is a certain marquis that I would like to see vanish from French soil," she agreed.

"Ah, then you'll fit right in, Katherine." Lucille's lips tightened over her yellowed teeth. "You shall fit right in."

It was near sunset when Katrina finally left the milliner's shop, moving smoothly through the crowds that had already gathered at the cafés of the Palais Royal to listen to the orators. She glanced around, then quickly lowered her head, fearfully wondering if any of the noblemen she had met in Poitou had decided to come to Paris for the fall. If the duchess or the marquis ever caught her, they would drag her to Poitiers to a fate worse then death. She would never go with them alive.

She could go to Rafe. Katrina closed her eyes at this thought. He had to be in Paris. All the dreams he told her in Poitiers—about building a new state, making a constitution for France—they were now happening here in Paris. If she tried, she was sure she could find him.

She shook her head in defeat, brushing away a tear that had slipped down her cheek. Why did she think he would change? He hated her—he blamed her for the deaths of three of his men. She could expect no more sympathy from him than she could from the duchess. Besides, her heart ached too much now, from all that had happened. It could not bear any more hate from Rafe.

Slipping through the stony arches into the gardens of the Palais Royal, Katrina slowed her step and lifted her head to the sky. The sun hovered tentatively on the horizon, not quite wanting to set, brushing the clouds russet and gold. She must return to her room soon, before night fell and she might be mistaken for a different type of woman.

Katrina hastened out of the Palais Royal and quickened her step toward St. Denis. She turned off into a narrow lane and followed the familiar paths as they twisted deeper and deeper into the *faubourg*. Katrina deftly avoided the showers of refuse that were thrown from the upper stories of the sagging brick buildings, while watching out for the gutter down the center of the lane, which held a swift stream of foul-smelling liquid.

A hawker gestured to her as she passed by, waving his nostrums and old hats. Katrina smiled and pressed on. She purchased dinner in a sausage shop, stopping once more to check the price of bread—nearly three sous a pound!—before turning into her lodging.

Mae, the concierge, stopped her on the narrow steps to her room. Placing her hands firmly on square hips, she asked, "Well, did you find a position, Katherine? Will you be able to pay my room and board this week?"

Katrina stepped down to get away from the harsh, musky scent of the woman. "Indeed, I did. At a small shop in the Palais Royal."

"The Palais Royal! If I had known I had such a rich boarder, I'd have charged you more." She laughed loudly, the cackle reverberating off the walls.

If I had more, I certainly would not live in this dungeon, Katrina thought. She pushed past Mae's solid frame and moved quickly through the dim corridor to her room. Sighing, she walked to the small dresser, the only piece of furniture other than a rickety bed with a dusty, straw-filled mattress. The water she had left in the pitcher that morning was full of grime that had fallen from the water-stained ceiling, but she was too tired and dirty to care. The water-woman might not be around for hours, and even her water was rarely better than this. Besides, fresh water cost money, something of which Katrina had precious little.

Katrina washed the day's grime from her feet, her fingers aching from sewing. She lay down on the bed, flexing her hands in the darkness, and soon fell into a deep sleep.

The weeks that passed were mercifully uneventful for Katrina.

She spent her days at the milliner's, her Sundays and Mondays walking through the streets of Paris or mending her meager wardrobe. She had pushed all thoughts of Poitiers from her mind—Papa, Rafe, Tante Helene, all those who had been good to her—because each brilliant day with one of them was overshadowed by darker ones with the duchess. The pain was too close and too harsh.

Paris kept her mind off her troubles. The city sprawled around the Île de la Cité, fanning out in all directions. The Seine, smooth but dirty under the bridges, was dotted with barges of strange shapes and brilliant colors. Katrina would spend hours on Pont Neuf, pressing close to the stone edge to avoid the constant rush of cabriolets, hackney cabs, and sleek berlines pulled by four horses. And when the spicy tongues of river men tired her, she would purchase a journal and read the political scandal of the day.

In Poitiers, without her father's quickness and interest to spur her on, how quickly she had fallen behind in her knowledge of current events! Weeks after the Bastille had fallen, the National Assembly had written a Declaration of the Rights of Man, abolishing nearly all feudal privileges. Some said the declaration even abolished taxes! The king had not yet approved the revolutionary declaration, leaving Paris tense for news.

Katrina inhaled the city smells gratefully, not once regretting her reckless decision to flee to Paris. Although she dressed in wretched rags and ate little but sausage and bread, Katrina relished her newfound freedom. Not for a million livres would she return to Poitiers to become the Marquise de Noailles.

Katrina walked slowly before the cafés, the most exciting places in Paris. Day and night, they overflowed onto the streets with noblemen, bourgeois, and peasant alike. The tables glittered with brandy glasses while men smoking virgin tobacco argued across the open rooms. As the evenings progressed, one or more speakers would rise upon the tables to address the crowd, the words booming out over the patrons to the passersby. Many an evening, Katrina had stopped to listen, her own heart quickening at their words. Few noticed the young girl alone in the crowded streets, and she reveled in her anonymity, reveled in the excitement of the burgeoning, fiery, tumultuous city that surrounded her.

And then the bread ran out in Paris.

"The crowds are worse than usual today," Lucille remarked, sitting down to take up the hat over which she had been laboring.

"Still?" Katrina remarked. "They have been rioting all week."

"But today smells of more serious upheavals," Lucille said, bending to pick up a long ostrich plume. "There's no bread or grain in any mart or *boulangerie* in the city. If I didn't have to work in this damned place I'd be out there, too. I'm hungry."

Katrina nodded her agreement. The milliners had been taking turns standing on the bread lines, trying to get their rations before rations were no longer there, and had been fortunate enough to get some yesterday. But today . . . Katrina remembered the thick loaves that Tante Helene had kneaded and baked in the stone oven. Her mouth watered and an arrow of pain twisted her stomach. She looked briefly at Lucille, whose dark head bent over the hat.

"Do you think there will be some tomorrow?"

"Probably not," Lucille responded, her jaw set in a stubborn line. "Unless something is done about it. If only the king would realize what he's doing. . . . He can't starve us into submission. We'll fight until we get our grain. Has he forgotten the lessons of July fourteenth already?"

"Perhaps the National Assembly can do something," Katrina ventured.

"They haven't helped yet. Lots of pretty words—all of them talking about 'The Rights of Man' and how we should be treated as equals," Lucille scoffed. "But that won't feed us. They should turn their attention to the hungry multitudes first."

Katrina smiled secretly. Lucille was getting excited again, as she did every time there was a riot in the streets. She had spent most of the past month in an agitated state—as had Paris.

"Perhaps there will be another turn of events such as the falling of the Bastille," Yvette said languidly. "It's too bad you weren't here for that, Katherine. It was glorious! The people of Paris taking down a fortress, almost solely with anger."

"The guns and knives we confiscated didn't hurt our cause, either," Lucille added. "Nor did the rope we hung the traitors with."

"Oh, Lucille. So violent—" Anne commented, her nose wrinkling.

"We have to be violent! We must get the king's attention!" Lucille replied angrily.

"Shouldn't the Assembly be given a chance—"

"The Assembly is full of noble fools, Emilie," Lucille spat. "Have they done anything? Do we have bread? They've been in session since June, and still Paris is starving. Only after the fall of the Bastille, in July, did any grain flow into this city. And now they are fighting over a piece of paper that the king will not sign and that will not bring bread to Paris. What fools!"

"Some of them are quite nice, Lucille," Yvette added slyly, straightening her tight bodice.

"You have been looking at them over too many bottles of brandy, Yvette," Lucille said sternly.

Flora entered, empty-handed. "I have just been to three *boulangeries*. There is no more bread in Paris."

"Is there wine?" Lucille asked.

Flora nodded.

"Good. I suggest we go to the cafés and see what Paris has to say about all this."

Katrina hesitated, glancing down at her reddened, pin-pricked fingers. She had intentionally avoided going on nightly forays to the cafés with the other milliners, although Lucille had invited her more than once. Too many mornings, Katrina had seen the girls stumble in, unwashed, stinking of cheap wine, struggling to keep their eyes open. Katrina suspected that several of the girls did more than simply talk to the café patrons. Their stories of their evenings out shocked her with their vulgarity—and often with their violence. Two nights ago they had witnessed the hanging of a *boulanger* who had run out of bread. Katrina shivered. She had to admit she feared these women, especially Lucille.

Lucille stared at her penetratingly. "Will you be coming with us, Katherine?" she asked.

The circle of women quieted, and six pairs of eyes turned upon her.

Katrina had read once that when wild dogs sensed fear within their ranks, the pack turned upon the offender and tore at him with bared fangs until death. Her instincts told her to answer with caution.

"Of course," she said slowly. "I would not miss this evening for two weeks' ration."

Yvette swayed into Lucille's wiry arms, releasing a gust of wine-tainted breath into her face.

"My God, she smells horrible!" Lucille exclaimed. "Come on, Yvette. We have work to do. We can't have you falling down drunk all the way to Versailles!"

"How long has she been drinking?" Katrina asked, appalled at the thought of drinking any more after the previous evening's debauch.

"All night, I suppose." Lucille's lips twitched. "I think some assemblyman didn't know that it wasn't necessary to ply her with wine."

"Just because I'm—I've had a brandy or two doesn't mean I'm drunk." Yvette lifted her chin high and stared with glassy eyes. "See. I can stand. I can walk, too." With a brave lunge forward, Yvette teetered and began to fall. Fortunately, Anne and Emilie caught her in their arms, squealing with laughter.

Katrina held her head in pain at the noise.

"Anne, Emilie. Take Yvette home. She'll never make it to Versailles." Lucille grumbled. "I'd bet the week's bread she did this on purpose."

"Send the king my best," Yvette said over her shoulder as Anne and Emilie lifted her up by the armpits.

Katrina stared after the drunken girl wistfully. Her own stomach ached from too little food and too much wine. None of the milliners had slept since the evening before. They had spent the wee hours in the cafés, listening to drunken assemblymen espouse their doctrines to the crowd. Yvette had slipped off with one of the orators, returning hours later, more drunk than when she had left. Fortunately, none of the milliners had to work Sundays. Katrina had looked forward to sleeping through the day, but Lucille had other plans.

"Why are we going all the way to the Faubourg St. Antoine?" Katrina asked, her weariness evident in her voice.

"The march is to begin in Antoine, where the hungriest are. They will be up and ready for such a trek." Lucille's eyes glittered. "That is also where the angriest people are—the ones who have suffered the most abuses by the aristocracy."

"Angriest!" Katrina exclaimed. "We want bread, not blood. That's what we are marching for, isn't it?"

"Sometimes bloodshed is necessary, Katherine. The last time bread passed into this city was after the Bastille fell. The king needs proof of our power before he unlocks his grain coffers. Since he's not in Paris, we'll bring the riots to him in Versailles. And if a few people are hurt along the way, well"—Lucille shrugged her shoulders—"It's a small price to pay for the Nation."

Katrina's skin iced, and her fear nearly eclipsed her hunger. The night before, in a moment of drunken insanity, she had agreed to march with the women to Versailles, hoping that the gesture might urge the king to open his grain coffers to the city of Paris.

"But the Assembly—surely they can do something." The wine and passion of the previous evening had left her blood, and the coldness of the early morning seeped through to her bones.

"Enough of the Assembly! The Assembly is in Versailles, as well. They need a taste of Parisian anger." Lucille's eyes blazed. "Now, you listen to me. I've got a mother and a sister who are starving in St. Antoine because I can barely feed myself, never mind two other women who can do absolutely nothing but look out their bottom floor window over the gutter's stench and watch other people carry bread rations home. There's no work for them—none! Thus no food. Believe me," she said, moving closer to Katrina. "I would gladly slit the throat of the man—or woman—who is causing this."

Lucille's eyes were colored with an unearthly light, emphasizing the dark hollows under her eyes and cheekbones. Her thin lips whitened into a snarl. Katrina stepped back as Lucille's gaze searched her face suspiciously, but a church bell in the distance grabbed the woman's attention.

"Let's hurry," Lucille said suddenly, motivated by the sound of the bell.

Katrina followed her in resignation. She knew that Lucille was testing her endurance, her patriotism, and she had felt the older woman's intense scrutiny throughout the evening. Katrina sighed. She wanted nothing more than to go home and sleep. Only her fear of Lucille and the hunger in her belly urged her on to this march.

"It is the tocsin of the church of Ste. Marguerite!" Lucille exclaimed. "Come, come, it has started."

Katrina stumbled after her. The streets were clear and quiet at this early hour, and a mist hung over the city. She heard voices mixed with church bells, which grew louder as they moved onto the Rue St. Antoine, the artery of the suburb.

Katrina stopped short when she saw the crowd of hard-faced women swarming toward them, filling the street. Lucille had said a few women were marching to Versailles, not this enormous group that filled the churchyard! Bludgeons, cutlasses, scythes, pitchforks, and pikes waved in the air, and Katrina caught sight of the dark metal of a musket, as well. Heat emanated from the crowd. Katrina remained rooted in her spot as the mass approached. Lucille embraced a woman, happily taking the bottle she offered and lifting it to her lips.

The crowd engulfed Katrina in its heat. Panic-stricken, she moved quickly within it, chasing after Lucille. Flora and Grace smiled drunkenly at Katrina.

"Wine?" Flora asked. Katrina turned away, her nose wrinkling at the stench coming from the goatskin, and Flora laughed. "Our little aristocrat has a weak stomach."

"That'll go away soon enough," Lucille said, gulping the wine freely. "When she gets cold and tired. Come, let's go to the king!"

Katrina moved warily in the mob, desperately dodging calico skirts and upraised arms to follow Flora and Grace. Her heart fluttered nervously at the sight of raised weapons. She started as she watched one young woman fiddle awkwardly with a gun. In such a large crowd, an accident could happen easily.

Katrina lifted her hand to her bodice, where the knife she had stolen from Poitiers nestled between her breasts, giving her confidence. *Besides,* she comforted herself, *I wear the cockade. These people will not harm me.*

But if they knew that I was also a duke's daughter, she thought, scanning the coarse, mottled faces of the screaming women, *I would never come out of this alive.*

The crowd slowed on Rue St. Honoré, and Lucille elbowed her way through the living mass. Fearing solitude more than Lucille's boldness, Katrina followed. She gasped upon seeing what caused the delay.

A row of French guards blocked the street, their black hats shading their faces from view. The early morning sun glinted off the buckles of their uniforms and the raised ends of their sharp bayonets. The women screamed at them.

"Ugly royal guards! Let us through!"

"Take off your black cockades in the presence of the Nation!" Lucille's voice rose distinctly above the taunts of the crowd. Her hair flowed wildly down her back, her bonnet long lost in the shuffle.

"We're telling you to move!"

A restless nervousness rippled through the crowd, and in a sudden burst they lunged toward the guards, whose horses skipped backward, rolling their eyes in protest. Scythes were raised high in the air, and even from her position, Katrina could see fear in the young men's eyes. Lucille whooped loudly and surged forward, pushing bodies aside.

The guards lowered their bayonets and turned them around, using the blunt ends to push off the women. The guards gave a little ground but remained tightly blocking the route. Katrina gasped as blood spurted from a horse's side.

"Pretty boys! Bet you don't have enough in you to please a goat," one woman yelled, cackling.

"Sons of whores! Aristocratic whores!"

"Move away, royalist pigs! Move away for the Nation!"

The woman behind Katrina pushed her until she pressed against the women in front of her. She stood on tiptoe to look over to the guards, who were now turning their bayonets around and pushing the women away with the sharp tips. The guards' faces were locked in ugly grimaces, and their thrusts and jabs became more violent as they threw curses into the crowd. Overwhelmed, injured, the women scattered into side streets, searching for a way to pass the guards. Moments later, the oppressive pushing of the crowd eased and the street cleared.

Katrina glanced around quickly. It would be so easy for her to get away from the mob now, return to her lodgings—and sleep, perhaps. When she awoke there might be bread in the bakery. Perhaps the whole horror of the riot would be over and she could return to her work in peace—

"Come, Katherine. Don't stand there waiting for something

to happen." Lucille wrapped a bony hand around her arm and pulled her into the darkness of a side street.

Katrina sighed and followed, hunger a sharp knife in her side.

They slipped through the winding roads in search of the heart of the crowd, moving ultimately to the Rue de Sevres which led to Versailles. French guards drove them into the side streets along the way, but the men could not control the flow of armed women toward the road. By the time Katrina, Lucille, Grace, and Flora arrived, a group had gathered that was twice the size of the one on the Rue St. Antoine. Gleefully, Lucille moved into the crowd and set off for Versailles.

"Du pain, du pain, parlons-nous du pain!" the women chanted, marching merrily. The sun blazed down from straight overhead, unseasonably warm, and the light glinted sardonically off the long, curved blades of well-used scythes.

Katrina wandered wearily among them. She reminded herself that all that lay behind her in Paris was a dingy room and a querulous concierge. Ahead, there might be food. Soon, she was able to ignore the weapons the women wielded with such carelessness.

The people laughed as if they were going to a parade, not to demand food from the King and Queen of France. Katrina gazed in awe as winebottles appeared from nowhere and her neighbors became more drunk as mile after mile passed. Her stomach churned violently, half out of hunger, half out of disgust. Her mouth was dusty from walking in the wake of hundreds of women, and she ached for a sip of cool, clean water.

"Some wine, *patriote?*" a woman offered, holding a dirty bottle close to Katrina's face.

Katrina licked her parched lips and reached for it. Only one sip. Or two. She couldn't walk all twelve miles without drinking something.

The sun blazed red and gold on the edge of the horizon by the time the first of the masses reached Versailles. Katrina thought they were never going to see the palace gates until finally, in the indigo twilight, they rose before her, covered with peasants shouting and laughing and taunting the king's bodyguard. Katrina limped to the gates, searching for a familiar face. The air had cooled, and she shivered in the dimness.

"There you are." Anne's figure bounced over to her. "Lucille was looking for you. You have to come with us. There's nothing happening here, but in the Assembly . . ." She didn't finish. Instead, she pulled on Katrina's arm and moved away from the gated walls of Versailles. "Come, come. We'll miss everything."

Katrina pulled her arm back, slowing her pace angrily. "Stop pulling me around," she retorted. "My feet are killing me from the walk. Is there food at the Assembly?"

Anne made a small *humph!* and walked quickly ahead of her. "Everyone else's feet hurt, too," she declared. "We all walked that distance. Most of us enjoyed it. As for food, you will have to come and see. Now, come on, we have to go to the *Salle des Menus Plaisirs—*"

"Where?"

"That's where the National Assembly meets. Look, it's right down the Avenue de Paris," she said, pointing to a building barely visible through the row of elms that lined the avenue. "On the Rue St. Martin. Come, come."

An aching half mile later, Katrina stumbled up the stairs of the National Assembly's meeting place and pushed through the throngs that hovered in front, dancing and singing drunkenly before a makeshift bonfire. Their noise could not cover the din that burst from the wide doors of the hall. Eagerly, Anne raced toward it, pulling Katrina in her wake. The first drops of rain had begun to fall when they made their way into the hall itself, high and wide and filled with assemblymen and the women of Paris, all talking at once.

On a small podium at the front of the room stood a speaker trying desperately to talk above the din. His words made no sense to Katrina, but she knew by the angry barbs thrown in his direction that he was not speaking on a popular subject. She glanced up at the second tier, surprised to find women still armed with the weapons they had toted from Paris. They stood straight and yelled angrily down at the speaker.

Katrina followed Anne to a spot right under the second tier and stood watching the proceedings. Someone had started the cry of "Bread! Bread!" and soon the chant filled the assembly. The President of the Assembly—Mounier—tried in vain to restore order, screaming from his tiny pulpit in anger, but the women would not listen. The call for bread continued.

"Who's that talking down there?" a woman exclaimed from above Katrina. "Make the chatterbox shut up, and tell him that we want bread."

"We want to hear our little mother Mirabeau speak," another cried.

Katrina closed her eyes and leaned her forehead against a wooden post. The chamber seemed to close in around her. She was tired, faint, hungry, and the incessant screaming made her head throb. She swallowed painfully and lifted one leg up to massage her cut, swollen feet. Someone passed her a small bottle and she drank deeply from it, ignoring the burn that ripped down her throat. She was too thirsty and too weak to care. She yearned for her bed in St. Denis, despite its hardness and the fleas that bit her at night. She longed to find a dry, soft spot to lay her head for the evening. But no one would return to Paris this night. It grew far too late to venture back safely.

Vaguely she heard the Assembly president speak to the women, and a slight hush fell over the crowd. Mounier claimed a deportation of assemblymen would be sent to the king. The petition would state that the people of Paris wanted bread, and that they wanted to speak to the king.

Cheering began again, louder than before. Katrina elbowed her way past Anne, out of the stuffy room and into the fresh, wet air of the night. She pushed her way through the crowd seeking shelter near the entrance and burst out into the street.

She walked aimlessly along the roads, aching for a bed. She considered curling under a tree, but then she caught sight of a church spire. Quickening her pace, she headed for it until she reached its open doors. Entering the hushed building, she eased her way into a pew and stretched out. In moments, she was asleep.

The dawn came cool and fresh, and Katrina tiptoed over the prone bodies littering the floors of the church to enter the dewy morning. The sun hovered over the tips of the elms, its clear rays lighting the profusion of early autumn red and gold leaves ablaze. She turned toward the chateau, visible at the end of the long, straight throughway. The people, clothed in dull colors, still swarmed about it, and the row was littered with stumbling,

lethargic passersby. Her stomach tightened painfully. Perhaps today the king would send them food.

How far she had fallen! Never in the chateau in Poitou had
she felt hunger. In the kitchens she had always eaten well. Although she had seen many a beggar in the past years, bony and
pale from starvation, she had never felt hunger's bite until now.
Her head swam and her legs wobbled dangerously as she walked
forward. Certainly the king would give them bread. He had to!

Katrina walked slowly, barefoot, toward the chateau. Small
pebbles poked her weary feet. She winced, ignoring the pain,
driven on by hunger. She dully passed a hand through her tangled, dirty hair. What a sight she must be—ragged, dirty, tired.
But as she walked through the manicured street, she realized she
looked no different from any other.

The restlessness of the crowd invaded her soul as she neared
the chateau. The crowds gathered in large, living clumps, moving aimlessly about. The soldiers behind the gates had moved
farther back to avoid the stones thrown their way. The gendarmes
bowed their heads in weariness, and their horses sagged tiredly.
Many of the women rioters looked fresh—as if they had just
arrived without a night of raucous drinking to dull their enthu-
siasm. A few peasant men barked orders loudly to the crowds,
and the women followed their lead.

Katrina neared the gates, staring enviously at the cold, stony
palace with its long windows and imposing entrance. So distant
and isolated. How easy it must be to forget the squalor outside
the gates. Moving idly along their length, Katrina closed her ears
against the taunts thrown at the bodyguards.

"I bet you don't know your father! Your mother opened her
legs for every idiot in Paris, hoping one of them would scratch
the itch!"

"Your wife—oh, she's cuckolded you many a time. I myself
have laid her till she screamed like a night owl!"

Katrina shook her head, blushing at the language. She searched
the faces of the ragged peasant women for Lucille or one of the
other milliners. They would know what was happening; perhaps
they had found food. Even wine—she winced—even wine would
be welcome now.

Katrina passed close to the fence, stopping to stare in at the
chateau. The pebbled yard seemed so immaculate. The men of

the bodyguard turned away from the gates and talked quietly to one another. Horses tossed their heads and pranced restlessly over the stones.

Her eyes caught movement toward her right. There seemed to be people milling into the yard with upraised arms. Katrina gasped as a cheer went up around her. The people had gotten into Versailles! She watched as the flood thickened, and scythes were raised in success.

People rushed by her. Katrina grasped the gratings of the fence, trying to keep her place despite the flow of the crowd. But, caught up by the movement behind her, she turned and followed the stream, ignoring the pebbles that stung her feet. The peasants laughed and cried out in joy, raising their weapons in victory as they rushed through the obscenely wide gate doors.

The bodyguards instantly lost their easy stances, straightening in their mounts and rushing toward the broken end of the dam. Their black cockades—black for the hated queen—fell upon the ground. The women jumped on them gleefully, spitting and digging dirty heels into the fabric. Lifting them up again, they tore the hats into ribbons and burned all that remained. Katrina careened through the gates, pushed by the masses. Pandemonium turned the serene courtyard into a circus, a wild theater, where many acts were played at once. The bodyguards retreated from the advancing mass in terror as the hungry, dirty faces moved toward them with intent.

"We are going to cut off her head and fry her liver!" someone cried, heading toward the sedate chateau. A dark door opened to the inky interior, and the screaming contingent rushed in, heedless of the guards that ran in their wake.

Katrina's blood chilled, and she backed away from a shying horse and its terrified rider and the women who chased them with raised clubs. She moved deeper into the courtyard.

She stopped, and just as quickly, her heart stopped.

An icy drop of sweat fell slowly down the length of her spine. She knew what the man planned to do when he raised his ax, already thick with blood. Yet she could not tear her eyes from the bloodied implement, the man's coarse-haired forearm coated with red human paint. His lips twisted oddly under the strain, and she could not help but watch as the ax finished its upward thrust and moved swiftly, heavily, down in a lethal arc toward the straining neck of a screaming guard.

Several women held the guard's arms and legs firmly against the pebbled yard. They laughed at him, raising his fear to frenzy as the ax fell down on his bulging throat.

The guard's cries stopped with the thud. His body writhed, headless, the movements slowing as blood poured from his gaping neck. His head, wide-eyed, rolled away, bouncing dully on the earth.

"No!" Katrina threw her hands before her eyes and turned to run as fast as her sore feet could move. To race away from the terrible, bloodied courtyard; to race from the women cackling at the sight, smearing the guards' blood liberally over their faces and arms; to race from the murderer who grinned proudly, his shirt and breeches soaked with the blood and gore of the fallen men. Katrina covered her ears with her hands, trying to deafen the next victim's cries, the sickly sound of the ax as it fell again, the screams of the spectators greedily calling for more. Her stomach heaved and she stopped as spasms shook her body. She choked on the bile that rose hot and acrid from her empty stomach, then fell to her knees in the mud. Cold sweat dripped from her nose and soaked her shirt.

But still she could hear the victim's cry. She could hear his boots kicking the stones of the courtyard across the yard, even as his head was severed from his body. Groaning, she lunged forward, propelled by some force that filled her veins with hot insanity. She breathed with difficulty, and her ribs pressed against her skin, heaving with the effort. Closing her eyes, she urged herself on, pushing through the revelers, passing close to the row of elms, her head lolling backward and her mouth open, gulping in the air that had suddenly turned stale and thick with smoke and dust and the tart smell of fresh blood. There was no aim to her flight, to her headlong rush of terror. A demon had taken her feet and made them work. She no longer felt the slashes that bled, leaving wet red footsteps in her wake. Her vision blackened. Only her mouth remained open as, unseeing, she gulped in what little air she could.

Two strong hands lifted her shoulders straight in the air, propelling her upward by the force of her flight. Her slight body slammed into his with the momentum, but he did not flinch at the slight weight. He stared into her glazed green eyes.

"What the hell—" he gasped at the wide, dilated pupils. Her mouth hung open, her face was filthy with mud and sweat, and her body was so thin he could see the whites of her bones through her wrists. He shook her. "What's wrong—" Suddenly, he recognized the color of those eyes, the locks of hair that, released of its haphazard plait, had fallen over a jutting shoulder. Her hair shone dully, but undoubtedly it was the same unique red-gold. Sparks exploded in his body.

Katrina looked up into the man's black eyes, vaguely hearing her name. Then oblivion—sweet, forgetful Lethe—claimed her.

Chapter 13

"Martha!" Rafe called as he entered the dark shop, carrying the limp, dirty girl like a sack over his shoulder. "Get water and linens—now!" He took the stairs two at a time, shifting Katrina's slight weight effortlessly, then pushed open the door to his room and marched to the bed. Chauncey strolled in from his own room next door, a wry smile on his face.

"What have you brought home this time, Rafe?" he asked drolly.

"A girl." Rafe flipped Katrina off his shoulder onto the bed, catching her head and gently laying it on the pillow.

Chauncey laughed. "It's not the first time you've brought home a girl, Rafe, but certainly you could wait until she's conscious before bedding her." He moved closer and stared down at the dirty bundle. "Good God, Rafe! What did you do, wrestle with her until she acquiesced?"

"Martha!" Rafe boomed, ignoring his half brother.

Chauncey jumped away as the servant burst through the door, her apron flying and water sloshing over the sides of a pail.

"Stop yelling!" she exclaimed, vexed. "What is wrong?" Her mouth dropped open as she saw the girl on the bed. "Look at her feet! She has to be cleaned up. My Lord, Monsieur! What will you be bringing home next?" Martha pushed her thick body between Rafe's and the bed. Kneeling on the hardwood floor, she reached for one of Katrina's muddied, swollen feet.

"What in the world made you bring her here, Rafe?" Chauncey peered quizzically at his brother's stern face. "Who is she?"

Rafe sighed, then tore his gaze away from Katrina and pushed open the jalousie blinds. Fresh air rushed in the room and tousled his hair. He had left Paris before the sun rose; now the sun had reached its zenith and he had returned. He had not expected to be back so soon, and especially not with *her!*

"I hired a carriage this morning to go to Versailles. I had heard rumors that the people had actually gotten in to see the king, that there had been some progress in their efforts to get grain into the city." He paused, pushing his hair from his forehead. "I had to see the progress."

"I expected no less, my half brother. You never could stay out of the thick of the action."

"As for her," Rafe continued, gesturing at Katrina's tiny form, "I hadn't even reached the chateau when she came tearing out like a demon from hell. I don't know who or what she was running from; there was no one behind her. She didn't even see me. She just ran right into me. I tried to revive her, but she fainted in my arms." His brows furrowed. "What was I supposed to do, leave her there?"

Chauncey's lips curved in amusement under his heavy mustache. "Many women have fainted at your feet and you haven't seen fit to bring them to your bed."

Martha glanced up at the men and scowled.

"This is different, Chauncey," Rafe said dryly. "Haven't you recognized her yet?"

Chauncey moved closer to the girl and then paled slightly. "My God, it's that girl—it's Katrina!" he said, whirling to face Rafe. "The one who betrayed us—"

"Yes."

"But . . ." Chauncey's eyes widened in confusion. "But last I heard, she—"

"She was to be married to the Marquis de Noailles, as we had predicted."

"No, no." Chauncey shook his head, his riotous curls bobbing in disarray. "No, I didn't tell you at the time, but . . ." He looked away from Rafe's intense gaze. "Well, I'm sorry I didn't tell you, but you *did* roar that day—quite loudly—that we were never to mention *her* name again."

"Chauncey . . ." Rafe warned.

"Very well, then. The last I heard, she had been kidnaped the day of her wedding and was presumed dead."

Rafe turned to stare at Katrina. Her face was streaked with

dirt and offal, her body bony beneath the loose, colorless dress His jaw tightened.

"Kidnaped?" he murmured. "Was there no ransom set? Who were the kidnapers?"

Chauncey shrugged. "I don't know. The story was suppressed only days after it had been told. The marquis sent search parties all over France for her, but no one seemed to know anything about his lost bride." He hazarded a glance at Rafe's haggard face.

Rafe frowned, rubbing his chin thoughtfully. "Perhaps she did not have the stomach for the marquis, after all," he remarked pensively. His gaze traveled over the girl, his eyes mirroring his conflicting emotions.

Chauncey tilted his head in confusion. "What will you do with her, once she is well?"

"That depends," Rafe said. "I want you to make some inquiries. Send someone down to Poitiers to see what happened. Find out if the marquis, or anyone else, is still looking for her." His back straightened. "She'll stay here until we know the situation."

"She looks more like a helpless, starving child than a traitoress," Chauncey observed. "But I'll do as you say."

"Chauncey," Rafe warned, "be discreet."

As Chauncey closed the door behind him, Martha continued to wipe the girl's feet and squeezed the water into the bowl, which was dark red with dirt and blood.

"How are her wounds?" Rafe asked, gripping the windowsill.

"Not too bad," Martha replied. "They're bleeding cleanly, so she won't get the fever. If we bandage them and she stays off her feet, they'll heal just fine. They look like she ran nails over her feet."

Rafe stared at Katrina's well-remembered face, the face he'd loved, then hated. Her lashes cast shadows on her pale cheeks. The hollows of her cheekbones were deep and dark. Her skin seemed translucent, her lips colorless. He reached down to brush a lock of hair off her cheek, and just as quickly pulled away.

Cursing loudly, he turned on his heels and slammed the door behind him.

* * *

Why the hell is she here? Rafe mumbled into his brandy glass. *And of all the people in France, why did she have to run into me?*

He had tried to forget the silk of her skin, the heavy length of her shining hair, the warmth of her body covering his own in the earthy must of the small shed. Her laughter rose unbidden in his head, and he looked around the alehouse to see if anyone else had heard it. How she would laugh if she knew his thoughts. Peasant turned aristocrat, looking down her elfish nose at him, sneering at his ink-splotched, work-hardened hands. How well she'd played her game. Hot anger rose in him. He clenched his glass and poured the fiery contents down his throat.

She had been so young, so innocent in Poitiers. Pure life, wrapped in peach skin and golden hair. How he had loved her! And still, still now—no woman could match her fire, her life, her abandon in the throes of love. The single night they had shared was etched forever in his mind. His hands itched to touch her, sweep her up and bring back that moment—

"No!" He slammed the empty brandy glass down on the table. The other patrons turned to look at him curiously, but quickly turned away, intimidated by his stubbled face and the massive width of his shoulders.

Refilling his tumbler, he glanced out of the dirt-encrusted panes of the alehouse to his shop. The printing shop had made him a rich man since he and the remaining members of his band had left Poitou. His newfound wealth had placed him in a position of power. Revolutionary journals burst from illegal presses all over Paris since the fall of the Bastille, and Parisians read them avidly. The embattled king did not dare try to suppress the papers. Rafe's own journal, *Révolution*, had quickly become the standard for all the others.

But the journal was merely a cover for more important activities. The secret room beneath the kitchen served as a meeting place for some of the most powerful men in the Assembly. Together, they planned events far grander than any Rafe had planned in Bordeaux or Poitou, and the results reverberated throughout the country, throughout the world.

No more forced labor. No more aristocrats feeding freely off the corpses of those who worked their land. No more tax collectors stealing coins from the peasants to fill the tax coffers for the queen's vanity. Rafe swore he would never see those injustices again, and neither would the rest of France. The new world he had strived for was rising before his eyes in all its glory.

Yet in all his years of planning, he had not anticipated anyone like Katrina: Katrina the traitoress; the false daughter of a wealthy duke; a woman pampered by servants who ran at her least command; a woman who dressed in the sheerest muslin, the dearest jewels.

Rafe shuddered. She had chosen that life, lusting after the money, the power. Fickle, flighty and, still worse, false. She had whispered sweet lies in his ears, taking her pleasure of him in a stormy night and then spurning him for the glitter of the aristocracy. Her hands were filthy with the blood of his ill-fated band. How foolish he had been to trust a woman who valued only the gleam of jewels.

The bitterness burned in his mind. He glowered at the other customers of the alehouse, wondering if they could read his thoughts, which felt as if they were blazed across his head.

"If you hold that glass any tighter, Rafe, you're likely to break it."

Rafe glanced up into his half brother's face. Chauncey's eyes sparkled and his usual wry smile curved his lips under his heavy mustache. Dressed in pale powder-blue satin breeches and a waistcoat trimmed with gold braid, Chauncey looked out of place in the crowded alehouse filled with peasants in rougher weaves. Yet the owner smiled, waved his greetings, and brought a clean glass to the table.

"Have you started the inquiries?" Rafe asked gruffly.

Chauncey nodded and his eyes flickered quickly to Rafe's face. "Duarte and Pierre will be taking a short trip to the country. I don't know how much they'll be able to discover. The incident was covered up quickly and completely, to save the marquis embarrassment, no doubt."

"No doubt."

"How much have you had?" Chauncey frowned at the dregs of the brandy decanter. "Looks like you'll drink old Chenier out. You know he serves brandy only to us."

"Then he'll buy more," Rafe snapped.

"Do you think she was really kidnaped?" Chauncey asked after a moment.

Rafe shook his head. "If she had been kidnaped, she'd either be with the marquis, or she would be dead,'' he said bluntly. ''Kidnapers would wait for the marquis's ransom, but they would never let Katrina go free without it.'' He leaned back in the creaking wooden chair. ''Of course, she could have escaped from the kidnapers—but I doubt it. They would guard the intended bride of the Marquis de Noailles with care.'' A humorless smile tightened Rafe's lips. ''I think the traitoress could not face her end of the bargain with the Marquis de Noailles.''

Chauncey crossed his legs and toyed with the end of his mustache. ''Are you so sure that Katrina was the cause of that disastrous raid?'' he asked slowly. As Rafe's heavy, drink-swollen lids lifted, Chauncey shrugged a shoulder. ''I'm just a bit skeptical, that's all. I can't believe the marquis would go to so much trouble to get rid of a few irritating brigands—''

''It goes much further than that, Chauncey,'' Rafe interrupted harshly. ''You're right: the marquis would never bother with a few brigands—if he didn't have some further aim.''

Chauncey lifted a questioning brow.

''Think, Chauncey—''

''You're the one with the brains, my dear brother.'' His eyes glittered in amusement.

''The Duke de Poitiers was known to be senile, known to have hallucinations of the ghost of his first wife. He had a daughter who would be Katrina's age if she were alive. All of this means nothing until the marquis finds a comely young girl who has the unusual coloring of the duke's first wife. The duke being without a blood heir . . .''

''I see,'' Chauncey said. ''The marquis decides to have the girl masquerade as the duke's daughter, then marry her, and—''

''And double his holdings,'' Rafe finished. ''Such a union would make the marquis one of the richest noblemen in the country: nearly as rich as the Duke d'Orleans or any of the king's other brothers.''

''Yes . . .''

''The marquis has trouble with brigands and needs to plant an informant so he can sabotage their plans. He takes the girl on a nocturnal jaunt through the woods in the middle of the night, tells her he will reward her if she discovers the brigands' plans, and then shoots me—with rather bad aim, I might add—and leaves us to our devices.

"As soon as she finds out about the final raid she tells the marquis, who instructs her to be the duke's daughter. Blindly, the senile duke takes her in.

"Months later, the duke dies in strange circumstances involving a liaison between the marquis and Katrina, and a few weeks after that, the banns for their marriage are announced. Do you see the devious cunning of the marquis? He rids himself of brigands and gains an estate and title all with one neat plan."

Chauncey sat, open-mouthed, as Rafe finished the story. He sat back and crossed his arms. "But Katrina escaped from the marquis," he mused. "That shows some promise for Katrina. Perhaps she had a change of heart."

Rafe's hand tightened on the glass until his knuckles whitened. "Women as treacherous as she don't change colors so quickly, my brother," he said quietly. "Don't trust her."

Chauncey looked away from his brother. "What will you do when she heals?" he asked. "It won't be easy having her in the house."

Rafe shook his head. "I'll watch her until we know the truth. Probably put her to work in the shop."

"Is that a good idea?" Chauncey asked. "She can read, and we've got revolutionary papers all over the place. She would know what we're up to days before Paris did." He leaned toward Rafe. "And if she overhears anything from the room below the kitchen, she could hurt us more than she ever did at Poitiers," he whispered. "We could all be in prison before the year is out."

"She'll know nothing," Rafe said harshly. "We'll guard her on meeting nights."

Chauncey leaned back and watched Rafe warily. Finally, he smiled and shrugged his shoulders. "Well, at least she'll brighten up that dreary shop," he remarked lightly. "We've been cooped up in there for so long that even Martha's massive wiggle has become strangely attractive."

Katrina slowly noticed the softness beneath her. Sunlight filtered through her eyelids, and she strained to open them, fighting against the darkness.

The room loomed strangely around her, made stranger still by the gray haze that framed it. A lyre-back chair stood near the large wooden door. Next to her bed stood a fine mahogany dressing table, the mirror tilted. Its smoothly curved legs reminded her of the dressing table in her room in Poitiers, and for a moment she wondered if she had been taken back.

But this was not her old room at Poitiers; it was far too small and bare. The writing table that stood in the corner looked nothing like her own, more ornate desk.

The room brightened as the sun emerged from behind a cloud. Katrina winced. If she were in Paris, this room had to be on one of the higher floors. Her own room never received so much sun.

A short, rotund woman bustled into the room with a tray in her dimpled hands. Katrina turned at the noise, her nostrils flaring at the aroma of rich soup.

"Ah! I see you are up, little one." The woman walked toward the bed briskly and felt Katrina's brow. "Good. No fever. Are you hungry?"

Mutely, Katrina nodded, suddenly realizing that she could not remember the last time she had eaten.

"That's a good sign," the woman continued. "I brought some cabbage soup. Rafe told me you were from the country, and I know how much you all like your cabbage soup. It took me days to find cabbage, and it was not cheap, I tell you—"

"Rafe?" Katrina squeaked. She trembled under the bedclothes.

The servant stared down at her oddly, "Why, yes, Rafe Beaulieu. You're at his house now. He brought you back from Versailles. Don't you remember?"

Katrina's body froze. *Rafe?* A flash of black eyes, the silky feel of thick, warm hair, and a smile that brought light into darkness. Memories, sweet and bitter, tumbled upon her in a confused rush.

The woman touched Katrina's arm in concern. "Katrina?" she murmured, reaching for the young woman's forehead. "You don't remember?"

"No, no, I don't," Katrina muttered.

"No wonder, really," the woman replied. "You were half-starved. Eat. Later, if you're still awake, I'll bring you something with more substance."

Katrina glanced up at her, her eyes a tormented mirror of her thoughts.

"Now, don't you worry." The woman shook her head reassuringly. "I'm Martha, child," she added, patting her hand. Then she left, closing the door quietly behind her.

Rafe? How in God's name had she come to Rafe's house? Katrina wondered. Her head ached painfully, vaguely remembering, out of the mist of terror, the sight of a familiar, angry face.

She looked down at the bed she lay upon. The same linens that were now pulled over her scantily clad body had also caressed Rafe's lean flanks. Unconsciously, her nostrils flared at the faintly familiar scent. She pushed the sheets away abruptly.

The chemise she wore was of the finest lawn. It certainly wasn't hers. Hers had been filthy, ragged—this one was new. She wondered whose hands had slipped it over her head and blushed from her toes to the roots of her hair.

The cabbage soup claimed her attention. Eagerly, she reached down and brought it onto her lap. In minutes it was gone, and despite the questions, fears, and worries raging in her head, she dragged the scented linens over her chin and settled into a deep slumber.

The days passed. Torturous days full of fear: would Rafe come today? Restless nights plagued by dreams of terror. Martha's food and medicines did little to ease Katrina's torment, but did heal her fragile body. By the end of the week, Katrina felt strong enough to sit up in bed.

"How are you feeling today, little one?" Martha came in with a tray full of food.

For the first time since Katrina arrived, she felt an urge to eat solid food. All previous attempts had been futile. "Much better," she murmured, flushing slightly. "How—how long have I been here?"

"A week to the day," Martha answered. "Now, you have to eat all of this. You've eaten hardly anything all week." Martha stood above Katrina, watching as she slowly dug through the mound of fresh bread and thick omelet.

A hundred questions surged in Katrina's head. One week. Had Rafe been in to see her during those snatched moments of sleep? The week seemed to be hidden in a fog, interrupted only by Martha's voice, the scent of rich soups and bread, cool cloths on her body, and dreams . . . nightmares. So many nightmares. Katrina bit back the questions. The answers would come soon enough, and for now, she feared them. She glanced up to find Martha staring at her oddly.

"Is something wrong, Martha?" Katrina asked as she bit into an omelet.

"Nothing, child," Martha replied nervously. "I was just admiring your hair."

"It's filthy."

"You're right. I'll send a bath up for you."

Katrina's eyes widened. "You can send a bath up for me?" New life surged through her veins. What luxury! When was the last time she had bathed? The gray vestiges of the groggy week dissolved.

"I most certainly can," Martha said haughtily. "There's a big basin in that closet. I'll be up in a minute to take it out and fill it."

"Don't—don't go to all the trouble," Katrina said quickly. If Rafe saw Martha lugging pails of steaming water up the stairs, he would know she was well. "It—I didn't . . ."

"Nonsense," Martha interrupted. "A bath will do your soul some good. Rafe bathes regularly, though I don't approve. Eat your dinner and your bath will be ready."

Rafe. The sound of his name sent shocks through her body. Katrina ached for his arrival, yet dreaded it each time she heard steps upon the landing. Certainly he must feel something for her if he went so far as to care for her in sickness. Surely he had learned the folly of his anger. Did she dare hope?

Could he love me again?

The bath was steaming invitingly by the time Katrina finished the last bit of her omelet. Hastily discarding her chemise, she skittered across the room and leaped into the scalding water. Martha had left a bar of soap, and Katrina rubbed it roughly over her itching, dirty skin. She dug her fingernails into the cake and scrubbed herself until every fleck of dirt had been washed off. Laughing, she ducked under the water, then lifted the heavy mass of her hair atop her head, soaping it until it stayed aloft of its own accord.

"You should be out of there by now, child!" Martha exclaimed, bringing in a thick towel. "It's mid-October. Not a time to be soaking in cold water."

"It's been such a long time since I bathed," Katrina gurgled, rinsing the length of her hair.

"You *were* filthy when Rafe brought you back from Versailles. What were you doing there with that nasty, rioting rabble, anyway?"

Katrina's face darkened. "I—I got caught up in it, that's all," she said curtly, pushing the memory of the horror from her mind.

"They managed to force the poor king and queen and the entire family to the Tuileries, did you know that? The mob came up through the streets of Paris with some poor guards' heads on pikes, drinking and raving like crazy people—Katrina, are you all right?"

"Please, Martha—" she stuttered, shivering, the murky water suddenly icy on her skin. She rose, wrapping thin arms around her chilled body.

"My dear Lord!" Martha exclaimed in surprise.

Katrina lifted her eyes to hers. "What is it?"

"My dear child, I mean—woman. I had no idea—Why, I thought you were only a child of thirteen or fourteen, but, well, now I see what Rafe sees in you!"

Katrina flushed and reached for the towel, wrapping it closely around her.

"What did Rafe tell you about me?" she asked, then turned away from Martha, overwhelmed.

"Nothing, child—Mademoiselle," the woman replied. "Only that he knew you in Poitiers."

Katrina searched her face carefully.

"I really must make dinner for the men," Martha said quickly. "I'll clean this up later." In a moment, she was gone.

"Wonderful," Katrina thought, drying her skin briskly and slipping her chemise over her cool skin. "She knows what a trollop I was with Rafe." She shivered in the smooth linen and searched for her clothes.

"Fallen from grace, Katrina?"

She straightened immediately. It was the low, husky voice that she had heard in love and in hatred. She would know it anywhere.

"Fallen from grace?" Katrina mimicked, her voice far huskier than she liked. "No, no. I ran from it, I think."

She had forgotten how tall he was. Rafe stood just inside the room, his shoulders so wide they nearly eclipsed the door behind him. His hair was only a shade blacker than his eyes, which were now blazing holes through her damp chemise. His hips were lean in black breeches; his chin arched proudly over a lacy cravat. One brow lifted at her retort as he stared at her boldly.

Katrina flushed and looked down. Her chemise stuck to the dampness of her breasts, clung intimately to her belly, her thighs.

Rafe's gaze swept brutally over her figure. From the light of the window he could see the blurred outline of her body, curving in sweetly at the waist, flaring out to smooth hips.

He slowly dragged his waistcoat off the bulk of his shoulders and tossed it casually at Katrina's feet. "I burned your clothes. They were little more than rags," he explained. "I suggest you cover yourself before I forget why I came here."

Clutching the top of her chemise, Katrina bent down and drew the still-warm velvet around her shoulders. Her blond hair swept over her back in a damp, heavy mass and nearly touched the floor, illuminated by the light from the window.

She could not look at him. Of all days, she had not expected him today. Her face flamed—she was nearly naked! As the silence stretched, she became uncomfortably aware of his strength, his heat, his anger.

"I—I appreciate all you have done for me," she said hesitantly. Her tongue seemed to swell in her mouth. She glanced once at his hard eyes. No sympathy emanated from the murky depths. "I—I'll be returning to my lodgings as soon as I am well—"

"And what are you going to wear on the way over?" he asked, a slow smile lighting his face. "I wouldn't suggest walking through the streets of St. Denis wearing nothing but a chemise."

"If you . . ." Katrina hesitated, torn between tears and laughter. After so long and so much, they were standing across from each other and speaking nonsense. A hundred charged words seemed to hover in the air between them. Katrina glanced at his set face, her eyes wandering over the familiar cleft in his chin, the deep-set eyes that even now sent chills rippling through her. "I'll pay you back for any expenses," she said quickly.

Rafe couldn't help admiring her pride. Huddled in his waistcoat, she looked like a helpless child. But her spirit betrayed her strength: her eyes were the eyes of a woman, full and ripe with promise. Suddenly aware of his own vulnerability, Rafe hardened his jaw and threw a small satchel on the bed.

"These are the things we found at your lodgings," Rafe said. "A few items of clothing, a brush, and a piece of jewelry."

Katrina's eyes widened. She moved toward the bed, then stopped quickly. This room was three times the size of her room in St. Denis, yet Rafe's strong presence made it seem as small as a closet. She backed up against the window.

"Why—"

"You didn't think you would get away so easily, did you?" he asked. "You're staying here, Katrina Dubois or Katrina de Poitiers or Katherine—whoever you choose to be—until I figure out what to do with you."

"Here!" Katrina glanced around the sparsely furnished room, terror dawning in her eyes. He still thought her a traitor—an enemy of the people. Would he arrest her? Throw her in one of Paris's horrible prisons? "Will you hold me prisoner?" she demanded.

"No need, Katrina." Rafe watched the clear play of emotions in her eyes. "You'll stay of your own free will."

"No." She shook her head, the drying tendrils of sun-streaked hair whirling around her face. Her heart pounded steadily but loudly. She could feel his anger like a physical force pressing her against the wall. Stay in this house? Never! She would die, crushed beneath the weight of such hatred.

"You have no choice," he said, stepping back. The fear in her eyes pierced his heart, and he clenched his fists in anger. Why couldn't he control his emotions around this slip of a woman? "Madame Bertrier has closed her shop in the Palais Royal. You no longer have a position with her."

Katrina's eyes widened. He had found out her home and place of employment in less than a week. What else did he know?

"I paid your board for the week in that miserable place in St. Denis." Rafe tensely folded his arms in front of him. "The concierge has already found another boarder."

"I—I'll find another shop—another house—"

"Don't you understand? Paris is in a state of revolution, Katrina. You won't find a respectable position, never mind a suitable room."

"I don't care," she said stubbornly, turning away. She pressed her forehead against the leaded pane. "It—it's obvious that I wouldn't be a welcome addition to your household. I'll go somewhere else."

"Where?" he asked, his eyes narrowing to dangerous black slits. "Back to the Marquis de Noailles?"

He watched her carefully as she stiffened under his voluminous waistcoat. She turned toward him, her tilted eyes full of pain and anger.

"I would not go *back* to the Marquis de Noailles because I was never *with* him," she said heatedly, her voice wavering. "I see time has not changed your opinion of me. You still believe I betrayed you, that I was allied with the marquis."

"Time has only made me more certain, my little traitoress."

His low voice sent shivers through her slight form. He stepped deeper into the room. She pressed against the sill, pulling his waistcoat more closely around her.

"I could be the Marquise de Noailles now." Katrina's gaze never left Rafe as he slowly approached. She could not stop staring at him. *Can a man be so heart-rendingly beautiful?* He stopped only a breath away from her. She lowered her eyes, not trusting her own heart, then rushed on, wishing he would move away, so she could breathe again. "I could be living in the richest townhouse in Versailles, Rafe." She took a breath. "If I were a traitoress, then why would I be starving in the streets of Paris instead of enjoying the rewards of my treachery?"

"Convincing, Katrina," he murmured. "But not convincing enough. I haven't figured out why you're here. The marquis is a clever man. Perhaps he has something to do with your sudden appearance in Versailles."

"Don't be ridiculous."

Rafe lifted one dark brow. "I will never underestimate the marquis again." His lips twisted. "I never expected him to use such a dangerously beautiful weapon."

"Don't do this."

"Do what, Katrina?"

"Don't force me to stay here."

Her eyes were like liquid green sparks in her diamond-shaped face. Rafe had forgotten the fullness of her lips, the quiver that softened the lower one until he ached to press his own against hers—

He reached out to touch her hair but dropped his hand before it could brush the drying strands. "I will not have to force you," he said curtly, stepping away to escape from her innocent allure. "You have a simple choice. You can either return to the marquis, stay with me, or . . ."

"Or what?"

Rafe glanced over her shoulder into the street below. "Or, my little traitoress, you will ply your wares on the streets of Paris."

Chapter 14

Katrina laced the silk-ribboned corset loosely around her tiny waist, gazing at her reflection ruefully. Her shoulders, her elbows, her cheeks all jutted out at painful angles. It had been a week since Rafe's visit, and though Martha's food was rich and plentiful, none of it seemed to stick to her bones. Sighing, Katrina pulled the dusky woolen dress over her head and slipped her arms through the sleeves. She reached back awkwardly to join the hooks and eyes.

The dress fit almost perfectly. A few more of Martha's meals and it would caress her like a second skin. Katrina flushed, realizing suddenly that Rafe must have described her to the *couturier*. She turned away from her blushing reflection in the mirror and collected the morning dishes. Today she began her job, or her indentured servitude, as she preferred to call it.

Nothing had changed since the last time she had seen Rafe. His vicious anger at the debutante ball had not diminished with time. He hated and mistrusted her.

Still, if Rafe hadn't offered her this position, she would have been thrown out on the streets of Paris. In such turbulent times it wouldn't have been long before she had to choose between eating and . . .

Katrina shook her head at the thought, but her chin hardened proudly. Rafe was not keeping her here to protect her, of that she was sure. He kept her for one reason only: to protect the Nation against *her.*

She straightened her thin back. She was innocent of all crimes, yet once again, fate forced her to rely on the protection of one who mistrusted her. She swore that she would not break under Rafe's cruelty; she would not succumb to his hatred.

But can you resist his charm?

She shook her head, squeezing her eyes shut against the glaring honesty of her thoughts. Resolutely, she glanced around Rafe's room one final time, then walked defiantly out the door. In the sudden darkness of the hall, she could barely discern the steep steps leading to the center of the shop. Taking a deep breath, she descended into the heated room.

"Ah, there she is," Martha said, approaching Katrina from the kitchens. "I told you she would be down."

A young man sat at a workbench, intent on a task. He looked up at her entrance, and Katrina nearly jumped in recognition. Chauncey! Rafe's half brother. She sent him a quivering smile, but he only glanced at his brother and then went quickly back to his work.

Her smile faded. Of course. Rafe had spread his hatred to his entire entourage.

Rafe stood behind a strange wooden and metal machine, his hand resting on a large handle, eyeing her dispassionately. "You certainly took your time, Katrina," he said evenly. "This is not a perfumed chateau. We rise with the sun."

"I had trouble with my dress," she retorted.

Rafe lifted a dark, winged eyebrow. "I forgot. You're used to a lady's-maid. There are none here. May I suggest, next time, that you rise earlier."

Katrina swallowed a sharp retort. A verbal dispute was no way to begin her stay under Rafe's auspices. She glanced toward Martha and found a sympathetic face.

"Come, child," Martha said. "I need help in the kitchens."

Katrina followed the servant and felt a brief rush of nostalgia at the aura that suffused the kitchen: the tart spices, the warmth of the hearth, the buttery smell of fresh-baked bread.

The kitchen windows faced a small courtyard, not over the stinking street, so Martha was able to open them fully. A sweet tart lay cooling on one of the brick sills, and Katrina's stomach growled at the sight. Then her eyes widened at the loaves on the table.

"There is bread in Paris!" she exclaimed, moving to the brick worktable.

"Indeed. Since the march to Versailles there has been much food in Paris. Though I don't approve of that rabble, at least they did some good."

"I've had some experience in kitchens," Katrina said, changing the subject. The nightmares plagued her still, and any mention of

Versailles brought back the terror of that day. "I can do just about anything."

Martha glanced at Katrina skeptically. She handed her a bowl of warm milk and chocolate. "Come. Whip the chocolate for breakfast, and whip it thoroughly. Chauncey hates lumps."

Martha watched in amazement as Katrina skillfully whipped the chocolate into a frothy, aromatic mixture and poured it into two porcelain cups. Katrina smiled at Martha's expression and moved to the hearth, where she seasoned a piece of beef until the scent of the rich, spicy meat filled the kitchen.

Martha stood back, her hands on her hips. "It seems Monsieur Beaulieu left out a few details when he told me about you," she said.

Katrina shrugged. "Rafe has a very distorted image of me, Martha." She felt the bite of tears behind her lids. "I would appreciate it if you tried to see me with your own eyes instead of his."

"I knew from the moment I saw you that you could not be the she-wolf he said you were," Martha whispered. "But I thought—I thought there might be some truth—"

"If the two of you have finished your tête-à-tête, we'd like to have our breakfast." Rafe's sharp eyes took in Martha's expression and the slight smile that lit Katrina's face. His gaze raked over the young woman's figure. The plain, unadorned woolen dress he had bought fit loosely on her slim figure. He had chosen the plainest design he could find; why, then, did she look so stunningly beautiful? He shook his head and stalked out of the kitchen.

"Don't mind him," Martha remarked, noticing the paleness of Katrina's face. "He's all bluster."

Katrina nodded, but she did not relax. She knew Rafe meant the angry words he directed toward her.

She brought the chocolate to the men. Rafe faced her from the end of the table, his hair tossed irreverently, his dark eyes inscrutable. Her hand trembled as she placed a cup before Chauncey, then moved toward Rafe. She swore he could hear her heart thumping above the crackle of the fire, above Martha banging pots in the kitchen.

She placed the chocolate on the uneven boards of the table. Rafe's hand brushed hers as he reached for the cup, and she pulled her fingers away as if burned. He stared at her, one eyebrow lifted in amusement.

"Excellent chocolate, Martha," Chauncey called, bringing the cup to his lips. "Not a chunk in the cup."

" 'Tis Katrina's doing," Martha yelled from the kitchen. "I've never seen chocolate whipped with such vigor."

Chauncey's brown eyes rested thoughtfully for a minute on Katrina, a slight smile twisting his lips. Though slim, she had all the curves of a full-grown woman. Her eyes, wide and exotically tilted, held his gaze innocently.

"My compliments, Katrina," he said quietly, lifting the cup to her in a salute. When Rafe scowled at him from across the table, Chauncey sobered quickly. He, too, must remember her role in the fateful final raid on the Marquis de Noailles. But she seemed too guileless to be at the root of such treachery.

"The Assembly has settled in the Riding School near the Tuileries," Rafe said abruptly.

Reluctantly, Chauncey tore his eyes from her beguiling figure and glanced with surprise at Rafe. "When did you find out?"

"This morning." Rafe glared at Katrina's flushed face. She flipped her long plait over her shoulder and marched into the kitchens. "The Assembly chose a place where they could keep out 'the rabble,' but the Parisians are already grumbling about the closed doors. It won't be long before they will be knocking them down."

"Ah, my pessimistic half brother," Chauncey mused, leaning back in the creaking chair. "The Parisians have bread in their stomachs. They'll rest quiet for a while."

"Perhaps." Rafe eyed Katrina as she burst into the room, broom in hand. Why couldn't she fade into the woodwork? he wondered with reluctant admiration. Her presence was proving to be a great distraction to him and, he thought with a twinge, to Chauncey. "The king cannot feed all of France. Since the king was brought to Paris, there have been innumerable reports of raids throughout France. The Viscount de Pleurean was hanged from his own chandelier in Gascony—"

Katrina gasped. Rafe and Chauncey stared at her sharply.

"Are you quite all right, Katrina?" Chauncey said solicitously.

She straightened. "Fine . . . fine," she stuttered, glancing at Rafe's curiously immobile face. "Do you know—have you heard anything of Poitiers?"

"I have heard nothing of the Duke de Poitiers's estate, Katrina, if that is what you fear." Rafe's brows lowered.

She bit her lip and moved away from the table, a gloomy sense of foreboding filling her. She bent to sweep up the bits of paper and sand spread liberally around each heavy workbench. Her nervous hands slipped on the smooth broom handle. She stood to calm herself, clutching her trembling arms until she could breathe easily.

Foolishness. All foolishness, she chided herself. Visions of the horrible morning at Versailles still haunted her waking hours as well as her dreams. That was all it was—just those violent, soul-shaking memories that were giving her such chills. Rafe spoke of other provinces, other chateaux. Katrina could not imagine the tiny village near the duke's chateau rising up against their seigneur.

Katrina leaned against a worktable, nearly upsetting a row of small iron pieces. She jumped away from it, then noticed the large piece of paper upon the table, entitled *Révolution,* and drew nearer.

"I see you are still interested in my politics, Katrina," Rafe said quietly.

She turned to him with startled eyes. "Not just 'your' politics, all politics," she retorted quickly. She bit her lip at her own audacity and turned her back to him.

Rafe fingered the crisp parchment. "Hmm, I remember," he murmured. A slight smile twisted his lips.

She flushed and quietly thanked God that the gloom of the mid-October morning hid her color.

"I remember you were very interested in just about anything I said to you," he said.

He leaned against the worktable, his arm flexing beneath the flimsy cover of fine-woven linen. A single taper lit his profile, tracing the straight nose, the firm, square chin, sculpting his lips in gray, stony pallor.

"I'd rather we didn't talk about it," Katrina whispered. She clutched the end of the broom close to her chest. Rafe's eyes flickered—dark, inscrutable. Then their eyes locked. Katrina tore hers away, unable to stand the pulse that throbbed through her body.

This man, this man. The only man who had ever made love to her. What had happened to bring such a gulf between them? Katrina hazarded a glance at him beneath her lashes. Not such a gulf. She could feel him. She could feel his admiration, his heat on her body. Slowly, she allowed her gaze to meet his.

A river of hot embers flowed through her as his eyes arrested on hers. The candle flickered.

"Rafe?" Chauncey's voice broke the silence. "We should be going to the Assembly—debate starts at nine."

"Yes." Rafe slowly backed away from Katrina, taking his woolen *redingote* from Chauncey's arm. With nary a farewell, he strode to the door.

Chauncey glanced at Katrina, then at Rafe. A slow smile spread beneath his mustache.

Katrina did everything in her power to stay out of Rafe's way in the following weeks. She rose before the men in the mornings to fill the inkwells on the worktables, clean the quills, and brush the tables free of sand and bits of paper. Then she escaped to the kitchens to help Martha in the day's meals.

Unfortunately, the meals brought her in direct contact with Rafe. She had to serve each meal, and Rafe seemed to be eating home more often these days, according to Martha. Katrina was sure he did that on purpose, just to antagonize her. He knew that her heart beat unsteadily every time she had to bend over him to give him his dish. His eyes followed her every move. His familiar, faintly musky scent rose to send her thoughts in dangerous directions. She shook her head against these thoughts.

Grateful to be alone now, Katrina wiped one of the worktables down, staring with curiosity at the plate lying on the desk. She tried to decipher the writing, but it was all backward. No, not backward . . . She tilted her head to one side to read the plate. Carefully, she lifted one of the letters out and turned it around.

"That's a plate for Marat's journal, *L'Ami du Peuple*," Chauncey said behind her.

Katrina started and dropped the piece. She hastily bent to retrieve it but collided with Chauncey. Off balance, they both fell ungracefully to the shop floor.

Katrina pushed her single ruffled petticoat back down over whitehosed legs and, despite herself, began to laugh.

As Chauncey struggled to get up, he glanced with amazement at her face, now bright with humor. "I didn't mean to startle you," he remarked, a small chuckle escaping him. He quickly gave her his hand and Katrina rose and dusted off her backside.

"I know, I'm sorry. I wasn't going to touch the letter, but my curiosity got the best of me."

"Hush," Chauncey admonished, brushing away the sand that

clung to his breeches. "You're talking to me, not Rafe. I encourage your interest. Perhaps he'll allow you to typeset. He's been such a damned workhorse lately, I have had no time to, ah . . ." Chauncey flushed suddenly.

"To flirt with the local women?" Katrina finished, a sparkle in her eyes.

It had been a long time since Katrina had seen such honest emotion in any man's face. Rafe always seemed suspicious, and Chauncey usually avoided her eyes. Suddenly shy, she turned away from him.

"Will *you* teach me how to typeset? I'm bored of these menial chores."

Chauncey looked at Katrina's bright face and nodded. "Of course," he answered. "It can't be during the usual hours—Rafe would never agree. Perhaps we'll sneak lessons when he's out." He winked conspiratorially.

Chauncey was a handsome man, Katrina thought, if a bit over-dressed and overperfumed. She remembered she had been quite intimidated by his rich brocade breeches and ivory-handled cane when she first met him in Poitiers. She laughed to herself, thinking how quickly that image had dissipated over the last few weeks. His round, chocolate eyes danced merrily whenever he spoke, and his flushed cheeks always reminded her of a boy fresh from the country air.

"I assume that you two are discussing business?"

Katrina turned to Rafe, who had descended into the room.

Chauncey lost all composure and flushed full to the roots of his riotously curly hair.

"Chauncey was just saying he'd like some of my chocolate for breakfast," Katrina lied smoothly.

Rafe lifted a sarcastic brow and glanced briefly at his half brother. "Yes," he murmured. "I've noticed you've taken to Katrina's chocolate." He moved over to the press and placed a fresh piece of paper beneath the plate. Reaching for the handle, he pulled upon it once, twice, his muscles bulging under the loose linen shirt. He was aware of Katrina hovering nearby, but eventually she returned to the kitchens.

He removed the print and tossed it on the table. The black ink smudged but he did not notice. His eyes lingered on Chauncey's brocade-covered back.

"You once valued my advice, little brother," Rafe said quietly.

Chauncey turned and lifted an arched, brushed brow. "I know what you have advised me—"

"Then why do you persist?" Rafe interrupted. He glanced toward the kitchens and crossed the room to Chauncey's side. "I've warned you that she is not to be trusted, yet I find you looking at her, *laughing* with her, like she was a *salonniere* to be courted." He ran an ink-blotched hand through his hair. "She must be watched, not pandered to."

Chauncey sighed and shook his head slowly. "Rafe, sometimes you show appalling blindness to the character of the people around you." His gaze traveled to the open kitchen door. He pulled upon his waistcoat and glanced up at his older brother, lean and dark and sinister-looking in his black breeches and open shirt. Chauncey spread his hands in appeal. "Haven't you been watching her, Rafe?"

"Of course," he said curtly. A muscle flickered in his cheek. How could he avoid watching her? She glided around the shop like an ethereal thing—a bright bit of light in the darkness of the day. Her laughter rang from the kitchens and her scent emanated from all the dusty corners. Rafe swore he could smell her in the ink, in the coarse grains of paper.

"Then you have heard her humming in the morning like the larks of Bordeaux," Chauncey said, noticing the tightening of Rafe's hands. "Have you caught her dancing around the kitchens yet? She rises before Martha to buy the freshest bread and eggs from the farmers' stalls. When she returns red-cheeked from the cold, arms laden with food, she runs to the kitchens to fix Martha's breakfast before she wakes." Chauncey shook his head. "I can't believe she betrayed us. It isn't in her heart."

"What do you know of her heart?" Rafe hissed.

Chauncey stepped away from the violence of Rafe's tone and lifted his hands in defense. "I cannot explain what happened in Poitou—I understand it less than you—but I know what I see. I see a young girl who has had more than her share of injustice in this life."

"Fool. You've always been too easily charmed by a pretty face. Why do you think she stays in this shop? She could have left weeks ago: she's healthy, and she has clothes on her back. Nothing keeps her here except the opportunity to betray us once again—"

"She sleeps as sound as a babe," Chauncey continued. "Not

once has she risen at the noise coming from below." He lowered his voice. "If she were to betray us, certainly she would have shown some signs by now. The group has met four times since she arrived."

"Perhaps she knows we're watching," Rafe said quietly. His eyes strayed to the kitchens. Katrina passed the door once, humming to herself. "She's biding her time. There's no other reason for her to stay. I have no hold on her."

At that, Chauncey turned to Rafe, staring at the familiar lines of his brother's face. Rafe's eyes held so much suspicion, tinged by anger and, yes, a bit of sadness. Chauncey's soft jaw hardened in resolution.

"Who plays the fool now, my brother?" he asked. "You do have a hold on her. Are you so blind that you cannot read in her eyes—"

"You've become much too enamored of Katrina," Rafe interrupted, his eyes hardening to black chips of onyx. "You will no longer guard her at night."

"Who will, then, Rafe?" Chauncey asked calmly.

Rafe rubbed his stubbled chin. "I'll take your place—at least temporarily," he replied. "Then I'll choose someone from the group who can be trusted."

Chauncey shook his head in exasperation. "For a man of justice, Rafe, you have condemned Katrina with neither judge nor jury."

Katrina woke suddenly. The room was swathed in darkness except for a faint orange glow spilling in from the shop. Voices filtered through the walls.

She pulled the linen coverlet and knitted blanket up to her nose and struggled with the dregs of sleep. Her dream still tumbled through her mind: mobs, pikes, bloodied hands. She closed her eyes tightly and willed the fear away, as she had done so many nights in the past.

The remnants of her dreams slowly disappeared, but the voices did not. She blinked several times, then lifted herself on her elbows. She tilted her head, straining to hear more.

Mobs.

Katrina sat up and peered into the darkness of the shop, but could see nothing but a small circle of light from the hearth. The voices continued, and she suddenly panicked that there was a mob forming outside.

Rafe had warned the household of the danger of living in Paris now. The advent of unemployed seasonal workers made the city a dangerous place. And the Assembly's announcement that the Nation had taken over the clergy's lands and was soon to sell them to raise funds for the new government increased the danger. Rumors of riots doubled as pious Frenchmen rebelled against such blasphemy.

Katrina rose from the bed, shivering in her peignoir. She ran her hands over the smooth silk, wondering again why Rafe had given her such a luxurious gift along with the coarse woolen dress and rough-woven chemises. The rose silk clung to her hardening nipples, and she reached for the dark knitted blanket. Wrapping it tightly around her, she reached blindly for the taper that stood at the head of her bed. Clutching its cold base, Katrina took a deep breath and walked out of the small room that she and Martha shared.

The soft glow from the dying embers of the shop's fire beckoned her, but her neck prickled in fear as she slid to the hearth. She dipped the end of the taper into the red embers. In moments, it flared and caught flame.

"Can't sleep, Katrina?"

She started, turning to the chair by the hearth. In the darkness she had not seen his long hose-covered legs.

"I—I heard voices." She pulled the blanket around her shoulders to hide her near-naked form. She suddenly realized that Rafe could see clear to her bed from the chair by the hearth. She flushed wildly. He must have seen her in the rose silk peignoir.

"So you came to investigate? Wrapped in a blanket?"

Katrina stiffened and faced him defiantly. "I was frightened," she said sharply. "Can't you hear those voices? I thought there was a mob." She stared at Rafe, his features slowly taking form as her eyes adjusted to the darkness.

He toyed with the edge of his untied cravat, the lacy end brushing gently against the hairs of his half-bared chest. His eyes glittered between thick lashes.

"Yes, I can hear the voices. Were you planning to eavesdrop, Katrina?"

His tongue rolled over her name sweetly, and Katrina pressed the blanket closer to her.

"Why should I?" she asked. "Do you know those people? Are you afraid I will betray you in some way?"

Rafe's eyes flickered. "I'll never allow you to do such a thing again, Katrina," he said quietly. "You need not worry about the voices. The only thing you have to worry about tonight, is me."

Katrina could not tear her gaze away from him. His loose linen shirt was open to his breeches. He leaned back in the chair, the muscles of his abdomen rippling up to the hard plates of his chest. His long muscular legs stretched casually in front of him.

Katrina's cheeks burned as she looked at Rafe. His eyes held a strange light, and he watched her, seemingly bemused.

"You were so subtle, Katrina. Your eyes, even now, hold such innocence. Yet you managed to squeeze from me every detail of my band's raids, my politics, most of my past."

Katrina glanced at the hearth. "I knew nothing of you," she said quietly, the darkness giving her courage. "I knew nothing of your cruelty, your distrust—"

"I had no distrust then. Your actions made me cruel."

Katrina bit her lip and turned away from him. There was no arguing with him; he had no logic when it came to her. Though Rafe Beaulieu was known for his moderation in the assembly, she had not seen him exercise that moderation at home.

Rafe leaned forward in his seat, pulling upon the knitted blanket. "I like the peignoir on you much better than the wool dress," he murmured. "Don't you wonder why I gave this to you?"

Katrina stiffened. The smell of brandy was strong on his breath. His fingers curled possessively around the blanket, edging it down to her bosom. His eyes probed her skin like hot fingers.

"I had hoped it was a gift."

"A gift?" he said curtly. "And why should I give you gifts, Katrina, when you have given me nothing but lies and betrayal?"

"I have done none of that," Katrina retorted, her eyes flaring. She tried to yank the blanket from his hands, but it only opened farther. He released the blanket, and the wool gathered about her hips. She knew she should cover herself, but her hands refused to move.

"Entrancing," Rafe murmured. "Like ambrosia: one sip brings both divine ecstasy and the bitterest death."

Katrina trembled beneath his unwavering stare. Her nipples hardened into peaked nubs under the caress of his gaze. "Why—why, then, did you give me the peignoir?'' Her shaking hand traveled over the silk warmed by the heat of her skin.

Rafe's eyes flared, and one side of his finely chiseled mouth lifted at her obvious arousal. He reached out to capture a lock of her hair. "You know the answer to that, *petite.*"

Katrina swallowed, her eyes widening at the passion burning in his. Gathering her strength, she turned away from his power.

"No," he murmured. "Don't play coy." He stroked her silken cheek with his work-hardened palm.

Her hair spilled riotously over her shoulders and down her back, brilliant against the dark blanket around her hips. The fiery highlights of her tresses reflected the dim glow of the red embers. He had never seen a woman so beautiful, so tempting as this dangerous Eve.

Rafe had sat for an hour while his revolutionary compatriots gathered in the secret meeting room below the kitchens. He simply observed Katrina as she tossed on the narrow pallet. He knew the revolutionaries waited for him—that was the cause of their restlessness—but he felt rooted to the chair, watching the enchanting wood sprite who he had taken into his home. When she had risen from the bed like a specter, he could do nothing but watch her sylphlike form in the gossamer silk as she walked gracefully to his side.

Katrina grew more uneasy as Rafe gazed at her intently.

"I wish you wouldn't . . . stare so."

"You should take it as a compliment, Katrina, that your charms have not faded."

Her light, winged brows drew together in confusion. She jerked away from his captive hand as a voice rose from the kitchens, higher than the others.

"Aren't you in the least bit worried about those people?"

"Not in the least," he replied, his eyes never leaving hers.

"Well, I am," she retorted, pulling the blanket away from her feet and rising to stand before him. She suddenly felt as if she were in more danger from Rafe than from the voices that had woken her. "I'm going to find out who they are and what they're doing out there."

"You're going to march out into a band of patriots and demand to know their cause for assembling?" Rafe asked. "Dressed in nothing but a slip of silk?"

Katrina's eyes flickered. "Then you know who they are!"

"I'd forgotten how quick you are, *petite*," he remarked, using the old endearment unintentionally. "Yes, I know who they are. And it would be wise if you stayed in your room on the nights you hear them. For if I find you so much as two feet from your bed, I will have no qualms about offering you to them freely—"

"I am not yours to give!" she hissed, suddenly realizing that Rafe had been guarding her that night—watching her to make sure she did not interrupt the revolutionary meeting. How many other nights had she been watched? "You are detestable!"

"No more than you, my noble traitoress."

Before she could retort, he gripped her wrist, pulled her toward him, and his lips descended in glorious heat upon her own. The blanket slipped off her shoulders, and she pressed against him, her near-naked body molding intimately against his hard, muscular frame. His hands caressed her shoulders and her back with undeniable need. Overwhelmed, she wrapped her arms around his neck, her fingers entwining in his silken tresses. His lips played magically against her own, sending flames of passion down her spine. She moaned—half in torment, half in ecstasy—as he crushed her slight form effortlessly against his own.

"Do you want me, Katrina?" he murmured huskily in her ear. He lifted her slight frame clear off the ground and pressed his lips to hers. "Like that night in the woods, Katrina—that wonderful night—"

Katrina's entire body shivered with the strength of her passion. She had known—since the moment she woke in Rafe's room—that they would come once more to this. She had denied the possibility; she had convinced herself he did not want her. But she could not deny the way he watched her in the shop, or the meaning of the silk peignoir. Her heart surged with hope. Perhaps he would see the folly of his mistrust and love her once again.

Rafe pulled away, gazing at her flushed face.

"Let me take you, Katrina," he whispered, running a hand through her thick curls. His eyes held raw, tormented passion as they searched hers for an answer. *Say yes, Katrina, say yes and let me love you again, like it was before . . .*

Yes, yes I want you, the thoughts surged in Katrina's head. But part of her held back, hoping for a glimmer of something more than passion.

"Not . . . ," she stuttered, her throat thick, "not like this."

Rafe's arms tightened around her, anger bursting in his chest.

"Not like this?" he hissed. "How do you want it, then, Katrina? On silken sheets with jewels studding your fingers, your throat—"

"I think Katrina has given you her answer," Chauncey said calmly.

Katrina twisted in Rafe's arms. Chauncey leaned against the kitchen doorframe, watching them with interest.

"This is not your affair, Chauncey," Rafe said dangerously, tightening his grip on Katrina.

She struggled against him, shame suffusing her cheeks. "Please, Rafe . . ."

"The men are waiting for you, Rafe," Chauncey said seriously. "I suggest you go down there and assert yourself before someone takes your place."

"None of them are clever enough to plan a simple raid, never mind run—" Rafe stopped in mid-sentence. Katrina had taken advantage of his loosened grip to struggle away from him and snatch up the dark blanket.

"I know that, and so do they. Nonetheless, they grow restless." Chauncey waved Rafe toward the back door. "Perhaps you should go down and calm them."

Rafe scowled at his half brother. His eyes flickered to Katrina's form, swathed now in the blanket, and his blood surged. He reached out to touch her cheek and she flinched.

"This is not finished, Katrina," he whispered. Flashing Chauncey a dark look, Rafe marched past him and out into the night.

Katrina buried her face in the blanket in embarrassment. She pulled the hem of the blanket up and moved toward her room. Chauncey walked to her side and placed a hand on her arm, and she turned to see his chocolate-brown eyes glowing with sympathy. Her eyes filled with tears.

"How much did you—"

"I heard everything, Katrina," Chauncey murmured. "I watched you on the other nights we held our meetings, but Rafe decided I was no longer a suitable 'guardian.' "

"So he decided to take over your 'job,' " she said sarcastically.

"He doesn't trust you, Katrina. Even though I've tried to convince him otherwise."

Katrina lifted tear-filled eyes and gazed at Chauncey with interest. "You've tried to convince him?"

"I thought something like this would happen," he continued. "Though Rafe says many cruel things, you must know he still feels something for you."

"Lust," Katrina retorted. "I am familiar with the word."

"Katrina." Chauncey whispered her name.

She glanced up into his deep, sympathetic eyes, which mirrored the secrets of her heart. She turned away, unable to face the truth.

"I know how you feel about Rafe," Chauncey said. He sighed and pulled her trembling form into his arms. She sobbed quietly on his shirt as he rubbed the length of her hair.

"I'll make sure this doesn't happen again," Chauncey assured her. "I promise."

Chapter 15

Rafe pulled the woolen manteau close to his skin and hunched his shoulders against the cold. He stumbled on the icy street but righted himself against a stone wall. The two delegates he left in the alehouse laughed uproariously behind the battered leaded panes and raised their glasses in a final salute. Rafe smiled tightly and lifted his arm in an unsteady farewell.

Fools! Rafe thought. *Young, reckless fools!* He shook his head, trying to clear the noxious fumes of cheap brandy. He had spent too much time with the Jacobin club, listening with growing disgust to their political policies. Too much time drinking their brandy, as well. At a time when the Assembly needed to join together to draft the constitution, Rafe watched it split into too many powerful, politically diverse factions. Although he had thrown himself headlong into the negotiations, he now felt powerless to mediate between them.

He frowned. The men who, like him, wanted a constitutional monarchy refused to negotiate with the young revolutionaries who wanted—Rafe suspected—to dethrone the King of France. Rafe feared that his efforts were in vain—that nothing but a second revolution would mend the rift that grew deep and wide in the Assembly.

Turning down a side street, Rafe angrily clutched his hands beneath the voluminous manteau. Winter had begun far too early this year; hordes of homeless Parisians huddled in narrow alleyways over flickering fires, warming their frozen hands and toes. Rafe glanced warily at each darkened doorway before passing, though he knew his height and breadth would deter even the most determined thief.

A carriage wedged in a small snowbank by the edge of the narrow street aroused his curiosity. The horses fought against their traces while the carriage driver brushed the mixture of slime and sleet from his dark cloak. A woman, her plumed bonnet askew on her ornate coiffure, pushed open the carriage door and fainted against it. A man in a silk waistcoat quickly caught her.

Rafe's brow darkened. Aristocrats. By the amount of luggage strapped onto the carriage, he could tell they were fleeing aristocrats—too fearful to stay in Paris and face the consequences of their ancestors' decadence. Rafe glared, the scorn evident on his dark face. The carriage driver glanced at him and urged the aristocrats back into the safety of the coach.

The streets grew more silent as snow accumulated over the uneven stones. Paris seemed so quiet this winter—as if it were biding its time, waiting for something. Rafe quickened his pace, his breath forming thick mists in the night air. He chafed at the lack of activity. His group had not met in the secret room for weeks; they awaited the changes the constitution would bring. Besides, Rafe's men had more pressing needs than forging a new government. They had to feed and clothe their families.

He scowled. His band had returned to the warmth of their own hearths. His home, however, had been turned into Katrina's home.

First you stole my heart, petite, and now you steal my home. Rafe felt like a prisoner undergoing torture. Forced to listen to Katrina's soft voice raised in laughter in the kitchens; forced to watch her and Chauncey exchange meaningful glances; forced to sit in thick silence while she wove her web of enchantment around him, charming his household under his very nose.

Rafe had thrust himself willingly into the thick of the Assembly's political negotiations. It allowed him to get away from Katrina's beguiling presence. She was driving him to madness.

His blood warmed at the thought of her and, despite himself, he thought of the kiss they had shared, wondering anew what would have happened if Chauncey hadn't interrupted them. She had said she didn't want him, but her body denied the words. He had not merely imagined the softness of her lips, her hair, her body as it pressed against his own.

I will have her.

He would not have her—she was a lying, deceiving traitoress.

Rafe gritted his teeth. He wanted her, he had no doubt of that. He wanted her like he had wanted no other woman. He wanted to feel her writhing beneath him, her hair spread out in a fiery halo around her exquisite face. He wanted her to stretch out her arms to him, with love in her eyes.

Rafe shook his head in amazement. *Love.* Yes, he wanted her that way. He could not imagine touching her, making love to her, without the glow of love between them. Why had he left so willingly the night Chauncey had interrupted them? He knew, but his soul cringed to admit it. He left her because she said she did not want him. He could not take her without her assent.

Not like this, Rafe.

Her words rang in his mind. Katrina knew her power over him, he was sure. She flaunted it with every move of her shoulders, the tilt of her head as she spoke to Martha. Her eyes seldom met his, but every glance drew him deeper into insanity. Only Chauncey's ubiquitous presence kept Rafe from pulling her into his arms and demanding she answer his question again.

Rafe stopped in the middle of the street and lifted his head to the sky. Flakes of snow melted on the heat of his skin. He cursed loudly.

She would not win this battle of hearts. Resolutely, Rafe turned deeper into the maze of St. Antoine streets and headed for the dangerous warmth of the shop.

"Still hard at work, Katrina?" Chauncey admonished as he breezed down the stairs. "It's nearly eight o'clock."

Katrina glanced up from the plate before her to smile brightly into his merry eyes. "I hardly noticed the time!"

"Time for me to leave for the theater, though I suspect the show will be terrible. This damned revolution has sent all the actors and actresses, as well as the aristocrats, out of France."

"Not *all* the actresses, I'd wager." Katrina smiled impishly. "Else you wouldn't be going to the theater."

"You'd better be careful not to catch the pox with one of those bits of fluff," Martha admonished severely from her chair. "Only the good Lord knows who they have—"

"Martha!" Chauncey interrupted, glancing meaningfully at Katrina and flushing.

"Oh, Katrina knows as well as I what you go to do," Martha

continued mercilessly, dropping her knitting in her lap and waving a needle at Chauncey. "You know I don't approve."

Chauncey winked at Katrina as Martha lifted her chin and went back to her knitting. The fire crackled high in the hearth, but Martha sat only a few feet from the blaze, apparently oblivious to the heat which Katrina could feel at her workbench, clear across the shop. Katrina watched with growing amusement as Chauncey knelt by Martha's side.

"Come, Martha. You remember what it was like to be young, now, don't you?" He reached for Martha's aged hand, brought it to his lips, and kissed it.

Martha snatched it away. "Yes, I do. And that's exactly why I don't approve," she persisted. Chauncey reached for her hands, forcefully taking the knitting needles out of her grasp. "Now what are you doing?" Martha cried querulously as Chauncey pulled her up off the chair and into the center of the shop.

"I am going to remind you what it's like to be young." With a bow toward Katrina, Chauncey began a country jig with the unwilling cook.

"Such foolishness!" Martha exclaimed, scowling ferociously as Chauncey hooked his arm with hers and whirled her around. "Oh!" Her apron flew up, wrapped around her waist, and fell over her skirts again, and she laughed unwittingly.

Katrina jumped up from her worktable at the uncharacteristic sound and clapped her hands in tempo. Chauncey winked at her. Mischievously, she clapped her hands faster until Martha finally gave in and followed smartly in Chauncey's wake. Laughing, he whirled her around until tendrils of graying hair slipped out of her plait.

"Enough! Enough!" Martha exclaimed.

Chauncey whirled her around one more time until she stumbled heavily against his slight form. He righted the stocky cook and then raced to Katrina's side.

"Come, now, Katrina," he teased, sweat gleaming on his brow. "You didn't think you would escape unscathed—"

Katrina clutched his hands and whirled around him, laughing wildly, her feet light on the hardwood floor. Martha's face split into a hearty grin, and she began clapping tempo as they kicked and whirled their way between the worktables. Chauncey lifted Katrina off the floor and set her back down again, only to whirl

her around till she staggered with dizziness. Her hair, which had
been caught up in a haphazard roll at the nape of her neck, now
tumbled down at the force of the dance and curled about her
hips.

"I didn't know you were such an accomplished dancer,
Chauncey." Katrina laughed, throwing her head back to expose
the long length of her throat. Her fichu had come loose of her
bodice and flapped uselessly around her neck. She ignored it,
caught up in the unexpected joy of the moment.

Suddenly Martha gasped and stopped her clapping. A cold
gust of wind chilled the room.

Chauncey and Katrina stopped in mid-twirl and stared at the
open doorway, where Rafe stood, gusts of snow-laden wind
pushing his manteau into a dark shroud around him. His fists
clenched at his sides as he took in the scene.

Katrina sucked in a ragged breath. She had not seen Rafe in
five days. Since the night several weeks earlier when he had
kissed her so passionately, he had spent most of his days and
nights out of the shop, only to return with wine on his breath
and an angry light in his eyes. But Katrina had never seen him
this mad. He glared furiously at her and his brother, and unconsciously they released each other and stepped away.

"Don't let me stop you," Rafe gritted, his eyes leveled hotly
on Katrina's flushed face. " 'Twas such a charming scene."

Katrina's hands trembled as she grabbed a broom and began
sweeping around the press. She felt Rafe's hot eyes on her body
and jumped as he slammed the door behind him and strode into
the warmth of the shop. Martha scurried to snatch up her knitting
needles and rushed into the kitchen.

Rafe tossed his sodden manteau to Chauncey and untied his
simple cravat. His eyes never left Katrina's form.

"I haven't eaten all day, Katrina. Bring me supper," Rafe
demanded. "In my room." After glancing once in silent challenge at Chauncey, he took the stairs by twos and slammed the
door to his bedroom.

Katrina dropped the broom and pressed her hands against her
heated cheeks.

"You shouldn't go up there, Katrina," Chauncey said firmly.
"Let Martha serve him."

"You saw his face, Chauncey." She struggled to return her

riotous hair to the roll at the nape of her neck. "He'd toss his food out the door and Martha with it. I'll go."

Chauncey shook his head, serious now, the merriment of moments before completely washed away. "I can't protect you there, and with Rafe in that state, I wouldn't send the dog up there."

"It's all right, Chauncey. I'll be quick." Katrina smiled. "Don't worry."

Nonetheless, Katrina was nervous as she climbed the stairs to Rafe's room. Since the night Chauncey had caught him kissing her, Rafe was never allowed a moment alone with Katrina. At first, she was grateful for Chauncey's protection, but she soon saw the folly of his actions. Chauncey and Rafe had always conversed freely and openly with each other, but now they could barely speak without exchanging bitter words. Katrina felt more than responsible; she felt incredibly guilty. If the truth were known, she had enjoyed every second of Rafe's kiss and, had Chauncey not interrupted their embrace, she knew she would have welcomed much more.

Katrina hesitated before the oak door, the meat stew in the thick crockery burning her hands. Then, bravely, she pushed the door open with her free hand and entered Rafe's bedroom.

Fortunately, Martha had the foresight to light a fire earlier. The light spilled through the bedroom, illuminating every piece of simple furniture. Katrina sighed in relief. At least they would not be caught in darkness.

"Close the door," Rafe barked. "There's a draft." He lounged on his bed, his chest bare, his breeches snug against his hips and legs.

Katrina shut the door, lifted her chin, and moved toward him, trying to ignore the breadth and power of his wide shoulders.

"Your stew," she murmured. Rafe looked over the steaming pot and their eyes locked. Katrina's hand trembled as his night-black gaze seared through to her soul. Katrina shakily placed the soup on the dresser beside his bed and stepped back.

"So now you intend to seduce Chauncey, *ma petite,*" he said, his voice low and husky in the room.

Katrina folded her arms before her and looked away. "You're foolish, Rafe. I don't plan to do any such thing."

"I don't believe you." He sat up and leaned against the carved mahogany backboard. "Especially after tonight's little scene."

"We were merely entertaining ourselves," Katrina said, her voice barely above a whisper. Rafe's reclining form, so perfect, so masculine, drew her like a charm. Unconsciously, she stepped back again, trying to resist his magnetic presence.

He snatched her wrist in his strong hand and pulled her effortlessly to the side of the bed.

Her green eyes darkened as she stared at him. His breathing was labored; the muscles of his chest rippled down to his abdomen with each breath. Katrina dragged her eyes away, pulling vainly against his grip.

"You will not destroy my brother."

"Destroy your brother?" she said, a note of hysteria entering her voice. Her hair fell over her shoulder and brushed Rafe's chest. His eyes wandered over its lustrous thickness, then back to her own pale face.

"You will not destroy my brother, Katrina, as you are destroying me."

Rafe reached for her, snatching her other arm as she whirled away from him. With a hearty pull, her body flew back to his, her arms pinned behind her. Ruthlessly, he pushed her body on the bed beneath him.

Rafe was lost in the translucent glow of her skin. Her lips were parted, her eyes wide with fear. Roughly, he pulled away her fichu and feasted his eyes on the exposed flesh. His fingers lightly traced the edge of her bodice, wondering at the softness of her skin.

"Rafe, don't . . ." she murmured softly. "Please . . ."

Boldly, his hand moved over her breast, the curve of her waist, over one smooth hip covered by dress and petticoat. His nostrils flared at the womanly scent rising from her every pore. It filled his head and heated his blood. She trembled, and the feel of her exposed skin so warm and alive under his hands drowned out all rational thought. He rolled on top of her, lowering his head to the pulse beating in her throat.

"No!" she cried, pushing against him. "Rafe, please, don't—"

"Hush, *petite*," he murmured, lifting his eyes to hers. He released her arms and brought his hand up to touch the soft skin of her cheek. He cupped her chin gently, memorizing the lines of her mouth before finally lowering his onto its soft, bewitching fullness.

So sweet! How could he have forgotten the honey of her lips? He traced them slowly with his tongue, moistening each delicate ridge before pressing against them, urging them open, speaking wordlessly of his need, of his passion.

Katrina groaned deep in her throat, her arms moving over his hard body. *Madness*, she thought, *all madness*. She could no more resist him than she could stop breathing. He lay heavily atop her, his long, strong weight pressing into her softness. His lips drank deeply of hers, demanding. For a moment, just for a moment, she let herself melt into him, caught up in his urgency.

Rafe's eyes shot open as her tongue tentatively touched his. Her body was molded to his own, the hands she had pressed against him for protection were now wound around his neck, running boldly through his hair. He groaned, pulling her closely against him.

"I knew . . ." Rafe said huskily. "I knew you wanted me. Your body speaks loudly, Katrina, and I have listened to it for weeks. . . ." He ached for much more than her lips. Mindlessly, he released her and moved down her body to kiss the long column of her throat.

Katrina's head fell back against the pillow as his lips burned a trail of fire to her aching, peaked nipples. She knew she should stop him, that this had already gone too far and that she would drown in this passion, but his lips teased her, they taunted her, they dared her to pull away from his magic embrace. She knew that if she let him continue, she would be lost, lost, and he would twist her heart into a burning, aching knot.

"Rafe . . ." she murmured. His name came out softly, like a caress. "This is madness."

"Ah, but such sweet insanity," he returned, his fingers lingering over the taut ridges of her nipple under her woolen gown. "All these months, I thought I had imagined the taste of your skin."

"Then you want me, too?" Her voice trembled. Rafe lifted his head from her bosom and stared into her eyes.

Ah, Katrina, I almost believe your innocence when you look at me like that. "Yes, *petite*. I have thought of little else—"

"Katrina!" Chauncey cried from outside the door. "Katrina, are you all right?"

"If you dare open that door, Chauncey, you will no longer have a brother," Rafe yelled, rising from Katrina's bosom.

"Do not do this, Rafe," Chauncey said quietly through the door. "Please—"

Katrina lay partially beneath Rafe, her gaze fixed on him.

Rafe's eyes, wild with passion, flickered to her. His breath grew warm on her cheek. His eyes asked her a silent, tender question.

"It's—it's all right, Chauncey," she said unevenly, her breath catching in her throat.

Rafe brushed the hair from her forehead and kissed the smooth skin. His eyes held both passion and suspicion.

"Katrina?" Chauncey's voice persisted behind the door. "Katrina, I can't—"

"Hush, Chauncey," she whispered. "It's all right . . . I'm all right."

Chauncey hesitated, then his footsteps could be heard moving slowly away from the door.

"So you've made your choice, *ma petite,*" Rafe whispered in her ear.

"There never was any other choice, Rafe."

His arms tightened around her. The weeks of pent-up desire burst upon him in full force. He pulled down her bodice and pressed her breast above the ribboned edge. He tasted the hardened nub of her nipple, rolling his tongue around its ridged bed. He lifted Katrina atop of him, deftly unhooking the river of hooks in the back of the woolen dress. Protected only by a thin chemise, Katrina felt the cool air caress her skin as his burning fingers traveled down the length of her spine. His hands hesitated at her hips, then roughly pressed her against his hardening loins. Katrina gasped, sudden panic flooding like ice through her veins.

"No!" she cried, pushing away from his demanding hardness.

His lips left her breast, and he lifted his slitted black eyes to her face. "Ah, my sprite, it is far too late for no," he whispered.

Katrina wished that she could think clearly, that he weren't so near, that his musky skin would stop rubbing so warmly against her own. His eyes mesmerized her as he moved back up to her face and once again claimed her lips.

A wave of gentleness rushed over Rafe as he felt her mouth quiver under his. He attempted to ease her fears with his kiss, with the tenderness of his touch.

The softness of the bed met Katrina's back as he slid the woolen dress off her body. Now nothing stopped the hard planes and ridges of his frame from molding intimately with her own, and he eagerly pressed against her, pulling her so closely against his own body that they seemed as one body, chest against chest, abdomen against abdomen, loins against loins. . . .

He pulled her tighter, sensing her surrender, his hands winning her, claiming her as his own.

Katrina sighed, allowing the flood of aching urgency to wash over her. She pressed her palms against the warmth of his chest, her fingers curling in the short hair, caressing the thickness of his shoulders and arms. Her nostrils flared with his full, masculine scent.

His blistering eyes seemed to burn the thin chemise from her body. Katrina shrank from the passion in his face as he lifted himself away from her nakedness to remove the last offending piece of cloth that kept him from claiming her fully.

She stared at his body outlined by the firelight. In the darkness of the shed the first night, she had seen only a glimpse of his magnificence. Here, nothing prevented her from gazing upon his nakedness, perfect in every hardened muscle, every moving sinew, every stretch of dark, taut flesh.

He covered her body with his, kissing the hollow behind her ear, tracing a path to her jaw.

"Katrina . . ." he murmured.

Her heart sang with the tenderness of his voice, and she arched up to him.

His hands brushed the hair away from her face. "I want you," he said huskily, searching her eyes, which were glazed with passion, for a response.

Katrina opened her legs wordlessly in ultimate surrender.

Rafe hovered over her for a moment, his hand seeking, probing her secrets. Katrina trembled in suppressed passion at each tender, searching touch. Shifting slightly, Rafe gently pressed until he filled her with his length, and her soft, heated walls contracted against him.

No pain, oh, no pain. Sweet, sweet pleasure!

Instinctively, Katrina bent her legs and lifted them high against his sides. Rafe moved deeper, then held himself motionless inside of her. He lifted his head to gaze at her face, which was turned away in the intensity of her passion. "Look at me."

Her eyes fluttered open. A dark lock of hair fell over his forehead, and a muscle twitched in his cheek. She stared at him lovingly, her face a bare testament of her heart. She searched his face, his eyes, veiled even now, for a sign of love.

He lowered his rough lips to her forehead, touching the silk of her skin gently. He moved and she gasped in pleasure.

He moved again. Then stopped. Katrina lifted her arms to his back, tracing the long, firm muscles. Still, he did not move. Her body shook beneath his.

"Love me, Rafe . . ."

He kissed the corner of her closed eyes as he began to move in that timeless rhythm, and Katrina moved with him, their bodies stretched achingly apart, then joined deeper, and deeper, and deeper. Katrina's nails bit gently into his back as she felt a faintly familiar wave carry her up. He pressed her still closer, his hand running over her skin, leaving sparks in its wake. She pressed tightly against him and gasped, throwing her head back, as he brought her to the dark, dizzying heights to which only he could bring her. He followed soon after, and they teetered at the top, crying out each other's names.

Rafe lay heavily on her, and Katrina instinctively pressed his head against her bosom. His ragged breath warmed the wetness of her breast. Katrina, gasping still, ran her hand through his hair and closed her eyes, still feeling the waves ripple through her body. Her body throbbed beneath him.

Sweet possession. Had she ever been truly free of this man? Katrina closed her eyes, basking in the soft glow of their lovemaking. He moved slightly atop her, and every touch of his roughened skin sent shocks of pleasure through her body. He shifted his weight off her slight form, a sheen of perspiration shining on their bare skin.

His hand rested over one of her breasts, his fingers softly teasing her. Katrina suddenly felt very small, very fragile, as the hard, large hand at her waist pulled her closer to his body. He moved his head to nuzzle her neck.

Slowly, the faint crackle of the dying fire invaded their silence.

The wind whistled low around the corner of the building, through the tiny cracks in the pane. Katrina heard Chauncey's feet shuffle on the stairs, pause hesitantly before Rafe's door, then continue to his own room. She stiffened in embarrassment.

Rafe felt her sudden stillness. He lifted his head from her breast and looked at her.

Suddenly shy, she could not meet his eyes. She reached for the sheet and pulled it up over her body.

"Shame so soon, Katrina?" he asked boldly as she turned confused eyes to him. "Why? You were not ashamed a few minutes ago."

He stared into her wide, tilted eyes. Suddenly the memory of her treachery washed over him, and he remembered why she was here, why she served him in a rough woolen dress. Hot anger rose within him, and he brushed away a fleeting sense of guilt as her eyes grew dark with fright. Roughly, he pulled the sheet away from her body.

The night air rushed over her, icy and cold. "Rafe!" she exclaimed, a note of pain seeping into her voice. "It's just that . . . well, he must know . . ."

"So what? Both he and Martha know that we were once lovers."

Katrina gazed at him with shock, the waves of their passion still throbbing in her blood. Her eyes searched his, only moments ago warm with tenderness and desire, but now as hard and flinty as black coal.

His hand reached for her breast, bared to the night air.

"No." She pulled away from him.

"You were not saying no earlier, Katrina."

His voice, soft and dangerously warm, frightened her. She glanced around for her chemise.

"You were as warm and as lusty as a tavern wench," he continued.

"I'm no tavern wench," she said proudly. She found her chemise twisted by the side of the bed. Sobs rose full in her chest, but she held them back. She suddenly felt used and then discarded, like old clothes. "So I suppose that just now, I was your whore, nothing more?" she asked, hoping he would deny her words.

A dark brow lifted as he watched her struggle with her twisted chemise. The silence stretched as he considered her question.

She stood to stare at him. "Well?" Her hair fell in confused wisps around her flushed face. Her hands clung together in a strange hope.

Remember Renauldo. Remember her treachery.

"This has changed nothing, my traitoress." Rafe watched her face as his words took effect. "Unfortunately, no matter how much I detest your treasonous soul, I can't resist your body."

"You—" she cried, anger surging hotly to her face. Rushing toward him, nails unfurled, she fell upon him, raining blows upon his body. He reached for her arms, but they moved too quickly, poking into his arms, shoulders, abdomen. Her hair flew wildly around them.

Finally he captured her arms and held her away from him. Her eyes widened and burned angrily into his. He tightened his grasp on her wrists.

"I hate you," she hissed, trying to wrench from his grasp in vain.

A surge of regret passed through him, but Rafe pushed it away, not willing to examine such disturbing thoughts just yet.

Katrina's eyes blazed liquid green fire, her hair was tossed wildly around her face, and her skin glowed beneath the chemise. His eyes flamed with desire, and unconsciously he pulled her upon him again.

She stiffened in his grasp, her passion long gone and replaced by icy hatred. Anger gave her strength, and she pulled her arms from his grip. Lifting herself from the bed, she reached for her woolen dress and struggled into it.

Rafe watched in interest and, as she tried to fasten the hooks, he rose to help.

"Get away from me," she ordered. "I'd rather go downstairs naked than feel your hands on me again."

Gathering her dignity about her like a cloak, she moved to the door, then hesitated. Turning to him, she stared into his eyes. "There will come a time, Rafe, when you will rue this day with every fiber of your soul."

As the door clicked shut behind her, Rafe knew that that time had already begun.

* * *

"Why don't you just admit that you are head over heels in love with her, Rafe?" Chauncey exclaimed, pouring the second bottle of brandy freely into Rafe's empty glass.

"Don't be ridiculous."

"You two have been quite entertaining, actually." Chauncey removed his coat and turned toward the tavern's blazing fire. Although Katrina and Rafe had never said a word, Chauncey had no doubt of what had transpired behind Rafe's closed door one week earlier. Since then, the tables suddenly had turned. Now when Rafe entered the shop in the morning, his gaze followed Katrina with softness rather than suspicion. But she held herself as aloof as a duchess, spurning his gestures of reconciliation. Her eyes held all the anger and hatred that Rafe's had held before. Chauncey frowned. Such foolish lovers' games.

"She is under my skin—nothing more," Rafe mumbled, sipping the brandy.

"I'd say," Chauncey remarked. "You've been an unbearable boor since she came back into our lives. She remained so quiet for so long, I thought she was a meek little thing. But after this past week—"

"You don't know the half of it," Rafe remarked. "You don't know her at all."

"Yes, I do, Rafe. You forget that I helped Katrina bring clothes to you in Poitiers. She seemed barely a child then, very frightened and guileless." Chauncey ignored Rafe's sharp look. "Though now, dear brother, those lucid, sparkling green eyes of hers hold all the promise of a fine, passionate woman." Chauncey tilted his head, staring at his brother with interest. "After all these weeks, after all that has happened, do you still think that Katrina was the cause of that disastrous raid?"

"I don't know, but as long as there is a doubt, I have to keep reminding myself of that raid, else it would be too easy to fall under her spell again."

Chauncey leaned back, rubbing his chin thoughtfully. "You really are in deep."

"Stop your muttering and tell me why you dragged me to this broken-down tavern in the middle of St. Antoine? It's damned cold out and I'd much rather be in my own bed."

"It's about the charming Katrina. I have received word back from Duarte and Pierre. They have just returned from Poitou."

Chauncey glanced around the tavern. "Apparently they have some shocking news."

Rafe's brows drew into a dark furrow. "Why the hell didn't you tell me earlier? What is it? Is the marquis still searching for her?"

"I don't know," Chauncey said, an amused smile spreading over his face. "We're to meet someone here tonight, and he'll fill us in on the details."

"Take that smile off your face, Chauncey," Rafe said testily, raising the brandy to his lips. "You aren't half as smart as you think you are. Come, now. What, exactly, did Duarte and Pierre tell you?"

A short, rotund man dressed in a rough, unadorned woolen waistcoat and breeches waddled over and turned toward Rafe. "Excuse me, could you direct me to Monsieur Chauncey de Chevreuse?" His small eyes searched Rafe's face.

"I am he," Chauncey said, rising to hold out his hand. "You must be Monsieur Forrestier."

"Yes. May I sit?" Forrestier pulled out a chair nervously, his movements surprisingly rapid for such a large man.

"This is Rafe Beaulieu, my . . . associate," Chauncey said, smiling at Rafe. "Have some brandy?"

"No, no, I'm afraid we must get straight to business. I understand you may know the whereabouts of Katrina de Poitiers?"

"Perhaps," Rafe interrupted, lighting a cheroot from the candle and examining the man through the blue-gray haze. "What do you want from her?"

"I'm not at liberty to say—"

"Come now, Monsieur," Rafe said. "You do not expect us to just hand an innocent woman over to you without knowing why you want her?"

Chauncey leaned back in his chair, a slow smile spreading over his face as he relinquished the conversation to his brother.

"But it is a matter of the utmost importance!" Forrestier exclaimed, his brow wet with perspiration. He snapped out a linen hankerchief and mopped his brow. "I've been looking for her for months. Everyone thinks she's dead, after being kidnaped so horribly on her wedding day. But when I overheard a man asking for her, I became suspicious. He gave me some hope that she may still be alive. But it may endanger her if I tell you why I must find her. These *are* dangerous times—''

''It's very simple, Monsieur Forrestier,'' Rafe began, swirling the liquid in his glass. ''Tell us why you want her, and then we'll decide whether to tell you of her whereabouts or not.''

''Then she is alive?'' Forrestier exclaimed. ''She has come to no harm?''

''Of course not,'' Chauncey said. ''She's in perfect health and quite safe.''

Rafe shot him an angry glance.

The older man sighed heavily, reached into his coat, and took out a crumpled piece of paper. ''Mademoiselle must appear in Poitiers very soon. Her stepmother and stepsister died quite horribly in a raid on the manor. There are no other heirs to the estate. By the old duke's will, if Katrina does not appear within a year, the monies and financial investments will revert to charity, and the lands and title, by law, to the Crown. Katrina is now the sole heir to the entire estate. If she returns to Poitiers, she will be able to claim all the estates and wealth left to her by the duke as her dowry, plus receive a yearly allowance until she marries. On that day, she will become the Duchess de Poitiers.''

Rafe watched the man wordlessly, his face unreadable.

''I cannot believe that she is alive!'' the lawyer exclaimed, wiping his forehead again. ''I couldn't believe the man I spoke to, when he said that there might be word of Katrina in Paris.''

''It is true, Monsieur. Katrina is quite well and quite alive,'' Chauncey said. ''In fact, if my associate agrees, I could take you to her now.'' He glanced at Rafe expectantly.

Rafe's eyes remained lowered, intent on his brandy. They lifted for a moment to meet Chauncey's. ''Go ahead,'' he said dully. ''Bring the good news to Katrina.'' He reached for the decanter and dragged it loudly across the splintered table. ''I am sure she'll be quite happy to hear she's nearly a duchess.''

Chauncey hesitated, slowly shrugging his shoulders into his waistcoat. ''You should come with us, Rafe,'' he said. ''At least to bid her farewell.''

Rafe's black eyes flashed up to him. ''Make sure she is gone by morning.''

''Rafe—'' Chauncey began, but at a glare from those dark

eyes, he threw his hands up in defense. Without another word, he shook his head and followed the solicitor out of the tavern.

Rafe's hand tightened around the smooth brandy bottle, his knuckles whitening under the pressure. A familiar vision of Katrina grew in his head: she stood in a ballroom, surrounded by a glow that seemed to emanate from her own soul, lighting her hair in shimmering waves; her eyes were sparkling jewels in a peach setting; her lashes fluttered lush and long; her bosom thrust up in gentle mounds from the lacy edges of her bodice. Katrina the aristocrat.

Rafe closed his eyes and another memory rose before him: Katrina against a lightning-striped sky, her eyes luminous and smoldering; her hair flowed in wet ringlets like a topaz river over the arcs and curves of her hips; warm, lingering lips and smooth, heated skin touched and teased him.

And still, another vision: Katrina, her eyes changing from the liquid glow of love to the bright hardness of hate, her hands pounding against him in frustration and anger. Rafe still could feel her tiny fists against his chest, as if they had left bruises on his soul. Why did he feel so much guilt for taking a woman who had betrayed him?

The morning after he had made love to her—if he dared call it that—he woke full of guilt and confusion at his own actions. Katrina had willingly given herself to him, and he had used her as he would use a whore. Sometime in the night, sometime in the middle of making love to her, he had known her innocence. He knew she could not be the one who had betrayed him, despite all the evidence to the contrary. Rafe battled with his own soul. His heart called her innocent, his head guilty—but over and above this struggle, he knew he had committed a grievous wrong by taking her that night.

"Damn!" he swore, nearly kicking over the chair as he rose from the pockmarked table. Chauncey was right. He was obsessed with her! The memory of her was forever imprinted in his head, and despite his efforts to tear her from his soul, he could not stop longing for the touch of her skin, for the feel of her silken tresses.

Swallowing the last of the brandy, Rafe moved toward the door, his brows lowered. He would *not* go home and look upon her again. She would be gone in the morning, and with her the obsession that had caused his restless nights and long, torturous days. No more . . .

A movement by the door caught his attention. A man in ragged breeches and a dirty shirt lifted his head. Rafe's eyes widened.

Renauldo.

Katrina sat in the worn chair by the hearth, picking at the edges of the satin robe Chauncey had given her as a gift. She stared wide-eyed into the red embers of the fire.

"The sole heir?" she asked softly.

Monsieur Forrestier, still dabbing his eyes in happiness at finding her, nodded. "Sole heir, Mademoiselle."

Katrina hugged her midriff. Her worst fears that the Poitiers lands were going to be raided had been realized, and her stepmother and her stepsister had been killed. Her father's lawyer had pointedly omitted the nature of their deaths, but knowing the violence of mobs, Katrina shivered in horror.

"But—but my stepmother had made an agreement with the Marquis de Noailles," she began. "Something about delivering my dowry to him if I married him. Must I honor such a document?"

"All the duchess's papers were burned during the raid," Forrestier said. "I've seen no marriage contract. Besides"—he shrugged—"after you were kidnaped, the marquis left France and has not been back since. You wouldn't be expected to honor such a contract after all that has happened."

Katrina sighed audibly in the small room.

Providence was suddenly shining brightly on her, she thought. One minute fate displayed a dismal face, and the next, shone like the sun.

For weeks she had been searching for a way to leave the shop. Where once she had enjoyed her days working in the kitchens, now she hated every moment she had to spend between these walls. Rafe's presence filled her with shame and fury. The night he had made love to her—Katrina thought of a coarser expression to describe the act—he had crushed her heart with his strong words, leaving her wounded and empty.

A cold, bitter fury had risen in her heart. She rebelled against the gross injustice that had been committed against her and all of Rafe's apologetic glances could not erase that night.

But nonetheless, Katrina's heart lurched in pain at the thought of never seeing him again.

Monsieur Forrestier held her future in his pudgy hands. Katrina smiled hesitantly up into his jovial, red-veined face.

"Can we leave tonight?"

"Tonight, I am afraid, is impossible. I have a few errands of business to take care of, but by tomorrow, mid-morning, we can return to Poitiers."

"So soon, Katrina?" Chauncey asked, approaching her from the hearth.

Her eyes flickered in hesitation. Chauncey had been a good friend, and she would miss him almost as much as— She shook her head to clear it of Rafe's image.

"The sooner the better, Chauncey," she said, determined. "I'm stifled here."

He frowned, his lower lip turning down. "Give him just one more day, Katrina."

"No," she said evenly. "One day, one month, one year—I don't know if I could forget, even then."

"Very well," he said, sighing. "I suppose I can't stop you. But when you tire of the country, Katrina, you must come back to Paris." Chauncey's eyes twinkled. "I'll miss having you around the shop."

Rafe burst through the door, the icy wind of January whipping through the room. Katrina rose instinctively, straightening her back. The low fire flickered and her robe blew open, revealing a fine cambric chemise beneath. Rafe's eyes never left her face.

"Katrina . . ." His voice dragged over her name, raw guilt and pain pouring raggedly through the syllables.

Chauncey hid a triumphant smile and rushed to close the door against the wind. "I'm glad you came," he said lightly, following Rafe's slow footsteps. "You must help me convince Katrina to stay a few days longer. Can you believe she wishes to leave in the morning?"

As Rafe stepped into the small circle of light from the hearth, Katrina stepped back and gripped the edge of the chair, nearly falling over it in her haste.

"Rafe!" she cried, clutching her chest. "Your arm! You're bleeding—"

Chauncey gaped at Rafe's bloodstained arm as his brother's manteau slipped off his shoulders and fell heavily to the ground.

"Chauncey, get water and linens." Katrina rushed to Rafe's side to push the bloodied linen sleeve up over the wound, but he pulled away from her touch, his tormented gaze never leaving her face.

"No, no," he said. "You must listen to me." Sweat gleamed on his forehead, emphasizing the strange light in his eyes. Katrina reached over again to help, but he held up his hand to stop her. "You mustn't stain your hands with my blood," he said weakly.

"You're talking foolishness," she answered as Chauncey reentered with water and clean linens.

"No, this is not foolishness." Rafe grasped her shoulder with one hand. "Foolishness was believing you could betray me."

Katrina wrested her arm away from him, her green eyes blazing in her pale face.

"It's too late for such words," she said firmly. Her robe had come loose with her abrupt movement, and Rafe's gaze lingered on the curve of her graceful collarbone.

"Rafe," Chauncey interrupted as he cleaned the deep knife wound. "How did this happen?"

Rafe glanced at his arm as if it were someone else's. His eyes registered no physical pain—but some deeper, inner torment was revealed plainly. "After you left, I found an old associate in the tavern."

"Who?" Chauncey asked breathlessly.

"Renauldo."

Chauncey hissed a deep breath, his eyes widening, and he shook his head in disbelief. "But Renauldo is dead—he disappeared at that—" His words died as a light of understanding dawned in his eyes.

"Right, Chauncey." Rafe turned to Katrina. "We thought Renauldo had been captured and killed by the marquis's men, but we were wrong. He collected the marquis's reward of a bag of gold louis, then disappeared from Poitou."

"So Renauldo informed the marquis of the raid," Chauncey

concluded. He turned and smiled brightly at Katrina. "It was not Katrina—"

"She is as innocent as the day she was born," Rafe murmured.

Katrina shook her head violently, her hair tumbling over her shoulders. "Too late," she said sharply, stepping away from Rafe's dark eyes, from the magnet of his strong body, which was scented with his own special smell and cold winter air. Her heart hardened at the memory of his brutal rejection. He reached out to her, but she stepped away from his outstretched palm.

"No." Her eyes glittered glassy and wide. "What if you had never discoverred this Renauldo?" she asked, her shoulders straight. "You would have spent the rest of your life believing I was guilty of treachery. Your brother knew, Martha knew—why couldn't you, too, see that I couldn't possibly have betrayed you?"

"I had begun to doubt, Katrina."

She shook her head violently, her brows knitting together over the bridge of her tilted nose. She threw her hands up in denial. "I will not listen to this."

A week earlier, Katrina would have melted to have heard Rafe speak such words. But that night had marred her heart far more deeply than he would ever know. As she gazed at him in the pale blue light of dawn, she knew she would always love him, but she wondered if she could ever bring herself to trust him again.

Katrina raised her chin. His dark eyes rested on her in a silent plea.

"Monsieur Forrestier," she said suddenly, turning to the lawyer, who had been watching the proceedings silently but with interest, "I'll be prepared by mid-morning. Please don't be late. I'm eager to go home." Katrina nodded to each of the men, her gaze stopping finally on Rafe. "Good night."

"Katrina—" Rafe stepped toward her as she retreated to her room.

Chauncey's arm shot out to hold him back. "Let her be, for now. She needs time alone."

"I must talk to her," Rafe insisted. "I must convince her."

A deep sense of loss loomed over him. "I've committed a horrible injustice—"

"Damn it, Rafe!" Chauncey swore harshly. "Don't you understand? You'll be fortunate if she ever speaks to you again!"

Chapter 16

Katrina waved one last time at Manon, her beloved servant. Sighing, she tapped her fan lightly on the roof of the new, polished berline, which then lunged forward down the long circular driveway. Katrina's eyes misted as she gazed through the carriage window toward the proud, strong, sandy walls of the chateau.

"So sad, Katrina," Monsieur Forrestier said softly at her side. "You know you could stay if you liked. You have been here only two years."

Katrina dragged her attention away from the empty manor, the trim lawns, and the clean, shining windows that winked like tearful eyes at her departure.

"I have been here too long, already," Katrina said. "My work here is finished."

"All the more reason why you should stay," Forrestier growled, his brows lowering. "You have a manor totally restored from devastation, yet here you are, off to a townhouse that hasn't been occupied for twenty years! Goodness knows what state we'll find it in." His cheeks reddened from his speech, and Katrina smiled tolerantly at his large form.

"I've sent people ahead to take care of such details."

"You'll spend everything your father left you—"

"I doubt that," Katrina interrupted, laughing softly. "Father left me enough to restore every chateau in France." Her gaze dropped briefly to a pile of papers tied in a blue satin ribbon. She grimaced in a quite unladylike manner, remembering the many papers she had left in Monsieur Forrestier's iron safe and all the time she had spent sorting through them. The sheets that

226

lay neatly beside her on the soft leather upholstery were the ones she deemed most important.

Katrina fingered through them yet another time: profits on the shipping line working out of Marseilles; the papers needed for the changes she had installed in the tenant system on the estate; titles for land in America; titles for the chateau in Poitiers and the house in Paris; last year's *rentes* collected on the duke's land.

"Have you studied any of those, Katrina?" Forrestier asked eagerly. "Despite my initial hesitation, it seems that by cutting down the tenants' *rentes*—from forty percent of their harvest to twenty-five percent—we still have come out with a small profit."

"Unfortunately, I have had little time to peruse those papers, Monsieur." She smoothed the rustling muslin of her petticoats, pulling the gold-striped skirt neatly around them. She puckered her forehead and turned inquiring green eyes toward him. "We received a profit off the sale of that percentage?"

"Indeed." The lawyer nodded.

"Next year, then, we will drop the percentage to twenty," she said, pulling off her kid gloves and laying them upon the sheaf of papers. She ignored the barrister's shocked look.

"But, Katrina . . . we will lose any profit—"

"Monsieur, these people work hard to stay alive. Don't you remember the lesson of my predecessors?" She lifted a brow. "All I want is enough return from them to maintain the estate. We will continue to drop the percentage we take from them until we are all even. Understood?" She gazed steadily into the solicitor's eyes, and he sat back, mumbling.

Katrina knew he would eventually agree to her terms. She and the lawyer had had many such arguments in their time together. Their first and most heated argument had been about money. She had spent an incredible amount of the duke's gold on the restoration of the manor, making few purchases that were not absolutely necessary, and had proved herself frugal. When Katrina had gone to Monsieur Forrestier, full of righteous injustice about the treatment of the peasants who leased the duke's land, she had thought he would have an attack of apoplexy. She smiled now. Another win for her; she'd judged correctly that the return on the *rentes* would be sufficient for upkeep of the estate.

"I'd like to ride as far as we can today," Katrina said, jolting the solicitor from his musings. "I'm anxious to settle down," she added. "It seems a century since I've been in Paris. So much has happened in my absence. The National Assembly finally has finished the constitution, and now the king has ratified it! I can hardly believe it."

"I cannot believe the king succumbed to the pressures of that rabble," the lawyer said wryly. "But at least, the revolution is over." Forrestier, she knew, was a royalist, and deplored the atrocities that had befallen the king since the start of the revolution.

"I wouldn't be so sure of that." Katrina pulled the pin out of the hat perched on her low coiffure and placed both on the seat beside her, atop the papers. "The last journal I read said that the new Legislative Assembly has all new delegates. I doubt they'll leave things as they are."

Katrina suppressed a sigh. She knew that she was doing the right thing, leaving Poitiers and returning to Paris. She had languished in the dark silence of the chateau, sewing or reading by the light of the fire in the kitchen with Manon. She'd felt isolated and, near the end of her stay, in exile. Her youth cried out for more than this conventlike existence.

When Katrina first arrived in Poitiers, she had wasted no time in visiting the flame-scarred manor, bravely marching through the hollow, mud-splattered rooms, hardening her heart against the jangle of hated memories. As if possessed, she raced through the halls, even daring to enter the kitchens. Only a few days later did the process of cleaning begin. One day, an older, careworn Manon came to the door, and without a murmur she got down on her knees with Katrina to mop the refuse from the once-shining parquet floors. Eventually a few former servants returned and lent a hand in the cleaning. Tante Helene, Katrina found out with great sadness, had perished in the previous winter's famine.

Pushing aside her grief at this news, Katrina worked the hardest. Her hands reddened quickly from the work; her feet and knees grew callused. Falling into a charred bed in exhaustion when the sun set over the western hills each night, Katrina would finally find some peace.

Monsieur Forrestier constantly rebuked Katrina for her behavior, insisting that she rise from the dirt and grime, and start acting like the duchess that she would be someday. Katrina refused until she became so exhausted from the work that she was forced to lay abed for two weeks. When she recovered, she spent her time finding furniture to fill the echoing shell. She became obsessed with the restoration, and in the process, she felt as if she, herself, were restored.

Not until the bulk of the work was finished did Katrina find time to think about her new situation. She rifled through her father's documents with an intensity that surprised the stodgy solicitor, who did not understand the relief Katrina found in filling her mind with anything but the resentment that welled when she thought of Rafe.

As the *clip-clop* of the horse brought her back to the present, Katrina unconsciously tilted her chin. She knew it would be hard to avoid him in Paris. Rafe had found her once before, and he had not even known where she was. This time, he would know where she lived because Chauncey would soon receive her card.

Katrina's full lips set in a firm line. Chauncey's first few letters had hinted of Rafe's misery, but she had hardened her heart against him. There would be no amnesty for that tall, dark man.

"Papers," the armed peasant demanded, his eyes peering into the darkness of the carriage to stare at Katrina.

Monsieur Forrestier moved his bulk between her and the guardsman, thrusting the well-creased traveling papers beneath the guard's nose. "I believe this is what you need?" His gaze wandered nervously to other citizens, all armed, loitering about the gates of Paris.

The guardsman sniffed and stared down at the papers, his mouth moving laboriously over the names. He lifted his eyes to stare again at the finely dressed woman who sat stiffly beside the solicitor. His nostrils flared as if disgusted at her perfume. He turned and gestured toward another who walked over leisurely to join him.

"Look here. We got a duke's daughter visiting Paris," the guard said loudly. "Another aristocrat returning from emigration." Heads encased in red caps turned to stare at the inhabitants of the rich carriage.

"I'm not an *émigré*, Monsieur," Katrina interrupted angrily. "I've lived in Poitiers for the past two years." She resented being called an *émigré*—an aristocrat who fled France in fear of the people. She was a full-blooded revolutionary, even if that blood was blue.

"You're sure you want to live in Paris?" the lawyer asked beneath his breath. "It seems the closer we get to the city, the more hostile these *sots* are!"

"And what is the purpose of your trip, *citoyenne?*" the second guard asked coldly, moving closer to the carriage and staring at Katrina's *décolleté*.

"I've come to Paris to live."

"You haven't left France in the past two years?"

Katrina shook her head. She had read that the National Assembly, before it dissolved, urged all *émigrés* back to France with complete amnesty. Why, then, was this guard so belligerent?

"Where are you staying?" he asked.

"I have a home . . . in St. Germain." Katrina hesitated, not wanting to publicize her address to the rabble that had gathered around her carriage.

"We will escort you, *citoyenne.*"

Katrina balked. She stuttered her protest as the men moved away from the carriage, calling for two National Guards in faded blue uniforms with frayed scarlet and white trimming to ride in front and behind of the dusty carriage. Then the carriage lurched forward through the stone gates and onto the ancient worn cobblestones of Paris.

Monsieur Forrestier lifted a thick hand to brush back his disheveled wig and turned a reddened face to Katrina. "Insolence!" he stuttered, bracing himself against the side of the berline as it turned off the Rue de Sevres. "An escort! As if we were criminals!"

Katrina moved to the window, shocked at their treatment at the gate. She pushed away a leather blind only to find red-capped men and women making obscene gestures at the carriage, yelling epithets that she had never heard, even in the seediest parts of Poitiers.

"I think it's best that we have the escort," she said breathlessly, dropping the blind as the old fear of mobs crept upon her again. "Only the presence of the National Guardsmen keeps these people from pulling upon the horses."

The lawyer stuck his face out the window, then pulled back quickly as a mold-tainted tomato flew past.

"I don't think we're very popular," Katrina said, her eyes wide.

"An understatement, my dear," he blustered. "You know, of course, that we could return to Poitiers."

Katrina returned her gaze to the city she had missed so dearly. Despite the calls of the peasants, despite the refuse that littered the streets and the stench that rose from the ground, Katrina wanted to stay. Her soul, long starved for excitement, drank in the sights and sounds and scents of the sprawling metropolis voraciously.

"Non," she said firmly. "I will stay here."

As the carriage rumbled deeper into the Faubourg St. Germain, she saw rich townhouses, their front gardens either tended meticulously or high in weeds and filth. The disparity was shocking. Katrina realized that the uninhabited homes were probably those of the *émigrés* who had not yet returned. The rest probably belonged to more liberal noblemen and perhaps a few delegates to the Assembly.

Katrina's excitement grew as the neighborhood became more lush and vibrant. Certainly her father's old townhouse must be beautiful, to be in such a wonderful part of Paris!

The carriage stopped abruptly. Katrina looked around, wondering which of the houses was hers. Her heart sank as she stared at the nearest one. The carriage door opened and she stepped down, assisted by the driver, clutching the fan tightly in her hands.

"Surely this can't be 110 Rue de Bac?"

The driver nodded.

She stared at the weed-choked fence and the tilt of one faded shutter, and then closed her eyes. The door opened and a servant from Poitiers came to greet her.

"Mademoiselle?"

"Certainly the men I hired came to fix the house?" Katrina asked.

The young woman nodded, perplexed. "Yes, Mademoiselle. They did as much as they could in the weeks before you came." The servant turned back toward the house. "It's much better now than before."

Monsieur Forrestier took Katrina's arm. "It has been twenty years, Katrina."

"I know. But I didn't expect . . ." She gestured toward the ivy-covered stone walls of the two-story townhouse.

Her solicitor hazarded a small chuckle. "It seems, my dear, that you have yet another house to restore."

Katrina straightened from sweeping as she heard a carriage stop abruptly before her house. Dropping the straw broom loudly on the wooden floor, she rushed to the stained curtains and carefully pulled them away.

"Therese, we weren't expecting anyone, were we?" she asked her newly hired servant.

"Not that I know of," Therese said curtly.

Katrina frowned as she stared at the shining carriage. Smoothing the rough, printed cotton dress over her thighs, she moved toward the large hallway. "Tell these people that I haven't yet arrived, Therese. I certainly cannot greet anyone in this state." She lifted dirty fingers to her hair, which was pinned haphazardly atop her head. "All right?"

Therese nodded sullenly.

Katrina did not like this servant, but Therese was the only help Katrina had been able to find in Paris. She wished she could bring the entire, loyal staff of the Poitiers chateau to the townhouse, but they had commitments in the country. This Therese would have to do for now, at least till Katrina found someone less sullen.

Katrina jumped at the knock at the door and turned to run back into what was going to be the parlor, if she ever finished cleaning the place.

"Remember, I have not yet arrived." She peered out the window. It was a hired carriage, so there was no clue as to the identity of the visitors. Many times in the past week neighboring residents—most of them newly returned *émigrés*—had come to the door after sending their cards, hoping to meet the future Duchess de Poitiers. Katrina had pretended that she had not yet arrived. How could she entertain guests in such a house?

A male voice drifted through to the parlor, and Therese's high whine lifted in anger.

"I know she's here. She sent me a card weeks ago. I don't know why she's hiding, but I'll soon find out—"

Katrina rose from the linen-covered chair just as the man burst past Therese and stepped into the parlor.

"Katrina!" he exclaimed. "Why have you been such a recluse?"

"Chauncey!" she cried, a smile lighting her face. Eagerly she moved into his waiting arms and hugged him, then just as quickly pulled away. "No, Chauncey, I am filthy. I'll ruin your clothes."

He laughed. "Ruin my clothes! Now, Katrina, how many waistcoats do I own? And how many cravats? And linen shirts?"

Katrina laughed and welcomed his embrace again. Over his shoulder, she saw Therese's stiff face. "That will be all, Therese. This man is an old friend." Katrina thought she saw one pale eyebrow lift on Therese's scowling face before she left the hall.

"Indeed! One old friend that you have refused to see twice already. What's the meaning of all this?" Chauncey gestured, pushing her away from him. "Katrina, you look absolutely marvelous."

"Always the gentleman, Chauncey. How can you possibly say that? I woke up at sunrise to wash the lower outside windows before the snows of winter set in. Then I returned to the house to pack up every linen in the closet for Therese to take to the launderer's. After that I washed the walls in this parlor. I'm filthy, and my hair is awry."

Chauncey's brown eyes twinkled brighter than Katrina had remembered. Only a light spray of lines from the corners of his eyes indicated any aging.

"Such a woman!" He released her and stepped back, studying her figure in a way that, if they had not known each other so well, would have bordered on insolence. "I say you look wonderful. Exceedingly so." He smiled. "My dear Katrina, you have changed!"

"Come, Chauncey." She rolled her eyes at his ebullience. "Please sit down and tell me how you are."

"I was so pleased when I received your card. The shop has been so dark and boring since you left," he remarked, "though I know you won't be returning to it.'

"Indeed not," she said stiffly, then smiled to soften her words. "I have other plans."

"I wager you do. You have an air of mystery, my dear, that is driving many of your neighbors into a frenzy. Do you know that even at Madame Roland's salon there has been talk about a certain young duchess who has arrived in the Faubourg St. Germain?"

"At Madame Roland's salon?" Katrina exclaimed. "I am establishing a notoriety before I have even tried! They don't understand that I am not a duchess yet—I have to marry, first." She sighed in frustration. "I've been receiving so many cards—"

"Why, in God's name, don't you respond to any?"

"Look around you, Chauncey. Do I seem ready to receive guests?"

He turned, noting the stained curtains, the linen-covered furniture, and the patina of dust that had settled over the mantelpiece. "Not quite yet, I admit," he agreed. "But still, you could appear at a salon—"

"Stop, Chauncey," she chided. "I think I like the mystery, so far. You see, I've come to Paris for more than just a visit."

"Well, do tell," he prodded.

As Katrina leaned back against the chair, apparently oblivious to the way her bodice stretched across her full breasts, Chauncey's eyes wandered over her figure. Why had he never noticed how much of a woman she really was? In the shop, she had seemed little more than a child until the last weeks of her stay. But here, in her own house, she was different.

"Katrina, what happened in Poitiers?" he asked.

"Poitiers?" she repeated, smiling softly. "I need not tell you the state in which I found the chateau. It was devastated, Chauncey. I could hardly believe it. In any case, I restored it to nearly its former beauty—there are some marks that can never be erased—and lived there, peacefully, for the past two years."

"Why do I feel there is more to this story?"

"Oh, there is much more, Chauncey. Not only did I restore the manor, but I also restored my father's estate, trying to right the wrongs that the duchess committed before her demise. . . ."

She discussed her changes in the sharecropper system, her attempts to reunite the families that had been evicted, and her relations with Monsieur Forrestier and some of their financial dealings.

"But enough of that," Katrina said, realizing how long she had gone on. "You must be terribly bored with my meanderings. I've had no one to talk to for a week, now, isolated as I am."

"Indeed, Katrina. This is fascinating. I never knew you had such a head for business." Was this really little Katrina, the waif who had flitted among the presses, her eyes a lucid mirror of her soul?

She smiled ruefully. "I had to acquire one quickly." She hesitated. "I felt as if I had to do it for my father, if not for myself."

Chauncey reached for her hand and lifted it to his lips. "Do you know how much you've changed, my dear?"

"Now, Chauncey, don't start that. You know I'm the same woman as before—"

"No, you weren't wholly a woman before. You bore the marks of your earlier tragedies so plainly on your face. Now . . ."

"Silly," she teased, and for a moment she was the playful elf Chauncey remembered. "But really, Chauncey, I am so glad you called. My lawyer left last week, and I've been so bored."

"So you miss him, do you?" he remarked suggestively, lifting a brow.

Katrina burst into laughter. "Come now, Chauncey! He's twice my age and three times my size! Though a sweet man, he's hardly my idea of a courtier." She blushed slightly. "In any case, he left last week, and with him went the last of the servants from Poitiers. Most of the structural work on the house is finished, so they were no longer needed. The only work that remains is interior, and the garden when spring comes. But that I'm fully capable of doing myself."

"Yourself?" he exclaimed. "Surely you will hire someone to do this work."

"Of course not. It's all quite simple, and I've done it before."

"Ah, Katrina. You'll never cease to astound me. I hope you never lose that touch of peasant blood. Why, what would Rafe say if he knew of all this?"

Katrina's back straightened at the name. It had been so long since she had heard it spoken.

"And how is Rafe?" she asked stiffly, breaking the silence.

"I wouldn't know. I haven't heard from him in months."

Katrina bit her lip. She would not, *would not,* ask Chauncey of his whereabouts.

Chauncey's face split into a quick grin. "You still have incredibly revealing eyes, Katrina," he murmured. Katrina flushed, then looked away. "Not long after you left, Rafe went to Turin, where many of the *émigrés* were gathered. He had hoped to gain access to the court they set up—"

"The court!" Katrina exclaimed. "How? Many aristocrats know he's a revolutionary."

"I know," Chauncey said, "but have you ever tried to convince Rafe of anything once his mind is set? He set off like a demon after you left. He returned last summer briefly, then left again, this time for Coblenz, where the king's brothers had gathered with many *émigrés* to scheme against the new government." Chauncey shrugged. "I've seen Rafe in many a tight situation, and he's always been able to come through, even when dodging bullets."

"Certainly he will come back soon. After all, the *émigrés* are also coming back."

"Not all of them, Katrina. I'm afraid the king's brothers are still scheming in Germany. They're trying to convince Leopold of Austria and Fredrick of Prussia to march against France."

"Even though King Louis has approved the Assembly's constitution?"

"Yes." Chauncey frowned. "Though that might all come to naught. I've been attending the new Legislative Assembly meetings. All these new delegates are anxious to make their own marks. I suspect they will challenge this constitution."

"No, Chauncey . . ."

"It took the last Assembly two years to write it up, and I fear it will be torn apart before the coming of spring. If Rafe were here, he might be able to help, but he's determined to stop the king's brothers from scheming in Coblenz."

"There is little he wouldn't do for the revolution," Katrina murmured.

"Yes." Chauncey toyed with his fobchain, watching her fingers pluck the roughness of her dress. Her nervousness was apparent. It seemed he had probed a painful spot. He searched her averted eyes for a flicker of the old emotion.

"So, with both you and Rafe gone from the shop," he continued, "it's been quite a boring two years. That is, with the exception of the king's attempted escape and a riot or two."

Katrina smiled. "I too, have been bored, in Poitiers," she admitted. "In fact, that's one of the main reasons I have come to Paris."

Chauncey looked crestfallen. "You mean you did not come solely to see me?"

"This is the second reason I came to Paris, Chauncey. The first was certainly to see you," she assured him, laughing. "In fact, I need to ask you a favor. I want to set up a salon, Chauncey. A salon like Madame Roland's. Will you help me become established?"

"Katrina, a *salonniere?*" he exclaimed. "You certainly have come up in the world, my dear!"

"Not Katrina, the *salonniere,*" she corrected. "The future Duchess de Poitiers, the *salonniere.* You forget, I am nearly a titled aristocrat."

Chauncey settled back on the chaise. "Indeed," he said contemplatively. "I do forget. You may want to start calling yourself 'Depoitiers,' Kat—the Assembly banned the separate prefix 'de' from all names. Silly, isn't it? But, my dear, I don't think you'll need my help in starting a salon. Your mysterious presence has already caused such a fervor that they will battle over the right to attend."

"But that will pass, Chauncey. I need more than mystery to keep my salon filled. I need you, I need your political friends, the writers, the publishers—"

"You want a serious salon, then," he said. "Very well. Yes, Kat, of course I'll help you."

She squealed and lunged over to hug him, babbling her thanks in his ear. Chauncey drew back as she pressed against him. Abruptly she pulled away and took his hands.

"Thank you so much, Chauncey. I won't be able to do this without you."

"Somehow, I don't believe that. But I must say, there is someone else who would be a much better contact than me. I tend to stay on the periphery of politics, believe it or not. This gentleman is out of town at the moment, but I may be able to lure him back to Paris."

"Who?" she asked. "I'd rather be obligated to you for such

a favor, but if you think this gentleman can help, then I'll ask him, as well. Who is it?''

"Rafe."

Katrina's face paled. She sat back in the chair and shook her head firmly. "Impossible, Chauncey. Out of the question."

Chauncey lifted his hand to protest, but her face was set in rigid lines as she called for tea.

"You must stay awhile," she continued, as if Rafe's name had not been mentioned. "There's so much I need to know! You'll fill me in?''

"How could I resist such an entreaty?''

The sun had sunk beneath the gray horizon before Chauncey left the townhouse in the Faubourg St. Germain. His throat ached from talking, but his mind churned with their discussion. Such a woman, this Katrina of whom he had only had a glimpse when she worked in the shop. Rafe would be devastated if he saw her now, in her full bloom.

Chauncey suddenly frowned in worry. He had not heard from Rafe in nearly two months. For the first time in his life, he began to doubt the immortality of his half brother.

Chapter 17

Rafe slumped wearily over the saddle horn as his horse ambled through the forest just east of Paris. His legs ached from days of riding, and his arm throbbed where a bullet had grazed his flesh. But he was near home now, and the royalist swine who had followed him through the German States, over the frozen plains of Belgium, lingered far behind him.

He squeezed his eyes shut. His undercover work in the king's brothers' court in Coblenz had come to a violent end. For two years he had worked to win the trust and confidence of a dozen *émigrés;* with two hundred thousand gold livres he had finally succeeded. How much of his life had he wasted in their perfumed salons, smiling like a benign courtier?

He shook his head. Not all was wasted. He knew he had succeeded in setting many of the court's plans awry, especially the first year in Turin. It hadn't been difficult to confuse these foolish aristocrats in their bumbling efforts to save King Louis XVI from France. Unlike Rafe, these men weren't skilled in the delicacy of secret missions.

They were, however, brilliant in diplomacy. After the king's failed escape, the aristocrats had moved their court to Coblenz. They had decided that only war would win back their country, and they soon caught the attention of Europe's leaders.

Rafe frowned, memories of the past year's events flashing through his brain. Once the Austrians and Prussians had sent well-trained, powerful troops into Coblenz to aid the *émigrés*, he had begun to fear he could do no more for France. He hadn't been able to stop the talks among the European leaders—any obvious attempt would have made him immediately suspect—yet he had tried, and for nearly eighteen months his cover had remained undetected.

Then the Marquis de Noailles had arrived.

Rafe's body tensed in anger at the memory. The marquis had boldly approached him in the middle of the Elector of Trève's palace. Rafe had expected him to denounce him on the spot, but the wily aristocrat had chosen a more subtle torture. He had had the audacity to ask about Katrina. He had watched Rafe carefully, obviously suspecting that Rafe knew of her whereabouts.

Rafe grunted, straightening stiffly upon his horse. Fury possessed him again, preventing him from sleeping. Even now, thoughts of the marquis made his blood boil.

After his casually cutting words, the marquis had walked away. He hadn't informed the Comte d'Artois, who stood nearby, that Rafe was a revolutionary. Not willing to find out what plans the marquis had in mind, Rafe had slipped out of the ballroom.

Three of the marquis's men had been waiting outside for him, but in Rafe's anger ten men could not have held him. Notably, the marquis didn't show his face during the altercation. He undoubtedly waited inside the protection of the palace. Stealing one of the men's horses, Rafe had galloped into the forests of Germany.

He rubbed his sore arm, checking the linens for fresh bleeding. Only one of the bullets had found a target. The marquis had wasted no time after he discovered Rafe's escape. The entire court sent soldiers to track him. Rafe had felt them heavy and hot on his back. Through the woods of Germany; through Alsace, where sympathetic peasants made a temporary home for him while his arm and body healed; out of their village under the cover of night while the Comte D'Artois's agents searched the houses—the mercenaries nipped hungrily at Rafe's heels, eager for the bounty offered for his head.

Rafe patted his steed, encouraging it. He'd stolen this animal from another royalist, as he had before. Their horses had served him well in his travels. He straightened in the saddle, peering through the thinning trees toward one of the customs gates of Paris. A bonfire burned high on one side, and several armed peasants warmed their hands by it. It would not be long now. Soon his report would be in the Assembly's hands, and he could settle down to consider his next mission, a far more difficult mission than the one he had just completed.

Katrina's face rose in his mind for the thousandth time, vibrant enough to send waves of guilt washing over him. He recalled a hundred hateful scenes from before his trip to Turin. How many times had he spit hatred at her when she deserved only love?

There was no doubt that Katrina hated him now, and that he had engendered that hate in her heart. He had acted atrociously—practically raping her then throwing her off like a whore. Chauncey had spoken the truth when he'd said he doubted Katrina would ever speak to Rafe again.

Rafe cursed loudly. The sound drew the attention of the soldiers at the gate.

"Who goes there?" One of the soldiers waved his musket toward the dark rider.

"A *citoyen*, like you," Rafe replied wearily. "Rafael Beaulieu, *citoyen*. I've come a long way."

"Beaulieu? If you be Beaulieu, then you have papers that say so."

Rafe reached into his *redingote* to pull out his traveling papers.

"Now, draw your hand out slow, else this musket might slip and let loose a bullet for you, *citoyen.*"

Rafe lifted his free hand and waved the papers. "Easy, *citoyen*. I didn't come all the way across France with the royalist dogs at my heels to be killed at the gates of Paris. Here are my papers. I assure you they're all in order."

The guard approached Rafe carefully, snatching the papers, then moving to the fire. "You may pass, Beaulieu," he said when he returned, the musket now propped on his shoulder. "Sorry about this. You know we have to be careful."

"I'm sure," Rafe said dryly, starting for the gates.

The guard walked alongside him. "We have to, sir. We've got to keep the spies out of Paris. We inspect everyone's papers and write down their name, occupation, and where they're living. Especially the returning aristocrats, though we haven't had many of those since the first of the year." He pulled on his musket strap.

"All very thorough, *citoyen*," Rafe said, offended at the martial state that seemed to have fallen over Paris in his absence.

"*Oui.* And you can wager we've got someone watching each

aristocrat." The man smiled. "We watch them as carefully as we watch these gates."

A thought nagged at the back of Rafe's mind. He reined in abruptly and stared down at the man. "You say you have a list of all the aristocrats who have entered Paris?"

"Yes, Monsieur. It's nearly twenty pages long now, but—"

"Let me see this list." As the man nodded vigorously and ran off, Rafe frowned. A list of suspects, indeed; as if being an aristocrat automatically meant that one was a suspect. Rafe dismounted stiffly and approached the gates. The guard returned clutching a thick book. Rafe took it and opened it beneath the yellow torchlight.

He wasn't sure what he was looking for until he found it. He stopped. His fingers traced the dried ink, and his heart pounded hard and fast in his chest.

The door crashed open, and Rafe entered the shop like a man possessed, the chill of the late winter wind following him.

Martha hurried to see what was the matter. "What is it? Who is it, here so late—Rafe!" she exclaimed, recognizing his tall, wide-shouldered form. He threw off his *redingote*, dropped it on the floor, and strode to the fire burning low in the hearth. Martha gasped as she caught sight of the bloodied rag around his arm.

"Where is Chauncey, Martha? I must see him immediately."

She ignored him and moved to get fresh water. "Chauncey's out for the night. He'll be back before long. Now, you sit down and let me tend that wound before it gets infected."

"Martha, the wound is the least of my worries." He sighed and lowered his head into his hands. His hair, long and unbound, fell around his lean cheeks. Weariness was etched in every hard, taut line of his body.

"Come, now, Rafe. You look a fright. You must let me tend that wound." Rafe allowed Martha to cut off the rag and wash the slash, now an angry purple. "I have a feeling that you were lucky to return with just this wound," she muttered. "Chauncey and I thought we'd never see you again. Why, we haven't heard from you in months—"

"I was unable to send letters for the past months. I spent most of my time hiding from royalists. Now, please tell me where Chauncey is. I must speak to him."

Martha rose from the floor and carefully folded the dirt-streaked linen. "You can't go and see him now, Monsieur," she said hesitantly, her hands fluttering over her apron. "Don't you worry, he will be back—"

"Martha," Rafe warned.

Her brows drew across her forehead in vexation. "Very well. Chauncey is with Katrina now, if you must know. She has set up a salon in the Faubourg St. Germain, and he is there now, helping her. Which is more than you ever did for the child." Martha cut off her speech and bustled to the back room.

Chauncey with Katrina? Rafe's eyes darkened. Chauncey had certainly wasted no time. Rafe scowled, his fists hardening. When he got his hands on his brother . . .

He shook his head. What right did he have to attack Chauncey? Chauncey had shown Katrina far more justice and compassion than he himself ever had. From the beginning, he had doubted her supposed duplicity. Rafe had seen the glances the two had exchanged while she lived in his shop, he had watched them dance like young lovers around the ink-stained worktables. There was little doubt that a bond had grown between them.

Rage shot, hot and urgent, through Rafe's veins. Katrina was *his,* not Chauncey's.

The fire had died to smoldering embers by the time a hired carriage pulled to a stop in front of the shop. Chauncey's lively whistle filtered through the door as entered. He stopped abruptly at the sight of the man by the fireplace. In a moment, he laughed in surprise and pleasure.

"Well, Rafe. You look like the devil," he remarked, moving toward the hearth. "You may be, for all I know. We thought you were dead." He reached for Rafe's hand.

"You were with Katrina tonight," Rafe said, ignoring the outstretched hand.

Chauncey's smile faded as he removed his manteau and placed it carefully across the opposite chair. "I suppose Martha told you. Katrina has opened a salon in St. Germain. She asked me to help." He shrugged and glanced at Rafe. "What the hell have you been doing? You look like you've spent the past winter in the woods."

"I have."

"You'd better get rid of that beard and put on a few pounds

before you go see Katrina. She'd be frightened to death of you like this, though I doubt if she would be frightened of anything now.'' Chauncey paused to see his brother's reaction. Encouraged, he continued. ''She's changed a lot, Rafe. She's not the same girl who lived here. She's very much a woman now.''

Rafe's lips tightened. ''Whose woman, Chauncey?''

''Her own woman. She has set herself up quite independently.''

''Katrina is in danger here. She's on the Assembly's suspect list. I was told at the gates that she is being watched.'' Rafe rubbed a callused hand over his forehead. ''I think it would be wise if you kept a very close eye on her. I have only been in Paris for a few hours, but I smell fear thick and heavy over this city. Before you tell me anything about what's going on in the Assembly, I can tell you that the city is preparing for war.''

''Yes, that is true. Perhaps we should keep an eye on the future duchess,'' Chauncey said, with an emphasis on *we*. ''I think you'll find it a very enjoyable pastime.''

''You know she will spit fire when she sees me,'' Rafe said curtly. ''This is one mission I delegate to you, at least until I right things with her.'' He frowned. ''I suspect that that won't be an easy task.''

Chauncey's lips quirked. ''Indeed not. She stiffens into granite every time your name is mentioned, my dear brother. But, by the looks of you''—he wrinkled his nose at the earthy scent emanating from Rafe's well-worn breeches—''you've already had plenty of practice in battle.''

A short smile creased Rafe's dark, sun-weathered skin. ''Battle of a different sort, Chauncey.'' His dark eyes flitted wearily to his half brother's face. ''After I have had two days' sleep, three of Martha's hearty meals, and a bottle of brandy, then I'll tell you of Coblenz.''

''You'll make me wait so long?''

''Yes,'' Rafe said shortly. ''Because right now, all I want to hear about, all I want to talk about, is a certain Katrina de Poitiers.''

Katrina perched on the edge of the powder-blue upholstered chair, feigning interest in the conversations that drifted around her. Glancing at the gilded clock on the top of the black-veined marble fireplace, she noticed that Chauncey was very late. And though fashion dictated that he arrive a bit past the hour, this was too much. Vaguely she wondered if he had abandoned her this night.

She smiled to herself. It would be the first night she "ruled" alone in the salon since the day she had opened it, one month earlier. Chauncey had become a fixture, as much as the lush, carpeted floor or the sculpted grisailles adorning the walls. He was probably with his new interest, Daphne d'Haliparte. Still, she missed his infectious laughter.

Remembering herself, Katrina scanned the room. Therese held a small silver tray with glasses of champagne, quickly snatched up by the men attending. It would soon be time to bring out the cold hors d'oeuvres as well as to replenish the champagne. She sighed. She needed at least one other servant to run this salon properly, but all her inquiries had come to naught. It seemed that the people of Paris feared working for a duchess-to-be, even a liberal one.

"You're worrying about your servant, Madame?" the gentleman across from her, Monsieur Bilbot, asked.

"It's only that she is overworked. I do need another, but I have found no one so far." Katrina shrugged, unaware of the effect the movement of those white limbs had on the men around her. "I suspect that many of the people fear working for an aristocrat."

"Perhaps," Bilbot said, musing. "I would watch that girl, if I were you, Madame. She has the face of a revolutionary . . ."

"Well, how silly, Monsieur. Of course she is a revolutionary. Aren't we all?"

Bilbot coughed over his large belly. "Indeed, Madame, but she looks as if she works for one of the more . . . radical factions. She has been rather rude tonight."

"And I apologize. I would dismiss her, but I've found no one else." Katrina's head perked as she heard a tap at the door.

"After the Jacobins' speeches in the Assembly against aristocrats, I'm not surprised it's difficult to find a servant," Bilbot continued persistently. His eyes lingered on her. "If I were you, Madame, I would take great care."

Katrina smiled distractedly and nodded her appreciation, her

eyes darting to the hall. Therese had still not answered the door.
"If you would excuse me," she said, rising from her seat.

In the hallway, she met her servant languidly heading for the
door. "I will answer it, Therese." Katrina cursed under her
breath. Insolent woman! Another tap dissipated her anger, and
she opened the door wide.

"Chauncey," Katrina said, holding out her hand. "You know
you're dreadfully late."

He took the proffered hand and lifted it to his lips. "Dreadfully," he repeated. "I was having a . . . discussion with someone. I quite lost track of the time. You'll forgive me?"

"Of course, but you must save me from the bores that sur-
round me. I've tried to keep your place free of others."

"Now, Katrina, do I hear a hint of cynicism?" he queried,
pinching her chin.

She laughed. "Come now, Chauncey. I don't have to like everyone in my salon," she parried. "Besides, I grow weary of
all this talk about what the king's brothers are doing in Coblenz.
Tonight Monsieur Bilbot announced that Leopold of Austria had
died, which means his son, Francis, will succeed as emperor.
These men have done nothing but speculate all night, and not
one of them knows anything about Francis's politics. Personally,
I think they should take better care of our own king, and then
we wouldn't have all these problems. They treat him abominably!"

"Don't speak too loudly, my dear. Someone may hear you
and suspect you have royalist tendencies."

"Pah!" she scolded. "I'm more of a revolutionary than any
of these men. Come, let us join this group and, perhaps, change
the subject."

Chauncey followed behind, tearing his eyes from the fetching
twitch of her skirt to glance around the salon. There were at
least thirty people present tonight, clustered in small groups
around the room. His brows raised a bit when he saw Madame
Roland and her husband seated at one of the card tables that
stood around the edges of the salon. He pointed the couple out
to Katrina.

"Yes," she noted, a smile spreading across her full lips. "I
am pleased. I guess this is her stamp of approval."

"Maybe. Perhaps she is just inspecting the competition. She isn't nearly as beautiful as you, my dear."

Katrina tapped him with her fan emblazoned with a scene of the fall of the Bastille. "Chauncey, you aren't the most unbiased man. Besides, people don't come here to look at me, they come to discuss politics."

"Don't be naive, my Kat. It's hard to ignore you whenever you're in the room."

Chauncey watched with interest as the color crept up her cheekbones. Tapping him again on the arm, she took her seat near the hearth. A young, angular man leaning against the fireplace began speaking in heated tones to his companion.

"We must fight against the king's brothers—we must go to war against the Austrians. Did you read the arrogant manifesto they sent us from Coblenz last fall? They have been planning an invasion of France for months, and waited only for the winter to pass."

"I agree with you that we must go to war," his older adversary said, leisurely crossing his legs before him, "but let us do it on our terms. You know King Louis is in favor of this battle. He never says as much, but he is eager to have the *émigrés* marching on French soil. That will give him time and opportunity to plan another escape. If he escapes and joins the *émigrés*, then France is doomed. I say, let's take care of the king first, then turn our sights to the enemies on our borders."

"Yes, let's take care of the enemies that remain in France, but not just the king." A third joined the discussion, quickly becoming the center of attention. "First, we should crush the priests that will not take the oath to the constitution, as well as the aristocrats who incite riots against patriots. We should strengthen the country from within and purge it of its diseased limbs; then, healthy, we can battle the Europeans."

A few cheers rose among the men and glasses were lifted in a toast to France.

Katrina smiled behind her champagne glass. "They seem to forget I will be a duchess," she murmured.

Chauncey laughed, nearly spilling champagne on his lace-trimmed cravat.

"Nonetheless," the first man interrupted, eager to regain the attention. "We may not have the time to do all that you say.

Now that Leopold is dead, we can no longer depend on Austria's hesitancy. This Francis, I hear, is young and hot-blooded. Let us crush him in his first battle—''

''There is an aspect you gentlemen are not taking into account.'' The deep voice came from the doorway to her salon.

Katrina's cheeks heated and her hands tightened on the short arms of her chair. Her breath hissed through her teeth.

Rafe leaned against the frame. Tall. Magnetic. His dark hair shone with blue lights, and one lock fell over his forehead. He crossed his arms in front of his chest as he scanned the room.

Katrina's hands tightened still more on the arms of the chair. Through stiff lips she addressed Chauncey. ''Did you know he was in Paris?''

''Yes. He's been here for two weeks. You aren't going to faint on me now, are you, Katrina?''

She pulled her hand away from his, her eyes blazing. ''Faint! How ridiculous.''

''If you grip the arms of your chair any tighter they will crumble,'' he murmured. She lifted her chin and released the chair.

''I was in Coblenz not too long ago,'' Rafe continued, his voice rumbling across the room, sending strange vibrations down Katrina's spine. For a moment she feared she *would* faint and embarrass herself before everyone. ''I have seen the *émigré* army, as well as the Austrian army and the Prussian forces. If they attacked France today, we would be destroyed in a matter of a week.''

''Chauncey,'' Katrina whispered, ''I'll have your hide for not telling me—''

''I thought you didn't care what happened to Monsieur Beaulieu, my dear.'' Chauncey watched the color ebb from her face.

''I don't,'' she said in a voice so low it was nearly unintelligible. ''But it's nice to know where one's enemies are.''

''I would hardly call Rafe an enemy,'' Chauncey replied, a smile playing around his lips. He had never seen her eyes so bright, her cheeks stained such an angry red. The battle to come should be entertaining.

''Why is he here?'' she continued. ''He's the one you were talking with before—the one that made you late, isn't he?''

Chauncey did not deny it.

"I knew it. You both planned this, didn't you? To embarrass me—"

"Quite the contrary, my dear, I encouraged him *not* to come."

Katrina turned to stare again. Tendons stood out in her neck, and a pulse jumped wildly in her throat. "What mischief is he here to perpetrate?" she asked. "Does he plan to embarrass me in my own salon?"

"You'll soon find out," Chauncey said, gesturing to Rafe's tall form as he approached them.

"Chauncey, this conversation isn't finished," she muttered.

As she moved to stand at Rafe's approach, Chauncey's hand stayed her. "Katrina, don't rise. Although he is arrogant, he's not a Prince of the Blood."

She flushed again and settled back. Chauncey was right, of course, but she felt at a disadvantage sitting beneath Rafe's looming frame.

"Mademoiselle," Rafe rumbled, reaching for her stiff hand.

She flinched as his warm fingers wrapped around her own icy ones, and his lips descended upon them. Resolutely, she stiffened her back. She could not lift her eyes above the top of his dove-white breeches. His faint, musky scent wreaked havoc with her senses. She stopped to count how many glasses of champagne she had drunk. Certainly that was what was causing her dizziness.

"Mademoiselle, I am sorry I intruded unannounced, but there was no one at the door." Rafe's voice brushed intimately against her ears.

Katrina cursed herself for trembling so in his presence. Lifting her eyes slowly, she steeled her heart against the devilish lights in his black eyes. Such a brutally familiar face: lean clean-shaven cheeks; lips that twisted up in mockery; eyes that read her very soul.

"My servant, Therese, is not the best," Katrina heard herself saying, her tongue thick in her mouth. "I didn't hear your knock over the conversation."

"Indeed, it seemed quite heated when I arrived." His dark gaze wandered over the stony beauty of her face.

She looked away again, pulling her hand away from his.

"I had heard that your salon was quite popular," Rafe continued, willing her to look at him, to grant him the favor of gazing into her eyes, no matter how cold they were. "Indeed, I notice quite a few delegates here, and Madame Roland in the corner with her husband. I congratulate you." Katrina's head jerked toward his, and one finely arched eyebrow lifted.

"You congratulate me?" A memory, cold as ice, washed over her. "Since when, my dear Beaulieu, have you ever wished me well?"

The dark eyes hardened slightly.

Katrina rose, no longer trusting her own lips. "If you will excuse me, I must see to Therese."

Rafe breathed deeply of Katrina's womanly scent as she passed, then turned to watch her muslin-clad figure march through the salon toward the kitchens. His brother's rumble of laughter lifted to him.

"The cat has sprouted claws," Chauncey remarked.

"I noticed."

"She just unfurled them for you. You'll know when you've felt their scratch. I warned you that your entrance wouldn't be taken well. You should have met her privately."

"Why? So she could tear me apart? At least here she must maintain some kind of civility."

"I never could tell you anything, brother," Chauncey replied, pulling on his fob chain.

"No," Rafe agreed. "You never could."

Katrina re-entered the room, her hair smooth upon her head, her chin tilted high. She carried a tray of steaming pigeon legs in her hand. Rafe watched as she glided gracefully through the knots of guests.

Circe. She was the enchantress Circe, the beautiful, the bewitching. With the power to turn men into swine. He could not tear his eyes from her glowing hair, the curve of her cheek. She bloomed tonight. In Poitiers, she had metamorphosed into the devastating woman he had always known was hiding beneath the elfin, innocent exterior. The vivid, sensuous memories of her body against his overwhelmed him.

"God, I had forgotten . . ." Rafe began, then checked himself. His gaze clung to her.

Chauncey leaned back in the chair, smiling. "If you keep staring at her like that, Rafe, I'll have to call you out."

"She hates me, still. Her eyes are as hard as jade."

"This will prove to be a belligerent match," Chauncey continued. "It will be interesting to see whose pride breaks first."

Rafe scowled slightly. "That should be no contest, my brother. I have more damned pride than . . . than the Comte d'Artois. You should know that by now."

Chauncey just chuckled.

The cold night air rushed over her heated body, lifting the curls from her nape and icing her skin. The muslin provided no protection from the chill, but she ignored the shivers that started in her spine. She walked resolutely into the garden. The night hovered moonless and dark, mercifully hiding the weedy, untended paths that wound unevenly through the small plot. Now that spring had come, small green shoots appeared around the woody stems that twisted aimlessly along the paths. She knew that soon she would have to tend this overgrown garden, but for now she was content in the growth. It reminded her of the wild forests of Poitiers.

Katrina closed her eyes, quelling the sudden urge to run recklessly through the garden. Why was he here? And why was Chauncey so nonchalant about the entire situation? Surely he knew what power Rafe held, how he could ruin her with one well-placed sentence. The swine! Rafe probably awaited her return now, smugly dropping notes of her decadence like acorns among squirrels.

And why couldn't he look old, battle-scarred? Why did he have to enter so straight and tall, his skin smooth, dark, stretched over perfect features? She was only a woman, and not unaffected by his rakish charm. What woman would not respond to the set of his wide shoulders, the large, hard bulge of his upper arm? He was a man. A strong one.

A distrustful one. Katrina shrugged, leaning her head back to face the sky. Such an old wound. Rafe had made her pay—for so long—for a sin she had never committed. Those months in the shop, working for him, answering his summons like a slave. And then the night he took her, took her like he would a prostitute and cast her away just as quickly. The resentment boiled up in her again. She welcomed it. With anger she could fight any battle.

"I didn't come here to argue with these men," Rafe said, rising like a ghost behind her. "I came to see you."

Damn Chauncey, Katrina thought. He had told Rafe of her garden. She would have a word with Chauncey soon enough.

"To see me? What business could we possibly have together?"

"Oh, *ma petite,* we have much business together." *The most important business,* Rafe thought.

"If I had my way, Monsieur Beaulieu, we would never interact again. You've caused me enough grief to last a lifetime."

"I could say the same of you, Katrina," Rafe replied, rolling his tongue over her name possessively. "These past years have been particularly difficult. Why do you think I ran off to Italy and then to the German States, little one?" He stared at her as her eyes widened and fixed on him. "I could not bear to be where your ghost haunted me. I could not face my greatest mistake, my greatest injustice. I returned to do just that."

Katrina stepped back, surprised at this assault. Had he ever spoken to her so gently? A memory nagged at her—a memory of a simpler time, of a quieter time, when they were younger and far more innocent.

Seduction! Of course. This was no return to the Rafe Beaulieu she had known in Poitiers. This was still the distrustful, hateful man who had kept her a slave in his shop. What better way to torture her? Now that she was on her own, not needing him, what better way to bring her under his sadistic wing again but to seduce her?

"Don't mock me. Didn't you have some other child to abuse while I was away? Someone else to accuse of treachery, to treat like a—" Katrina hesitated, swallowing the word *whore.* Rafe's face darkened at her words, and her chin quivered.

"I plead guilty to all charges," he said softly, his gaze stroking her hair. "And though it is quite late, I'm sorry."

Katrina came close to snorting. "After all those months at your shop, all you can say is 'I'm sorry?' What has caused such a change of heart, Monsieur? Are you perhaps in need of money and have come to court one of the few aristocrats in Paris? Or have you had a premonition of death and now you are atoning for your sins?"

Rafe pushed away from the trellis and brushed twigs and bark from his velvet waistcoat. He walked toward her, his gaze unwavering.

Katrina caught her breath. A breeze ruffled the lock that fell over his forehead, then followed to lift the curls from her neck. His eyes imprisoned her own. Their dark, soft velvet held, for once, no hint of hatred.

"I nearly lost my mind the day you left," Rafe said. "I . . . I used to pride myself on my sense of justice." He lowered his eyes in embarrassment, and her heart lurched. "I treated you abominably. I never could think quite straight when you were around."

His nearness was affecting her far more than she liked. "I suppose you expect forgiveness."

"Hardly. I expected your hatred. What I did to you was unforgivable." He searched the stiff lines of her face for a glimmer of softening. Could she have forgotten everything? Could she have forgotten that brief, brilliant spring in Poitiers? "You loved me once."

"I will never let you manipulate me again."

"Never is a long time, *ma petite.*" He pulled her close against him, swiftly but easily. His strength left her no choice. "I won't wait that long."

He bent his head to kiss her rounded mouth. *Sweet texture, ah, sweet, precious love!* He loved this woman, he had always loved her. He coaxed her lips into softness.

Katrina closed her eyes against the gentle, tender touch. Was she imagining it, or were his hands clasping her shoulders in silent restraint? His body trembled slightly against hers, and she spread her fingers against his chest. As he pulled away, her heart cried, *No, don't stop!*

He tilted her chin up with one finger. "We have plenty of time, my love." He pulled her full against his body and cradled her head on his chest. She could feel her heart melting against him, his nearness wrapping silken cords around her soul.

He cannot—he must not seduce me like this—and I must not let him.

Caught off guard, Rafe did not expect the violence of her sudden struggles. She pushed against him, broke his hold, and landed a stinging blow to his cheek. Shocked, he turned to stare down into the fury etched on her exquisite face.

"How dare you!" Her bodice rode dangerously low on one side, and a few curls had escaped from the smooth coiffure. Her blood-red lips curled to reveal small, pearly teeth.

A heartbeat ago he had felt her, warm and vital, against him. His eyes sparkled. She would love him, in time. He had the hope he needed.

"As I said, Mademoiselle, I seem to have difficulty controlling myself around you. Once again, I apologize." His eyes glowed with warm memories. "My aim is simple, little one. You were mine once. I want to make you mine again."

Katrina gaped, shock pushing her over the edge of anger. "I am not the child you tortured before, Rafe. You'll find that you'll have far more difficulty conquering me this time."

He reached to touch her cheek. "I don't want to conquer you."

"Stop! Leave now. Leave me alone."

"Very well." His eyes glittered on her. "I will, until next week. On Saturday I will escort you to Daphne d'Haliparte's ball."

"Like hell!"

"A bit of the peasant comes through, eh?" he teased, laughing. "I'll pick you up at nine o'clock. Dress well."

"You'll be wasting your time."

"Next Saturday. Nine o'clock," he repeated. Bowing formally before her angry form, he strode out of the garden.

The bastard!

Chapter 18

Katrina pursed her reddened lips in the mirror, frowned, and applied a dot of rouge. Her hair cascaded in ringlets over her shoulders. The hairdresser, obviously eager for her patronage, had worked on the golden locks for three hours this afternoon, arranging the lighter, sun-streaked hairs around the deeper golden tresses. The result shone magnificently.

"Very well, Monsieur Beaulieu," Katrina murmured in a honey-coated voice. "Two can play at the game of seduction." She rose from her dressing table with a rustle and swirled before one of the larger mirrors. A half-dozen petticoats whooshed beneath the smooth blue satin trimmed in gold ribbons. Stopping to judge her appearance, she pulled the bodice down an inch more and smoothed the satin over the tight, whalebone corset that thrust her breasts up high on her chest. Blond lace peaked out from under the dress and dripped from her elbows. She spread her fan before her.

"The man's been waiting near a half hour," Therese whined rudely, entering without warning. "He told me to tell you that if you don't come down soon, he'll come up and get you himself."

"Very well, Therese," Katrina said, smiling. "Go back down and tell him that I'll be there momentarily." Her smile deepened. All was working as planned. Rafe had been waiting for thirty minutes and his ire was up. He'd be primed for the sight of her.

It had been a long time since she'd been so dressed up—not since the balls in Poitiers. She looked forward to dancing, but

most of all to capturing Rafe's attention so thoroughly that he
would be hers: mind and soul.

*Then, Monsieur Beaulieu, you, too, will feel the pain of be-
trayal.*

Twirling once more before the mirror, Katrina practiced one
last seductive glance then strode gracefully out of her room.

Rafe toyed with the brandy glass, tapping it against his fingers.
He would give her one more minute to appear before he went
upstairs and carried her bodily to the carriage. His brows lowered and he took a healthy sip of the fine brandy, enjoying the
burn through his throat. The minx! She was toying with him
now, and he didn't like it.

He stood up abruptly, scanning the morning room. The interior reflected Katrina's coloring so well: warm maroon upholstery blended in with the precious shine of the gilt edging the
chairs and the curved feet of tables, and gold-trimmed drapes
hung in front of the high French windows. A fire blazed in the
hearth, and two portraits hung above the mantel. The first was
easily the Duke de Poitiers in younger years; his intense eyes and
trim physique showed an energy Rafe never knew he had possessed. The other painting was of a beautiful woman; she was
so much like Katrina that any doubt Rafe had had about Katrina's
heritage ended.

"My father and my mother." Katrina's melodious voice drifted
from across the room. "My father gave my mother this townhouse before they married."

Katrina demurely spread her fan in front of her bosom. She
waved it a few times, and the breeze lifted soft tendrils from
the long, arched column of her neck. She took advantage of
the diversion to let her gaze linger over the wideness of Rafe's
shoulders, set easy under the dark blue velvet waistcoat.

"Mademoiselle," he said quietly, bowing.

Katrina lifted her eyes from her avid regard of his well-
muscled legs and blushed.

The fire crackled loudly behind Rafe as he straightened to
stare openly at her. The young promise of her coltish, angular
body had come to full, lush bloom. A lithe grace touched her
limbs, and her shoulders rose round and fair above the mounds
of her bosom.

As if sensing his stare, Katrina slowly lowered her fan. Her bodice dipped deeply between her breasts, leaving no doubt as to their authenticity. The lace peeped beneath the bodice, barely hiding what he ached to touch. The satin clung to her sides, down to her tiny waist, where it moved out in flounces to the floor.

"Rafe?" Katrina asked, trying to draw his attention from her bosom to her face.

His eyes danced with reddish lights. "Charming," he said, reaching for her hand.

Katrina pouted. *Just charming?*

Rafe brushed his warm lips over the smooth surface of her hand, then rose to stare more closely at her face. "You overwhelm me, my dear."

"Come now. Overwhelmed by a peasant girl?"

"It wouldn't be the first time," he countered, taking her hand and settling it firmly in the crook of his arm.

She squeezed the hardness of his biceps, and a thrill coursed through her. Quickly, she stifled it. *Tonight,* she swore to herself, *I will be the seducer.* She gripped his forearm with her other hand, pressing her bosom against his side. She raised tilted eyes to his face.

"Are you surprised that I decided to come?" she asked.

His eyes flared at her, at the dip of her bodice and the fruits it nearly revealed. "No." He smiled mysteriously. "If you hadn't come down by now, I would have gone up the stairs and carried you bodily into the carriage, regardless of your attire."

An angry flush suffused her cheeks, and she bit her lip to still her retort. Her hand tightened on his arm. "Well!" she replied, a mite too boisterously. "We'd better be getting to the ball. I am eager to meet this Daphne d'Haliparte."

Rafe smiled wryly, enjoying the view from his height. "Daphne, as well, is eager to meet you," he replied. "But come, the carriage driver must be getting impatient. Your pelisse?" He gestured to the ermine-trimmed cape hanging in the foyer.

She nodded, turning her back to him.

Rafe lay the pelisse across her shoulders. His fingertips brushed her neck, his breath ruffled her hair, and she became suddenly aware of him, his maleness, his strength looming behind her. His fingers toyed in her hair a moment, and she closed her eyes, leaning back.

It's all part of the game, she told herself as she met the resistance of his chest. His hands traveled over her shoulders, down her arms, then around her body, pressing against her midriff. She arched her neck back into the crook of his shoulder.

"You are indeed bewitching tonight, *ma petite,*" he murmured against her ear.

Chills rippled through her body as his breath heated her throat. She released a throaty laugh. "Bewitching, bewitched," she said softly. "What is the difference?" Her legs suddenly weak, she stepped away from him and pulled the soft fur tightly to her chin. She glanced at him from beneath lowered lids. "Shall we?"

She preceded him out into the cool spring air. Her heart pounded far too hard for her taste. She must stay in control, she told herself, opening the cape to allow the air to soothe the sudden heat of her skin.

Rafe opened the carriage door for her, taking her hand firmly in his own and helping her to her seat. He followed, blowing out the lantern on the side of the carriage.

Katrina was too involved in watching the light dance off his lean cheeks to notice. As he tapped the roof with his ivory-handled cane, she lifted her eyes to discover that his face was now swathed in purple shadows, yet the light of the lantern on the outside of the carriage shone brightly on her.

He had the advantage yet again.

"So what brings on such a change of heart, Katrina?" he asked softly, watching the breeze toss her hair into a golden fury.

"Change of heart?"

"Yes. Last week you strike me with your fists, this week you strike me with your beauty, baring your magnificent bosom for my perusal."

"Why—" she stuttered, appalled at his audacity. "You—"

"Do you deny it?" He laughed. "That dress is cut dangerously low, wouldn't you say? Not that I mind, of course. Though I wanted to show you off, I did not mean it quite so literally."

Katrina's rage broke and she tossed her gloves across the carriage at him. "You are an insufferable—"

He lifted a hand to her mouth. "Now, Katrina. A true lady wouldn't say such things." He leaned over to press his lips against hers, then pulled away again, making her gasp. "Then, again . . ." Catching her flailing arms, he dragged her across his lap, her cape falling off her shoulders. "I never did like 'true' ladies."

"Let go of me!"

"Not yet, *petite*," he murmured. "You tempted me too much in that house. If your damned servant hadn't been hovering around the door, I would have done this then—"

His lips claimed hers again. The sweet silkiness of his tongue pressed against her honeyed lips, demanding entrance. Katrina stiffened in his embrace, not prepared for the rush of sensation, for the roughness of his hands on her back, the hardness of his chest against hers, the sweet scent of his breath. Alarms rang in her head like the tocsins of 1789, and she weakly pushed against him.

Rafe lifted his head to stare down into her face, which was captive in the curve of his arm. Sparks emanated from her eyes, but he saw the smoldering light of passion beneath the anger.

"You have not changed," she muttered through kiss-softened lips. "Always forcing yourself on me." She struggled to control the trembling of her body, cursing herself for her own weakness. Unmercifully, his lips lowered to kiss the tip of her upturned nose.

"And you, *petite*, always tempting me. If you play the part of a coquette, you must also accept the consequences." His face hovered only inches above hers.

"Well, then, I'll stop playing the part," she replied tersely, "if you would please stop doling out the 'consequences.' " His teeth flashed above her, and his fingers idly traced the edge of her bodice. She gasped as the rough ends brushed over the most sensitive area.

"Stop!" she demanded. "I should have never come—I should have known that I was only inviting trouble." She swayed against him as the carriage jolted over an irregular stone in the street. He tightened his hold.

"Easy, Katrina," he said. Her eyes blazed a vibrant green, but he ignored their warning, lowering his lips to kiss them closed. Her ebony lashes cast shadows over pinkened cheeks. He pulled her tighter against him, willing her response.

Katrina reluctantly pressed her forehead against Rafe. This

scene was not going *at all* the way she had planned! His nearness was affecting her senses like too many glasses of champagne.

"Please," she said quietly. The velvet pelt of his waistcoat brushed against her bosom, the heat of his skin burned her own. She turned her face away from the scented nook of his throat. "Please, will you let me go?"

"Soon, my sweet," he said gently, "but not just yet. There is something I want from you."

Her eyes fluttered open again, and she searched his face, her gaze following the cleft of his chin up to hard lips, over the perfect, patrician nose, to rest in the blackness of his eyes.

"What?" she whispered breathlessly, afraid of the answer. His muscular arms against her back and beneath her head, and the way he held her against his body added to her confusion, sending ripples of fire through her veins. His eyes mesmerized her. She prayed that he would let her go before she could no longer control the demon he had woken in her.

He did not answer, but instead kissed the rose of her cheek, the hollow beneath her cheekbone, the delicate lobe of her ear. The fire of his lips trailed down her neck to rest in the indentation of her throat. Her head fell back against his arm, and her eyes fluttered shut.

Why not? Why not let him seduce her, let him taste the fruit, she thought vaguely, softening. The rumble of the carriage wheels seemed suddenly very quiet. The horses' hooves beat out a rhythm that matched her heart, and the sway of the carriage lulled her. Unconsciously, her ungloved hand lifted to his hair. She spread her fingers in its thickness.

Rafe groaned. He tasted the smooth, perfumed skin of her chest, rising over the upthrust mounds of her breasts. He felt the hardness of her nipples beneath his chin and rubbed against her. Her body flinched, her hand tightened on his head.

"Katrina," he murmured, lifting his head to hers. "I had forgotten how sweet your skin tastes." He rubbed his shaven cheeks against her. His fingers teased the edge of her bodice. "Let me . . ."

Katrina's eyes flew open as he pushed her breast above the restraint of her bodice. Her hands tightened on him as his lips lowered to claim the taut peak. She groaned as her blood heated to a fever pitch, and she arched, wildly, in his arms.

Rafe burned for her. He had wanted only to prove that he was not a boy to tease. He had vowed never to take Katrina again without words of love between them. But once he enfolded her softness in his arms, he lost all control. He had to touch her, to taste her, to make her want him as he wanted her.

Katrina sighed at the sparks that heated her body. Rafe's dark head bent on her chest, and his hair brushed her neck. She knew that she should push him away, that she should stop this madness, but his touch intoxicated her.

Remember the night when he used you like this, then tossed you away like a whore.

Anger surged, icing the passion racing in her blood. Of course. That was what he wanted. He wanted her again, wanted to abuse her, to toss her off like a worn coat. She pushed him away.

"Let go of me!" she cried, pummeling him with her fists. Off balance, Rafe released her and she fell with a hearty bump on the floor of the carriage. Flushed, confused, she lifted herself up and moved to the opposite end.

"Katrina . . ." he said softly, his deep voice rumbling in her ears. "What—"

"No!" she cried, frantically adjusting her bodice to cover her shame. She lifted trembling fingers to smooth her curls back into place. The cool air rushing through the windows dried the memory of his kisses and left cold spots over her bosom. She snatched her pelisse and covered herself. "I know what you want from me. You will not have it." She tried frantically to adjust her clothes and control the beating of her heart. "You took me once in anger and tossed me away like refuse. That won't happen again."

Rafe moved toward her through the purple shadows. She held out a white hand to stop him.

"Katrina, it isn't what you think," he said, the power of his own passion still pounding in his head. He reached out, but she slapped away his hand. The carriage stopped abruptly, and they were swathed in silence.

"All I wanted from you, *petite,* was a response." He could not help the smile that spread mischievously over his face. "It seems I got it."

* * *

"My goodness, I'd say Daphne and Katrina hit it off famously," Chauncey remarked. "They have barely left each other's side all night."

Rafe drained his fourth brandy and placed it loudly on the sill of the nearest window. "Except when Katrina's dancing with some doting boy," he said, watching her as one of the guests asked her to dance.

"It's the oldest trick in the world, Rafe. I'm surprised you don't recognize it." Chauncey clicked his tongue. "She can't possibly like those fops. Can't you see she is trying to make you jealous?"

"Well, she's succeeding. I'm jealous as hell, though I'll kill you if you tell her."

"Come now, Rafe. You know me better." He eyed his brother speculatively. "What happened at her house that has you so tense and has her flirting like a courtesan?"

"It's very simple, Chauncey. The woman hates me, and is wreaking her revenge the one way she knows how. She wears a dress cut down near to her waist, thrusts herself at me in a way I cannot resist, and then, once at the ball, does the same to every lecherous idiot in the crowd." He snatched another glass from a passing servant.

Chauncey's brows lifted and he suppressed an amused smile. "Somehow I know there's more to it than that, but I won't press. Look, here comes Daphne." Chauncey moved to greet their hostess, kissing her hand and exclaiming over her fine dress and the color of her eyes.

"Hush, Chauncey," Daphne admonished. "You grow wearisome." She softened her words with a smile. "Besides, I have come to speak to your friend."

"It's because he's taller that he gets all the women," Chauncey murmured into Daphne's ear. "But that says nothing for other parts—"

"Chauncey!" Daphne exclaimed with a laugh, stopping the ribald comments that were sure to follow. Her gaze slipped to Rafe. "Mademoiselle Poitiers is charming, Monsieur Beaulieu. I'm pleased you brought her."

"So are most of the guests."

"Now, don't be so harsh on her! You have been, you know. She's so angry at you right now, she's near to bursting."

Rafe tore his eyes away from Katrina's graceful dance to turn to Daphne. "Katrina is perpetually angry at me, Mademoiselle. Hasn't she told you?" He lifted his glass to his lips.

Daphne laughed again, her violet eyes sparkling with secrets. She lifted a hand to her dark hair, tucking in a loose curl. "How foolish you two are," she began. "She hates you no more than you hate her. It is foolish pride that keeps you apart."

"I don't see that this is any of your affair."

"No, it isn't," Daphne agreed lightly. "But I absolutely couldn't let the evening pass without telling you this." Her dimpled smile faded into seriousness. "Don't push her too far, my dear Beaulieu. She has a spine of steel that will break before it bends. Do you understand?"

Rafe's eyes glittered strangely. "I am intrigued, Mademoiselle. How could you possibly find so much out about the dear duchess-to-be in such a short time? You've only known her for a few hours. I've known her for years."

Daphne chuckled again. "I pride myself on being an outstanding judge of character, Monsieur Beaulieu," she replied, turning away to take Chauncey's hand. "Mademoiselle Poitiers is a gem. Don't be a fool and lose her."

Rafe cursed beneath his breath, searching for Katrina's fair head among the crowd. After leaving the carriage, she would not tolerate his presence, and she held herself so stiffly he feared she would break if he touched her. She had found a kindred soul in Daphne and soon excused herself. Rafe had seen her only twice since then, both times in the arms of another man.

The wench! *He* was her escort this evening. Pride prevented him from forcing his attentions on her, but if he saw her once more, laughing easily with some other doting suitor . . .

He moved out of the shadows and into the thick of the ball. He would find her and claim at least one dance. He would show her the difference between a man and the weak boys she had chosen for the evening.

Rafe picked Katrina easily out of the sea of swirling couples, for her hair shone brightly under the glittering chandeliers. He leaned negligently against a column, but his hands tightened into fists. A tall, burly man was holding her far too closely.

They waltzed gracefully through the crowd, her laugh drifting over the strains of the violin, teasing Rafe. He calculated their path, waiting for them to swing by his side of the ballroom.

"Beaulieu?" A portly man stared quizzically at Rafe's darkened face. "Beaulieu, that is you! Where in God's name have you been for the past year?"

"Monsieur Monsteiul," Rafe replied curtly. "I should have guessed you would be here. You never seem to miss a party."

The older man chuckled, the brandy sloshing close to the rim of his glass. "Course not. But you didn't answer my question. I haven't seen you in—Lord, it has been so long I can't remember." His gray-streaked eyebrows lowered between his eyes. "What have you been doing, eh?"

"Just off on business."

Monsteiul's face broke into a smile. "Business, my ass!" he replied loudly, drawing the wide-eyed attention of several ladies, who moved nervously away. "I bet you were off with some filly. You always did have a way with the fairer sex."

Rafe smiled, his eyes traveling over the dancers again, searching for Katrina. "Not always," he said ruefully.

Monsteiul followed Rafe's gaze. "What a goddess!"

"Yes, she is."

"Now I see. I was correct: there is another woman. She's stunning, Rafe. Have you lent her out yet?"

Rafe turned hard eyes to the corpulent man. "You will mind how you speak about the lady," he said harshly, his eyes hard as flint.

Monsteiul backed away, holding up a reddened hand. "Now, now, Beaulieu, no offense meant. She's quite a beauty, that's all—"

"That's quite enough, Monsteiul. Unless you want to be called out for that remark, I suggest you retract it."

"Yes, yes of course. I didn't know. I meant no harm—" He bowed effusively and backed away from Rafe.

Rafe moved away from the offensive delegate and again searched for Katrina. He discerned the glow of her hair as she disappeared outside a set of open French windows. His forehead creased.

She was with a man.

Katrina breathed deeply of the fresh summer air, knowing that the movement drew Robert's attention. She reveled in his stares.

"It was so hot in there," she commented, running a hand lightly over her brow. "The air feels good."

"We could go deeper into the garden. Mademoiselle d'Haliparte has the most intricate garden in the area. I've heard that her gardener has also done work, years back, for the royal family."

Katrina smiled politely. How quickly this man bored her. "Yes," she agreed bravely. "Let's find the wisteria. I can smell it from here."

She followed the brick paths into the darkness. The thick vines clinging to the trellises muted the music drifting from the French windows, allowing the night sounds to reign: the call of a nightingale, a swish of muslin as a lover's cove was found, silken slippers gliding over smooth stone. She heard Robert's heavy step following her, and she quickened her pace, hoping he would get lost among the paths. She had wanted Rafe to see her with another man, but this one had proved to be such a bore.

Finding a wrought-iron bench, Katrina sat down demurely, pulling off her gloves and placing them neatly beside her. Although Rafe had hid in a dark corner of the ballroom most of the night, Katrina had felt the incessant heat of his gaze. She smiled. Perhaps her plan was working, after all.

Robert emerged from the brush, his face florid even in the dim starlight.

"Oh!" she exclaimed. "I thought you'd gotten lost."

"Your hair is like a beacon, Mademoiselle. I followed its light to you." Robert reached for her hand and planted a wet kiss on its palm. Katrina flinched as his tongue flickered over it.

"Robert, please! I didn't come out here for you to—"

He lunged for her, pulled her against his large body, and forced her head back with wet lips.

Katrina screeched. Pummeling his back with her fists, she finally managed to push him away. "How dare you!" she said breathlessly.

"Katrina, Katrina, do you know what you do to me?" He knelt at her feet.

She turned to his open, pleading face, wiping his taste from her lips. She pulled at her skirt, trying to loosen his hold on the silk. "Get up, Robert. Stop pawing at my dress."

"I'm sorry, Katrina. You don't understand. You are so . . ."

He swallowed. "So incredibly beautiful, I couldn't help myself—"

"Robert, please! You are embarrassing me."

"Please, tell me that you forgive me, my heart—"

"Yes, yes, I forgive you!" she cried, finally freeing her skirt from his hands. "Now please, Robert, get up and control yourself."

He rose to his feet and sheepishly turned away. "I—I will make it up to you, Mademoiselle," he said, stronger now. "It won't happen again—"

"No, it won't," she agreed flatly, adjusting her bodice.

As Robert turned once again to her, his hair tossed and his mouth slack, Katrina realized how young he really was. She bit her lip in remorse. She had thought he was at least thirty, but now he looked no older than herself.

"Will you please attend the Brussiers' salon with me next week?" he asked.

Katrina smiled slightly, feeling guilty for using him. She certainly had been a Jezebel tonight.

"I'm afraid Katrina will have to decline that invitation."

Katrina whirled around. Rafe stood at the turn of the path, a cheroot burning between his fingers. He watched them through amused eyes.

"I think that is for the lady to decide," Robert replied, suddenly rising straight and firm.

"The lady will decide the same, I am sure."

"I wouldn't be so sure of that, Monsieur!" she snapped, then bit her tongue. Although she wouldn't let Rafe get the best of her, she certainly didn't want to go anywhere with Robert.

"The lady, you see, is here under my escort," Rafe explained, amused at Katrina's crestfallen expression. "Yes. My escort."

Katrina shrugged and tossed her head. "And what does that matter?"

Robert moved away and bowed to Rafe. "My sincere apologies, Monsieur. Had I known—"

"I suggest you leave now. The lady and I have things to discuss."

When Robert had disappeared into the darkness, Katrina stepped toward Rafe, then away as he moved closer.

"What was the meaning of that?" she snapped, her hands rising to her hips. "What right do you have—"

"Don't talk to me of rights!" Rafe exclaimed. "I hear it each day in the Assembly, in the journals. When it concerns you, I have every right, my dear. I even have the right to call him out for what just transpired."

Her eyes glittered behind the dark netting of lashes. "And you would, wouldn't you?" she replied. "You'd almost enjoy killing that boy—"

"Ah, you admit it, then," he said, drawing on the cheroot. "You admit that he was just a boy."

Katrina turned away from him. "I didn't notice until we were out here. He is no older than I am."

"He is a few years older," Rafe corrected. He threw the end of the cheroot on the ground and moved to Katrina. Her back stiffened at his approach. "Relax, Katrina. I won't throw myself upon you." He chuckled. "That's happened once too often this night."

Weary of battling with him, Katrina's shoulders slumped and she sighed. For some strange reason, she believed that Rafe would leave her alone. She flinched slightly as his warm hands gently caressed her cold shoulders.

"You are cold," he stated. His fingers left her, and then returned, wrapping his waistcoat firmly around her.

She pushed her chin into it. His musky scent rose from its folds, not unpleasantly. A nightingale, oblivious to their presence, began to sing in the tree beside them. They lifted their heads to listen to the sweet melody piercing the dark silence of the night.

Rafe lifted his hands to her shoulders, gently massaging them beneath the waistcoat.

"In Poitiers there were hundreds of nightingales in the forest," Katrina murmured, shutting her eyes.

"Hundreds?" Rafe's breath ruffled her hair.

"Umm," she replied. "Hundreds. When I was a child I used to slip into the woods and sit very still beneath the trees to listen to them. The other girls were afraid, but I didn't mind. I liked being alone with them. It was as if they sang for me."

"I remember those nightingales," he said. "I remember one particular night in that same forest . . . one very special night."

"You aren't angry at me for luring Robert out here?" she said swiftly, changing the subject.

"Furious." Rafe moved away from her. "If you hadn't pushed him away I would have torn him off of you myself."

Katrina turned to him, her eyes widening. "You mean—you mean you saw all of that?"

Rafe's smile shone as he nodded.

"Even, even when he was—"

"Everything," Rafe replied. "Do you think I'd let you out of my sight with another man?"

Katrina burst into laughter, lifting her hand to cover the sound.

"I love when you laugh like that," Rafe said abruptly.

Her laughter stopped and she stared at him.

"You used to laugh like that with Chauncey all the time," he said. "I always hoped that I would be able to make you laugh like that with me."

Katrina smoothed her skirt and darted quickly to the wrought-iron chair, where her gloves still lay. Pulling them to her breast, she avoided Rafe's eyes.

"We should get back to the ball," she said quietly, as his dark eyes probed her face with disturbing intensity. "If we stay out any later, people will begin to wonder."

"Come here," he murmured. "Come to me for a moment now, while there is still calm between us."

His gaze invited her and he lifted one hand. Her heart tumbling in her breast, she stared at the hand, at the fine lace dripping from his wrist. Slowly, she raised her eyes to his face again. Her feet moved of their own accord.

He caressed her cheek, moving a thumb over the fine, high cheekbone. Her lips trembled.

Rafe's dark eyes held secrets, loving secrets, soft, dark secrets whose wings brushed her now. His gaze touched her face tenderly, slipping over each sweet curve, the arch of her nose, the fall of a wayward lock. Their lips merged, sweetly, and this time Katrina did not pull away. He stroked her nape, moving against her warmly, and she lifted languid arms to touch him, to feel the rough matting of hair beneath his fine linen shirt.

A thousand memories drifted, unhurried, through her mind. How many kisses had they shared? So many in passion, in anger, in punishment. None had tasted so sweet as this one that continued so gently. Rafe pulled her lightly against him, and her body thrilled to the arms that tightened around her.

Reluctantly, he released her lips. One hand toyed with her curls while another held her easily against him. Her eyes fluttered open. Another nightingale joined the first, and their song rose above them.

"Is that the kiss of a man who wishes you harm?" Rafe murmured above her, running his fingers through the fiery blond curls. "Or is that the kiss of a man who seeks your forgiveness . . . and your love?"

"N-no," Katrina stammered, confusion filling her eyes. "I mean . . ." Her body stiffened and she pulled away. Bereft of the heat of his body, she shivered and wrapped her arms more tightly around his waistcoat. The moment had passed.

"We must get back to the ball," Katrina said finally, his question humming in her head. "I'm afraid my reputation will be sorely compromised."

Rafe smiled in the dark. "That will just bring more men to your salon, *petite.*"

"Yes," she agreed, confused.

"Come. We have a whole night ahead, and I have not danced one dance with you. I am eager for a waltz."

Katrina smiled, bemused, still trying to sort out Rafe's strange words, the surges of emotion that wrestled in her breast.

As they emerged from the garden into the warmth of the ballroom, Daphne's eyes sparkled a deep indigo. "There you two are! You've been gone so long I thought you might have left."

Katrina blushed. "I danced too much. I needed some air."

"But she is not finished dancing," Rafe corrected. "She has promised me a waltz."

"Yes, I did," she confirmed.

Daphne's gaze jumped back and forth between Rafe's dark, smiling face and Katrina's flush. "Well, you mustn't dance just yet," she interrupted. "There's someone you must meet, Katrina."

"Oh, no," Rafe insisted, blocking Daphne's approach. "You've had her most of the night. The rest is mine."

Daphne stared at him, and burst into laughter.

"What's all the fuss?" Chauncey asked, moving behind her and pulling on one of her raven curls.

"It seems Rafe has claimed Katrina for the rest of the evening," Daphne explained. "He won't let me introduce her to anyone."

"A waltz," Rafe demanded, gesturing to the orchestra. Bowing slightly to Katrina, he led her onto the floor.

Daphne's eyes shone as she watched them.

"It seems a truce has been called," Chauncey remarked.

"Indeed. Far more than a truce." Daphne arched her neck to watch the stunning couple. "They were in the garden for a long time."

"I'll never understand Rafe. One minute he's cursing her, the next practically making love to her."

"It's called love, dear Chauncey," she said. "Or have you forgotten about love?"

Chauncey watched her as she moved haughtily away into the crowd. *Oh, no, sweet Daphne*, he thought sadly. *I haven't forgotten about love.*

Katrina's head still swam from the kiss in the garden when Rafe pulled her out to dance. Only his hard arm around her waist and the strength of his hand in hers brought her back to the present. Her gaze fluttered up to meet his.

"You haven't forgotten how to waltz, have you?" he teased.

"Of course not. But it's been so long since we . . ."

"Do you remember our last waltz?" he asked, pulling her along in the first steps. "You danced like an angel."

"I seem to remember that you were very angry at me that night."

His face clouded and he swung her around, pulling her against his body. "Yes," he said through tight lips. "I had forgotten."

I wish I could, Katrina thought, frowning. *I wish I could forget your hateful words, the words that made scars I can still feel now, years later. I wish I could forget your distrust, your hatred. I wish I could forget all of it, all of it except our time in the forest of Poitiers. . . .*

They danced in silence, the memories spoiling the music's magic. Rafe loosened his hold on her, and they swirled in stiff grace, their eyes locked over the other's shoulder. He released a ragged sigh.

"That was a very long time ago, Katrina."

"Yes."

Damn! Rafe's arms tightened around her. *What can I say to erase those bitter memories?* He glanced down at her. Her pale face seemed stony in the golden light. The music stopped, and when she looked up at him, he lost himself in the pained depth of her green eyes.

"I think you'd better release me before we make a scene," she whispered. Rafe planted a light kiss on her forehead, forgetting for a moment where they were.

"Rafe!" she exclaimed. "Do you want people to talk?"

"I never paid much mind to idle chatter," he said, bowing to her. "Besides, I couldn't resist."

"Finally!" Daphne's imperious voice rose. "I hate to break up such an intimate tête-à-tête, my dears, but I must introduce the future duchess to my new guest." She bustled to Katrina's side and pulled her away from Rafe. "Come, Katrina, this man has been asking about you. He says he knew you before the revolution—"

Katrina's gasp stopped Daphne's reckless pace across the length of the ballroom. Still, he came nearer, that insolent, icy gray stare pinning her to the spot.

The Marquis de Noailles smiled, his face twisted in that terrifying, familiar grimace. He reached for her hand. "My dear, lost bride."

"Marquis . . ." Her voice sounded weak, high, strange to her own ears. "How—Why . . ."

"If you touch her, Noailles, I shall kill you on the spot." Rafe's tall form stepped between Katrina and the wiry, barrel-chested aristocrat. A muscle moved stiffly in his cheek.

Astonishment flickered briefly over the marquis's face, then just as quickly disappeared. He leaned back and glared insolently at Rafe's tall form. "Well, Monsieur Beaulieu. I see you've eluded the mercenaries we sent after you." He shifted his weight, his eyes hardening to unyielding silver. "How unfortunate."

"Yes, unfortunate for you and the king's brothers," Rafe said. "You are either very brave or very stupid to return to Paris, Marquis. The Assembly no longer looks favorably on returning *émigrés.*"

"I have been in France since last fall, Beaulieu. Since before the New Year's deadline. Would you like to see my papers?"

Rafe's dark eyes narrowed. He knew that the Marquis had been in England until February of 1792, for that was when he had gone to Coblenz and discovered Rafe in the *émigré* court. Rafe did not doubt the marquis had papers that said otherwise. In the Assembly, as in the *émigré* court, men could be bribed.

"Papers won't tell me anything that I don't already know. I know you are a treacherous aristocrat, and mean only harm to France." Rafe reached back to touch Katrina. Her small hands, so cold, curled around his wrist. His heart surged with the need to protect her. He pulled her close against his side. "I also know you mean only ill to Mademoiselle de Poitiers."

"Certainly not. I've wanted nothing but good for Mademoiselle. Tell him, my dear. Tell him how I saved you from your stepmother's whippings."

"For a worse fate," she whispered, her throat dry from the shock of seeing her nemesis. Rafe's fingers tightened around hers.

"I think she has made herself quite clear, Noailles." Rafe lowered his voice to a dangerous softness, and Katrina felt his muscles stiffen beneath the velvet pelt of his waistcoat.

The marquis's gaze never wavered from Rafe's. He did not seem to notice the curious, hostile stares of the other guests. Rafe's comment linking the marquis to the king's brothers had been made on purpose: now everyone would suspect the marquis of treachery against France. The king's brothers were actively planning a campaign and were rumored to be gathering in Belgium, near the borders of Alsace.

Katrina shivered as the marquis's gaze locked with her own. *What does he want?* As soon as she formed the question, the answer rang loud in her ears: *Me. He wants me.*

The marquis bowed suddenly. His eyes lingered on Rafe, and Katrina gasped at the hatred that sizzled between them. Frightened, she pulled on his arm.

"Rafe . . ."

"Hush, *mon ange.*"

The marquis's eyes blazed when he heard the endearment. He turned his stare toward Katrina, and her heart pounded furiously in her chest.

"Get your filthy eyes off her, Noailles—" Rafe growled.

"Gentlemen, please!" Daphne, standing nearby, wanted to

break the intensity of the hostility that had erupted between the two men. She fluttered her fan before her face, staring at one, then the other, wondering how she could diffuse it before they began to fight on her polished floors. "Please, Messieurs, surely there is a better time and place—"

"Of course, Madame." The marquis bowed toward Daphne and smiled. "I hope you will not think me rude if I leave a bit early?"

"No, Monsieur, no, that will be quite all right—"

"Then I bid you *au revoir*."

"*Adieu*, Marquis," Rafe corrected. "I suggest you leave Paris before the Assembly seeks you out for your crimes."

The marquis turned on his heel and left. Katrina's hands tightened on Rafe's arm, but he did not relax until he saw the marquis's black figure pass through the open doors of the ballroom. Only then did he turn to her.

Rafe's eyes, only moments ago as hard and black as onyx, grew warm as he stared at Katrina. He touched her cheek.

"You are so pale, *petite*. He frightened you."

"I was just surprised, that's all," she explained, lowering her gaze. "I haven't seen him since I escaped from Poitiers."

"You have nothing to fear from him, do you understand?"

Katrina's green gaze clung to his. Tears stung her eyes, and she swore beneath her breath for allowing her weakness to show.

"Come." Rafe pressed her hand against his arm and led her through the ballroom to a dark corner near the table of hors d'oeuvres. He sat her down on the wide windowsill and placed a crystal glass of brandy in her hands. "Here. Drink."

"But—"

"All of it."

Katrina did as she was told, wincing as the fiery liquid burned a trail down the back of her throat. She coughed once and Rafe laughed softly.

"There. Now there's color in those cheeks."

Katrina blushed, adding more. Rafe sat beside her, pushing her skirts out of the way so he wouldn't crush the satin. He reached for her hands, warming them between his own.

"Why is he here, Rafe?" Katrina met his steady gaze.

"You nearly fainted when you saw him, didn't you?"

She smiled, and the golden light from the candles anchored

to the wall reflected off the curve of her cheeks. "Would it be a sign of weakness if I said yes?"

"No, love, it would be honesty." He entwined his fingers with hers, and wondered at the smallness of her hand. "You know why he is here, Katrina. There is only one reason he would risk so much."

She could not speak. The terror gripped her by the throat and made her dizzy.

"Katrina, love." Rafe reached for her and pulled her against him, pressing her close enough so her head rested in the crook of his neck. Her hands flattened against his chest. He felt a tremble ripple through her, and he kissed her brow tenderly.

"Will he always torment me, Rafe? Will he always find me, no matter where I run?"

"He will never harm you. That I promise you, Katrina." Rafe took her shoulders and pushed her away from him. "Do you hear me? I swear to you—the Marquis de Noailles will never hurt you."

Katrina gazed at Rafe through tear-filled eyes. *I shouldn't trust you, not you of all men.* She lifted a hand to brush a tear from her cheek, but Rafe pulled out his handkerchief and wiped it himself. *Why do I feel so safe here in your arms?* she wondered.

"I'll send someone to watch your house," Rafe said quietly, "though it may not be necessary. If I have my way, the Assembly will arrest him under the rules of the New Year's resolution."

"It will be too much trouble—"

"Nonsense." Rafe released Katrina's arms and leaned back against the wall. "There is another option, one that will be even less trouble."

"I am frightened to death of him. Tell me what to do."

"Come live with me."

Katrina's eyes widened. In the darkness, his face was all shadow, but from the set of his profile, she could tell he was serious.

"I couldn't!" she gasped, lifting a hand to her chest and pressing it against the lace that rimmed her bodice. The anger started again, strengthening her. "Absolutely not! Rafe, if I—"

"Katrina, you're in far more danger than you think, and not only from the marquis." Rafe shook his head. He knew he shouldn't tell her about what he had discovered at the customs gates; it would only make her more frightened. But if he could convince her to stay with him in the shop, he could protect her. Moreover, he knew he could win back her love. He slid along the sill until their legs pressed against one another. "I don't want to frighten you, but if it will convince you to come and stay with me, then I'll have to—"

"No!" Katrina's eyes flashed with anger. "Don't tell me anything. I won't come and stay with you like . . . like a woman of the streets of St. Denis!"

"I won't lie to you. I want you under my roof for more than one reason, but the most pressing reason is your safety. Katrina, your name is on a list of suspects gathered by the Assembly."

"Suspects? Why am I a suspect?"

"Because you're an aristocrat. You might be a returning *émigré*, and to them, all returning *émigrés* are suspect."

"That's foolish. I made it quite clear at the customs gates that I was living in Poitiers—"

"Love, listen to me." He reached for her shoulders and squeezed her. "You've read the journals: you've heard how vicious the Jacobins in the Assembly have become. They want to wage war against the *émigrés* in Coblenz and their borrowed Austrian armies. How long do you think it will be before the Assembly turns on the aristocrats living in their own city?"

"But I'm a revolutionary. . . ." She shook her head, lifting a hand to press against her temple. "This is too much."

Rafe brushed his fingers against her cheek. Her eyes opened, and in the lucid depths he saw fear and hesitation and doubt. He released her and stood.

"Just tell me you will think on it, Katrina."

"Think on it?" She nodded. "Yes, yes I will think on it."

Rafe smiled, a wide, devilish, bright smile. *A victory. A small one, but a victory nonetheless.* "Come then, Katrina. Dance with me. Let us seal our bargain."

The sliver of the moon shone through the western windows by the time Rafe wrapped Katrina's pelisse around her drooping shoulders. She buried her face in the fur. Rafe helped her into the carriage and then followed, seating himself opposite her, so close that their legs intertwined. Katrina felt too tired to protest. Not that she wanted to protest. Rafe had stayed at her side since the incident with the marquis, charming her like she had rarely been charmed. She sighed. The meeting must have addled her, for she couldn't seem to dredge up the anger, the distrust, that she should have against this enigmatic man.

"Did you enjoy the ball?" Rafe asked.

"Yes." She gazed toward the eastern sky as it slowly lightened to indigo. "Daphne is charming."

"Chauncey thinks so, too."

"Do you think so?" she asked. "He flirted with her just as he flirts with any woman, even me—"

"Which is probably why Daphne is so oblivious to him. She's heard Chauncey's outrageous compliments used on too many other women."

"Oh, Daphne isn't so oblivious," Katrina said mysteriously, looking back to the window. "She mentioned Chauncey's name more than once during the evening. In fact,"—Katrina hesitated—"I think she was relieved to see you with me. With all the time Chauncey has spent at my salon, I think she was a bit jealous."

"She wasn't the only one speculating," Rafe said roughly. "Chauncey has spent an inordinate amount of time in your salon."

"Jealous, Rafe?"

"Yes."

Katrina's smile faded, and she pulled her hand away. Her gaze flitted to the passing scenery, but not before Rafe read the doubt plainly in her eyes.

The horses' hooves clopped loudly on the street in the still spring morning, echoing on the stones of the houses lining the route. Katrina shut her eyes and dozed quietly, letting the boat-like sway ease her into slumber.

Rafe watched her quiet features. Her hair tossed about her face, and her lips were parted in slumber. He ached to reach out and wind a silken strand around his finger, but he feared waking her. She was so beautiful. The taut pain that edged her features in waking disappeared in repose. He wondered if that pain came only when she looked at him.

The carriage eased to a stop in front of Katrina's townhouse, and the driver waited patiently as Rafe shook her awake. Her eyes fluttered open, confused.

"Home so soon?"

"Yes, *petite*. We're home." Rafe helped her out of the carriage, wrapping his fingers around her slender waist. Her hands fell to his shoulders. Pulling her pelisse tightly around her, he walked her into the townhouse. As he closed the door behind him, she turned to him nervously.

She met his eyes and her heart thumped painfully. The evening hadn't turned out the way she'd planned. Katrina hadn't expected Rafe's tenderness. She shook her head. The hour was late—or early—and she'd been awake far too long. Tomorrow she would examine this evening and answer the questions he had posed to her.

"Thank you for taking me to the ball, Rafe," she said, draping her pelisse across the balustrade. "I haven't had such a fine evening for a long time."

"Is Therese here?"

Katrina hesitated, then walked into the morning room. "No. She takes Sundays off to be with her family."

"You'll need help undressing."

"I assure you that I'm capable of undressing myself."

"Katrina, I have had some experience with undressing women, and I know that it's near impossible to undo all those hooks without some help. And as for the undergarments—"

"Rafe, please!" She moved deeper into the room. A bluish light diffused through the leaded windows.

"Now, Katrina," he urged. "You know I'm right."

Katrina knew that she could not undress easily, at least not without damaging the garment, but she also knew that she would rather sleep in her whalebone corset until Monday than have Rafe's fingers on her bare skin. She turned and stared at him through tilted, suspicious eyes.

"I can do it myself."

"Come here."

Katrina stiffened into stone, her eyes flashing defiance.

He closed the distance between them in two strides, and his hands moved firmly to her shoulders, turning her back to him. Startled, she lifted her hands to her bodice.

"Rafe!"

His hands locked her in place as they worked swiftly on the river of hooks. His fingers brushed her back as they traveled downward. Just as quickly, he released the ties of her corset, loosening it enough so she could take if off easily. Despite her anger, Katrina sighed as the binding garment loosened around her ribs.

Rafe stayed behind her when the work was done, his fingers running over the laces. She turned to him and pressed the dress carefully over her bosom.

"Are you quite done?" she asked quietly, only a faint note of annoyance in her voice.

"Nearly." He kissed her swiftly, possessively, not daring to linger over her mouth. Grasping her chin, he brought her face up to his. "There will come a time, my sweet, when you will trust me."

Chapter 19

"The Assembly has declared war on Austria." Rafe slammed the heavy door and strode across the shop.

Chauncey looked up from the printer's plate, "Already? You would think they would have enough sense to wait until our troops are ready."

"Sense? What do they know of sense!" Rafe pulled off the top of the brandy decanter and poured himself a liberal draft. "All they know about is words—pretty, florid, useless words!"

Chauncey pushed away from the workbench and lifted his ink-stained apron over his head. Rafe exuded rage as he paced in front of the fire. The amber brandy sloshed dangerously close to the rim.

"Words started the revolution, Rafe—"

"Perhaps, but they cannot fight the Austrians. I have seen their troops, Chauncey. I know their power." Rafe sat down in one of the worn upholstered chairs. He finished the brandy with one swallow and threw the crystal glass into the fire. The flames leaped high and blue. Chauncey poured him another glass and handed it to him silently.

"There were only seven votes against the declaration," Rafe brooded. "Only seven sane men in the entire Legislative Assembly—and all of them mine. How foolish of the old Assembly to rule that their members could not be re-elected to this one. By doing so, they doomed their own constitution to failure." He pulled off his blue waistcoat and tossed it onto the opposite chair. His linen shirt was stained from the long night in the assembly halls.

"Surely they have some plan to defeat the Austrians?" Chauncey lifted Rafe's crumpled coat and folded it neatly across the back of the chair. He watched his half brother's face with concern; it had been days since he'd seen him sleep. Rafe leaned back in the chair and closed his eyes.

"We're going to attack immediately, in Belgium, while the enemy forces are still unsettled. That may be the most sensible idea the fools had: strike now, before the *émigrés* are fully mobilized." Rafe shook his head. "Even so, we can't possibly succeed. Our troops are undisciplined and depleted by desertions. The Assembly has also decided to call for volunteers from each department to come to Paris, but you and I both know the king will never approve of so many troops in this city."

"If the king goes against the Assembly, at this time . . ." Worry creased Chauncey's brow. "There's no limit to what the Assembly may do."

"Legally or not," Rafe agreed. He opened his eyes and fixed a dark, intense gaze on his brother. "I'm worried about Katrina."

Chauncey's lips quirked. "Of course you are. You've done nothing but worry about her since the Marquis de Noailles returned to Paris."

"With good cause, Chauncey."

"I don't know. For a month we've had her townhouse watched, and not once have we seen the marquis, or any other suspicious people. Except for her hideous maid. I wouldn't trust that woman any more than I would trust the marquis."

"There's more reason to worry about Katrina, Chauncey, now that war has been declared." Rafe's frown deepened and he ran a hand through his unruly, unbound hair. "That damned list of suspects that they have—it could be used against her. She's on that list as the Duchess de Poitiers."

"There must be a way you can get your hands on that list. After all, you're a member of the Assembly."

"Don't you think I've already tried that?" Rafe reached over to a small table where several cheroots lay. He picked one up and rolled the thickness between his fingers. "The Jacobin contingent has become very powerful, Chauncey. They seem to have control of that list."

"But surely the name Beaulieu can shake it from them."

"Not anymore, my brother."

Chauncey's chestnut brows disappeared beneath the curls that fell over his forehead. He reached for a taper that stood on the narrow mantelpiece and touched its tip to the flames of the fire. Although the April sun poured through the thick crystal panes of the shop, a chill had permeated the room. He sat on the chair across from Rafe and held his hands out to the flames.

The brothers exchanged knowing glances.

"So it's happened."

"Yes," Rafe mused. "I knew it would happen eventually, but I never expected it now of all times."

"Can't this be kept from the Assembly? After all, they have other events to worry about—the upcoming battle with the king, the war with the Austrians. . . ."

"It's too late, Chauncey."

"What are you going to do?"

Rafe shrugged. "I'm going to continue my work as always. I fear only for Katrina." He leaned forward. "You must promise me you'll protect her, should anything happen to me."

"You're going to tell her, aren't you?"

"No." Pain flitted across Rafe's hard features. "If I told her she'd be in more danger than she is now. I must keep this secret to myself."

"Rafe." Chauncey said quietly, "she deserves honesty, not secrecy. If she should find out—"

"If she should find out, then nothing will change, will it? She doesn't trust me now, and she won't trust me then." Rafe's eyes hardened. "But at least she'll be safe."

"And how can you be so sure that something will happen to you? After all, Katrina is on that list of suspects, and no harm has come to her. You're not even on the list."

"Yes, I am. That's why the Jacobins won't let me touch it."

"But they wouldn't dare expose you."

"No, they wouldn't. But I know someone who would."

Chauncey sat back in his chair. "Who has the audacity to implicate you as a traitor to France?"

Rafe smiled wryly. He sipped the last of the brandy and placed the glass on the floor by his feet. "Ironic, isn't it, that the most dangerous man in France can implicate me as a traitor? It's the Marquis de Noailles, my dear brother, who knows my deepest, most insidious secret, and I fear he will use it to destroy not only me, but also the woman I love.''

Katrina clutched the thick velvet curtains. The morning sun shone brightly outside the window of her townhouse, but she could not appreciate the beauty of spring. Her eyes reflected turbulent, disturbing emotions.

When will he get here? she wondered, scanning the length of the Rue de Bac. Rafe had promised to take her outside the city gates for a dinner in the country with Daphne and Chauncey. She closed her eyes. *How good it will be to leave Paris for a day.*

Although it had been nearly a month since she had seen the Marquis de Noailles at Daphne's ball, Katrina knew he would eventually come for her and was only biding his time. Everytime someone knocked at her door, even on the nights of the salon, her heart leaped to her throat. She sighed and closed her eyes.

Paris seethed with mobs since the Assembly declared war on Austria and the *émigrés*. The previous evening, a crowd of red-capped, drunken *sans-culottes* had walked through the quiet street, their tattered pant-legs fluttering around their thin, bony legs. Katrina, alone in the townhouse, had run about snuffing out every candle; she didn't want them to know she was here, for if they did, they might break in. . . .

For the first time, Katrina, seriously considered Rafe's proposal. Perhaps she should stay in his printing shop. Then she would be safe—from the wild-eyed, reckless Parisians and from the icy, methodic scheming of the Marquis de Noailles. She would be safe from everyone—everyone but Rafe.

His words drifted back to her, over the years, over the pain and anger.

I have little to offer you, Katrina, but my protection.

Protection from what?

From everyone but me, for if you choose to come, you will never be safe from me.

How prophetic. Katrina wondered if Rafe remembered those words he had whispered to her in the woods of Poitiers, back when she was younger and so very innocent.

Katrina closed her eyes. She was innocent no more; now she understood the implication of his protection. He would keep her like a mistress. Her breath caught in her throat. He would keep her like a mistress until he tired of her.

A carriage rumbled around the bend and headed toward the townhouse. Pushing away from the window, Katrina shook her head to clear her mind. Why did she dwell on it? She knew she couldn't put herself under Rafe's care—it would tear her apart, and this time there would be nothing left. The wound was still too raw, too tender. But perhaps . . .

Stop! she chided herself. Katrina walked to the gilt-edged mirror by the door and inspected her simple coiffure. Her face was pale and drawn from sleepless nights. She patted her cheeks and smoothed her pink and white striped muslin dress over her fluttering stomach. *A day in the country will do me good,* she thought, *even if that day is spent with Rafe.*

Rafe tapped on the door.

"Good morning, *petite.*"

Katrina's heart tightened. Dark circles surrounded Rafe's eyes, and his skin seemed drawn taut against his features. She'd seen little of him since the ball—he claimed he'd been spending many days in the Assembly. By the look of him, he'd also been spending many nights there, as well.

"You shine like the morning, Katrina," he whispered.

She shrugged prettily, one pink muslin sleeve slipping lower on her shoulder. "It must be the light. I do not feel very rested. It seemed like a mob of peasants spent the entire night in revelry in my front garden."

A strange flicker danced in Rafe's eyes. "You were alone here last night?"

"Of course."

Shaking his head, he closed his eyes briefly, then opened them again. "I'll send another man to watch the house."

"Rafe!"

"It's done." Suddenly, he smiled, and the whiteness of his teeth brightened his face. "Now, I've promised you a day in the country. Come, Chauncey grows restless, I'm sure."

"Yes, he finally has a chance to get Daphne away from her suitors."

The spring burst gloriously around them as they sauntered down the stone-laid path through the front garden. Katrina examined her handiwork critically, noticing the new weeds rising to choke her pink roses and the violets lining the path. The heady mixed fragrances drifted lightly over the grounds and excited the birds nesting in the boughs nearby. Their chirps and warbles mingled with the low buzz of the bees humming around the blossoms.

"Chauncey told me he convinced you to come on this picnic with me so Daphne would agree," Rafe said, glancing down at Katrina's glowing head. Her eyes—so clear, so guileless—shone on him. "I fear that's the only reason you came."

Katrina laughed, a bright, tinkling sound in the brilliance of the spring morning. Rafe's gaze rested warmly on her upturned face.

"Though what Chauncey told you is true, I had my own reasons for coming out with you." Rafe lifted a brow, and Katrina tapped him on the arm with her free hand. "Don't let your thoughts get the best of you, Rafe, my reasons aren't what you think."

"Mmm. That's what I was afraid of." He sighed and reached over to brush a lock of hair from her forehead. "Someday, my sweet, you'll tell me what I want to hear."

Katrina suddenly felt lighthearted, buoyant. She knew she shouldn't let herself flirt with him; it was a dangerous game. But right now she felt like a reckless debutante.

Chauncey half rose out of his seat in the carriage as Rafe handed her in. "Well, Katrina, you look positively delicious today—a virtual pink and white confection!" He bent over her hand.

"Chauncey, you always overdo it," she replied.

He looked up at her with a small scowl. "I think Daphne agrees with you," he said. "She'll be the death of me."

"Chauncey!" Katrina exclaimed, arranging her muslin skirt around her and placing her hat on her lap. "You mean you haven't won her over yet? And you've not been to my salon for the last two weeks."

"Believe me, Kat, I'm trying. But she's a cruel woman, keeping her love from me, her—"

"Chauncey . . ." Rafe warned as the carriage jerked forward onto the cobbled streets.

"Ahem." Chauncey stopped himself and restlessly toyed with

a button on his silver-trimmed blue waistcoat as he searched for words. "She keeps her love from me," he repeated simply.

"Which is probably best for her," Katrina added. "A rake like you—"

"Katrina! You call me a rake?"

"Yes! You forget that I lived under the same roof as you for five months. I know of your amorous adventures—"

"Another cruel woman come to torture me!" Chauncey exclaimed.

Rafe rolled his eyes. "You confuse *cruel* with *smart,* my brother," he remarked. "Daphne is protecting herself from the likes of you."

"And look, the wolf speaks!" Chauncey said. "He'd like to have you think he's the gentleman and me the rake."

"How very silly," Katrina replied, her lips curving into a slight smile as she gave Rafe a sidelong glance.

Chauncey broke into laughter. "It seems the woman knows her foe," he remarked, then glanced out the carriage window at the silent townhouses. "It's so quiet here, unlike the Rue St. Honoré."

"And why is the Rue St. Honoré so noisy?" Katrina asked, fearing the answer.

"There's been news from Belgium—"

"The Austrian troops have been sighted there," Rafe interrupted, giving Chauncey a dark glance. "Our own troops retreated because their forces were far too large."

Katrina nodded, now understanding why Paris seethed with tension. Everyone seemed to be waiting for something. Even the delegates who graced her salon could feel the strain that was stretching the city, threatening to tear it apart. An ominous cloud loomed, ready to explode, portending the signs of anarchy. Was it not the same before the fall of the Bastille? Before Versailles? Before the king's attempted escape?

"Katrina?" Rafe asked solicitously. "Are you all right?"

"It's nothing." She looked away from his probing gaze. The last thing she needed was for Rafe to see her fear.

The carriage stopped in front of Daphne's house. Daphne walked out regally before Chauncey could escort her. He bowed over her hand, spouting a pretty speech as she stepped into the carriage.

"Katrina, you look absolutely ravishing even in the light of day," Daphne remarked, barely acknowledging Chauncey's eloquent words.

"And you, as well," Katrina said, admiring the silk dress that dipped dangerously low. The echo of blue and gray sparkled in her eyes.

Chauncey agreed and began another long string of outrageous compliments.

"Stop babbling, Chauncey," Daphne quipped, smiling. "Isn't it the perfect day for a picnic?" She gestured to the bright, sun-warmed streets.

"It certainly is," Katrina agreed. "I haven't been in the country since Poitiers."

"I've never been there," Daphne said. "I've always enjoyed larger cities so much, but it's pleasant to go out and do something . . . rustic . . . like this once in a while."

Katrina hid a smile.

"Since the revolution, though," Daphne continued, "the city has become a bore. There's hardly ever an opera, and I can't remember the last time I saw a ballet—even the street players have disappeared."

"But certainly the salons are entertaining enough," Katrina remarked. "I swear some of the Assemblymen have missed their calling—they gesture like prima donnas rather than politicians."

"Could you be bored of your salon?" Rafe asked.

"Not in the least," she replied quickly. "Though all the men ever do in my house is argue! One side wants to restore some power to the king, and the other wants him completely deposed. So many extremists—no moderation."

Rafe raised his eyebrows. "A pearl of wisdom," he murmured moving to touch the curve of Katrina's neck. "It seems we have the wrong gender ruling the Assembly."

"Indeed," Daphne agreed. "Don't scoff. There'll come a time when women will do more than make intelligent comments."

"I look forward to the day," Rafe said. "There have been many times when I've been in the Assembly and have urged moderation. Perhaps if the words came from lips as sweet as these—"

"Rafe!" Katrina exclaimed as he reached to trace her lips.

"—then worlds would be changed."

"How charming!" Daphne remarked as Katrina glared at Rafe. "Katrina, I congratulate you on your success. You have made the catch of the season. Why, several seasons ago the Baronness d'Aureville was throwing herself shamelessly at Rafe—and she's an attractive, rich woman. Before that, Mademoiselle d'Honoré had claimed publically that she would make Rafe her husband before year's end."

"Daphne . . ." Rafe warned.

"No, go on, Daphne," Katrina urged. "This is all very informative." She was happy the conversation had turned. Rafe's intimate caresses in the presence of both Chauncey and Daphne had annoyed her. She'd forgotten, in her ebullience, what he was.

Daphne looked back and forth at the two in amusement.

"No, don't stop, Daphne," Chauncey prompted, a twinkle in his eyes. "Let Katrina know the whole black past of the man who sits beside her. This gentlemanly facade is only a veneer."

Katrina turned to stare out the window, letting the cool air rush through the hair gathered coyly around her shoulders and neck. Hmm! The catch of the season, indeed!

The carriage turned sharply on down the Rue de Sevres, heading southwest to the customs gates. Katrina gazed on the tightly spaced brick buildings that lined the streets, wondering at the lifeless windows.

Alarmed, she stiffened against the seat. There was not a sign of life in the street—not a child or a dog, no flicker of a curtain over dusty windows, no flash of dull calico through half-open doorways. She searched frantically for movement.

"Rafe, there isn't—"

"I know." He leaned past her to pull the leather blinds together. Katrina pressed against the back of the seat, but still the warmth of his body penetrated her thin dress. She flushed as he brushed her arm and bodice.

"It's dreadfully quiet," Daphne said softly.

"Too quiet," Rafe said. "I suspect there's a crowd ahead."

"Perhaps they're all at the Palais Royal," Chauncey said, "or at the City Hall. There was quite a large group there this morning."

"What matter? Certainly they wouldn't harm us," Daphne said emphatically. "After all we're patriots!"

These words brought little comfort to Katrina. She knew what mobs could do, knew the twisted sense of wine-induced justice that prevailed in the crowds.

A noise could be heard in the distance. It first sounded like the rumble of carriage wheels over a pockmarked section of a cobbled road, but Rafe's ears were trained for such sounds. He knew, as the noise grew louder, that the rumble was more than what one carriage and two horses could make. As the foursome continued down the Rue de Sevres, the noise diversified. Coarse, raspy voices, slurred with wine, yelled loudly and huskily over the general din. Vulgarities flew through the air and seemed to penetrate the walls of the carriage shamelessly. The sway of the leather shades gave glimpses of red Phrygian bonnets and raised, hairy arms and distorted faces. Katrina squeezed her eyes shut and grasped her belly. It was too late to turn back; they were moving into the thick of the mob, and she prayed they would not be stopped.

As if sensing her dread, the carriage slowed. The driver received his share of jibes, and Katrina could feel bodies bumping against the hackney's rattling sides.

Unconsciously, she clutched Rafe's arm.

"They certainly are rambunctious today," Daphne remarked, moving the shade slightly and calmly observing the crowd.

"Mobs are like that by nature," Katrina said, a tight knot of fear hardening within her. "Loud and drunk and violent."

"You sound like you know that from experience, Katrina," Daphne remarked. "There's a story I have yet to hear."

"Another time, perhaps," Rafe said, staring down in concern at Katrina's pale face. He covered her cold hand with his own. "First we must get through this crowd unmolested."

"This crowd isn't nearly as bad as the one we battled through near the Palais Royal," Chauncey commented. "These people seem to be simply whiling away a Sunday morning."

"Crowds that join aimlessly soon find an aim," Rafe said, watching the windows warily. The carriage lurched to the side, throwing Katrina bodily upon Rafe. As she clutched his shoulders to regain her balance, his eyes flickered darkly over her form.

"Really, Katrina. So forward," he teased to lighten her mood, helping her to a sitting position. A lock of hair had fallen in front of her blazing green eyes.

"You're a beast," she retorted, but her voice shook. She rearranged her hair, smoothing it back into place.

"I suppose this beast should find out why we're stopped."

He opened the carriage door, and Katrina gasped as the noise increased and the eyes of drunken men gazed avidly into the carriage.

"What the hell is going on?" Rafe asked the carriage driver.

"Don't know, Monsieur. They won't let us pass the gates. Say they need to check the carriage for traitors."

"There are no traitors in here. Tell them that—"

"I've tried, Monsieur. They won't listen."

"And look what we have here." The raspy voice came from the crowd as Rafe moved out onto the street and closed the carriage door firmly behind him. Curious, Katrina leaned to watch his broad shoulders through the separation between the window and the blind.

"Looks like a friend of the Baker!" someone shouted.

"Certainly, if you knew me, you wouldn't say such things," Rafe began, scanning the crowd. "Now what's this foolishness? Why are we being detained? We want nothing but to leave the city for a brief afternoon—"

"Just for an afternoon?" the first man cried. "That's what all the aristocrats say, and then they hie off to Austria and join the traitors to plot against the Nation." The crowd echoed his anger.

"If I were leaving for good, certainly I'd bring luggage. Do you see any here?" He gestured to the top and boot of the carriage.

As looks of bleary confusion passed over their faces, Katrina smiled despite herself.

The leader, a short, round man with thick arms, gazed angrily up at Rafe. "It's a trick, I'm sure," he said. "You dress like an aristocrat. What else do you want but to restore the Baker to his throne? Those times are gone! We'll not take them back!"

Rafe lifted a hand in vain to still the crowd. Their anger roared around the coach.

"We'll check your carriage," the leader continued, "to make sure neither the king nor queen, nor any of the royal pigs are sneaking out of Paris to join their allies."

"Yes! Pull them out!"

"Hang the traitors!"

"I'm not an aristocrat. I'm Beaulieu. Certainly you've seen my name."

A hush moved over the crowd as Rafe's name registered.

He watched them and nodded slightly. "And now, if we may?" He moved to enter the carriage.

"Not so quickly." The man's raspy voice pained Katrina's ears. She moved away from the light of the open door. "We don't know for sure that you're Beaulieu. Shall he make fools of us and ride away freely, perhaps harboring the royal family?" The crowd turned hateful, suspicious eyes on the carriage, and a grumble began again. "We'll see everyone in the carriage."

Rafe's hands rose to his hips. "As a patriot, you should take my word."

"We know nothing of you!" The angry yells continued.

"This is foolishness," Chauncey whispered from inside the carriage. "If we go out there and show them that we are not the royal family, they'll let us be." He rose and joined Rafe.

Daphne grimaced at the audible gasp that filtered through the crowd at the sight of Chauncey's chestnut curls and buckled shoes. Smiling, he moved around the small open circle and winked at a few of the women, who giggled in response.

"Men are so vain!" Daphne snapped, watching him strut before the crowd.

"You see?" Chauncey remarked. "Neither one of us is of royal blood. Thank God."

"There are others there," the leader persisted, squinting into the carriage. Katrina dropped the blind. *"Une blonde,* like Marie Antoinette!"

The crowd's growl grew in intensity, and Katrina stared across at Daphne.

"I can't stand this," she said, pulling her wrap tighter around her shoulders.

"The men are trying so gallantly to save us, and all they're doing is causing more trouble. Come." Daphne pushed open the door and stepped regally into the circle.

Katrina hesitated on the step, overwhelmed by the burst of heat and anger. Heads bobbed at them as they moved down into the filthy street.

Rafe whirled to stare angrily at Katrina. "Don't be a fool," he said under his breath, moving to help her down. Her face paled at the size of the crowd, and he squeezed her hand tightly. "You should have stayed in the carriage."

Katrina lifted her chin, a touch of anger bringing color to her cheeks.

"They would have forced their way in if you had persisted."

"Why don't you trust me, *petite?*"

Katrina glanced up at him towering over her. A heavy breeze lifted her hair around her face. His dark gaze was serious now, far more serious than she liked. He did not ask the question rhetorically; he wanted an answer. As she stared up into his familiar face, she searched for the answer in herself.

"See?" Daphne said to one of the men that surrounded them. "We are naught but a few bourgeois out for a Sunday afternoon."

"I don't know," the leader said, his eyes fixed boldly on Katrina's curvaceous form as he inched closer. "This little filly here could be Marie Antoinette, wouldn't you say?" He pulled on her arm and dragged her closer to the crowd.

Coughing as the stench of unwashed bodies rushed to greet her, she struggled against the man's greasy grip. Her eyes darkened to a deep pine-green in fear.

"Let her go." Rafe's voice rumbled low and dangerous, and for a moment the man checked his advance.

Bruising her arm with his grip, he turned to face his adversary. "You lust for this filly, Monsieur? I'd say she's a mighty fine piece—"

Katrina had not a moment to scream before Rafe pounced upon the revolutionary. Shoving her away roughly, the man reached in vain for the club that hung by his side. Katrina fell heavily on the cobblestones, and a sharp pain ripped from her elbow to her shoulders. Pushing herself from the mire running in the crevices, she turned to see Rafe throw a red-capped man into the edges of the bloodthirsty crowd. The man who had held her now lay motionless on the stones. Rafe's face stretched into a violent scowl as he crouched, facing another adversary.

"I know this girl," a woman yelled.

Startled, Katrina lifted herself up to a sitting position and squinted at the women around her. Her mouth dropped in recognition. "Lucille!"

Although Lucille's face had sunken into deep hollows and her eyes bulged yellow and wild, there was no doubting her identity. As Katrina struggled to her feet, Lucille's gaze roved slowly over her rich dress, now covered with the street's murky refuse.

"Sold yourself to the highest bidder, eh, Katherine?" Lucille said bitterly.

Katrina flushed, glancing briefly at the worn, mended shift Lucille wore—the same one she had worn two and a half years ago when they worked together in the milliner's shop. Katrina stared at the other women around her—Yvette, thinner, older, her breasts sagging unbound beneath a linen dress spotted with stains that looked suspiciously like blood; Anne, once so fresh-faced, now had skin webbed with red veins, and her eyes blazed out of blackened sockets.

"Surprised to see us?" Lucille's lips curled to reveal gaps between her feral teeth. "Thought you had gotten away at Versailles, didn't you? But no one ever escapes their fate, Katherine. Now you are with aristocrats. Or perhaps you are one? I wonder at a girl who goes from a revolutionary to an aristocrat in such a short time."

"My fate differed from yours."

Ignoring Katrina's words, Lucille added, "There are only two ways you could move so high so quickly. Either you're a whore," she said, smiling at Katrina's angry flush, "or a traitor."

"Who are you to call me traitor?" Katrina spat, a ball of anger loosening in her chest. Forcefully she pushed Lucille out of her way and began her march to the carriage. Lucille lifted a bony fist, but Katrina warded it off and kicked her in the shin. Lucille's eyes widened, but as she lunged at Katrina, two strong hands lifted her away and tossed her to her companions.

Rafe turned to face Katrina. Lucille's angry epithets mocked them, and before Katrina could lunge back at the stringy-haired shrew, Rafe lifted her high in his arms.

"No time for this, *petite,*" he said, pulling her over his shoulder.

"Let me go!" she yelled, pounding his back. "Let me get the—*ow!*" Rafe pinched her exposed calf.

"Shut up, Katrina. We have enough trouble as it is."

Katrina looked around at the moaning bodies scattered around the street. Others shouted curses from safe distances, waving their fists and clubs in threat. Rafe pushed her roughly into the carriage, her skirts flying above her knees. Then, barking directions to the driver, Rafe thrust himself in, nearly atop her, and quickly slammed the door shut. The carriage lurched forward, then turned completely around to head the opposite way, back into the city.

From the floor of the carriage, Katrina pushed down her skirts and lifted fiery eyes to Rafe's stoic face. "Who do you think you are, picking me up like a sack of grain and throwing me over your shoulder!" Painfully she pulled herself up on the seat next to Rafe, fists clenched.

"What did you expect me to do, Katrina? I'd just finished battling the men who handled you, and when I turned around, you were in a tuffle with a bunch of women. Not much for hitting women, I decided to remove you from the situation."

"You're a brute. I was doing quite fine on my own."

"I would say," Chauncey remarked. "I saw her give one of those demons a good kick on the shins before you interrupted, Rafe."

"Katrina, your arm!" Daphne exclaimed.

Katrina twisted to stare at the back of her arm. A trail of blood dripped off her elbow to stain her already mud-stained dress.

Rafe pulled her to his side despite her resistance and examined her arm. "That swine. You shouldn't have pulled me off of him, Chauncey. I'd kill him for this."

Katrina's stomach churned a little at the sight of the blood. "It's nothing, really," she said woodenly.

Rafe turned to look at her face, only inches from him, and his nostrils flared. "It's something," he insisted. "Chauncey, pull out that bottle of water." Rafe bent to lift Katrina's skirts.

"Rafe!"

"Hush," he said, ripping a long strip from one of the cleaner layers of her petticoats. "I'll buy you a new petticoat. Right now it's more important that I see to that wound."

Katrina winced as he poured water over her arm. Her skirts became soaked with the dirty, bloody water as he wiped the gash clean.

"Must you be so hard?" she asked through clenched teeth.

The pain radiated from her eyes, though she tightened her lips to deny it.

"I don't want it to fester." Rafe continued the cleaning, but more gently.

Katrina leaned against his strong shoulder, the bruises of the scuffle suddenly flaring up. Her knee ached from the fall, and her head pounded. Idly she lifted her good arm to massage her temples. She felt strange, lightheaded.

Rafe leaned down to rip off another piece of her petticoat and watched Katrina's face. She did not murmur a complaint as he fumbled with her dress, and her eyes fluttered in pain. She'd been hurt worse than he thought. Grasping her wrists, he forced her to look at him.

"Katrina," he said softly.

"Are we home yet, Rafe?" she asked quietly, opening her eyes. "I'm feeling quite strange."

He muttered a curse.

"Please, Rafe—"

"Why the hell didn't you stay in the carriage?" he chastised, pulling her against his shoulder.

"Because they would have entered forcefully," she argued weakly, her head throbbing too hard for a sharp retort. She hissed in pain as Rafe continued swabbing the gash. "Must you continue?"

"Chauncey, brandy. There's some under your seat with the wine."

Chauncey and Daphne stood carefully, holding on for balance against the sway of the carriage, and he pulled out a bottle. "The finest," he noted.

Rafe gently pushed Katrina away from his shoulder. "Here. Drink," he demanded.

Katrina's stomach churned at the smell.

He pushed the bottle to her lips. "Drink."

Too weak to argue, she obediently took a healthy gulp and swallowed, wincing as the liquor burned through her chest. While the color rose to her cheeks, Rafe poured the fiery liquid liberally over her arm.

Katrina's tortured cry died under Rafe's hard lips. Hot tears slipped out from beneath her dark lashes and fell upon his

smooth, lean cheeks. His lips clung mercilessly to hers, clinging, clinging until the pain dulled to a tender throb.

When Rafe pulled away, Katrina's head fell upon his shoulder
again. He deftly set a makeshift bandage in place and tied a linen
around it. Immediately, blood began to stain the white material.

"It will do until we get home," Rafe said gruffly, his heart
still pounding from the kiss. A feeling of tenderness washed over
him. Ignoring Daphne and Chauncey's presence, he held Katrina's face and wiped the smudges off her perfect skin.

Daphne sat stiffly in a corner of the carriage, two red spots of
flame high on her cheekbones. Chauncey looked inconspicu-
ously out the window. The brightness of the day waned, though
the sun still shone in its late morning splendor.

Katrina sighed with relief as the carriage stopped its incessant
swaying before her townhouse.

"I guess we'll go to the country another day," Chauncey said
lightly, trying to ease the tension.

"Yes. Another day." Daphne glanced at Rafe. "You'll take
care of her, won't you?"

"Yes."

"I just need some rest, that's all," Katrina insisted, smiling
courageously. "I'm sorry for all of this—"

Daphne waved her off. "Don't be silly. It's not your fault."
Her lips pursed in anger. "It was those damned people."

The birds had quieted since earlier that morning, and it was a
silent garden Rafe and Katrina walked through to the door of her
townhouse. Rafe tempered his pace to Katrina's, opening the
front door for her.

"Really, Rafe. All this attention is foolish. I have a small cut
on my arm—"

"That's no small cut," he began. "You forget how many fights
I've been in."

Katrina lifted a hand to her pounding temple. "I think my
head is worse than my arm. I need to sit down—" She murmured
a weak protest as, wrapping his arms around her back and legs,
Rafe lifted her bodily against his chest.

"Hush," he soothed her. "I'm taking you upstairs." With
quick strides he carried her to her room and placed her on the
bed.

"Where's Therese?" he asked.

"It's Sunday, her day off."

He suppressed a curse. "Well, it looks as if I'll be the one to lug up the pails of hot water—"

"Pails of hot water!" Katrina exclaimed. "Whatever for?"

"Your bath, of course. You must ache all over. You were pushed around like a doll this afternoon."

Katrina smiled hesitantly up at him. "You're being terribly kind."

He rubbed her cheek. "I think I like you wounded," he murmured. "You lie quietly and accept my directions, you look up at me with a twinkle of trust in your eyes, you accept my caresses . . ."

"It seems you like the helpless type," she quipped, then winced at the pain that shot to her head from the effort.

"Ah, you're feeling better already," he said, smiling. "But I won't spar with you today. Not while I have you helpless before me."

Katrina sighed. She was in no mood to argue. Besides, it was nice having Rafe waiting on her. "My bath, kind sir?"

His smile illuminated his face. "Very well, m'lady."

She closed her eyes as he trotted down the stairs to the kitchens. As the sound of banging pots and muffled curses rose from the lower floors, she smiled, but even that effort pained her. She drew her brows together in frustration. Surely she could not have been hurt so much—she must be imagining it. But as she tried to lift herself from the bed, she knew the pain was real. Giving up, she relaxed against the soft comforter.

Of all people to see in Paris. Lucille. She looked so bitter and hardened. The revolution had treated her harshly, whittling her into a wiry, suspicious woman. A tremor of fear shook Katrina's pain-racked body. Those eyes. They had seemed somehow . . . not human.

How could she have once befriended such a woman? Was she so blind and desperate in those early, harsh, glorious days of the revolution to fail to see the bitterness in Lucille? Katrina sighed. Those days blurred in her mind; all she could remember was the hunger, the constant hunger. She could hardly blame Lucille for/ her bitterness. Had it not been for Rafe, Katrina would have turned out the same.

Katrina opened her eyes wide, surprised at her own unconscious admission. *If it weren't for Rafe* . . . She resisted the urge to continue this line of thinking. She had to remember that though Rafe had saved her in Versailles, he'd proceeded to make her his slave, to punish her for treachery she had never committed.

Still, what she remembered most was the image of his face before her in Versailles; the feel of his hands soothing her heated skin; the look on his face when he first laid eyes on her there. Why did the memories of that moment seem so vivid now, while those of the months of servitude faded into obscurity? Even the night he bedded her—why could she so vividly recall his tender, whispered words, yet only vaguely remember the angry ones that followed?

She frowned. The knock on the head must have made her daft. When she recovered, she'd remember why she didn't trust this man who kept entering her life with brutal force.

His heavy step approached the door.

"Up, up!" Rafe demanded, dropping the pails and pulling the tub out of its alcove. He poured four buckets of steaming water into it. "Get out of those filthy clothes and into this tub before the water gets cold."

Katrina gingerly lifted herself from the bed, the sight of the steaming, boot-shaped copper tub inviting her. The dark wood and red lacquer hinged partition stood far on the other side of the room, and she wondered how she would get from one side of the room to the other without exposing every inch of her naked flesh.

Rafe turned and, noting the perplexed expression on her face, picked up the partition without hesitation and placed it in front of the tub. Katrina smiled gratefully and moved past him to hide behind it.

She pulled the pins from her hair and placed them on the small footstool next to the tub. Her hair fell heavily onto her shoulders and down her back. As she moved to undo the hooks of her dress, she groaned, her arm throbbing in protest.

"Rafe?"

"Yes?"

"I need . . . help with this dress."

Growling, he moved around the partition. His fingers flew deftly over the long row of hooks, shaking slightly as they moved over the curve of her lower back.

"You'll drive me to madness, *petite*," he said huskily, lifting his shaking fingers to unlace her corset. He moved swiftly to the other side of the partition before she could meet his eyes. Hastily, she shrugged off the filthy dress, her corset, the ruined petticoats, and the cambric chemise that clung familiarly to her curves. Unconscious of her shadow cast against the paneled partition, Katrina lifted her head and gently shook her hair free. She tested the water with her toe, then moved deeper into the soothing heat.

"Keep that upper arm out of the water, Katrina," Rafe instructed. "I'll dress it later. Is there anything else you need?"

Katrina, buried to her neck in the water, glanced around the tub. "I need some lye. There's a bar on my dressing table." She suppressed a giggle as he fumbled with the atomizers and jars lying about the table. The faint scent of jasmine and roses drifted to her, followed by her favorite lemon and spice oil. His steps moved toward the partition, then stopped.

"And how am I going to give this to you, *ma petite*, without getting an absolutely unforgettable view of your incredible body?"

"Close your eyes."

"I can't do that."

Katrina lifted her gaze as he came around the partition. Too much in shock to do anything but gape, she made no move to cover herself. He'd taken off his waistcoat and cravat and now stood before her in breeches and a clean linen shirt, open enough to show the slight pelt of dark hair rising between the plates of his chest. His eyes roved over her, over the dark golden tresses that clung to her shoulders, the roundness of her breasts rising above the steaming water, and the promise of long, coltish limbs blurred in the bath.

"Chauncey was right," she said in a quiet, shaking voice. "You are a rake."

"Sometimes," he agreed, not yet daring to move closer. His gaze caressed her intimately, longingly.

Katrina shivered with strange, yet too familiar sensations. Bashfully she crossed her arms over her breasts. "Are you just going to stare while the water grows cold?"

He moved closer to the bath and poured a liberal amount of the oil in the center, sending ripples to brush against her skin.

Katrina lifted her eyes to him as he sat down on the footstool near her, the pins she had gathered so carefully falling in a glittering array on the floor. He opened his palm to show her the lye.

"How can I take that, Rafe? Without—"

"I'll wash you," he murmured, moving behind her and pushing her back from the side of the tub. He scowled slightly. "I told you to keep your arm out of the water."

"I told you to close your eyes."

"Touché."

Rafe sucked in a ragged breath.

"Is something wrong?" she asked.

Reaching out, Rafe slowly traced a long, thin scar on her back.

"A gift from the former Duchess de Poitiers," she said swiftly. "And if you do not mind, I don't want to talk about it."

Rafe sat behind her in silence for a moment.

"I . . . I can do this myself," Katrina protested, her stomach churning, as Rafe brushed the rough bar over her tender skin. "Please, Rafe, let me—"

"Hush." His voice brushed her ears lightly, and his hands massaged her back, rubbing the lye over her bruised skin.

"You have a bruise here," he said huskily, tracing an irregular circle over her shoulder blade. "And here." He traced another, larger one, on her side. "And here." His hand moved lower, beneath the water line, to move gently over her hip. He continued his caresses, without the lye, his large hands massaging the aches from her body.

Katrina lifted her knees and rested her head on them. The day had grown brighter. Her room, facing south, caught most of the sunshine of the spring day and reflected it in every mirror and every polished surface—from the gilded dressing table to the smooth green porcelain insets of her writing table. She was aware of the birds chirping in the apple tree outside her window, but all her senses were tuned to the man who leaned over her, his dark hands soothingly rough on her back, his soft breath brushing her ears. She strangely felt as if she had been here before, as if she was reliving an old, happy time.

She shivered as a cloud passed over her.

"Water cold?" he asked quietly, reaching over her shoulder to dip his hand in the bath. He brushed her breast, forcing her to suck in her breath, and he retracted his hand, moving away. "I'll get you more hot water." He turned and left the room.

Katrina quickly dipped her hair under the water, scrubbing it clean with the lye. Just as quickly she ran the bar over the rest of her body—granted, it wouldn't be as clean as her back—and stood up to squeeze the excess water out of her hair.

Hearing him gasp, she swirled to see him, as two pails laden with steaming water dropped, upright, to the floor. Instinctively, she wrapped her arms around her breasts, and his eyes widened.

"Sweet Katrina . . ." Rafe stared with unabashed admiration at her glorious naked body. Water ran in rivelets over her smooth curves, clinging to the tips of her breasts and pooling in the soft indentation of her navel.

"I'm freezing and covered with soap, Rafe. Please, pour that water over me." She wondered at her own shamelessness. Mutely he moved to her and poured water over her shoulders and head. Katrina closed her eyes and threw her head back, letting the hot water baptize her.

The pail fell loudly to the floor as his arms wrapped tightly around her. Katrina groaned as, tingling from his touch, she pressed her body wantonly against the rough length of his. She gasped at the force of her own response and lifted her arms to cling wetly to him. Her body shook with tremors she had never expected to feel again, tremors only he inspired. The woman in her rose in full force and demanded fulfillment, demanded Rafe.

"Katrina, you tempt me too far."

"Rafe." The name trembled on her lips. Her body sang for him, called to him, ached for him. Mutely she sought his lips, lifting her face to his. His eyes burned feverish into hers.

"Katrina, I'm only flesh and blood," he warned, seeing the passion glowing in her eyes.

She pulled his head gently toward hers, ignoring his words.

Their lips joined eagerly. Rafe's hands moved over her softened skin urgently. The kindling took flame and lit the fire which heated their blood. Katrina gasped as he released her lips to trail kisses down her neck.

How could she have denied this? Was it not inevitable from the moment she set eyes on his tall figure again? Had they not shared the sweets of love already, unable to deny the needs that drew them together in spite of all that happened around them?

Katrina pulled him more tightly against her and moaned his name.

His head shot up and he stared down at her, his hair falling over his forehead in shadowed waves. He searched her face.

Once again, Rafe had vowed to protect this woman—his woman—from his lust. Once again, he faced failure. His entire body ached to join with her, to force her to love him. She wanted him. He wanted her. But he had sworn never to take her without words of love between them. He had made that mistake once—he vowed never to do it again.

"Katrina, my love, come stay with me. Tell me you love me and will come stay with me."

Katrina closed her eyes. *No words,* she thought. *No words—not now. Now I need more than words.*

"Tell me, Katrina."

"Rafe . . ."

She'd hesitated too long. He wouldn't take advantage of her weakened state. Gently, he pushed her away from his body, which was blistering from her kisses.

"Get dressed," he said hoarsely, pulling a towel from over the partition. "I cannot stay here any longer and still call myself a gentleman." Not waiting for her response, he stormed out of the room.

Katrina listened until his heavy step stopped downstairs. She heard him fumbling with the brandy decanter in the parlor. Painfully she rubbed the rough towel against her skin. She couldn't fool herself anymore. She loved Rafe Beaulieu. No matter what had passed between them before, she couldn't deny this. Sighing raggedly, she sank down on the small wooden stool.

He must never know. . . .

Chapter 20

"It sounds like thunder up there, the way he's rumbling around," Martha said, looking toward the ceiling. She clucked her tongue. "It's a wonder the floor holds out."

Chauncey stared into his coffee, gazing with idle fascination into the dark depths.

Martha's hands rose to her hips. "And what's the problem with you?"

"Me?" he asked, looking blankly up at her.

Martha leaned back on her heels and shook her head. "Yes, you." Pulling a linen from her apron, she mopped a ring of coffee from the wooden table. "You've got a scowl as dark as his, though you're much quieter about it."

Chauncey returned his attention to his coffee, shrugging his shoulders beneath the rich brocade of his finest waistcoat. " 'Twould not be polite to discuss it in a woman's company."

"Ah, then," Martha said, a smile of satisfaction spreading across her face. "It's as I thought." She sniffed loudly and waltzed across the rough floorboards. "I should have known. There's a woman on your mind. Katrina, I'd wager. Are you protecting her from him again?" Martha gestured toward Rafe's room.

"Katrina's now fully capable of protecting herself." Chauncey leaned back precariously on the legs of the lyre-backed chair. "The last time we saw her at her salon, she was involved with an older delegate from Marseilles. Rafe nearly ran the man through with a brass poker when the delegate dared to call her by her first name. You should have seen the sparks in Katrina's eyes!"

"Now, why would she be flirting, I wonder? Lord, she must know how murderous Rafe can be—" Martha stopped in mid-sentence, a smile crinkling her wide-cheeked face. "Yes. She does know how murderous he can be."

"I swear I'll never understand the ways of women. First Daphne, then Katrina—"

"You'll understand one day," she said curtly, "but by that time, you'll be trussed up and wedded."

"It'll be a dark day indeed when a woman calls me husband. I have enough trouble with one woman in particular—"

Martha chuckled. "That's when you are in the most danger. When it's 'one woman in particular.' "

"This fool cravat!" Rafe stormed down the stairs, a river of epithets bursting from his lips. His lace-edged cravat lay, untied, around his neck. "Martha, tie this for me. But not so intricate that I look as much a fop as my brother."

"Might do you some good with the ladies to dress like me," Chauncey retorted, fingering the soft brocade of his waistcoat. He curled his lips at Rafe's sober attire. "Instead of looking so dreary."

"I don't see that your attire has won any hearts."

"Hush, you two!" Martha interrupted, bustling to Rafe's side. "Sit down so I can reach that neck of yours. I'm in the mood to strangle it."

Chauncey laughed.

"And you'll be next!"

"I've half a mind not to attend her salon tonight," Rafe said, lifting his close-shaven chin. He winced as Martha's hands pulled tightly on the cravat.

"I'll hear none of that. You've both been entirely lax in attending her salon." Martha sighed. "Poor Katrina. And after all the abuse she received at the Parisian gates—"

"Ach," Rafe said, " 'twas nothing but a scratch and a few bruises. The duchess-to-be is heartier than that. She may not remember it, but I do. When I met Katrina she was a kitchen servant, strong-armed and wiry—"

"Don't be so hard on her. She was barely a woman then."

"Well, she certainly is one now, Chauncey," Rafe retorted. "With a woman's dangerous wiles."

"Not near as dangerous as Daphne," Chauncey said. "Daphne was born a woman, born with a treacherous heart—"

"No more of this!" Martha interrupted. "You don't do the ladies justice." Chauncey opened his mouth to speak, but Martha glared at him, stopping his words. "You'll both go to the salon tonight, you'll treat your women cordially, and if either of you has any drop of gallantry in you, you'll apologize to Katrina for your continual absences. The poor girl must be wondering what she's done to deserve such neglect."

Rafe turned to Chauncey, a twinkle entering his eyes.

"Seems that we've been given orders," Chauncey teased.

"I'd say so," Rafe agreed.

Martha harrumphed and tied the last row on the cravat.

The mood hung much heavier in the careening carriage. Rafe watched the passing streets, oblivious of the hackney driver's recklessness. A lamplighter lowered a lamp to the ground and made an obscene gesture at their driver as the carriage flew by, only inches away. They turned onto the Rue Saint-Jean, and prostitutes lifted their skirts high to expose pale legs swathed in bright petticoats. Despite the humidity of the July evening, Rafe pulled the leather blind closed.

"It would seem we've lost our taste for ladies of questionable virtue," Chauncey mocked lightly.

"Indeed."

Katrina. Her name echoed in his head. The mere thought of her kisses, of her sweet, warm body pressed close against his, drove him to madness. It had taken strength he'd not known he possessed to push her warm, vital body away from his own. Days had passed before the fire in his blood had lowered to a simmer, before he could breathe evenly enough to speak. This wasn't a passion that could be slaked on any willing body.

Rafe closed his eyes. How could he go to her salon tonight and not sweep her out of that room full of leering delegates, carry her up the stairs to her bedroom, and finish what they'd started on that spring day? The last visit to her salon had ended bitterly, harsh words passing between them on the taut strings of their passion. She had flirted—outrageously—with that old man, Resault, a lecherous delegate from Marseilles. How dare she rise up like a fury when Rafe had set Resault in his place!

Rafe could see the desire in her eyes. He had known her long enough to probe the depths of her expressions: anger that deepened her smoldering eyes to pine-green; joy that brightened her face into a sparkling, peach and white jewel; hatred that hardened her eyes to emeralds—cold, glassy, unforgiving.

He knew her hatred well. How many kisses, how many times must he pull himself away from her nectar before that hatred dissolved into love?

The carriage stopped abruptly before Katrina's townhouse. The French windows glowed bright gold from the plush interior. Through the crystal panes, Rafe could see her gleaming coiffure.

"Come, Rafe. The sooner we arrive, the sooner we can gracefully depart," Chauncey said, stepping out into the fresher air of the St. Germain quarter. He pulled on his waistcoat nervously. "I can see Daphne next to Katrina. I often wish I'd never introduced them. Daphne is constantly at the salon."

"I, for one, am glad they've taken to each other so well. It gives Katrina someone else to talk to than those leering delegates." Rafe stepped onto the small cobbled path. A breeze rustled the verdant garden, moving low in the full bushes, high in the heavy boughs. It danced restlessly among the leaves.

The door, as usual, was left open. No servant arrived in the foyer to take their tricorn, no butler to introduce the newest arrivals. The two walked to the edge of the parlor and waited at the door for their hostess to notice them.

Rafe drew in his breath at the sight of Katrina, as he did every time he saw her. Had she ever been anything but the beauty she was now, tonight, perched like a resplendent bird on the edge of a gilded seat? Her smile softened the point of her chin and cheeks into a sweet, heart shape while her eyes smoldered vital and warm from beneath a dark fringe of long lashes. Rafe scowled. She was smiling at Resault.

"But, really," Katrina said, turning to the room at large. "Why do you think the Austrian troops are hesitating in Belgium?" She lifted her eyes to a delegate by the hearth. "They've been there nearly two months!"

"Indeed, it is a bit long," the delegate said graciously. "But don't mistake this delay for hesitation, Mademoiselle. I fear the Austrians and the *émigrés* intend to march into Paris soon and restore the monarchy."

"Certainly there are dangers in waiting so long," she continued, turning to Resault, who leaned over the edge of the plush blue and white striped couch to stare avidly at her *décolleté*. "Their delay has already allowed us to assemble troops, despite the king's protestations."

"Yes," Resault agreed. "In spite of the king's objections, we had twenty thousand members of the National Guard in Paris for the celebration of the Jeu de Paume."

"Twenty thousand!" Daphne exclaimed. "Where were they when the peasants entered the Assembly? And the Tuileries?"

"Probably among those protesting the king's dismissal of his ministers," the delegate by the hearth said, scratching under his powdered wig. "The king cut his own throat by dismissing all his ministers last month in protestation of the new troops. The Assembly has appointed new ministers from our own ranks. With new ministers, and the traitor Lafayette fleeing the country, the king no longer has a friend in court."

"Perhaps he will see the error of his ways and begin to cooperate," Daphne murmured.

"Perhaps," the delegate remarked dubiously. "But I must admit that possibility is slim. I suspect the king is either preparing for another attempted escape, or hoping the Austrian and *émigré* troops will restore him to power."

"I agree with Mademoiselle that the Austrians are foolish for hesitating on the borders of Alsace," Resault said, glancing possessively at Katrina. She smiled in encouragement, and Rafe felt his rage set in again. "Their hesitation lends weight to the theory that the king is planning another escape. Perhaps Francis II of Austria and Fredrick William of Prussia do not truly want to embroil their troops in war. Perhaps their presence is just a ruse to distract our attention to the king's schemes here, in Paris."

"Nonsense," a third delegate said from across the room. His rich cheroot scented the still air heavily. Katrina wrinkled her nose, wishing he would smoke outside her home, as the other delegates did. "The *émigrés* are itching to march victorious on French soil, and the Austrian emperor would love nothing better than to have King Louis indebted to him for returning his throne. Perhaps the king is planning an escape, but it's more likely he's waiting for the *émigré* troops."

"Personally, I wouldn't blame the king if he fled the country to join his brothers,'' Katrina said bluntly, gazing with what she hoped was disapproval at the man smoking so heavily in her house. ''He's held like a prisoner in the Tuileries for no other reason than the mistake of his birth. What kind of justice is that?''

The silence that followed stretched. Katrina's eyes went from delegate to delegate.

''Ah . . . I think the Tuileries are a bit luxurious for a prison,'' Resault said awkwardly.

''The king is a weak, useless aristocrat who has done nothing in his life but live off the blood and sweat of 'his people,' '' the man near the windows said.

''Pardon, Monsieur?'' Katrina said politely.

The man, wearing clothes that hung on his thin frame, moved into the center of the room. His pinched features focused on Katrina, who straightened under his glassy green stare. ''The King of France is not a man to be pitied,'' he continued. ''It is right that he's treated like a prisoner. We've all been prisoners of the nobility for centuries.''

''You will remember, Monsieur, that you are speaking to a lady,'' Rafe said harshly.

Katrina stood abruptly, forcing the men to stand with her. She stared, open-mouthed, at Rafe's dark silhouette. He moved deeper into the room and bowed over her hand.

''Mademoiselle, it seems I'm constantly protecting your honor.''

Katrina caught the glitter of anger in his dark eyes before he turned to the delegate, whose face had visibly paled at the sight of Rafe.

''Indeed, Monsieur,'' he stuttered, suddenly losing the cold poise that had held him so rigid. ''Mademoiselle, my apologies.''

''It's always best to keep a wild beast in captivity, Monsieur,'' Katrina retorted. ''But if you let it see its bars, it will begin pacing and planning. Though I don't approve of the way the king has been treated, I do see the necessity of watching him. But no one seems to have the grace to do it surreptitiously.''

The man bowed. ''If you'll excuse me.'' Moving in sharp, jerky steps, the delegate left the salon.

Sighing in relief, Katrina returned to her seat, the rest of the gathering following her lead. Bubbles of conversation erupted across the salon.

"You should watch what you say, *petite,*" Rafe whispered.

"You've been neglecting me," Katrina said simply, pulling her hand from his warm, enticing grasp. "Both you and Chauncey."

"I admit to sloth," Chauncey said, approaching her from behind Rafe and taking her hand. "And I have no excuse."

"But it's been weeks since you've been here!" Katrina scolded. "Tell me you'll come more often."

"Daphne," Chauncey said in greeting, bowing.

Daphne lowered her eyes, her cheeks strangely flushed.

"Katrina, how's your arm?"

Katrina smiled and lifted the softly rounded limb for Chauncey's inspection. The opposite sleeve of her muslin dress slipped to reveal the curve of her shoulder. " 'Tis nothing," she said. "In a few weeks there will barely be a scar."

"Thanks to Rafe's fine care," Chauncey added.

The color rushed hotly to Katrina's cheeks.

"Chauncey, I smell some sweet tobacco. Shall we go out front?" Rafe's gaze settled on Katrina's bright cheeks. He suppressed an urge to trace the line of her cheekbone with his finger. Chauncey agreed quickly and they excused themselves.

"I suppose they'll sneak off now," Daphne said sullenly.

"You don't think they will, do you? They've just arrived."

"Perhaps not Rafe. I know not why he stays away. But I think Chauncey is still angry at me. I said some horrible things to him that day we tried to leave Paris."

Katrina lifted her fan to cool her skin, letting the self-made breeze lift tendrils of hair from her neck and temples. "I've never known him to hold a grudge, Daphne. Certainly he'll come around soon."

Daphne shrugged and her gaze followed Chauncey's chocolate-brown curls out of the room.

Katrina sighed, snapping her fan shut. She felt Resault's eyes on her, but she refused to turn to him. He had grown tiring. She flushed a little, embarrassed at her own behavior the last time Rafe was at the salon. Piqued that he had ignored her and spent his time in discussion with delegates, she had flirted outrageously with the nearest person, the rotund, pockmarked Mon-

sieur Resault. Since that night, Resault had become rooted to
her blue and white striped couch.

She tried to pay attention to the delegates' current discussion,
but now that Rafe was near, the conversations seemed banal. His
presence wiped out all other thoughts. Katrina sat straight and
set her face into the attentive, interested expression that satisfied
her guests.

What brought him here this night? she wondered. And what
had kept him away? Were her kisses so disgusting that he couldn't
bear to see her? He'd hardly spoken to her since the day he
washed her back—

Katrina took a sharp breath. Dangerous thoughts, these. Her
heart had already began its erratic flutter, sending her blood
flowing too quickly through her body. She closed her eyes.

"Katrina?" Monsieur Resault said, placing a thick hand on
her arm. "Are you all right?" Her eyes fluttered open. "Yes,
I'm fine," she said. "If you'll excuse me—" Abruptly, she rose
and moved out into the foyer.

Glancing about the empty hall, she lifted her muslin skirt and
scampered to the back of the house, where the darkness was
eased only by the light of a few tallow candles. Checking her
surroundings once more, she pushed open the door to the back
gardens.

The fresh air burst upon her, still warm but so much cooler
than the stifling salon, even with the French windows open wide
to the outside air. She moved quickly into the paths, losing herself among the twisting layers of vine-covered trellises. She
breathed easier, the fire in her blood cooled by the rapid escape.

He must know. He must know she loved him. Why else would
he play such games? He'd not come for weeks, while she waited,
bored nearly to tears by the constant arguments that rose and fell
in her salon. She ached for him, even now, even after all the
pain. Clutching her fists, she swore she wouldn't submit to that
again.

She heard herself laugh at her own absurdity. Covering her
mouth quickly, she whirled to see if she'd been found.

He stood, immobile, at the head of the path. Katrina clutched
her bodice and stepped back, wondering for a moment if it were
Rafe or some demon sent to torture her.

She'd known he would come.

"You laughed," he said simply, moving closer to her.

Katrina gasped and tried to catch her breath. "You startled me."

"It was a sweet sound, your laugh," he continued. "Laughing in the dark and quiet of your garden, alone."

"I was thinking . . . of foolish things."

"Nothing you think can be foolish, Katrina," he murmured, moving closer.

Her breath shortened and she wondered if he would touch her.

"There have been many times when I've wondered what thoughts run behind that pretty brow." He moved near enough to smell the light perfume emanating from her skin.

Katrina tilted her chin to stare into the hard planes of his face, now softened in the darkness. "You should have asked."

"Ah, but would you have told me the truth?" He stared at the glow of her hair for a moment before returning his gaze to her eyes. "Or would you hide behind your hatred, lie through your anger?"

Katrina opened her mouth to protest, but his lips silenced her, pressing softly against her own. She moaned deep in her throat and placed her hands against his chest. Grasping her shoulders, he pulled her tight against the length of his body.

What exquisite torture is this? she asked herself as the kiss deepened. Her mind battled against her treacherous body, one telling her to push away from his chest, while the other urged her hands up to circle his neck. She weakened in his arms and fell against him.

The night air suddenly moved heavily between them, and Katrina opened her eyes.

Rafe watched her as he moved away from her pulsing body. The fine arches of her breasts heaved against the constraints of ribbon-trimmed bodice. "I seem to have a hard time controlling myself around you, *petite*," he said huskily.

Katrina choked down the urge to tell him to come to her, to walk by her side, to kiss her lips, to share her bed. Her hands balled into fists and then relaxed, although her pulse jumped wildly in her throat. Her entire being cried out for him. *I must not submit to his torture again.*

Rafe wondered at her silence. Her hair shone even in darkness, but her eyes were squeezed shut. Was she feeling passion? Or anger?

"What are you thinking?" he asked softly.

Katrina's eyes flew open, her internal struggle evident in their luminous depths. She opened her mouth to speak then closed it quickly.

How easy it would be to tell him she loved him, she needed him. The words surged to her throat, but she swallowed them again. She would die if he laughed at her.

"You see?" he said, when she did not answer. "I asked you what you were thinking and you said nothing." An edge of bitterness entered his voice. "Was it anger this time, Katrina? Or was it hate?"

"How little you know of me," she bit back caustically. Her cheeks flushed in frustration. "You tease me, kiss me like a lover, then pull away coldly. And you wonder at my confusion?"

"So," he murmured. "You want my kisses to continue?"

"Well, no. I mean . . ." She glared at him beneath her thick lashes. "My guests are waiting. I should return."

"There's something I must say to you," Rafe said, "before you return to your treasured guests."

"Yes?"

"Your guests are not always your friends, Katrina. You must watch what you say in their presence."

"I'll say what I damned well please in *my* salon." Her body began to tremble with anger and restrained passion. "No one— least of all you, Rafe Beaulieu—will tell me otherwise."

"Don't be a fool, Katrina," he said through stiff lips. "The man you spoke to tonight—he is no friend of yours. His name is Regat. He is a Jacobin."

Katrina crossed her arms stubbornly. "And what of it?" she persisted. "I invite people of many political philosophies to my salon. A tart Jacobin adds spice to the evening."

"You know nothing of them. They foment riots in the streets, urge death for all aristocrats, call for the king's head—"

"I know of the Jacobins," she snapped, clutching her hips. "They are revolutionaries. Their tactics may be unorthodox—"

"Fool." He grabbed her arms.

Her eyes widened in anger, and she twisted in his grasp. "Let me go!" she hissed, pushing against his solid, firm bulk.

"Not until you hear me out." He held her without effort. "After he left, Chauncey and I saw him in your front garden, in conference with Therese. Now what would this Jacobin have to do with her?"

Katrina struggled in his grip. "How do I know?!" she exclaimed, enraged. "They could be out there for any kind of tête-à-tête. Perhaps they are enamored—"

"He is using—probably paying—Therese to spy on you. Can't you see that?"

Katrina shook her head, the golden ringlets flying in hopeless disarray. "And why would anyone want to spy on me? I say whatever I please in front of a good part of the Assembly every Wednesday night. There's no need for a spy."

"And when have you become so naive? Don't you remember the irrational anger of the crowd at Versailles? They don't ask for justice, they mete out their own."

"What are you saying? That Regat will ask for my head?"

"Precisely," Rafe answered. "Especially if you continue to spout near-royalist sentiments."

"I'll not believe a word of it," she said stubbornly. "I prefer to believe they're out there for more . . . romantic reasons. After all, revolutions make lovers out of enemies."

His black eyes narrowed, and she knew she had pushed too far.

"I didn't think we were enemies, Katrina."

"Neither are we lovers."

"That can be changed."

The sound of raised voices and a crash distracted their attention from the passion that stretched taut between them. Katrina started and pulled away, heading toward the house with Rafe at her side. Another crash resounded in the still night air, and they ran through the cobbled paths, through the rear door, through the foyer. A knot of delegates had gathered before the entrance to the morning room.

"What's going on?" she exclaimed, trying to push her way through. One by one, the delegates turned to her and moved away. "What's happened?" she asked again, trying to keep the hysteria from entering her voice. The faces that surrounded her grew sober.

Rafe stepped in front of her as she burst through the crowd and into the room. He grasped her shoulders tightly.

Katrina looked up at him, wondering how he had gotten through the crowd before her.

"Katrina," he said quietly. "Perhaps you should go into the other room—"

"No!"

She lifted a hand to her throat. The room was in shambles: the dark maroon drapes were ripped into long, thin slices, one still smoldering where someone had quickly doused a small blaze. Refuse covered the cream-colored carpet, and the stuffing of the chaises and sofas still fluttered on the air. She lifted her eyes to the mantelpiece and gasped at the portraits of her mother and father. The canvas had been poked savagely through their eyes, their throats, and sliced down their bodies in innumerable slits. It was as if someone had stabbed them over and over.

Katrina stared in horror at the mutilated paintings. Rafe's strong arms moved around her, and gratefully she turned to burrow in the strength and comfort of his chest.

Rafe stared up at the destroyed paintings, the only reminder Katrina had of her parents. As she trembled in his arms, he held her tighter, oblivious to the crowd that watched. A seed of bitterness took root in his heart. How tired he was of this revolution!

Katrina pushed away from him, then straightened her back and moved to the delegates. "Does anyone know what has happened here?" She asked the question as calmly as if she were asking the name of a street or a shop.

One delegate stepped forward. "It seems that the ruffians were here for some time before we discovered them," he began. "None of us heard anything until the window was broken. There was so much noise and banter in the other room. We all raced in here, doused the fire the scoundrels had started—but they had already gone out the window."

"Did anyone see them?"

The men shifted their eyes and weight, but no one answered.

Katrina's lips tightened. "I am sorry for the inconvenience, my friends, but I think it would be best if you departed early tonight."

The delegates breathed a collective sigh and began gathering their hats.

Rafe watched Katrina with renewed admiration as she graciously bid each guest good-bye. A small, pained smile lingered on her otherwise immobile face. She moved with quiet grace in her butter-colored dress, holding her head erect.

"I will stay with you tonight," Rafe said, moving behind her.

"You will ruin whatever reputation I have left," she whispered. "Especially after that scene in the morning room. I can almost hear the delegates speculating when they look our way."

"I don't give a damn what they think."

"I do," Katrina replied without conviction.

"I will not leave you alone in this house tonight."

She lifted a fine shoulder. "I hardly think the ruffians will come back. Certainly they'll expect me to be on my guard."

"Then it's best that you have a guard with you. Me."

"Fine protection you'll be," she whispered, smothering a weary laugh. "I'll have to bring someone else in to protect me from you."

"No, *petite*," he whispered into her ear. "You'll never have anything to fear from me."

Katrina gazed at the soft velvet of his waistcoat, then slowly lifted her eyes to his. Her heart began a steady thump. "I have everything to fear from you, Rafe," she whispered. "Don't you understand?"

Understanding dawned in his eyes like silver stars bursting onto night. He grasped her arms, and she was overwhelmed by the passion rushing through him to her.

"Katrina?" Monsieur Resault's chalky voice broke into the strange, charged atmosphere that had settled over them.

Katrina stepped out of the warm circle of Rafe's arms and lifted her hand to the delegate. "I'm sorry for the inconvenience," she apologized, for the twentieth time.

Resault eyed Rafe behind her. "We've searched the house, Katrina. I hope you don't mind me taking the liberty."

She immediately thought of the stockings she'd left hanging over the lacquer partition, the chemise discarded on the floor of her room. "No," she answered graciously. "That was kind of you."

"The house is bolted and secure. We boarded the broken window in the morning room. You need not fear their return," he added, staring at Rafe's mocking smile. "If you want me to stay—"

"Monsieur!" Katrina said, rising up in dignity. "I think it's best we say *au revoir.*"

"Very well," he said, bowing slightly. "Beaulieu? Will you be leaving?"

"Momentarily, Monsieur Resault."

Katrina moved to where Rafe's tricorn rested on one of the tables in the foyer. She lifted it and brought it to him. "Monsieur Beaulieu will be leaving now," she said distinctly, lowering her eyes before Rafe's dark gaze.

He grasped the tricorn, crushing one of the corners in his grip. "Thank you for finding my tricorn," he said, his eyes searching her face. "I have no more excuse to linger." Fitting the hat beneath his arm, he followed the delegate out the door.

Katrina clasped her hands, watching his broad back with regret.

He stopped to turn to her. "I'll be back."

Chapter 21

Katrina listened at the door until the last carriage rumbled into the darkness. The silence fell heavily over the house, and she suddenly wished she had let Rafe stay to guard her.

She turned to face the interior, daring to let her gaze travel to the destroyed room. She could feel the draft from the hastily boarded window moving her skirts restlessly. Pushing away from the door, she braced herself for the results of the horrible, useless display of anger. It was no coincidence, Katrina was sure, that the ruffians chose her favorite room. They had torn through it like they would tear through her, if they were sotted enough and had the opportunity. A tremor of fear racked her limbs. She wished again that Rafe were here to comfort her.

Katrina shook her head. Rafe said he would return, and he had always been one to keep his word, despite her objections. Sighing, she picked up a piece of the curtain that lay on the carpet. Perhaps she could clean away some of the destruction while the shock still numbed her senses.

She glanced up at the portraits of her parents, her heart lurching at the sight. The flicker of candlelight made their empty eyes move in pain. Tearing her gaze away, she brought a chair to the hearth, pulled the paintings off the wall, then leaned them against the edge of the hearth. The spaces above the mantelpiece seemed so lifeless, so devoid of any warmth, that she sank down upon the ruined couch and buried her face in her trembling hands.

For the first time since her father had died, Katrina cried. A deep mourning song rose from her soul, bursting forth in rivers of tears that flooded between her fingers and dropped in dark circles on her dress. She thought of all the time that had been stolen: between her mother and father, between her father and herself. She thought of what little snatches of happiness each member of her family had had before death reached out its cruel claw to take one of them away. She thought of Rafe and the painful words that kept them apart—of all the time they had wasted.

Much later, Katrina rubbed her hands, sticky with dried tears, through her tousled hair. Her limbs felt heavy with weariness, and for a moment she leaned back against the couch, letting the exhaustion of her emotions wash over her. Now, when Rafe returned, she would have herself in control. The baptism of tears had made her a stronger woman.

She rose firmly from the chair and lifted her hands to her hips in determination. She surveyed the room around her.

"Now, where should I begin?"

The night had moved deep into the witching hour before Katrina left the morning room, her butter-colored dress streaked with dirt and ash. Her coiffure fell about her face riotously, and she wearily brushed a curl from her eyes.

Katrina nearly gagged when she returned to the salon. The smoke hung sticky in the air, mingling with the odor of warm wine grown sour on the card tables, on the mantel, and the windowsills. Needing the activity to keep her mind from other things, she moved into the room determinedly. She picked up a glass from the windowsill and darted a glance out the smoky, leaded panes of her tall windows.

She gasped.

A pair of eyes glared at her through the darkness of the moonless night.

Lucille was standing outside, her thin body a shadowy ghost in the blackness. Her eyes speared Katrina, ripping her breath from her throat and thrusting her back to the middle of the room. Lucille's mouth opened to reveal an evil, toothless grin.

Katrina stumbled back against a card table, her hands raised to ward off the sight. Lifting bony arms, Lucille began banging on the thick panes, the vibrations shaking the walls. Gasping, Katrina whirled away from the vision and threw herself through the kitchen doors, then leaned against them, closing her eyes in terror.

She opened her eyes.

Through the kitchen windows, Therese's bright eyes seared holes through her. Therese laughed as Katrina stumbled through the kitchen to dash into the safety of the halls. More hands pounded on the windows, and soon the beat reverberated not only through the salon and kitchen, but also in the parlor and on the heavy oak door before her. She fell against the stairs in fear.

Then she heard the voices.

"Traitor!" Lucille's scratchy voice rose above the din of the pounding. "Royalist sow and enemy of the people! She would help the king! Let us bring her to justice!" The chant echoed around the house, and Katrina pressed her hands against her ears.

Dashing to the upper floors, she slammed her bedroom door tightly behind her. After dragging over the chair to her dressing table, she lodged it firmly under the doorknob, fear running cold in her blood. What was happening? How had Lucille found her way here? What had Katrina done to provoke such an attack?

Suddenly Rafe's words of warning flooded in full force to her. If only she had listened to him. . . .

The banging stopped suddenly. Katrina's heart beat loudly in the silence that followed. What was she going to do? Certainly she couldn't just sit and wait until they broke the bolts that held the doors secure.

Katrina hid her head in her hands. Had her stepmother and stepsister felt the same when hordes of peasants raided the chateau? Certainly the title of the Duchess de Poitiers must be cursed: her own mother died too young in childbirth, her stepmother was murdered by peasants, and now Katrina, next in line to inherit the wretched title, sat in her room, waiting for assassins to burst through the door.

She shook her head abruptly. No. She would not hide in cowardice. She rose from the bed and pulled open the doors of her armoire. On the bottom lay the papers Monsieur Forrestier had entrusted to her and a simple calico dress she'd had no use for, until now. Quickly, she reached behind her and struggled with the clinging hooks of her gown, tugging on them until the material tore loudly. Shrugging out of the gown, Katrina left it in a glimmering heap on the floor. Her hands trembled as she pulled the calico dress over her head. Reaching down to collect the papers, she felt an icy smoothness.

Katrina lifted an antique gold knife off the floor of the armoire. It glittered in her hands. Without hesitation, she nestled it between her dress and corset. The hard coldness gave her strength.

Gathering the papers securely in their satin ribbon, she warily approached the window. She could see the outline of skirts, still in the front, rustling in the night. She must escape this house, go to Rafe. To Rafe. Her heart fluttered. There would be no more foolishness between them.

Katrina sucked in her breath. She could hear footsteps—close to her door.

The floor boards outside her bedroom creaked again. She snatched a heavy porcelain vase from off the dressing table and lifted it above her head, watching as the knob slowly turned. The chair fell away as Therese burst through the door, her teeth bared in her sour face.

Katrina threw the vase blindly. Therese lunged toward her, oblivious to the pot until it shattered against her head. Blood stained the pale fragments, and her body sank heavily to the floor. In the silence that followed, Katrina stared at Therese's lifeless body, a knife from her own kitchen still clenched in the servant's hand. The shards of porcelain glittered around her.

Katrina fell heavily to the bed. If Therese had broken in, then certainly there were others. She must—

"You may have gotten her, 'Katherine,' but you still have me to contend with." Lucille's raspy voice brought Katrina's head up sharply. The dark-haired woman's silhouette loomed darkly in the doorway.

"You should leave, Lucille," Katrina said, hoping she could bury her fear, "before you meet with Therese's fate."

"Therese was foolish. Much too eager and stupid." Lucille stepped over Therese's body and moved toward Katrina.

Katrina rose and pulled the knife from her bodice. "Get away from me."

"What, Katherine?" Lucille taunted. "We were once friends, remember? But that was before you decided to become a duchess. Or were you one already? Were you a spy sent by the king to see the plans of the people? Were you sent, perhaps, to sabotage them?''

Even from the distance that separated the women, Katrina could smell the stale wine on Lucille's breath. ''You wouldn't believe anything I said,'' she retorted. ''Your mind has already been made up.''

''Traitoress,'' Lucille hissed, lifting her arm to show a long, glinting silver knife. Katrina's blade was tiny in comparison. Lucille fingered the curved edge of her weapon. ''This knife has already disposed of many traitors. It shall now do the same for another.''

Katrina stepped back, her blood freezing as she stared up at the blade. As Lucille moved toward her, her eyes avidly gazing at Katrina's neck, Katrina knew the woman would kill her, right here, in her own bedroom. Katrina would never see the glitter of Rafe's dark eyes, never again feel the strength of his arms crushing her, never again experience the joy of their mutual passion. She stumbled back against the bed as Lucille continued her approach. Katrina could not tear her eyes from the dark, biting steel. Various images filtered through her head: Rafe's face as he bent over her bloodied body. Father Hytier reading from his Latin prayer book over a fresh grave—was it her father's or hers? The duke's sweet, crinkling face smiling toward her with open arms. Rafe, his expression loving, angry, passionate, reaching toward her with determined arms, screaming for her, screaming—

''No!'' she cried as the knife began its deadly arc. As she fell heavily to the floor and rolled away, an explosion filled her ears. She heard a heavy thump near her, and something fell across her leg. The acrid smell of sulphur burned her nose, and she wondered if it were really so easy to die.

''Katrina!''

As she was pulled onto her back, she closed her eyes in fear, and she nearly blacked out, so overwhelming was her terror. A gray fog obscured her vision, but she fought to rise above it.

''Katrina!''

Could it be Rafe's voice that called to her from the realm of life? Or had he found his way to her even in death?

''Katrina! Look at me!'' Arms encircled her body and lifted her from the floor.

She focused on the face before her, the dark eyes warm, soft, filled with concern. "Rafe?"

"Katrina, my love, my dearest—" He brushed his cheek against hers, and his fingers probed her body as he placed her on the bed. "Did she hurt you? Katrina, talk to me!"

The fog lifted, and vaguely Katrina realized she was alive. Her heart still pounded, and Rafe's fingers were very real on her flesh. "How did you get here?" she asked. "Where's Lucille?"

"Dead," he said curtly, lifting a long-muzzled pistol and replacing it at his side. "She will never hurt you again." His eyes swept her body one last time. "Are you sure she hasn't harmed you?"

"I don't think so," Katrina murmured, lifting herself to a sitting position.

"There's little time, love. I don't know how long my men can keep the attention of the women in front. Can you walk? I have a horse waiting out back. Come." He took her hand firmly and pulled her toward the door.

"Wait!" Katrina said suddenly, reaching for the pile of papers on her dresser. She avoided the two bloodied bodies and reached desperately for Rafe's hand.

He pulled her sharply against him. "Walk with me. Don't leave my side."

She followed in his shadow through the darkened house, jumping at every creak. He led her around the stairs and through the garden door, the night air moving cool and swift over her sweat-stained brow.

The women still yelled, and their voices traveled to the back of the house. Katrina stiffened as she and Rafe moved through the midnight-black lanes of the garden toward the far back, where he had cut a small entrance through the bushes. Ignoring the branches that poked her and tore at her thin calico dress, she rushed through after Rafe. He pulled her up into the saddle, and the horse pranced beneath them. Without a word, Rafe whirled the mount around and sent him racing through the streets. Katrina sighed, fainting against the hard, living man whose arms closed possessively around her body.

Rafe picked Katrina up off the horse and carried her into the shop, where he set her back on her feet. Darkness enveloped her warmly, and she pulled away from him to move deeper into its safety. She could feel his eyes on her. Suddenly her panicked thoughts of the evening seemed silly. How could she tell Rafe of her love? Uncertainty seeped into her heart again.

"Rafe," she murmured, not daring to meet his eyes. "I suppose I should apologize for not listening to you earlier, when we were in the garden. I—I know now that Therese was watching me all along."

"Hush." He stepped toward her, then stopped, waiting. "That doesn't matter anymore. Nothing matters but . . ." He tugged on her arms until she stood before him. He struggled with words.

"But what, Rafe? Nothing matters but what?"

He pulled her up to display the passion and love on his face. "Nothing matters, my love, but this." His lips fell on hers, teasing them open. As he squeezed her hard against him, she gasped, burying her fingers in his soft hair.

"Katrina," he whispered, rubbing his lips over her brow. "I nearly died when I saw you motionless on the floor. When I saw that black-haired witch raising a knife, I only knew that she must die for taking you away from me."

"Rafe . . ." Katrina was nearly overwhelmed by the love pouring from him.

He ran his hands up the length of her back. "When I saw you moving on the floor, when I realized you could actually be alive, I felt like you had been ripped from death—"

"Rafe, I—I could think of nothing but you tonight, nothing but you as Lucille approached me—"

"You are not leaving me—ever." Rafe lifted her chin. He rubbed a thumb softly over her tear-stained cheeks. "You are mine, my love, and tonight I will prove it." He swung her easily into his arms and climbed the steps to his room.

Their clothes melted from their bodies, leaving their flesh naked and yearning. With wonder his hands traveled over her soft curves, just as her hands stroked his hard, defined muscles. It was as if they were touching the lengths of smooth skin, the locks of tousled hair, for the first time, rediscovering what neither had been able to forget. Gentle fingers ran through tangled tresses, lips eagerly sought lips and their breathing deepened to gasps as the coals of desire kindled and rose to a raging blaze of passion. Katrina cried out as Rafe set her on the bed and covered her with his body. Though lightning did not streak the night sky, she felt the storm building inside her as his fingers sent bolts of sensation rippling through her. Gentle became urgent, urgent demanding, demanding undeniable. Flesh yielded to flesh, joining them together in an ardent ache that grew until the thunderous storm exploded, soaking their bodies with its power.

Rafe's breath teased her ear as he rolled over and pulled her close.

"I have waited forever for this," he whispered, kissing a pert earlobe.

"Me, too," Katrina agreed, still breathless. "I thought that I would never touch you again."

"That is over now," he said. "As long as I live, I'll protect you from anyone who wishes you harm." His hands moved over her skin avidly, thirsty for her warmth.

"I love you so much," she whispered, her fear shaking her words even now.

He leaned upon his elbow and gazed into her face. "And I love you. I shouldn't have waited so long to tell you, *petite*. I have loved you since the first time I saw you, that darkened night in Poitiers." Katrina's hands rose over his lean hard hip, tracing the leg that nestled possessively between her own.

"The waiting is over," she murmured.

"Yes," he agreed, kissing the hollow of her neck, the light of passion dancing in his eyes. "It's time to make up for lost time."

Katrina yawned sleepily as the first rays of afternoon light slipped up the twisted linen sheets to touch her raven lashes. Languidly she turned away from the annoyance to lie on her side. A warm weight anchored her body to the bed, stretching across her flat abdomen. Her brows drew together in confusion, and she reached down to push the weight away.

She smiled slowly as she touched the skin peppered with a fine spray of hair. Her fingers caressed the deep indentation of his forearm, moving slowly up past the strong elbow and over the muscled expanse of his biceps, which hardened under her touch. Pressing herself closer to him, she rubbed her nose between the smooth bulges of his chest. The arm tightened.

"You're awake," she murmured, daring to kiss one dark nipple.

"Again," he said, his lips moving against her hair. "If I wasn't dreaming, we woke several times during the night."

"But it must be near noon now, Rafe," she whispered, pressing her legs against his and reveling in the feel of his skin against hers. His hand moved to tilt her chin up. Her eyes were heavy-lidded, but her cheeks flushed full with life and her lips curved softly. "We really should rise."

"Now, so soon, *petite?*" Rafe said huskily. He dipped down to capture her lips, which clung eagerly to his.

"Well," she said, lifting her arms to draw his head to hers. "Maybe not just yet . . ."

Much later, Rafe reluctantly drew the linens over Katrina's flushed body and rose, naked, from the bed. She shamelessly watched his leonine body through tilted eyes as he searched for the clothes they had shed so quickly the night before. Finding a heap of cambric, he tossed Katrina her chemise and lifted the calico dress.

"It seems, my sweet, that I now owe you a petticoat and a dress." He tossed the shredded dress over a chair. "I must have been quite overcome."

"You were," she teased. "But I didn't stop you."

He flashed a wide grin, gazing a bit too long on her scarcely covered body. Gruffly he turned away and continued the search for his clothes. "Are you hungry, *petite?*" He pulled his breeches over well-muscled legs.

"Starved." She reached for her chemise. "Though I can hardly go downstairs with you like this."

His eyes twinkled as he looked to her. "I think not."

"*Dieu!* I forgot about Martha!" Quickly Katrina pulled the chemise over her body. "What will she think? And Chauncey—" She flushed deeper.

"Chauncey will be congratulating both of us. Martha, however, is another matter. She'll be quite shocked." His lips twisted devilishly.

Katrina looked around for something to throw. "You're horrible!" she exclaimed. "You're enjoying this!"

In two steps he was beside her, pinning her against the bed. "Every minute, my love." His gaze raked her face. "Every minute.'' He brushed his cheek against hers. "I'll get us some breakfast. Don't you dare move.''

She giggled softly. "I can hardly leave this room without clothes.''

"Perhaps I'll leave you without any, then,'' he teased. "That will keep you by my side.''

Rafe whistled loudly as he walked down the narrow stairs into the heart of the shop. The smell of Martha's rich coffee wafted from the kitchen while two golden-brown loaves of bread lay on the wooden table. As he walked into the room, Chauncey struggled with a smile.

"Good morning, Chauncey, Martha.'' Rafe moved past Chauncey, ignoring the grin splitting his face, and placed a hard kiss on Martha's floured cheek.

"Now what in the good Lord's name was that for?'' she asked with a flustered laugh. "And what has you in such a dandy mood? After all that happened to Katrina last night—''

"Especially after all that happened to Katrina last night,'' Chauncey said, snickering.

"Katrina is fine, Martha. She's awake now.'' Rafe seated himself at the table.

"Well, why isn't she down here to eat? The poor girl must be famished. I'll go bring her some bread—''

"No, Martha,'' Rafe interrupted. "I'll bring it to her.''

Martha looked at him strangely, her face puckering into a frown. "What foolishness! I'll bring her the food. I haven't properly greeted the child yet—''

Rafe pulled her back by her skirts. "Katrina's not, ah, properly dressed just yet.''

Chauncey's face reddened with the effort to hold back his laughter.

"You're acting decidedly strange this morning, Rafe. As if I haven't seen the child without a stitch on! I'll just tell her to get properly dressed. It's far too late for her to be a-lying abed.''

"Martha. You don't understand.'' Rafe hesitated, fruitlessly looking to Chauncey for support. "She doesn't have . . . anything to wear.''

"What happened to last night's clothes?''

"There's nothing left of them.''

Chauncey's laughter burst through and filled the room. He rose, with effort and patted Rafe heavily on the back.

As she stared at Rafe, Martha's face paled, then turned bright red.

"You rake, you devil, you seducer—" Chauncey began, laughing, but stopped as Rafe lowered his brows in anger.

Chauncey turned his attention to the woman whose face flushed darkly. "Martha, are you quite all right?"

She struggled with her emotions, rubbing her hands over her muslin apron, then twisting them together. She lifted her chin haughtily, but her lips did not move.

"Eh, Martha? What do you think?" Chauncey teased, moving toward her.

She struggled some more, unintelligible sounds coming from her throat. Finally, she straightened her back and faced Rafe squarely.

"It's about time!" Martha burst out, and Chauncey's laughter began anew. "You two have been marching around each other like enemies in battle for too long. Mind you, I don't like this, not at all! She's a good girl, and besides that, she's nearly a duchess, a lady, and this is no way to treat a woman of her standing. No, I can't say I approve of this, but I do say that it's about time you two got . . . together. You better treat her right, Monsieur. Yes, you'd better do the right thing by her. She's had enough misery in her life—"

"Martha, please," Rafe interrupted.

"No, no, hear me out! You'd better do right by her, or . . . or . . . or I don't know what!" Martha finally ran out of steam, and Rafe moved to join Chauncey at the table.

"It *is* about time," Chauncey said, unable to suppress a smile.

"No more on it. Katrina will never forgive me."

"Martha—some coffee for us, and some for Katrina, as well." As Martha turned away from them, shaking her head, the smile faded from Chauncey's face. "There is some news, Rafe," he began seriously. "I couldn't interrupt you, obviously . . ."

"What is it?"

"I returned to Katrina's townhouse this morning." Chauncey hesitated and looked away.

"What happened? Tell me."

"The house is nearly burned to the ground, Rafe. There was

a crowd around it, including some delegates taking notes from the people.''

"Do they know—did anyone mention Katrina?"

"I didn't stay long enough to ask."

Rafe sighed heavily. "Let's hope that she isn't suspect. I grow weary of this revolution and its endless rounds of suspicion and accusation.''

Chauncey's brows shot up under the chestnut curls. "You grow weary? My, my, I never thought I'd hear those words from you, my dear half brother."

"It's been three years since the revolution began, Chauncey. How many years were we fighting before that? Too many. Now there are people more extreme than we are, ruling in the Assembly. Some kind of fateful cycle.''

"You wax philosophical, Rafe. Perhaps that has something to do with your evening—'' Chauncey stopped at the warning in Rafe's eyes.

"Sometimes," Rafe said slowly, "even I become nostalgic for security, for something quieter and easier, for an end to this constant battle.'' He sipped his coffee, and smiled rakishly over the rim. "But not too often.''

Chauncey laughed, and Martha shook her head in disapproval as she handed Chauncey his cup.

"I have a request for you, Chauncey," Rafe said in a more authoritative tone. "Katrina will need clothes. She'll be moving in here for an . . . indeterminate amount of time. Martha, you can go with him and make sure he buys all the appropriate articles. Though he knows enough about dressing—or should I say—*undressing* a woman, it would be nice if you were there to moderate his tastes. Then go by Katrina's townhouse again, Chauncey. There might be something to salvage.''

Katrina wandered through Rafe's small room, restless already after a morning's confinement. The heat of the summer day beat through the windows, warming the wooden floorboards. She pulled off her light chemise, tossed it casually upon the bed, and stepped over the heated wood, letting the warmth caress her toes. She wished Rafe would return from his mysterious excursion. After sharing breakfast in bed, he'd left with only a promise to return before sundown.

She smiled slowly, closing her eyes and hugging her arms to her body. The memory of his whispered words caused her blood to race, the recollection of his touch . . . Katrina shook her head, letting the tangled curls brush the small of her back. Such thoughts would be of no use until Rafe's return.

She stretched out on the mussed bed and pressed her face into the pillow. His scent emanated from the warmed linens. She smiled, unable to remember when she had felt so happy, so full, so totally whole.

Steps resounded on the stairs, and Katrina quickly pulled the bedclothes over her naked body, flushing with the thought that Martha might come up and greet her. The door opened and a dark head peered into the room.

"Rafe!" she exclaimed.

He turned to her, his black eyes bright as he saw her hair tumbling in confused waves over her shoulders and the bedclothes slipping enticingly over her breasts.

"Don't move," he said softly, and returned to the hall.

Katrina heard the bump of packages dropping on the floor, and in a minute, Rafe returned, one hand hidden behind his back. Carefully, he closed the door behind him.

"I thought you wouldn't be back for hours," Katrina said, her eyes settling on the hidden arm.

"Lay back," he whispered huskily, his eyes focused hungrily on her.

Smiling slowly, she lay back against the pillow, letting the linens drop lower on her body. Rafe stood over her for a moment, his eyes caressing the outline of her body.

"You're beautiful," he murmured. He reached for the roughened edge of the bedclothes, slowly pulling them off her. As if they, too, wanted to be near her skin, the linens clung stubbornly to the peaks of her breasts, then fell beneath them, moving smoothly over the silk of her midriff, her abdomen, then resting just above the curve of her hips. His eyes drank in the sight.

"And so are you," Katrina whispered, the touch of his eyes making her tremble. She reached for him, running a hand over his thigh. He captured her hand, bent down to kiss it, and returned it to her side. Smiling, he brought his hidden hand before her.

Katrina gasped as he fluttered fragrant blush-colored rose petals over her breasts, her belly, and upon the sheets. Their velvet softness kissed her skin.

"Rafe!" she exclaimed, picking up one of the delicate petals. "Where—"

He placed a finger upon her lips. "Hush," he said huskily. "I stole them from an unsuspecting delegate's garden." He reached for a petal, rubbing its softness against her cheek, then her jaw, following the line of her throat. Katrina's eyes fluttered shut as his caresses moved lower, to circle the hardening tip of her aureola. He silenced her gasp with his lips. "These petals look far better on you than they did on the stem."

Katrina ran her hands through the thick warmth of his dark hair. "I missed you," she murmured as his lips followed the path of the petals.

"And I missed you." His voice rumbled over her belly. "That's why I'm early. Chauncey and Martha are gone."

"Both of them are gone?" Katrina whispered as Rafe's hand moved over her hip.

"Yes," he said softly. "For most of the afternoon."

When they finally rose from the bed, much later, the rose petals clung tenaciously to their skin and left faint pink stains on the white linen. Katrina's face flushed as deeply as the color of the petals.

"I have a present for you," he said.

"Another?" she asked, reaching for her chemise.

His smile flashed for a moment before he pulled on his breeches. "This one is just for you, *petite.*" He opened the door and pulled in a large dress box.

"Rafe, what have you done?" she asked, approaching him. "I have so many dresses at my house—"

"None like this," he said, placing the box on the bed. "Come, open it."

Katrina, impulsively, threw herself upon him. His arms tightened around her body.

"Petite . . ." he whispered, overwhelmed. "I love you." He rubbed his face in her tangled hair. "But come, open your gift."

Katrina moved quickly to the bed and tore open the box. She gasped, pulling up the dress.

It was made of gold and white striped muslin; the sleeves were a mere whisper of white and clung to the bodice by golden ribbons; the cleavage dipped provocatively low. Katrina held the gown against her, unaware of the breathless effect the color had on her shining hair.

"You like it?" Rafe asked, a bit hesitantly.

She smiled. "It's exquisite."

"There's more," he urged. She dug through the box, lifting the dress entirely out. Rows of lace-edged petticoats followed, then corsets, two near-sheer chemises, and lacy, beribboned undergarments.

Katrina blushed. "Rafe . . ."

"You like them? For you, nothing is good enough."

"And when, my dear Rafe, am I going to wear such confections?"

"Tonight. At dinner," he said. "Martha thinks I'm not treating you right. I'll prove her wrong."

"If this is not treating me right," Katrina began, moving to his side, "then I don't want you to stop."

Their kiss was interrupted by an insistent knocking. Rafe pulled away from Katrina for a moment.

"Who is it?"

"It's Chauncey. And it's important."

Reluctantly, Rafe released Katrina who struggled into her chemise and pulled a new wrap around her figure. Rafe touched her cheek and smiled, then moved to a safe distance across the room.

"You can come in, Chauncey."

He entered without comment and shoved a folded journal into Rafe's hands.

"Look. Not one day has passed and the Jacobins have already derided Katrina in their rag of a paper." He paced the floor as his brother began reading.

When Rafe tossed the paper angrily to the floor, Katrina reached for the journal and scanned the front page for her name. She gasped.

Katrina d'Hausseville Depoitiers, who also calls herself the Duchess de Poitiers, said at her salon last night that the king "should not be caged up at the Tuileries" and should be allowed to roam free in France and abroad. As a member of the ancient order, she must indeed fear that she, too, will lose her power and estates if the Nation rises to power. Perhaps she has already helped our enemies at the borders. . . .

Katrina let the paper drop, her mouth agape. "What lies!" she exclaimed. "How dare they!"

"They dare anything, my love. Jacobin swine. I've a mind to—"

"Don't," Chauncey warned. "You can't say a thing to them, nor can you print anything to the contrary."

"Why not?" Rafe growled, his brows lowered in anger. "They have no right to abuse Katrina. They'll see what happens to—"

Chauncey's hand curled around his arm, pulling him to a stop. "Listen to me, Rafe. It's worse than you think. What was left of Katrina's house has been dismantled, stone by stone."

Katrina gasped, sinking down into the sheets. "No," she moaned. "No, not again. Not like Poitiers—" Rafe moved quickly to her side, and she clutched his hand.

"Rafe, they did it because they found two women, two 'patriots,' dead, in the house. But it's worse, Rafe—"

"Chauncey . . ."

"Rafe, if they find her, they'll have little mercy." Chauncey warned, turning in frustration.

"That's enough," Rafe snapped, tightening his hold on Katrina's hand.

"No, Rafe. You must hear this all." He took a deep breath and sat stiffly in the lyre-backed chair. "I went to the Jacobin club today. There was talk about arresting her for treason. Mind you, it's not just Katrina—many royalists are becoming suspect. There are reports that the Prussian forces are preparing to march into France. The Assembly is up in arms—they're calling for a national convention to write a new constitution, they want to set up a new Paris Commune with their own people in charge—"

"Stop, Chauncey. I'll hear no more." Rafe's command broached no argument, and Chauncey remained silent. Rafe's hands balled into fists.

"What is this? The Assembly may arrest me? For what crime?" she asked, wide-eyed, rising to stare at Rafe. "Treason? But there's no proof. I'm innocent—"

"In times like these, justice doesn't always prevail, Katrina," Rafe said soberly. "They seek people to blame for the war to come. The night before, you spoke in favor of the king—who they suspect is urging the *émigrés* to invade. And two *citoyennes* were found in your house, dead. And now you have disappeared.'' He stood, the anger evident in the taut lines of his body. ''If I know the Jacobins, they will be crying next for the execution of the king.''

''Right now they're only demanding his imprisonment,'' Chauncey stated.

Rafe shook his head, walking over to the windows. Chauncey and Katrina watched him expectantly.

''Katrina is safe here with me,'' he began slowly. ''If anyone asks, we know nothing of her whereabouts. Tell Martha this. Perhaps this will blow over in time—''

''Rafe . . .'' Chauncey interrupted.

Rafe ignored him. ''Katrina, you must stay in this room, away from the windows, at least for a while. Too many people come in and out of this shop for you to wander downstairs.'' He moved toward her again. ''It shouldn't last long. Perhaps the crowd's anger will pass on in a week or two.''

''Rafe,'' Chauncey repeated. ''It will be difficult to keep her presence a secret—''

''Quiet, Chauncey.''

''I won't be silent until I tell you this.'' He gripped the back of the chair. ''When I went past Katrina's townhouse this afternoon, there was someone there.''

Rafe's eyes flickered.

''Yes, Rafe,'' Chauncey said. ''The Marquis de Noailles.''

Chapter 22

The Marquis de Noailles stared at the delegate with a mixture of annoyance and distaste. "What are you trying to tell me, Monsieur? Haven't I given you enough information with which to accuse Beaulieu?"

The delegate shifted uneasily on the embroidered seat. "Beaulieu is a powerful man."

"A powerful traitor, you mean. I've paid you nearly ten thousand louis in gold—not in your worthless assignats—and all you can do is get his name on the list of suspects?"

"Money cannot suppress fear, Monsieur." The delegate glanced greedily at the crystal decanter of brandy resting on the silver tray before him, but the Marquis made no move to pour.

"Fear of what? His power wanes, and you know it." The marquis reached for his own glass of brandy. The golden cherubs and flying satyrs that shone on the ceiling of his study made a distorted reflection in the surface of the amber liquid. He swirled it, dissolving their mocking smiles.

"But what you've told us, Monsieur . . ." The delegate swallowed dryly. "It seems unbelievable. You've not shown us documents—"

"The documents are forthcoming. Do you doubt my word?"

"It's not my place to doubt you, Monsieur, but the other delegates . . . I've had difficulty keeping your own name off the list of suspects. The delegates are suspicious of all men of title."

"All the more reason why they should suspect Beaulieu."

The delegate's gaze shifted nervously to examine the gold silk covering the walls.

The marquis frowned. He had been in France since spring,

and he still hadn't succeeded in his goal. He was a patient man. He'd waited years to find Katrina again, but this delay sorely tested his endurance. Though the delegates thirsted for his gold, they gave little satisfaction in return.

"Has the future Duchess de Poitiers been found yet?"

The delegate, eager for a change in the topic of conversation, shook his head vigorously. "She's disappeared. She's now branded an *émigré* and will be arrested if found."

"You'll inform me when that happens."

"Of course."

The marquis unlocked one of the drawers in his gleaming mahogany desk and pulled out a soft leather bag. It clinked as he placed it on the veneer surface.

"This is the last payment I'll give you until you have arrested Beaulieu."

The delegate stared hungrily at the sack but tightened his hands. "I'm afraid, Monsieur, that Beaulieu will not be arrested, at least not based on what you have told me." He swallowed. "It's not enough to override the fear of the delegates."

The marquis's eyes narrowed. "Are you telling me it cannot be done?"

"No," he remarked. "I'm telling you we need more proof. If you had those documents—"

"Those documents will come anon." The marquis leaned over the desk. "Would it help if I told you that the Prussian troops have, just this morning, stepped onto French soil?"

The man's eyes widened. He clutched the edge of his cravat. "Today? They're now on French soil?"

"They're in Alsace and moving closer." The marquis smiled. The news had struck home—the delegate's face had paled to a deathly white. Terror, rather than gold, seemed to be the best form of coercion in Paris these days.

"I must—I must tell the National Convention," the delegate stuttered, rising to his feet.

The marquis rose stiffly and extended his hand. "You'll be discreet, of course." He handed the bag of gold to the delegate, who took it with shaking hands.

"Of course." Determination suddenly lit the delegate's eyes. "If Beaulieu is indeed a traitor, Marquis, I assure you that he will die before the Prussians ever reach the gates of Paris."

The marquis's thin lips spread into a smile as his guest exited through the high doors of his study. He sat down in his chair and twisted it to face the window to his garden.

It seemed he'd found a way to incite the men of the Assembly. He'd lied to the delegate—the Prussians did not plan to start their campaign for three weeks. The marquis knew the false information would not harm the *émigré* campaign; the French forces were weak and undisciplined. It would take years to form them into a strong, viable army. The *émigré* victory was inevitable— as inevitable as the death of Beaulieu and the marquis's marriage to the Duchess de Poitiers.

The marquis closed his eyes, remembering the sight of Katrina at the spring ball. She had hardly changed, only become more beautiful. He had once fancied himself in love with her, back before the revolution when she was still just a child.

Anger surged in his blood as he remembered her treachery. She had jilted him, left him at the altar of the church of his ancient marquisate, with hundreds of aristocrats to witness his shame. He would never forgive such an insult. *Never!*

He would have his vengeance, not only on Katrina, but also on the blackguard who had plagued him since before the revolution. The marquis traced the rigid scar that traveled from his forehead to his temple and around to beneath his cheekbone. Rafael Beaulieu was the cause of this disfigurement. He would pay for it with his life.

He rose and paced methodically over the thick rug. This time, Beaulieu would die. No man had ever wounded the Marquis de Noailles and lived to tell the tale.

How foolish the man had been to pit his small, useless band of brigands against him all those years ago. How foolish, even more so, to wound him—to scar him—and then continue to raid his estates. Every time the marquis learned of another raid, he knew the brigand mocked him. The marquis had finally bribed one of Rafe's men and set a trap for the brigands, but Beaulieu had escaped.

Three years later, Beaulieu had escaped again, from Coblenz. The marquis closed his eyes, anger rushing through him. Beaulieu had escaped twice. He would not escape a third time.

And now, with undiminished audacity, the brigand dared to take his woman. Katrina was with Beaulieu, he was sure. No one, least of all an aristocrat, could leave the city without the knowledge of the newly formed Commune. She was in Beaulieu's house, living with him, sharing his bed. If travel around Paris were not so dangerous, if trustworthy royalists were not so hard to find, the marquis would not hesitate to steal her away himself.

He closed his eyes as fury flamed his veins. *Patience,* he counseled himself. *Patience.* In a matter of weeks, if all went as planned, Beaulieu would be dead and Katrina de Poitiers would be writhing beneath him like a wanton.

"Monsieur." A liveried servant entered without ceremony, carrying a piece of dirty parchment on a gold tray.

The marquis scowled. His servants of yore would never have dared interrupt him without knocking first. The insolence of these Parisians would drive him to murder.

"What is it?"

"A courier has just delivered this, Monsieur. He says it's important."

The marquis quelled the urge to snatch the paper from the tray and gestured to the desk. "Set it down and close the doors behind you. I wish to be left alone."

The marquis stared at the note. Miraculously, the wax seal was unbroken. Gold could buy a trustworthy courier, at least. He fingered the grain of the parchment for a long time, testing his own patience. Finally, he reached for the ivory letter opener and slipped the smooth blade beneath the wax.

A slow smile twisted his face.

"Well, Beaulieu. Your time has come."

"And what of the Prussians?" Rafe asked, watching with disgust as Etienne shoved food between his parched lips

"Prussians took Longwy a week ago, as you probably already know," Etienne muttered, tearing off some white meat and pushing it down his throat.

Rafe nodded and sat back, moving away from the sack of food he had brought to this darkened forest, waiting until his associate had eaten his fill.

"When was the last time you ate?" he asked, his gaze wandering from Etienne's tousled hair, which was full of twigs and nettles, to his face, which was unshaven and drawn in hunger.

"Before Longwy. I found some berries in the forests on the way here, but barely enough to sustain me. I was followed and was unable to lose them until yesterday, but they know I am in this forest."

"Are they French or Prussian?"

"What matter?" Etienne asked, bringing the wine to his lips again. "It seems in Paris we are all enemies of one another. I've heard some bitter rumors, my friend." He sat on his rump, breathing regularly for the first time since Rafe had opened the sack before him.

"Not rumors," Rafe said. "I'm afraid it is all truth."

"The king and queen, imprisoned?"

"Put in the Temple. Danton and his damned Commune's work. That municipal authority grows far more powerful than the National Convention. They own the police and the National Guard."

"My mother's house was searched," Etienne said harshly. "They took her kitchen knives and my father's musket."

"The Commune has searched Paris for days, house by house, confiscating weapons. They have arrested hundreds of men and women on a whim. The prisons are so full that some of the people arrested have been put in monasteries and empty convents."

"And now, they've confined the citizens of Paris to their houses? What kind of law is this, my friend, that holds its people imprisoned in their own homes, locked within the walls of their city?"

Rafe shook his head, running a hand through his thick hair. "Since Longwy fell, Paris has been engulfed in some strange terror, Etienne. The Commune uses its police to seek out traitors, to confiscate weapons, to force people into submission. There's crazy talk of prison plots. The world has gone mad, and suddenly I'm powerless to do anything."

"If Beaulieu is powerless, I fear the monster that must have taken over Paris." Etienne settled back, his stomach swelling from the food he had so ravenously devoured.

"I fear I've come under suspicion, Etienne. It would be best if you dissociated from me. It won't be long before the Commune's agents knock at my door with a warrant for arrest."

"They wouldn't dare!" Etienne scoffed, wiping his mouth on the back of his dirty sleeve.

"You haven't been in Paris, Etienne. Since Danton and his cohorts orchestrated the attack on the Tuileries, which ended with the royal family's imprisonment, the power in the Assembly has shifted. Suddenly, this Commune has taken all power into its hands. I tried to dissolve it tonight, but from the look I received from Danton, it will be impossible." Standing, Rafe sighed and stretched his cramped limbs. "When Longwy fell, it strengthened Danton's policies. It justified the arrests, the searches, the stay on passports, the closing of the Parisian gates."

"Aye, then my news will not please you," Etienne said, finishing the last of the wine. "As I left the battlefield, the Prussians were advancing deeper into France, toward Verdun. I suspect they will have success there, as well. Their supply lines are thinning, but if they continue their rapid advance, they'll enter Paris and won't have to worry about supplies."

Rafe moved to his horse and patted its steaming neck. *So it comes to this.* The Prussians advancing without hindrance, and Paris being choked to death by its own government. And himself, nearly bereft of power, considered an enemy of his own country, watching in frustration as his life's work collapsed.

Rafe sighed heavily. What was left in Paris for him? He could stay and pull the last powerful strings he could, work with Roland and the other Girondists to dissolve this bestial Commune, and pray that the French troops would rise up and conquer the stronger Prussians. But more than likely, Rafe would end up in one of the many overflowing prisons in Paris, awaiting the invasion of the triumphant *émigrés*. Either way, the result was death: death at the hands of his own countrymen, or death at the hands of the *émigrés*, ironically his own countrymen, as well.

He feared more for Katrina. Rafe closed his eyes, and a smile flitted across his face. *Sweet Katrina.* How precious the last month had been, with her presence always in his house, always near, even now in his heart.

"Don't mourn so, Beaulieu," Etienne said behind him. "Do you think the people will ever willingly submit to a king again? What we've done was for the best."

"Perhaps. I'm just getting old and tired of this, Etienne. I yearn for something easier."

"I suppose your lady does, as well," Etienne said. "Perhaps it's time for you two to leave this place."

"No, Etienne. I must see this damned revolution through to the end, no matter how bitter."

"Yes, it's like that with men like you, Beaulieu,' Etienne said sagely, rising to his feet. "You die fighting in the flames of your own home." He spread his hands. "As for me . . ."

"As for you," Rafe said authoritatively. "You must remain in this forest for some time. I'll tell your family and the others that you are safe. You mustn't try to enter Paris. I can't get a *certificat de civisme* for you—only the Commune can write them, and they do not approve of me." He sighed. "In a week, you must leave France. It's no longer safe for you here."

"I feared you would say that. My wife—"

"If you wish, I'll arrange for her to leave with you," Rafe said. "But you must remember the danger you'll put her in."

"She's a strong woman. She'll do as you bid."

Nodding, Rafe turned away from Etienne and kicked his horse into a gallop. Seconds later, Rafe's shape merged with the darkness of the forest.

"Ah, Beaulieu," Etienne said sadly, listening while the horse's hooves faded into the distance. "I'm afraid that's the last I'll see of you. The shadow of death dances darkly on your soul."

Katrina squinted in the dull light as she placed another letter in the printer's plate. Her fingers were stained from the ink made of linseed and lampblack, but she didn't care. All she cared about right now was finishing this plate before Rafe returned from whatever new political development was keeping him away from her.

She flushed at the thought of him. He had treated her like a precious, fragile loved one these past weeks, buying her rare, expensive books to entertain her while she stayed hidden in his room. Every moment he didn't spend with the National Convention or with his own men, he spent with her. She could see the exhaustion on his face. Many a night she had eased the aches from his shoulders and brushed his dark hair until he slept upon her breast.

Chafing at the inactivity of her isolation, she had begged Rafe to give her some work—something that would help him. Reluctantly, Chauncey and Rafe had pulled a workbench near the back of the shop, hidden from the door by the stairs. Here she could set up printer's plates for Rafe's paper, *Révolution*, yet still be close enough to the stairs to hide if a stranger arrived.

Martha bustled around the kitchen, preparing the midday meal. She hummed as she worked in the sun-drenched room, and the sound seemed odd to Katrina, considering all that was happening outside these walls.

She closed her eyes and pushed the worries from her mind. She wouldn't think of what could happen—she must not. She must live each day, one at a time, and thank God that she and Rafe had finally been reunited.

The door to the shop opened, and she quickly pulled her dark shawl over her hair. She peered around the edge of the staircase.

"Rafe!" Tossing off the shawl, she scampered around the stairs and flung herself into his arms.

His deep laugh rumbled in his chest. "I should leave and return more often," he laughed, "just for the reception you give me."

"Don't you dare!" she warned. "You spend enough time away."

"I know, *petite.*" His dark eyes glowed at her. "But not willingly, I assure you. You've got ink on your pretty face, my sweet. You've been working on that plate all morning, haven't you?"

"Oh, dear. And I wanted it to be a surprise." She reached up to rub her nose, only making it worse, and Rafe laughed.

"Here, let me." He led her away from the windows into the depths of the shop, noting that Martha tactfully disappeared deeper into the kitchen. He reached for a clean linen from one of the workbenches and straddled a bench beside Katrina. He tilted her chin up and gently rubbed the tip of her nose.

"How was your meeting?" Katrina asked, wrinkling her nose to make his job more difficult.

Rafe's lips parted into a smile at her antics. "It went well enough. I didn't learn anything new. The Prussians are still marching into France."

"How close are they?"

Rafe finished his cleaning and wadded the linen in his hand. "They are nearing Verdun." He kissed her nose as she gasped.

"So close?"

"I'm afraid so." Rafe released her chin but did not move away. "How would you like to take a trip to England, my love?"

Katrina's eyes widened. "England? You mean emigrate?"

Rafe winced at the word. "Not emigrate, but leave before the *émigrés* and the Austrians and Prussians march into Paris. Most of the National Convention will do the same, otherwise the king and his cohorts will kill everyone who was involved in the revolution. We'll go to England and plan how to reclaim France."

"You really think the Prussians and *émigrés* will win?"

"Yes, barring some miracle." Rafe ran a hand over her bright hair. "Either way, it is dangerous for you to be here, Katrina. I want you safe."

"You're coming with me?"

"Of course." He kissed her soft cheek. "I promised I would never leave you, my love. I meant that."

"Now, now, none of that." Martha bustled out into the main room and looked at them sternly. "We'll be eating dinner soon and I want you both at the table, not upstairs."

Katrina flushed, but Rafe smiled rakishly. "Martha, could it be that you are jealous?"

Martha glowered, then laughed and returned to the hidden depths of the kitchen.

"Come, Katrina," Rafe said. "Show me what you've done today."

"I've nearly finished. I know you wanted to print these leaflets before the next Convention meeting tomorrow."

"You work far too hard, *petite.*" Rafe leaned over her shoulder and stared at the plate. "I feel like I'm taking advantage of you."

"By all means, do so," she teased, her eyes shining as she looked up at him.

He tore his gaze away from her dancing eyes and examined the plate. "I'll have to tell Chauncey that you are besting him at his own craft." He reread the plate, this time more slowly. "I cannot find a single error. Chauncey always has one or two letters in reverse."

"Chauncey has his mind on other things," Katrina remarked. "On Daphne, in particular."

"Yes, women have a way of stealing into a man's heart and distracting him from his work." Rafe wrapped his arms around her and pulled her against him.

She closed her eyes and rested her cheek on his fine linen shirt. "Are you objecting?"

"Heavens, no." He kissed her hair and rocked her silently in his arms. He stared over her head at the plate and frowned. The article addressed the need for moderation: in the Convention, in the Commune, in the ranks of the National Guard. The words seemed empty and useless, considering the current state of the city.

"I think it best that we leave Paris, Rafe," Katrina said quietly, her voice muffled against his shirt. "Even if we stay, you're in danger."

Rafe did not deny it.

"And this article will put you in more danger."

"You are far too bright, *petite.* Here I stand thinking I've kept all that worry away from you."

"I know you, Rafe," she whispered, "as I know my own heart. Did you think you could keep such a secret from me?"

His lips curved in a soft smile. "And you, my love, do you think you can keep secrets from me?" He reached down to gently stroke her stomach, and Katrina flushed to the roots of her hair.

"How did you know? I mean . . . I am not sure yet, but—"

"I have spent the last month, day and night, by your side, Katrina. I know your body well enough to see the signs."

He knew! Katrina reddened anew and looked away. He knew that she was carrying their child!

"You don't regret it?" he asked softly, lifting her chin up. "You're happy for this?" Doubt and hesitation clouded his eyes.

"Of course I am, Rafe. I've never been happier. I just didn't know if you'd be pleased."

"Ah, my sweet Katrina." Rafe hugged her tighter and nuzzled the silky warmth of her hair. "Nothing could please me more than the fruit of our love." He pulled away and a devilish smile spread over his face. "Now you'll have to marry me."

"It's about time you asked," Martha said as she peered around the edge of the kitchen.

Rafe and Katrina gaped at her.

"Have you been eavesdropping?" he asked with mock anger.

Martha's dark eyes sparkled. "These walls are as thin as the parchment upon which you print, Monsieur."

"Really, Martha!" Katrina exclaimed, blushing.

"You haven't answered him yet, Mademoiselle. I suggest you do so quickly before the rake changes his mind."

"I won't change my mind," Rafe assured Katrina. "But I'd like to hear your answer."

Katrina's heart pounded with love, and she was sure she was dreaming. She smoothed her new calico dress over her still-flat belly.

"Yes, my love."

As Rafe swept Katrina into his arms, Chauncey entered the shop with a whistle. He stopped short and frowned.

"Are they at it again, Martha?"

"Hush! Monsieur Beaulieu has just asked her to marry him."

"Was she fool enough to say yes?"

"Indeed, I was," Katrina said breathlessly as Rafe released her. She glanced at Rafe then hurried across the uneven floor-boards to embrace Chauncey. "Aren't you going to congratulate your future sister-in-law?"

"I think the correct response is 'good luck.' " He bent down to kiss her on the cheek. "I think you'll need it."

"Well, brother! Home from another night of debauching fine young women?" Rafe slipped an arm around Katrina and pulled her back against him.

Chauncey glanced away and reddened.

"My goodness, Rafe!" Katrina exclaimed. "I believe Chauncey is blushing!"

"I would say so. That is definitely a rose color on those tender cheeks."

"Nearly scarlet, I think," Katrina persisted unmercifully. "Would it be due to a certain Daphne d'Haliparte, I wonder?"

Chauncey pulled off his waistcoat and turned his back to them. "Well, Martha, it's two o'clock. Is dinner ready yet?"

"It seems the gentleman will not speak on the subject," Rafe teased. "Perhaps the lady has jilted him."

"Indeed not!" Chauncey burst. "But I mustn't talk about it— not even to you, my brother. *Sacre bleu*, let's have *some* respect of privacy in this house!"

"Sounds as though there will be another wedding in the family before the year's end," Rafe murmured.

"I certainly hope so," Katrina agreed as she sat on one of the wooden benches next to Rafe and joined hands with Martha and Chauncey to say grace before dinner. Rafe and Katrina ceased their teasing, for Chauncey had grown so red-faced they felt it would be cruel to continue.

Martha bubbled as she fussed over the newly engaged couple. "Come, Mademoiselle, eat some more meat. You'll be needing it for the years to come." She spooned more stew onto Katrina's overflowing plate.

"She'll need more than meat to fortify her," Chauncey jibed. A light glowed in his eyes—a gleam that portended ribald stories. "She'll need—"

"Hush!" Rafe said, lifting his head sharply.

"Come now, Rafe. You've had your fun with me—"

"Quiet, Chauncey. Listen." Rafe stood up from the table and strode across the shop to the door, his legs tense beneath his dark breeches.

Katrina's heart pounded. She strained her ears but could hear nothing except the usual sounds of the mid-afternoon streets.

"Katrina, go down to the secret room. Don't come up until we tell you." Rafe glanced at Chauncey. "I think we're going to have guests."

"No . . ." Katrina let out a half-strangled cry.

Rafe took her firmly by the arms and led her to the kitchen, out of sight of the front door. He pushed away the worn rug and lifted up the trap door. "Come, *petite,* there's no time to waste."

She reached for him, and he kissed her hard and full upon the lips, then lowered her onto the ladder into the secret room.

"Remember: don't come out until we tell you."

"Open up!" The voice boomed from behind the heavy front door. "Open up, Beaulieu, in the name of the Commune!"

"Rafe! Please, you must hide with me!"

"I'm an innocent man, Katrina."

"What do they care about that?"

"We'll knock this door down if you don't open it, Beaulieu!"

Rafe bent to kiss Katrina's cheek. "Don't say a thing, Katrina. Not a thing." He closed the door above her.

As Rafe moved into the main shop, Chauncey opened the door. A group of National Guards rushed in. They brandished their muskets before them, as if protecting their bodies from some invisible onslaught.

"You're under arrest, Beaulieu," the leader said, his large belly barely confined within his uniform.

"And what are the charges?" Rafe asked, crossing his arms before him.

The man looked blankly into his piercing eyes. A few of the guards behind the leader shifted their weight, averting their gazes from the fierce glare of the famed Beaulieu.

"Treason, Beaulieu. You are an enemy of the people."

"I don't believe I've had a trial yet, Champetre," Rafe spat.

The man seemed to recoil at the knowledge of his name. "Come peaceably, Beaulieu," Champetre retorted. "Else we'll have to force you along."

"I'll come peaceably," Rafe said, "but you'll leave these people and my shop untouched."

The man hesitated, eyeing Chauncey and Martha. He obviously wanted to retort but decided against it. Everyone knew that Beaulieu was not a man to trifle with. Reluctantly, he nodded.

In the darkness of the secret room, hot tears burned trails down Katrina's smooth cheeks.

Chapter 23

The guard at a side door of La Force leered at Katrina as he accepted the coins from Chauncey. Katrina's skin crawled as she pulled her shawl over her head, trying to ignore his stare. Chauncey stepped before her and smiled into the guard's face.

"Come now, good patriot. We've paid you your due. Let us in to see the famous Beaulieu."

The man eyed Chauncey with some annoyance, but turned to open the door. It screeched against the pressure. Katrina choked at the stench rising from the dark interior and took Chauncey's arm before descending into the prison.

The guard led them down a dimly lit hallway lined with rooms full of prisoners. Their voices, some raised in raucous singing, others in prayer, echoed over the damp, thick walls. The heat and sweat of a hundred bodies filled the reeking hall. A few of the prisoners poked their heads through the doorways, whistling at her. She moved closer to Chauncey, wondering if the prisoners could leap out and accost them as they passed.

A thin sheet of sweat bathed her body. The odor of the prison made her feel faint. *So many prisoners,* she thought. *How many more will the Commune arrest before they are satisfied?*

At the end of another hallway, the guard reached out to unlock a door which opened onto a wide courtyard. Katrina gasped for air and lifted her face to the dim evening light. The sky was streaked with pink-tinted clouds, and for a moment she watched them float across the darkening heavens, then came to her senses and rushed to catch up to the guard. He opened another door, and Katrina gulped in one last breath of fresh air in preparation for another stench-ridden hall.

346

But this door opened to a wider hallway, the walls glistening with cleanliness rather than infested drops of dew. The lingering scent of a man's rich cologne hung in the air, and across the hall moved several well-dressed gentlemen, some in powdered wigs, silks, and brocades. There was none of the din of the lower wing, nor the confinement. Along the walls were openings to rooms that had no doors.

Katrina looked at Chauncey in surprise. It seemed as if these well-dressed, calm men were preparing for an afternoon of cards, nothing more. She wasn't sure, but she thought she could hear the clatter of silver against porcelain coming from the large room at the end of the hall.

"Prison can be quite tolerable if you have the resources," Chauncey stated, his voice low. "This is where the aristocrats are kept, along with other wealthier prisoners—lawyers, deputies with means . . ."

"It doesn't seem like a prison."

"Don't be fooled, Katrina," he said swiftly. "This is indeed a prison, and these men are in more danger than the ones in the other wing."

The guard pointed at an open doorway. "Fifteen minutes," he said gruffly, pulling his red hat over his eyes.

Katrina rushed through the door. The light of the sunset, bursting through the small, high window, lay across Rafe's broad shoulders. He opened his arms to her.

"Have they hurt you?" She pressed against him and felt his lips on her head.

"No, *petite.*" His voice was raw.

"Rafe, we must get you out of here." She pushed against the hardness of his ribs. "I've brought gold—"

"We will talk of this later, my love."

"We must talk now. We must get you out of this place—"

"Rafe, there's not much time." Chauncey's calm voice came from the doorway.

"Yes." Smoothing his hand over Katrina's temple, Rafe gazed into her green eyes. "I asked you a question yesterday, Katrina. Do you remember it?"

Her lips curved into a shy smile. "Of course."

"Then, do you still want to be my wife, even though I'm now a prisoner?"

"Of course I do."

Rafe motioned to the pallet that was his bed and Katrina started. A man sat upon it, watching them. She observed his dark habit, the prayer book, the crucifix about his neck.

"Mademoiselle, I am Father Vignerot." The priest bowed, clutching his book.

Katrina returned the salutation, and turned to Rafe with questions poised on her lips.

"The *curé* is in prison because he wouldn't take the constitutional oath. He's agreed to marry us right here, right now." Rafe's eyes softened. "If you're sure it is what you want."

"Rafe, of course—"

"Katrina, please. Before you agree, think of what you're doing. If I'm convicted, then you will be in danger, too. And our little one."

"I'm already in danger, Rafe, and I want our child to bear your proud name. But why are we rushing? You will be out soon enough, and then we can have a proper wedding."

Chauncey and Rafe exchanged glances.

"Just tell me, love, will you marry me now?" Rafe reached for her hands.

Katrina's head spun at the sudden strange turn of events, but she could think of no reason why she shouldn't marry him now. She looked down at her coarse calico dress, which was stained from brushing against the ink-smeared worktables. So much for marrying in ivory satin and pearls with fragrant pink roses and a velvet-clad man at her side. . . .

She glanced up at Rafe's dark features, the lines of his strong chin blurred by the growth of his beard. His eyes radiated with love, and she smiled, her heart warming.

She'd waited for him for so long.

"Yes."

Rafe led her to a table that would serve as an altar. They knelt, and Katrina barely listened to the *curé* as he droned in Latin. She turned to stare at the man who would soon be her husband.

His gaze grew warm on her face. He noted the fading rays of sunlight dancing in the thickness of her hair, then probed her eyes, searching for and finding the love he needed, the love that he returned to her in full force.

A strange feeling captured her as she watched the light linger in his blue-black hair. An evening breeze slipped through the high window and moved lower to encircle the kneeling couple. For a moment she was transported out of the prison cell to a clearing in the forest of Poitiers. The leafy-green canopy above them rustled in the wind, ruffling his linen shirt and tossing her curls in disarray. His precious, dark eyes swept her figure and she felt his glance like hands on her skin.

"Do you, Katrina d'Hausseville de Poitiers, take this man . . ." The priest droned on, his voice faint.

Katrina swore she smelled the scent of jasmine drift to her as the man, her man, moved closer, his eyes asking wordless, tender questions.

"I do," she murmured, lost in Rafe's velvet gaze. The fantasy entwined with reality as Rafe came closer, as his hands clutched her own and drew her body against his.

". . . for as long as you both shall live?" The priest's voice was a mere buzz in Katrina's head as Rafe's hands moved behind her, pulling her shawl and letting her hair fall freely over her shoulders.

"I do," he whispered, his face inches from hers.

She reached up to trace the edge of his jaw, loving the feel of his rough beard beneath her hand. He caught her hand in his own, raised it to his lips, and pressed a fervent kiss on her fingers.

". . . with the power vested in me . . ."

Rafe lifted her hair like a veil to reveal the smooth, glowing skin, the radiant smile, the eyes that were not big enough to hold all the love she had for him.

"I now pronounce you man and wife."

A smooth cold band slipped on her finger before Rafe's lips descended upon her own—clinging, merging, joining them in the eternal bonds of matrimony.

Katrina swore that somewhere, beyond the damp prison walls, she heard a lark sing its approval.

Rafe rose from the lumpy pallet that served as his bed. He rolled his shoulders to unwind the kinks that had knotted in them during the restless night. It seemed like weeks since he had slept. Although only the first rays of the morning were filtering through the dusty air, Rafe knew that there was no use in trying to sleep any longer.

Some wedding night, he mused, rising to splash his face with stale, dusty water. *I'm in a prison cell and she's in my room.* His last image of her, as they sealed their union with sacred vows, was etched in his mind. A few words from a priest and their union was sanctioned. Suddenly Rafe realized that he had been bound to Katrina long before, that this ritual was only the verbal realization of all that had already passed between them, and that somehow their ties would reach further and deeper than the grave.

He shook his head free of the morbid thoughts. He sensed the edgy hysteria in the air. Paris bordered on another explosion, and he feared he would be one of the casualties. It seemed somewhat ironic that he would become a victim of the kind of riots he had once provoked.

Rafe lifted his chin and rubbed the thickness of his beard. His mouth curled under the dark stubble, one side lifting higher than the other. It seemed, then, that his life was coming to a head. All would be determined in the next few days, if that long. If he were convicted, his head would roll and his soul would be consumed by the fires of this damned revolution. If he were acquitted, then he would leave all this, take Katrina away from this stinking city, and raise their children in a far more peaceful place.

He gazed out the prison window, his eyes lingering on the gray eastern sky. The city was still and airless this morning. The few boys that flitted through the Rue St. Honoré ran on soundless feet, as if afraid to break the silence of the misty September morning.

Rafe's black eyes softened as he thought of Katrina, his wife, his lover. The thought of being with her in a calm village many leagues from Paris sounded like the closest thing to heaven on this earth.

The sound of scurrying footsteps inside the prison riveted his attention. Through the cell door he watched wigmakers, covered with powder, racing to their patrons on the other end of the hall. The smell of strong coffee drifted across the room, and Rafe's stomach growled in response. He reached for his linen shirt, now quite dirty, and pulled it over his unruly hair.

"Beaulieu."

Rafe jerked to his feet and stared at the figure in the doorway. The man's features were covered by a perfumed handkerchief, but there was no mistaking that barrel-chested form.

"Noailles," Rafe said with a sneer. "So the Commune has finally come to its senses and imprisoned you." Rafe's voice, low and bitter, cut through the cell's dampness.

"How foolish of you," the marquis remarked. "They wouldn't dare imprison me." He dropped his handkerchief and tucked it into a small pocket in his waistcoat. His gray eyes glittered with a mad light as they traveled over Rafe's disheveled form. Two guards stood behind him, their arms crossed.

"What do you want, Noailles? Say it and leave."

"I want what I've always wanted." The marquis stepped into the dim room, his gaze never wavering from Rafe's. "And this time, I shall have it."

A muscle twitched in Rafe's cheeks. He wanted to lunge at this aristocrat and tear his limbs from his body, but he knew that to do so would mean instant death. The armed guards would pounce on him immediately. *Perhaps that is why he has come.*

"You overestimate your own power. This is Paris, Marquis, not Coblenz."

"That matters little. Soon enough the *émigré* troops will be here. Or haven't you heard? The Austrians have taken Verdun."

Rafe remained silent, but the news hovered heavily in the air between them.

"Yes, Beaulieu. The army is now on a crest overlooking Paris." The marquis laughed and toyed with his golden watch chain. "One could say that the wolf is at the gates."

"I see it pleases you to bring me such news."

"It always pleases me to see you in pain, Beaulieu. And I shall see you in much more pain before the day is through."

"What, does the Commune now hand its prisoners over to aristocrats? What a surprising twist of logic."

"The Commune has already begun the process of your trial. I've merely asked for the privilege of prolonging the sentence. I've been allowed to watch your death, Beaulieu, and I intend to make the show a long and delicious one."

Rafe's lips quirked. "Should I be frightened? Did you expect me to grovel at your feet?" His insolent smile gleamed in the dim light.

The marquis frowned. "You'll grovel at my feet when I'm carving your heart out of your body."

"I shall spit blood at you."

"Really? I suspect you'll tell me anything to ease your torment," the marquis continued. "Including the whereabouts of Katrina de Poitiers."

Rafe's eyes flared. The smile disappeared and his powerful chest heaved.

"Ah, I see I've hit a nerve."

"I won't hear her name from your filthy lips!"

"You'll have no choice after you're dead. I know you're hiding her now, but after you're dead, Beaulieu, I'll find her and force her to marry me."

Rafe crossed the distance in a blink. He lunged and the marquis fell heavily to the floor. Rafe's teeth bared white in his dark face as he squeezed his fingers around the marquis's neck.

The two guards raced in and pulled Rafe's arms, but even the combined strength of two men could not release Rafe's deathly grip. The marquis's eyes bulged out of sunken sockets, yet Rafe continued the pressure. Two other guards, hearing the struggle, ran in and pried Rafe's fingers from the marquis. Rafe struck out, knocking one man to the floor and sending another sprawling across the bed before he lunged once more for the marquis. But the aristocrat retreated to a safe distance while another guard pressed a pistol against Rafe's face. He stilled.

The marquis brushed dust off his velvet waistcoat, breathing heavily from the attack. This was just one more reason to extend his torture.

"You'll regret this, Beaulieu."

"The only thing I regret is that I didn't kill you."

"You'll be dead before sunset." The marquis straightened and pulled upon his waistcoat. "If you're lucky."

Katrina stamped her foot in frustration as she whirled away from the guards. No one would let her in, no matter how many gold louis she waved in front of them. They glanced greedily at the money but shook their heads, warning her to leave. She knew she shouldn't show such agitation, but she had to see Rafe, and these fools wouldn't let her.

The hawkers had announced that Verdun had been taken by

the Austrians. The enemy was close, and the knowledge had brought all the people of Paris into the streets, where they milled about in hysteria. Katrina shrank away from the sweeping crowds, her eyes wary on the pikes and scythes they all seemed to carry. The scene reminded her all too much of Versailles.

She moved into the Rue St. Antoine, staring in fear at the swarms of people heading in the direction of the Seine. Barefooted women, their hair loose and their voices raised high against the "enemies of the people," led a large contingent of pike-wielding peasants. Katrina noted the multitude of red caps worn by the lower class, the men with their scarred legs sticking out of their *sans-culottes*. She was thankful she was wearing her faded calico rather than the gold striped muslin hanging in Rafe's armoire. Bravely she stuck her chin in the air and marched with the crowd, praying she would be ignored.

"Pretty wench, would you like some wine?" A hand encircled her arm, and she looked up into the dirt-smeared face of a peasant. His red cap was drawn low over his greasy hair and his mouth gaped loosely. She reeled back at the smell of his breath.

"Non, thank you, patriot. If I drink any more of that, I'll be falling in the streets!" she said, forcing a chuckle, hoping her story convinced him.

He threw his head back and laughed. "Oh, a little more won't hurt, wench." His gaze roved over her fichu, but she moved away quickly and lost him in the crowd.

She noticed a man with a paste pot and brush fastening an announcement on the pillar of one of the gates of La Force. She moved through the drunken crowds to get a closer look.

Katrina skimmed the report on the loss at Verdun, catching her breath when she reached what she had feared.

The people must execute justice themselves. Before we hasten to the frontier, let us put bad citizens to death. . . .

She clasped a hand over her heart, whirling to stare at the wild-eyed patriots that jammed the streets.

They could not—they would not! But as she searched the angry, hard faces, she knew they would.

There would be no justice here, just the hysterical mass murder of prisoners to ease the minds of the bloodthirsty Parisians!

Her heart thumped painfully in her chest, and she grasped the pillar for support, resting her hot forehead on its cold surface.

"*Sacre bleu!* They will kill Rafe," she said, the idea bringing sweat to her palms. "What am I to do?" Grasping her skirts tightly, she raced into the center of the crowd and followed its inevitable flow.

Choruses of "*Ça Ira, Ça Ira*" burst around her ears, loud and raucous. Her head was spinning. She knew she had to get into La Force, get to Rafe, and pull him from prison before a tribunal was set up. *Get to Rafe.* She stumbled toward the front gates of the prison, ignoring the scythes that glinted in the sun, the pikes waving in the air. Her nose flared at the stink of hundreds of unwashed bodies marching in the sweltering afternoon. Her hands bunched her calico skirt and lifted it out of the mire. She squinted against the sun at the crowds gathering around the mouth of La Force.

Oh, no. My dear God, no!

She ran, dodging the lowered scythes, the bodies that milled around the prison. Her eyes settled on the darkened stone walls, willing Rafe to feel her presence, willing herself to feel his. She ran into a thicker group of people, knocking and elbowing them out of her way as she passed, ignoring the sharp curses that pounded in her ears. *Get to Rafe.*

Sweat poured from her face, down her neck and back. The salty drops stung her eyes. Her chest heaved from running, her feet were torn by the street, but she could think of only one thing. . . .

Suddenly her breath was cut off as a strong arm fastened around her waist. Her body folded in two from the impact. She was pulled against a hard body and she slumped, dark spots dancing before her eyes, as someone forced a bottle to her lips. She drank the water greedily.

"Stop struggling, Katrina."

She whirled around, staring into Chauncey's brown eyes, which were partially hooded by a red cap. He was clad in coarse workclothes, his pants ending in ragged edges at his knees.

"Chauncey! We must get to Rafe! They're going to kill the prisoners."

"Hush, Kat," he said. "I know. Some prisoners were going to be executed in the Abbaye de St. Germain, but they never made it. They were killed in the streets by the mobs.'' Her hand flew to her throat. ''But what the hell are you doing here when you should be home waiting for me?''

''I had to see Rafe. You were gone all night. I was losing my mind in worry. Did you expect me to sit home like a wilting flower?''

''I suppose not.'' His chin hardened has he looked toward La Force. ''This means I'll have to tell Martha—'' He stopped himself.

''What are you talking about?'' Katrina asked, her brows drawing together in confusion.

''Later, Kat. Do you still have that gold you tried to give Rafe yesterday?'' She nodded, reaching under her skirt to retrieve the coins from her garter.

''We're going to need it. Come with me.''

''But what's going on?'' she cried.

Chauncey pulled on her arm, moving through the dense crowd. His voice floated back to her. ''You'll see.''

Katrina squeezed into a space near the front of the hall where the impromptu trials were in progress. Chauncey followed her, his eyes searching the room.

Katrina gasped at the sight of the tribunal. Four men were sitting at a table, one wearing a red sash. She supposed he was the head judge. She stared in horror at the brandy bottle discarded under the table, and at the snoring, gaping mouth of one of the jurors. The juror farthest from her was flirting with a young girl in a neat peasant's cap, ignoring the proceedings completely.

''Your profession?'' the judge asked the rag-clad man standing before the tribunal.

The wretch twisted his hands nervously. ''I'm a cobbler's apprentice, Monsieur.''

''You have been charged with stealing from a grocer. How do you plead?''

''Not guilty, Monsieur.''

The crowd erupted in hisses, and Katrina swirled to stare at Chauncey, who paid her no heed. Drawing her brows together, she followed his gaze but couldn't see anyone she recognized. The crowd was still yelling in joyous accusation, waving their red caps in the air, and tilting their heads back to pour wine into their mouths.

Katrina sucked in her breath as she once again scanned the tribunal.

The marquis!

He tightened his hold on his gold-handled cane, his lips curving in a smile of recognition. Katrina gasped as he lifted himself from the lathed chair and nodded in her direction. He sat down again, crossed his satin-clad legs, and brushed a fleck of dirt from his sleeve. As she watched in horror, he reached into his waistcoat and drew out a piece of folded parchment.

"Chauncey!" Katrina choked, reaching back to clutch his coarse shirt.

His hand fell upon hers, stilling her. "Kat, please," he whispered close to her ear. "You must relax, else they'll pull you from the crowd and set you before the tribunal. Keep your shawl tight on your head. They must not see your hair."

Katrina paled slightly and straightened. "The marquis is here," she said. "He's sitting in the back, nearly behind the judge's table. Look."

Chauncey lifted his eyes until he saw the nobleman. His lips tightened. "I should've known that bastard would be here," he said harshly. "While in Turin, the marquis told Rafe he'd be present on his judgment day."

"The marquis has some kind of document with him—"

"Don't worry, Katrina. We've outwitted the marquis before."

"But—"

Chauncey's finger on her lips silenced her. She turned back stiffly. For as long as she could remember, the marquis had terrorized her, his gray eyes and twisted, scarred face haunting her darkest nightmares. Now, today of all days, he appeared in the flesh to torture her once more. Her body flooded with anger and she turned to face him. *At least he will not know that I am afraid.*

"This man is guilty as charged," the judge said, tossing the paper in his hand to one side. A thick sheaf of parchment lay before him. As the man was led off by the guards, the observers shouted obscenities.

Minutes later, his piercing scream echoed through the stony hallways, reverberating through the judgment chamber and lingering in Katrina's mind.

She would have fainted if Chauncey's arms had not held her up. He swung her around and brought his lips down on hers. Startled, she pushed forcefully away from him. He released her, a rakish smile spreading across his face.

"Nothing better than a wench with the taste of wine on her lips," he said loudly, winking at the men who were watching the scene with interest. Katrina stamped her foot and turned her back to him, but he moved up behind her and encircled her in his arms.

"You'd better not faint again, my sister-in-law," he whispered in her ear. "Else I'll drag you out of here bodily and put you in Martha's care."

"You will not drag me out of here!" Katrina said loudly, bringing more laughter from the eavesdroppers.

"I certainly will, Kat," Chauncey whispered. "I do have some of Rafe's blood in me. Besides, I didn't go to all the trouble to save my brother to have you endangered, as well."

"Don't fear, brother-in-law. I won't faint again."

"Pity," he said, teasing, a smile playing around his lips. "I rather enjoyed that kiss."

"You're guilty as charged," the judge said, sending another man off to the guards.

Katrina gasped. That man had hardly had a few minutes before the tribunal. . . .

Another scream soon filled the room, and the observers added their excited cries to the agonizing yell.

Another prisoner was led to the tribunal, and the judge began his questions anew, without even glancing at the paper before him. Katrina watched in fascination as the judge pronounced him guilty, to the joy of the spectators, and sent him off with two guards into the hell in the courtyard below. More prisoners were led in: a hairdresser who had dared to work for the aristocrats; a young boy caught stealing an apple from one of the vegetable carts; a girl accused of spying for the Austrians because of her relationship with an *émigré;* a dozen refractory priests who still refused to take the oath to the constitution. Hardly had the screams of the last victim died away before the death cries of the new filled the room.

Katrina shook her head free of the terror, stiffening her body against her faintness. The screams came regularly now and were almost indistinguishable from the raucous yells and cries of the people who swarmed around the judges' table. She opened her eyes and stared at the marquis.

Satan. He sat there, ruling these hellish proceedings, his pallid face a deathly white, his eyes the color of granite. How fixed his gaze was on her, as if she were the next victim. She trembled, nervous laughter rising to her lips.

Chauncey's hands gripped her shoulders roughly. "Hush, Katrina," he whispered. "Don't break down now. It's nearly over."

"We've been here for hours, Chauncey. Hours, while dozens of men and women and children have—"

"Shh." He pressed a finger to her lips. "Come. The judge is nearly at the end of his list. Rafe will soon be—"

"Soon?" she said harshly. "Then I shall hear his scream, too, as he dies?"

Chauncey's eyes softened as he saw the hysteria in her bright eyes. "Don't lose hope, Katrina."

"Rafael Etienne Beaulieu," the judge said.

Katrina straightened. She pushed past Chauncey and moved near to the front of the group, ignoring the curses of the women she displaced. She searched the dark entrance of the prison for Rafe.

Rafe's hands were tied behind his back, and his dirty linen shirt was torn and open to his abdomen. He glanced around the room as he entered, swaggering into the light. He stopped, smiling toward the crowd, but a guard poked him with the end of his bayonet and urged him to the middle of the room.

Even disheveled, Rafe cut a fine figure. The white of his teeth flashed, and his dark eyes shifted with annoyance to the judge and then back to those in the room.

His jaw tightened when he saw Katrina. He looked over her head and flashed a warning glance at Chauncey. Just as quickly, he turned and stared at the other side of the makeshift courtroom, so as not to bring suspicion to them.

The judge waited patiently for the giggles of the women to cease. Yawning, he glanced down at the paper before him and lifted his red-rimmed eyes to Rafe.

"State your name, prisoner."

"Rafael Beaulieu."

"Your profession."

"Delegate to the National Convention, St. Antoine section."

"Traitor!" yelled someone in the crowd.

"Beaulieu, you are charged with treason against the nation," the judge said over the din of the crowd. "How do you plead?"

"Not guilty." Rafe watched the judge stiffly, riveting his eyes on the man's emotionless face. From the corner of his eye, he could see Katrina, but he dared not turn to her.

"I have a signed deposition here that says you have spent years in the employ of the king's traitorous brothers, the Comte d'Artois and the Comte de Provence. I have another which says you spent eight months in Coblenz—"

The crowd erupted at the sound of the enemies' headquarters. Katrina paled and turned to Chauncey. "Chauncey . . ."

"Hush, Katrina."

The judge waited patiently for the eruption to end, running his fingers over his dirty sash.

"Do you deny this testimony from a good patriot?"

"I do not deny that I spent time in Coblenz," Rafe said carefully, his back flexing as if he could already feel the blows the crowd wanted to rain upon him. "Anyone who was in the Assembly at the time knows I did so to spy on the king's brothers. My lengthy report proves it."

"How do we know you did not submit a similarly lengthy document on the plans of the National Assembly to the *émigrés?*" the judge persisted. The crowds' yells grew louder at the insinuations.

"If you read my report, you would see it contained information about the *émigré* and Austrian military moves in the Rhineland, information vital for the continuation of the Nation." Rafe's eyes flickered in anger. "Why would I give such information to the Assembly if I were a traitor?"

The crowd, mindless, hissed at Rafe's speech, shouting his guilt to the tribunal. The judge lifted his brows and picked up the piece of paper that lay before him.

Katrina swallowed nervously. The marquis stood up, and his glare was so intense it took her breath away.

"There is more evidence against this man," the marquis said calmly. He pulled some papers from his waistcoat and placed them before the judge. "You may find these of interest."

Rafe's eyes hardened to onyx as he stared at the Marquis de

Noailles. The marquis returned his stare, and the flow of hatred passed unhindered between the two men. Katrina clutched Chauncey's arm and bit her lip, fearing Rafe would lunge at the marquis and be murdered on the spot.

The judge read the papers the marquis had thrust upon him, then handed them to a juror, whose eyes ingested the contents laboriously. The crowd grew restless at the delay and threw taunts at Rafe, eager to get a reaction from the prisoner. But the cries fell on deaf ears. Rafe's full attention was on the marquis, who watched the proceedings with a small grin of satisfaction.

Rafe's frame vibrated in anger as the marquis paced leisurely behind the tribunal, his eyes glinting with a joyous light. Rafe burned with fury and cursed the ropes that bound his hands. If he were free, he would end this hell by ending the marquis's life.

No. He stiffened, swallowing his anger. He must remain calm. If he stepped any closer to the table, he would be run through with a pike without a second thought. There was no justice to be found in these half-sotted judges. He suppressed a harsh laugh. He'd known it would end like this. Yet, out of a sense of misguided pride, he had stayed. He should have left Paris months ago.

He stared at the marquis's insolent face again, wishing he could tear the skin off those aristocratic bones. Though the marquis wore the grin of victory, Rafe knew that the battle was not over yet. Even if he had to rush to the marquis with a pike stuck through his own body, he vowed he would inflict the last blow.

Katrina's soft hair glowed out of the corner of his eye. Rafe stiffened, willing himself not to turn to her. If his eyes fell upon her for more than a few seconds, she would be instantly accused, for he did not fool himself. His verdict was inevitable. Although he longed to set his eyes on Katrina's face one last time, he would not drag her down with him in death. She must live, care for their unborn child, and find her happiness without him.

The papers were handed to another juror, and the three who already had read them conferred among themselves. They cast suspicious, accusing glances at Rafe.

"I'm forced to ask the accused again, under pain of perjury, what is your full name?"

"My name is Rafe Beaulieu," Rafe said distinctly, tilting his head at the marquis.

"Your full name," the judge reiterated.

Rafe glanced at the judge, his irritation evident. "That is my full name."

"You have no title, no other name by which you are addressed?" the judge persisted.

Rafe sighed, shrugging his shoulders. "I've been called many names by many people, *citoyen*," he said calmly, turning briefly to the crowd. "Some of those names I wouldn't repeat in front of female company." A few laughs spread around the room. "But I have no other official name."

"None?" the judge repeated. He turned to glance at the other jurors, who were now wide awake. The judge toyed with the papers in his hand. "We have evidence, donated by this good *citoyen*, that says you are actually the reigning Duke de Libourne."

A hiss passed through the crowd, and the observers tensed, straining against the roped-off area where the prisoner stood. Rafe did not flinch. The judge sat back, letting the peasants denounce the man, the nobleman, who stood before them.

Katrina sat numbly, unable to believe this turn of events.

The Duke de Libourne? The name rang in her head. That was the name Rafe had used at her debutante ball. No, no—he had said he was the illegitimate son of the Duke de Libourne. Her brow puckered.

Chauncey clutched her shoulders. "Later, Katrina. I will explain it all later."

"I am not the Duke de Libourne," Rafe said evenly, his voice loud enough to cut through the riotous calls of the crowd. He waited until their yells quieted before he spoke again. "My mother, who was a printer's daughter, was raped by the Duke de Libourne when she was hardly a woman. I am the result of that assault."

"So you are the former duke's natural son?"

"I claim no ties to the duke." Rafe's eyes wandered to the marquis. "When the duke died six months ago, I fully renounced his title and his estates. I've taken not one bloody sou from that aristocrat."

The Duke de Libourne? Katrina stood, shocked, senseless, watching the proceedings in horror as the crowd became restless.

"Traitor!" someone yelled. "Traitor to the people!"

"You should have joined your relatives in Coblenz, Beaulieu," another screamed. "You'll die here."

The judge examined Rafe's tall, straight stance and steady eyes. He reached over to shuffle the papers before him.

"You are guilty of perjury, Libourne," the judge said solemnly. "There are papers here, signed by you, that recognize you as the sole heir to all of the Duke de Libourne's estates."

"Forged," Rafe snapped. "I signed no papers." He glanced angrily at the marquis's grinning figure. "I'd wager you don't even know what my real signature looks like."

"You're an aristocrat and a spy, Beaulieu," the judge said, ignoring Rafe's statement. "You are accused of treason, and from the facts I have examined—"

"If your evidence were true, it would make me an aristocrat, not an enemy of the state," Rafe interrupted angrily, his eyes flashing black daggers.

"We can only assume that you hid your true identity to conceal your communications with Coblenz. The people must rid themselves of spies in the city before we can march against those at our gates."

The crowd roared in approval, waving their red caps. A brandy bottle hit Rafe, cutting his arm. The sight of blood brought the crowd to a frenzy, and they strained against the meager bindings that kept them from the prisoner. Rafe turned as the ropes were pushed away and the crowd exploded, jeering and yelling and rushing toward him.

"Chauncey!" Katrina cried, rushing forward. "Chauncey!"

She pushed forward with the crowd, but Chauncey swept her up by the waist, ignoring her screams, and dragged her away.

"Chauncey, Chauncey!" she cried. "Please, let me go, let me get to Rafe—"

"Shut up, Kat," he snapped, pressing her to his chest. "We've got to get you out of here."

She gasped, searching over the heads of the mob as she and Chauncey moved away. She released a long, agonized wail, barely audible above the roar of the crowd, and struggled valiantly in Chauncey's arms until she wiggled out of his embrace. Flinging herself through the masses, heedless of the pikes that pricked her sides, the elbows that bruised her ribs and arms, she pushed desperately through the mass of people, scratching, tearing her way through to Rafe.

Chauncey found her again and lifted her high upon his shoulders, pulling her away from the brutal onslaught. From her high vantage point, Katrina looked over the heads to see Rafe's blueblack hair disappear behind rows of raised pikes and red caps.

Chapter 24

Katrina sucked air into her lungs as Chauncey carried her out into the night. Her body strained against his shoulder. She looked back into the court, where Rafe was buried under the attack of drunken Parisians. Tears rolled down her face and her wracking sobs twisted Chauncey's heart.

He pushed brutally through the crowd, using Katrina's kicking feet as weapons against those who dared get in his way. There was no time to waste. He had to get her safely away from here. A hackney cab stood across the square, surrounded by singing sots. He sighed in relief as he caught sight of Martha, who was clutching a small satchel.

Katrina stretched her arms out, reaching toward the prison. Her body shook with pain, until finally, mercifully, she shuddered one last time and her body fell limply over Chauncey's shoulder. He mouthed a silent prayer of thanks. At least she would be given a brief respite from the torture that twisted her soul.

"*Sacre bleu*, the child looks like death," Martha exclaimed as Chauncey approached her. He pushed open the hackney's door and placed Katrina on one of the hard seats.

"There's no time for talk."

"But what of—"

"I don't know," Chauncey said bitterly. "I couldn't see a thing as I left." His eyes fluttered to hers, then away again. "We must pray that all went as planned."

"Oh, dear God," Martha sobbed.

Chauncey gripped her shoulder. "Martha, you must return to the house now. Don't go outside. I'll be back as soon as I can."

Composing herself, Martha stepped away from the hackney. "Go. And Godspeed."

The carriage lurched forward at Chauncey's direction and weaved into the street. The driver cursed liberally at the riotous peasants. The dark night air was thick with the smoke of a hundred fires. Between the bottle-waving groups of singing, drunk peasants, the *falots* bravely carried their pinpoints of light, as if the small beacons could ward off thieves and beggars. The horses' hooves clopped unevenly on the cobblestones, tapping a staccato rhythm that conflicted with the weaving melodies of *"Ça Ira, Ça Ira"* and the brisk *"Marseillaise,"* the new national anthem to which the troops marched. Katrina and Chauncey's bodies jolted side to side against the interior of the coach.

She woke, rising to stare wild-eyed at him, then out the open windows. She recognized the wide Rue St. Honoré, and up ahead rose the Palais Royal, its courtyards swarming with people. She glanced in confusion at Chauncey's averted face.

"Where are we going?"

"We're leaving Paris, Katrina," he said, running a hand through his mussed curls. "It's too dangerous to stay."

Katrina started, feeling like she'd heard those words before. "But . . . but . . ."

"Katrina, there's still hope," he said softly, reaching over to squeeze her hand.

"But I saw the crowds cover him." She squeezed her eyes shut against the memory.

Chauncey's hand tightened on her wrist. "Listen to me, Kat." He glanced away from the desperation in her eyes. "Rafe has always been the leader, always—since we were boys, growing up in Bordeaux. Tonight, for the first time, I was the leader, and I pray that what I've planned has worked."

"Chauncey, please, don't tease me," Katrina cried. "What are you telling me? What have you planned?"

"Rafe has as many friends as enemies, Kat," he said. "Probably more. I gathered them together tonight and spread them through the hall where the tribunal at La Force was set up." He clutched his red cap in his hands. "There was hardly any time before I knew what the Commune was planning. I had them dress appropriately, brought them in, and spread them around.

We were going to rush upon him, just the twelve of us, and carry him off into the crowds. But things got out of control . . .''

"Out of control?''

"Yes, but the plan will still work, if . . .'' He hesitated. "If they got to him before the rest of the crowd.''

"If?'' she exclaimed. Her free hand flew to her burning face. "They had to. They must have. Rafe must be alive.''

"Let's hope so, Katrina.''

"How will we know? When will we find out?'' Her eyes sought the dim streets, staring at each tall, ragged figure, seeking Rafe.

"We arranged a meeting place a few leagues from Paris. We will wait there for Rafe or . . . or for news.''

Katrina clutched her chest, willing her heart to stop its hard, painful pounding.

The carriage veered off the main road and plunged down a bumpy path that could barely accommodate the width of the black vehicle. The horses whinnied against the sudden change in terrain, tossing their heads against the holes and the threat of the thick, close trees. Not even the light from the stars could penetrate the leafy canopy, and they rode in a darkness pierced only by the lanterns that shone a dull yellow from the sides of the carriage. Katrina stared uneasily into the blackness as the vehicle made its way through the brambled path, protected only by the driver and one unarmed man.

The driver cursed as the horses stopped, their way blocked by heavy undergrowth. Chauncey jumped out to help the man clear the rotted logs, twigs, and woody vines that had woven a net across the narrow road. Katrina shivered in the empty carriage, painfully aware of the branches that reached out to her. Her eyes avidly searched the undergrowth for signs of movement, and her ears strained to hear alien noises above the hoot of the owls, the crickets' incessant chirps, and the rustle of a light breeze in the treetops. The men's grunts seemed to scream through the forest.

Chauncey returned, his shirt wet with sweat and his hands blackened. The carriage lurched forward again and the horses picked their way among the debris. Chauncey stuck his hands outside the window and rubbed them briskly together, a sneer of distaste on his face.

"What I do for Rafe . . .'' he mumbled, brushing the dirt off his smooth palms and examining his manicured nails. "These hands were made for writing poetry, not for clearing woods." He attempted a smile to lighten the mood, but it looked more like a grimace.

The carriage entered a small clearing and stopped. Katrina stepped out, her eyes never leaving the dark perimeter of the woods that surrounded them.

"Is this where we are to meet him?" she asked. The chill of the night cooled her skin and she wrapped her arms around her for warmth.

Chauncey nodded abruptly, his brows drawing together. "I suggest you go back inside and rest, Katrina. It may be a very long night."

"Just another five minutes, Chauncey," Katrina pleaded, touching his arm. "Please."

"Katrina, we've been here hours already," he said, tightening the traces with short, violent pulls.

"Chauncey—" she cried, bending to catch his eye. "Please, Chauncey."

"Katrina, we've been here all night. Soon dawn will break, and then we'll not be able to move. We're too close to Paris to take that chance."

"But—"

"Katrina, perhaps . . ." He sighed raggedly. "Perhaps Rafe didn't make it out of the prison."

"No!" she said, not nearly as adamantly as earlier in the evening. Starting deep in her abdomen, her sobs began, hard and heavy. Chauncey lifted her high in his arms and walked to the carriage door. She hid her face in his rough coat.

She sank wearily upon the seat, burying her head in her hands. It was time to face the truth. Rafe was gone.

She had never felt so alone, so weak, in all her life. Her sobs ceased slowly, leaving her face wan, her eyes shadowed by dark circles. She wondered at the steady beat of her heart in her hollow chest. It was strange how her body could still work when her life had shattered around her. She felt her veins rush with blood, her skin shiver at the cold, while her mind was black and blank and emotionless, frightened to face reality.

Could it be that Rafe's spirit had been extinguished? Her eyes fluttered shut as his face rose strong and sure in her mind, the dark eyes lit with tiny flames as he took her, or gentle in tenderness as he brushed tendrils of hair from her face. She smiled, her hand moving as if to run through the silk of his hair.

The carriage left the earthen path and entered the main road with a burst of speed, the horses brisk after the night's rest. Katrina's eyes flew open and she stared at the countryside. A small lake shone through pine trees, and her gaze lingered on the soft ripples. Its depths were black, as black as *his* eyes, while the eastern sky reminded her of the indigo highlights in his ebony locks. She turned to Chauncey, whose face was thin and pale in the early morning light. His eyes fluttered to hers, endless grief in their brown depths.

They both looked away. Katrina watched the trees rush by them, each one that passed putting more and more distance between Rafe's beloved city, his shop, his body . . . and his family, who raced silently away from the danger that had made him its victim.

She touched her stomach. At least Rafe's seed had found a home in her womb. God had granted her that one gift to ease the pain of his loss, and Rafe would live on through their child. The thought brought a touch of color to her cheeks.

The carriage raced over the pitted road. They stopped only once to feed and water the horses before hitching them up again to continue their journey. Katrina and Chauncey ate little of the bread and chicken that they had purchased from a nearby inn, but both drank liberal glasses of wine.

"It will be some time before I taste wine this good again," Chauncey said, savoring the burgundy.

"Where are you going, Chauncey, that will bring you so far from your beloved red wines?"

He cradled his cup so the movement of the carriage would not send its contents splattering over his cut-off breeches. "After you are safe, Katrina, I will return to Paris, take care of a few affairs, then follow you to England."

"And what of Daphne?"

Chauncey nodded. "One of the affairs I have to take care of is Daphne. I'm going to ask her to come with me. I've suddenly realized the importance of being with her."

Katrina's face sobered. "I'm glad you're going to her," she said. "Daphne loves you, though she speaks little of it."

"I doubt it," he murmured. "But I'll find out for myself."

"How do we get to England?" Katrina asked, the thought of Daphne and Chauncey together and happy casting a glaring light on her own loss. She stared blindly at the passing scenery.

"First we're going to Le Havre, Katrina. From there you'll catch a boat to the British shore."

"I hope I can remember my English. Father Hytier—my old tutor—used to scold me for being so lax in my studies."

Chauncey jolted upright, moving to the window.

"What is it?" Katrina asked, jumping from her seat.

"Riders. Several of them. And they're headed full speed this way." He reached under the seat and pulled out a musket.

"Who—who are they?"

"I want you to stay behind the carriage, and I don't want you to move—do you understand?"

Katrina nodded, and Chauncey's head disappeared out the window as he yelled for the driver to pull over into the woods and stop. Katrina caught sight of her satchel that Martha had prepared. She reached for it, searching through her clothes and papers for her knife. Gripping the smooth handle firmly, she laid it on her lap. Chauncey stared at her in surprise.

"I'm not leaving this carriage without some kind of defense," she said sharply. The carriage lurched to one side as they moved off the road. Chauncey leaped out agilely, peering at the forms raising dust down the road. Katrina stumbled out after him and peeked from behind him, her eyes squinting against the sun. The forms moved out of the dust, and with terror she recognized the marquis.

"Chauncey!" she screamed.

"I know, Kat," he said, turning to her briefly. His eyes burned. "I'm going to kill him for Rafe."

"Not if I get him first."

Chauncey placed the musket high on his shoulder, aiming for the marquis. His coat flapped in the wind behind him, making him look more like an evil demon than ever before. Chauncey squeezed the trigger and moved back, bumping into her at the report. Katrina cried out in surprise at the loud noise.

The group pulled back and a cloud of dust obscured their numbers. Chauncey swore. He had missed.

"Beaulieu!" the marquis cried loudly over the men. "Beaulieu, come out and fight like a man!"

"Beaulieu is dead, Noailles," Chauncey yelled. "And he is dead because of you."

The marquis's laughter traveled over the short distance. "Good. That's one goal accomplished."

Chauncey lifted his musket and fired again. One of the men next to the marquis grunted and fell below the feet of his horse.

A volley of shots rained on the carriage, and Katrina cringed behind it. The driver and Chauncey moved to shoot, their efforts hampered by the bullets that flew past them on either side. Katrina screamed, but the sound was drowned by the noise of the muskets. Pulling on Chauncey's arm, she turned him to her.

"Listen to me. It's me he wants, not you. Let me go and stop this shooting before we're all killed."

"Don't be foolish, Katrina."

"Do you want to die, Chauncey? That's what will happen if I don't go," she shouted above the loud crack of the muskets.

Chauncey grabbed her. "Listen to me: I will not allow you to do this."

"Listen to *me*," Katrina spat, waving the small knife. "Let me go to the marquis. He will not see the sun rise again." The marquis's men had slowed their shooting, and the marquis gave the order to stop completely.

"No," Chauncey insisted.

"I must—" Abruptly, she moved away from the carriage. "Marquis! Don't shoot!" she cried, ducking from the carriage driver. The marquis lifted his arm, and his men warily lowered their muskets. In the silence that followed, she stood staring into her nemesis's icy granite eyes. Chauncey tried to grab her, but a shot grazed his arm, and he fell back behind the carriage. Katrina gasped and raced farther away.

"Katrina, come back here!" Chauncey cried. "Don't be foolish!"

She ignored his words, moving closer to the riders.

The marquis stared at her, his eyes resting on her tangled hair, loose and heavy down her back, the dust that settled on her face and dress, down to her dirty, bare feet.

He had found her. This woman would be his.

"If it's me you want, Marquis, then I'll go with you willingly," she called. "On one condition."

The marquis's smile lifted higher to one side, showing yellowed teeth. "You're hardly in the position to make bargains, Katrina."

"You could kill me now and I could care less." Her green eyes darkened as she stared at the nobleman. "You've already killed me once by killing Rafe."

The marquis digested her words, moving his horse out of the circle of men to approach her. "Very well, *lapin*," he said softly. "What is it that I trade for you?"

"Their safety," she said, pointing at the carriage and the two musket butts extending from the sides. "Guarantee me their safety and I'll go with you with no further trouble."

"We do not hide behind your skirts, Katrina," Chauncey said harshly. "Run from him!"

"Shut up, damn you. I'm saving your lives."

"That's all you want, *lapin*?" the marquis mocked her. "Their safety?"

She nodded.

"Very well," he said. His voice, crisp and authoritative, rose over the carriage. "I'll spare your hides for now, Messieurs. By the request of this woman." He handed his musket to one of his men and dismounted.

Lost in his icy eyes, Katrina froze as he approached her, his steps slow and sure. She must do it. If she surrendered to him, then Chauncey and the driver would be spared. Her fingers curled over the cold knife.

Suddenly, crashing out of the deepest part of the forest, a black steed jumped over the underbrush. His sides heaved and foam flecked his mouth. The beast flew over the few feet that separated it from Katrina's small form. She screamed as a hard, strong arm swept her against the side of the animal, bringing her up swiftly into a solid chest, wet with sweat. Gasping for breath, she watched the ground fly across her field of vision and she clung desperately to the beast, her abdomen banging against his neck. An arm came around her and brought her upright, holding her against the bolt of muscle that was his chest. Gasping, Katrina lifted her head.

Rafe!

The black eyes seared her face and his midnight hair flew around him like a shroud. Katrina's heart burst in joy, and she threw her arms around his strong, proud neck. The horse flew across the road and into the forest. Hidden by a thicket of trees, she glimpsed the angry volleys of musket fire, doubling the din and dust, but she could think of nothing but Rafe's warm breath on her cheek. He reined in the horse and placed his rough hands on each side of her face. Lowering his head to taste the honey of her lips, he pressed her against the long length of his chest and abdomen, pulling her tightly to his warmth.

"I love you," he said, breathless. "I told you I would never let you go."

"Beaulieu." The icy voice stiffened Katrina's spine, and she turned to see the marquis approach them slowly through the trees. He was unarmed and his gray eyes burned.

Rafe twisted to see the man who had tormented them for so many years.

"Upset, Marquis?" he asked warily. "Upset that you find me alive, instead of dead by some executioner's pike?" He slid off the horse, and Katrina gasped, reaching for him. He turned to her. "This is something I must do, *petite.*"

"How touching," the marquis said, sneering. "And don't be so gleeful about your miraculous escape, Beaulieu. My men outnumber yours, and I am here to ensure your death."

"How silly of you," Rafe said snidely, "to think that you'll ever be able to kill me. Your men were on open ground when I passed by. My men were behind the trees. Do you think I escaped alone, Marquis? You must have great faith in my powers."

"You simply have luck, Beaulieu," the marquis said angrily.

"I have brains. I always get what I want, don't I, Katrina?"

Rafe's body tensed at the mention of her name. "Don't you dare utter her name—"

"I will do as I please, Beaulieu," the marquis interrupted. "And I assure you Katrina will please me, often, after you are gone."

Rafe lunged at him, his body flying across the space that separated them. The force of the impact sent both men sprawling hard against the solid forest floor. The marquis reached for Rafe's throat, but Rafe clutched his first.

Thrusting his knee into Rafe's stomach, the marquis loosened himself and twisted Rafe's arm behind his back, pulling it up until Katrina screamed. The sound gave Rafe strength and he swung out of the marquis's grip, bringing his opposite arm hard against the man's jaw. Rolling away, Rafe rose to his feet and warily watched the older man as he crouched near his coat.

"Come on, Noailles," Rafe taunted. "Out of breath so quickly?" The marquis rose and they circled each other. The marquis's arm lashed out, but Rafe twisted and took the blow harmlessly on the shoulder. Off balance, he righted himself with a blow to the marquis, who staggered, but lunged forward to grip Rafe.

Falling to the forest floor again, the two rolled over and over. Katrina gasped as she saw something glitter in the marquis's hand.

"Rafe!" she cried, sliding from the horse and backing away from the men. "Rafe, he's got a knife!"

Rafe saw the silver of steel shining amid the nettles. Pushing Rafe off him, the marquis lunged forward, smiling as he gripped the knife in his hand. Rafe jumped away.

The marquis laughed, waving the blade before Rafe. "A little hesitant, Beaulieu? How many death sentences can you avoid?" The knife made small silver arcs before him. Katrina's heart hammered and she reached up to clutch the musket on the horse's saddle. The marquis stepped nearer and swung at Rafe, the knife cutting a swath in his shirt. Rafe glanced down to see a drop of blood ooze from the scratch.

"That's the last blood you will draw from me, Noailles." With a swiftness that startled Katrina, he reached for the arm that held the knife, grasping it in a viselike grip and holding it away from their bodies. The marquis sneered at Rafe, his mouth open, his arm straining against the strength of the younger man. Once more they fell to the earth, moving stiffly in a twisted horizontal waltz.

Katrina raised the heavy musket, then lowered it when Rafe rolled to the top. She raised it again at the sight of the black-clad marquis. They were moving too close and too fast . . . if only they would separate for a minute. She sobbed in frustration as she saw the glint of sun shine off the knife before it plunged between them.

For a moment neither moved, the knife lost between their bodies. Katrina gasped as she watched Rafe's face under the marquis, waiting for the horrible signs.

The marquis lifted his head and rolled away. Katrina gasped at the knife rising out of the man's chest. His eyes grew wide and disbelieving as he stared over the handle. For a moment the marquis's eyes turned to Katrina. He reached out for her. She watched in horror as the arm fell and the satanic light left his icy gray eyes.

Rafe rose to his feet, his body blocking her view, and she lifted her gaze to his. He pressed her face against his blood-stained shirt.

"It's all right now, Katrina. It's all over."

Epilogue

Katrina lifted her face to breathe in the salty sea air that rose riotously over the bow of the ship. The captain had said that land was only a few hours away, and she was eager to be one of the first to sight it. She clutched her swollen belly as the baby kicked vigorously. The babe had been doing that a lot lately, and she feared that if they did not reach New Orleans soon, the baby would be born in the cramped, cherry-wood scented cabin that Rafe and she had shared during the arduous trip.

A smile curved her full lips. Not that she minded sharing the berth. She enjoyed seeing the look of surprise in Rafe's eyes when she moved to him in the middle of the night, her extended middle keeping them a few inches apart. He would caress her soft skin and lightly stroke the evidence of their love, his hands smoothing over her abdomen in wonder.

She sighed in contentment, staring over the choppy water. Soon they would have a new country. America. France had long sunk into anarchy. This past January, the French had killed their own king, and rumor said that Queen Marie Antoinette would soon follow. The French army had beaten off the Austrian and *émigré* forces, but that victory had done little to ease the country's reign of terror. France was not a place for the Beaulieus, not anymore.

They had left just in time. The trip to England was mercifully uneventful, and the couple spent most of their time in their new bedroom, reacquainting themselves with each other in a far calmer environment than Paris. Rafe told Katrina the secrets of his birth, and explained that the only reason he had kept his heritage hidden from her was to protect her from the Convention.

While leafing through the papers Katrina had taken from Poitiers, she rediscovered the deed for a tract of land in America. She vaguely recalled seeing the parchment once before but had forgotten it, having never considered leaving France as an option. It seemed their salvation: a new start. They had booked passage within a week.

Chauncey had written from Paris, where he still lingered, miraculously unmolested. He hinted of another wedding in the family soon, and Rafe was saddened that he could not be there. There were so many people to whom they had never given a proper good-bye—Daphne, Martha, Monsieur Forrestier. To write was useless; the letters would never make it to their destination.

Katrina shook her head to clear it of the depressing thoughts. Today was no day to be depressed! Their future stretched bright before them. She lifted a hand to shade her eyes from the intense sun. Although it was only early May, the sun beat hotly on the blue-green water, and her hair hung heavy against the nape of her neck.

"There you are," Rafe said behind her.

She twisted to smile up at him. His hair shone with blue highlights and his face was clean and free of the beard that had obscured it during their last days in France. She reached up to trace the strong line of his jaw.

"Aren't you warm out here?" he asked, his hands lifting the heavy golden mass off her neck.

She sighed at the pleasurable breeze. "A little."

"You should be downstairs resting." He studied her flushed face with tender concern.

"I know, but I wanted to see the first glimpse of land."

His gaze lifted toward the horizon. "Then look, love. There's our new home."

Catching her breath, Katrina stared across the water at the thin strip of land silhouetted against the horizon. She smiled, her eyes bright.

"Our new home." Her hand moved to her belly, quelling the answering kick. Rafe pulled her against his chest and touched her swollen abdomen.

"I think he likes it," she said.

"I think she does, too," he whispered, his hair falling in thick locks over his forehead. His eyes lingered on her upturned face. "And I love you, my sweet, precious Katrina."

LISANN ST. PIERRE

LISANN ST. PIERRE was born and raised just outside Boston Massachusetts. She's always dreamed of being a writer, but she put her aspirations on hold to finish her studies at Vassar College, where she received a degree in chemistry. After graduating, Lisann moved to San Francisco, helped to organize the local Romance Writers of America chapter and began writing DEFIANT ANGEL, her first novel. Lisann is engaged to her college sweetheart, Tom, and although she's currently employed as an analytical chemist, she looks forward to writing full-time in the near future.